the
LAZARUS
PROJECT

the
LAZARUS
PROJECT
a novel

JOHN BAYER

BROADMAN
& HOLMAN
PUBLISHERS
Nashville, Tennessee

Published by Broadman & Holman Publishers, Nashville, Tennessee
Page Design: Anderson Thomas Design, Inc.
Typesetting: PerfecType, Nashville, Tennessee
Editorial Team: Vicki Crumpton, Janis Whipple, Kim Overcash

Dewey Decimal Classification: 813
Subject Heading: Fiction
Library of Congress Card Catalog Number: 98-49223

Scripture citation is from the New International Version, copyright © 1973,
1978, 1984 by International Bible Society, and KJV, the King James Version.

Library of Congress Cataloging-in-Publication Data

Bayer, John F., 1947—
    The Lazarus Project: a novel / John Bayer.
        p.   cm.
    ISBN 0-8054-0172-5 (pb)
    I. Title.
PS3552.A85868L39   1999
813'.54—dc21

                                                                    98-49223
                                                                        CIP

1 2 3 4 5 03 02 01 00 99

DEDICATION

To Chip, Peggy, and Megan

ACKNOWLEDGMENTS

Thanks to Vicki Crumpton, Janis Whipple, and Kim Overcash, whose work has made this a better book.

PROLOGUE

Second Flotilla U-Boat Base
Pointe de Keroman
Lorient, France
17 June 1944

The U-Boat *Eins Zwei Drei* rocked gently in the oil-stained water of bay B5 of the Keroman I bunkers. Her fourteen previous patrols into the North Atlantic had twice taken her as far as the eastern shore of the United States. Her captain, a thin-faced Kapitänleutnant named Reinhard Hardegen, had skippered the *Eins Zwei Drei* to within half a mile of the North American shore from Cape Hatteras to New York City. Those had been exhilarating and dangerous times, *expectant* times Hardegen recalled. He had sunk nine allied ships during one patrol, sending more than fifty-seven thousand tons of U.S. shipping to the bottom of the Atlantic, including the *Esso Baton Rouge.*

But those had been war patrols, something that Hardegen understood. This was different, frightening, almost sinister. Hardegen self-consciously glanced over his shoulder.

As the lights burned away the darkness of the bunker, two men watched from the surrounding catwalk. The first, a man in his early fifties, with studiously intense gray eyes behind rimless glasses, appeared particularly uncomfortable to be standing where he stood. His large square head, set on narrow shoulders, continually rotated to take in the activity of the crew as they prepared the U-boat for its mission.

The second man wore a pale-gray Litewka tunic with the runes of the Schutzstaffeln—the SS—on his right collar tab and the three diamonds of a Haupsturmführer—captain—on the left. The high-intensity lights of the bunker added life to his penetrating brown-green eyes; his dark brown hair was impeccably groomed beneath the gray SS cap. His right hand continually went to the tunic pocket where he carried an untouched package of cigarettes. He was a chain smoker, but smoking was forbidden within the confines of the bunkers, which only added to his discomfort.

"That is Hardegen?" the man in the rimless glasses asked. His accent was that of one who had been well educated in the northeast United States, and his dark business suit and matching felt hat marked him as a prominent businessman or a diplomat. His German was flawless, the guttural tones softened by his accent.

The second man nodded. "In the conning tower, wearing the white sea cap. He oversees every aspect of the preparations. They will be ready to leave in the morning."

"What does he know?"

The Haupsturmführer hesitated before answering. "He knows only that this patrol is not a war patrol. He will know the details when he opens this after passing twenty degrees longitude." The man revealed the large, blue, sealed operations envelope he held in his right hand.

"But he suspects," the man in the suit stated, his gaze returning to the thin-faced man in the conning tower.

"He suspects," the Haupsturmführer replied quietly. "He is too intelligent not to, and speculation cannot be avoided in this case," he continued. "Too much is going on; too much is different."

The two men fell silent. Too much *was* different. Mechanics, technicians, armorers, welders, and refit specialists swarmed over the cigar-shaped vessel, preparing it for its final patrol. Already, the 10.5-centimeter cannon on the fore casing and the smaller 3.7-centimeter gun on the after casing had been removed, leaving the U-Boat with a stripped-down, somehow more deadly, profile.

As the men watched, the final G7 torpedo was hoisted from the interior of the submarine. Each of the massive projectiles had to be manhandled from the forward torpedo room, attached to a chain hoist and trolleys, and lifted free of the forward torpedo hatch with care. Free of the additional weight, the Type IXB U-Boat would significantly increase its range, which was of paramount importance to the mission.

"The crew?" the man in the glasses asked.

"All volunteers. They know the Third Reich is dying."

The man in the suit nodded only slightly, acknowledging the significance of the Haupsturmführer's statement.

"There's a certain irony there, I think," the bespectacled man said. "A kind of poignancy."

"Perhaps. There are many who do not understand what we have tried to accomplish here, how we have attempted to enlighten the world. I fear our motives will forever be shrouded by other factors."

The man in the glasses said nothing. No reply would be adequate. He had heard the names—Auschwitz, Belsen, Colditz, Buchenwald, Dachau, and others. Names that would forever live in the darkest reaches of men's memories. And he had heard the stories, seen the photographs, known the men who had died there. Just being in the presence of the Haupsturmführer was distasteful enough.

The uniformed man sighed. "Perhaps one day we will be vindi-
cated in our actions. Until then, we will change to meet the circumstance. Change like you are seeing right here, right now. That is the
future, the continuity," he said, indicating the U-Boat gently rocking at
its moorings. "History will have the final judgment."

"When will our passenger arrive?"

"*Herr doktor* will arrive shortly. He was three hours outside
Lorient at last report." The Haupsturmführer checked his watch. "He
should be here inside an hour."

The other man nodded, his attention drawn back to the dark hull of
the U-Boat as if some mystical force possessed the craft. He'd traveled
from Basel, Switzerland, the day before yesterday. There he'd met with
the American Vice-Consul, Nancy Reichman, before proceeding into
German-occupied France. The meeting had been more than just a minor
stopover. Reichman was his single link back to a world of sanity. His
orders to her had been succinct and specific: If he failed to return within
a specified period of time, she was to notify the State Department and
the overseas headquarters of the OSS, the Office of Strategic Services.
Given his current assignment, notification to any other agency was not
wise and could prove fatal. The "niceties" of political expediency were
sometimes misunderstood by the military minds of the times.

A sharp clanging drew the man's attention back to the U-boat. The
crew was beginning to dismantle the chain hoist and lift trolley. The torpedoes that had been removed from the *Eins Zwei Drei* were positioned
in racks alongside the U-Boat, against a wall of the bunker. They represented the last offensive weapons carried by the boat; without them, the
Eins Zwei Drei was completely defenseless. That was the plan.

A flurry of activity announced the arrival of the single passenger. The
two men on the catwalk, as well as Hardegen, made no move to greet the
new arrival. The passenger was escorted by two blue-clad crewmen to the
hatch on the fore casing. With a brief glance backward toward the men
on the catwalk, he disappeared into the bowels of the boat.

"That's that, then," the man in the glasses said.

The gray-uniformed Haupsturmführer nodded without looking at the man. "I wish it were me," he said evenly.

"May God have mercy on our souls," the man said, not wishing to reply to the Haupsturmführer's last statement.

"On your soul, Mr. Dulles. When that passenger reaches his destination, it will be on your shoulders. You will have to justify this action, not I, nor anyone else here."

"That is true, *Herr doktor.* But success *will* require your complicity *and* your silence. Never forget that. And the actions we are taking today will not justify inhuman atrocities, should they occur. This is not over. It is only the beginning."

The Haupsturmführer smiled slowly. "I will not forget my part. And you will not forget your promise either. When this war is over, I may require your help to survive. That has been promised, has it not? You will not forget. I think somewhere in South America, should it come to that. Argentina, Paraguay, or Brazil perhaps."

Allen Dulles, head of the United States Office of Strategic Services in Europe, nodded as a deprecating smile crossed his face. He had not forgotten the promise made to the Haupsturmführer, the man now standing next to him in the immaculate gray uniform. As distasteful as that duty would be, he would follow through with it. After all, there was too much to gain by cooperating with the man and too much to lose if he did not. That was one of the things Dulles despised about his current position. The expediencies of war were forced on the unsuspecting. Acceptance was guaranteed as much by the fate of the defeated as by the fortunes of the victorious. At the moment, the OSS director wondered which category was his.

"I will not forget you," Dulles said dispassionately. Then added to himself sadly, "I could never forget you in a million long nights."

■   ■   ■

Kapitänleutnant Reinhard Hardegen unconsciously fingered the Knights Cross at his throat as he watched his passenger being escorted into the hull of *Eins Zwei Drei*. With that done, Hardegen turned his attention to his chief engineering officer, who had joined him on the conning tower. He glanced at the two men standing on the catwalk of the bunker, wondering if he was as crazy as he considered them to be.

"The torpedoes have been removed, Herr Kaleu," the engineering officer said, using the diminutive form of Kapitänleutnant with his commanding officer, "and the chain hoist and gears will be removed within the hour."

"Well done, Theodor. Carry on," Hardegen ordered.

The engineer started to turn, hesitated, and spoke. "Herr Kaleu, this is a strange voyage. You know about the fuel?" he asked, immediately regretting his choice of words. There was nothing on the *Eins Zwei Drei* Reinhard Hardegen did not know.

Hardegen allowed his engineer to absorb the full impact of his inquiry, then said gently, "Yes, I know about the fuel."

"I do not understand. We have barely three hundred cubic meters of diesel fuel in our bunkers. Barely enough to reach our destination, if what I have been told is true. How are we to return?"

Hardegen felt an instantaneous wave of remorse sweep over him like a cold North Atlantic swell. *"That* is not our concern. We have a job to do, and we have been provided with the tools to do that job. It is not our place to question those orders or the manner in which they are to be carried out. Perhaps," Hardegen continued, "we are to be given a vacation at the end of this journey."

Chief Engineer Theodor Bleichrodt nodded to his captain. He had volunteered for the mission because of Captain Hardegen. Bleichrodt had been with Hardegen in 1942, during Operation Drumbeat. He had jumped at the chance to serve with a true hero of the Third Reich once again. But this was not what he'd expected. Not at all.

The boat had been stripped of all armament, leaving it totally defenseless. Because he was the chief engineering officer, he had been told the destination of the boat. With that knowledge, Bleichrodt had calculated the amount of fuel necessary to reach their destination and return. Three

PROLOGUE

hundred cubic meters of fuel would get them there, but that was all. It meant abandoning the *Eins Zwei Drei* once the destination was reached. It was inconceivable—unless abandonment was somehow the idea.

The arrival of the single passenger compounded the mystery. But Bleichrodt knew enough not to question his captain beyond those details dealing with the actual operation of the boat.

"There is something else?" Hardegen asked politely.

"The crew, Herr Kaleu."

"Speak."

"It's just that, . . . well, we are shorthanded, sir. At last count, we have only forty-one crew members, including us. That leaves us at least twelve short, sir."

"As you can see, we have no use for gunners or torpedomen."

"Yes, sir, I know. Nevertheless, we are still short. And the stores are sufficient for only a month. My calculations show thirty-three days, one way, Herr Kaleu."

"Your destination calculations are based on what grid?" Hardegen probed, already knowing the answer.

"The one I was given, sir. Grid DA 58."

"That is the correct destination. Perhaps we will need to conserve what rations we have on the crossing. Maybe we will all lose a little weight," Hardegen said lightly, his attempt at levity failing.

Bleichrodt did not smile this time.

"You knew the circumstances and the possible consequences when you signed on for this voyage, Theodor," Hardegen said, ignoring military protocol once again and using his friend's first name.

"That is true," Bleichrodt acknowledged. "Perhaps I should return to my job. These are your worries now, I think, Herr Kaleu."

"Yes, my friend, they are," Hardegen replied in a low voice. He watched Theodor Bleichrodt turn and scramble down the exterior ladder attached to the conning tower. Everything aboard the *Eins Zwei Drei* was his worry, including the successful completion of the assignment at hand.

He knew the basics, just as Bleichrodt did. It had been necessary to confide those to certain members of the crew. He knew, for example, that the mission involved nothing more than the delivery of a single passenger to the shores of the United States. The grid DA 58 mentioned by Bleichrodt corresponded roughly to the shoreline near Galveston, Texas. The fact that the fuel bunkers contained only three hundred cubic meters of diesel fuel meant there was to be no return trip to the French port. It made no difference. Eleven days ago, the allied invasion had begun on the beaches of Normandy. The death knell had sounded, Hardegen knew. If what he had heard about German atrocities was true, this mission might offer him and his crew a degree of absolution. Not absolution in a criminal sense, but in a moral sense. If the rumors were true, the German Reich would die a horrible death, and the German people would need an absolution that might be difficult to find in the post-war state.

This voyage would most certainly take his crew out of harm's way, if he could successfully navigate the Atlantic without being sunk by allied warships. *That* would be a miracle in itself. At this very moment the identification numbers on the conning tower were being painted over. Not that it made much difference. There was not a ship's captain plying the Atlantic who did not know the profile of an IXB U-Boat on sight, regardless of markings.

It would be a precarious voyage, but one that must be made.

Hardegen looked once again in the direction of the man in the suit and the Haupsturmführer-SS who stood on the catwalk. They were gone. At the same instant, a messenger scrambled aboard the *Eins Zwei Drei.* Hardegen could see the blue operations envelope he carried. The envelope would make it official. For a brief moment, Reinhard Hardegen wondered whether he would ever see Germany, *his* Germany, again. The thought provoked a sense of profound nostalgia within him.

The messenger climbed the conning tower ladder and handed the blue envelope to Hardegen. Hardegen signed the single cover sheet and returned it to the messenger.

The order on the outside of the envelope indicated he was to open it only after reaching twenty degrees longitude. It made little difference; Hardegen already knew the essentials.

Tomorrow, when the engineering department fired up the nine-cylinder MAN diesel, the *Eins Zwei Drei* and Hardegen would say farewell to their homeland. With luck, one day, they would both return, but luck was not something Reinhard Hardegen believed in.

A Valley in the Ozark Mountains of
north central Arkansas
1965

A chilled wind snaked in and around the mountaintops, whistled through the deep valleys of the Ozark Mountains. The house in this remote valley of north central Arkansas had been constructed for comfort and solitude.

Built in 1812, the house had been burned to the ground during the Civil War when the armies of the north swept into Arkansas destined for an obscure location known as Pea Ridge. The house was rebuilt in 1868, surpassing even its former grandeur. White columns rose three stories, anchored to a two-inch-thick marble portico. Wings right and left balanced the enormous facade and added more than two thousand square feet each to the already huge floor plan. A single balcony graced the front of the house, providing air circulation for the entire second floor complex of bedrooms. The roof, in those days, had been tin, and the present owner had remained faithful to the original design when the time had come to replace it.

Had the Historical Society of Arkansas ever seen the house, they would have unanimously voted it into the Historical Register of Homes. But the number of people familiar with the house numbered less than two dozen, and the remoteness of the valley ensured its continued obscurity.

But what had, up to this point, been a singular advantage was now proving to be a drawback for the owner of the house.

"The papers have been executed?" the middle-aged man asked, his English still tinged with German undertones.

"An hour ago," his assistant answered.

The men stood on a short knoll overlooking the mansion. From their vantage point, they could easily see the small river that flowed through the valley. The trees were beginning to change color, signaling the first frost and the onset of autumn.

"I will notify the others then," the first man said.

"What about *him*?" the assistant asked.

The man thought for a moment. "I am told he has prepared for contingencies. Is this true?"

The assistant shuffled, uncomfortable with having to bring such news to his superior. Finally he said, "It is true."

"Then we must wait for the proper timing. He is no fool. Perhaps this is something our friends from Langley can assist us with," the man said, his eyes never wavering from the house.

"I will contact them, but I suspect *he* is too well-known for us to attempt anything at this time."

The man turned to his assistant and clamped one hand on his shoulder. "You are probably right, but we will have to try. We cannot allow anything to stand in our way. Now that we have what we have sought for so many years, we must see to it that nothing jeopardizes our plans. Is that understood?"

"What do I tell Langley?"

The man turned back to stare at the house. "What those men do not know cannot hurt us. Not even *they* can be allowed to know what goes on here. We will provide them with the information they think they so desperately need, but we will do what is necessary for our survival."

"Should I make the call?"

The man acknowledged the question with a nod. "I will talk to him. I have not talked to my friend for some time. He is often difficult to locate. Try the house on Calle Arenales in Buenos Aires."

The assistant nodded and walked briskly to the house. The phone call would take some time. Procedures had to be followed, procedures assuring total security for the man being called, for an angry world still sought the man in Buenos Aires.

The man on the knoll watched his assistant disappear into the house, then turned his thoughts to what was about to happen. At last, the facilities had been acquired. Other such facilities already existed, and one other was slightly ahead of the progress here in the Ozark Mountains. Seclusion came with a price.

The equipment would arrive in a few weeks via railroad. It would then be transferred to trucks driven by trusted men—men of *Die Gruppe,* The Group—who would never reveal what they had transported nor the location. With luck, within a few months, the work would begin; destiny would be fulfilled.

PART I
ESCAPE

CHAPTER ONE

The Valley
1998

The sound reached her through the barren trees and the falling snow—muted, softened. With the sound came a new wave of terror.

In the beginning, the snow had been welcome, peaceful, providing a blanket that seemed to cover the horror, if only for a short time. But the terrible reality was never far away.

This place was not like her home, where a honey-lemon sun warmed the broad beaches, and brown-skinned children rolled and tumbled in the warm waters of the Gulf of Mexico. Not like the narrow streets of her village, where ochre-colored dust settled over everything in sight. Where the soft red hues of the tile roofs announced each morning with their changing colors. Where old men lined the plaza in mid-afternoon, drinking coffee, and women bustled about with babies tied to their backs like bundles of firewood.

The sound of the pursuing dogs found her once again, snaking through the trees like a demonic creature on the loose. The thoughts of home vanished, and once again she began to run. She had never known such fear; it clawed at her like an insane beast loosed from the very bowels of hell.

Gaby Ibarra swallowed the sob that threatened to escape from her throat. Despite the paralyzing fear, she knew what she had to do. She rose from where she had stumbled and ran on, forcing exhaustion from her mind. Escape was her only option, her only course of action. It had not been planned; it had been a reaction, a survival reflex gleaned from deep within her. She had to escape the evil that seemed to hover over this secluded valley like a loathsome creature.

El valle de la sombra. That's the phrase she'd heard when she'd first been brought to this place. What was it in English? She sometimes forgot. The valley of the shadow, that was it. The name was appropriate. A shadow cast by the creature that lived in the protective confines of the surrounding mountains. The creature—the beast—was evil, that much she knew.

Gaby stumbled on, her foot coming down on a snow-encrusted tree root. She fell again. This time the sob escaped; hot tears flowed down her cheeks. She looked around, searching for hope she knew she would not find in the gray landscape of mountains, snow, and barren trees.

The sound was closer now. Though still no more than a whisper of wind in the lifeless trees above her, it was closer, nonetheless.

The men were coming, searching, hunting.

Hunting *her.*

They would be methodical and disciplined in the search. Nothing would escape their notice, not the slightest sign. They would find her just as they had found all the others. About this, she held no illusions.

But death, even death in the snowy mountains, was preferable to living with the nightmare that possessed the valley.

She knew about the dogs. All the girls did. She had heard them howling in the night, felt their presence while she lay in her bed during the chilly nights. They were horrible, black-and-tan monsters trained to hunt and kill. Trained to destroy.

Gaby picked herself up again and ran.

The snow was not as deep here in the forest where even the naked branches offered some protection, so she kept to the wooded spaces. The alternatives were less inviting—deep snow piled into massive drifts against fence rows in the open pastures.

Gaby stopped to rest. Her panting breath was expelled in small clouds of fog. The cold air hurt her lungs and her breathing was coming in measured gasps, short and ragged. The howling of the dogs was still there, in the background, small and quiet. And deadly. *Eternal.*

She looked behind her, hoping there would be nothing to see. Nothing yet, no figures moving among the distant trees, but they would come. For now there was only the muted sound, the persistent, relentless reminder that the men and dogs were still there.

Gaby's heart thumped inside her chest, an incessant beating that no amount of self-will could quell. This was not the way it should be, not for a girl of her age.

She had fourteen years. That's how her people phrased it in Mexico. She *had* fourteen years when she arrived in the valley, but time was a blur after that. She'd started counting the days on the wall of the room she shared with Tia, until one of the guards had discovered the small, vertical marks near the head of her bed and had erased the evidence of time's passage. Since that day, time had become irrelevant, fluid. Maybe by now she had another year, maybe two. She couldn't be certain, and it bothered her that she didn't know.

It was beginning to snow heavily. The large white flakes drifted down through the barren tree limbs as if an unseen force was trying once again to eradicate the evil that gripped the valley.

Gaby was cold. Cold and tired. Her feet were numb. She briefly thought about sitting down and letting the cold work on her, letting it numb her even more, taking away the pain and loneliness. Would the cold work before the dogs caught up with her? Was there a chance the beasts would catch her before she froze to death? It was a risk she could not take.

A sharp crack echoed through the forest. The men! *The dogs!* They were closing in on her.

Terror energized her; panic forced her into action. This time she moved more slowly, her feet hindering her movement.

Maybe she should pray. It had worked before. Not here in this valley, but before, when she and her family had been on the road, seeking the migratory work that had led them from Mexico deep into the southern United States. She'd prayed then, asking God for work, for food and for safety. He had answered her prayers then. Maybe it was time to pray again. She needed to know someone was watching over her, even if it was someone she could not see.

But the cold was relentless and bone-chilling, forcing even the idea of prayer from her mind. Stinging sleet began to mix with the snow. The sleet ticking in the tree limbs reminded Gaby of the rat claws clicking across the tile floor of her Mexican home. She crouched at the base of a large oak and surveyed her surroundings. Nothing but rolling hills, rounded mountaintops shorn flat by the wind, and barren forest devoid of color. For her, the gray sky and leafless forest were as alien a landscape as she had ever imagined in her most terrifying nightmare.

But this nightmare was true.

Her thoughts returned to Mexico.

Her land.

Her home.

Gaby visualized her small village ensconced between mountains and sea. The sounds of children playing in the streets and the smell of onions and meat frying on the street grills. She wondered whether she was beginning to hallucinate. Maybe she was dreaming. Was she asleep? Could one dream while totally awake? The same sky and trees surrounded her. No, it was all in her mind, this quiet specter of times past. She longed to return, to see the face of her mother, the weathered features of her father, and the innocent smiles of her two brothers and younger twin sisters. She wanted to see the golden sun rising over the jagged peaks, to be warm again. Oh, to be warm just once more.

The cold gnawed at her like a rabid animal, and she knew without a doubt she would die in this horrible place, alone, in this *valle de la sombra.*

Gaby scanned the horizon, forcing her mind to forget all thoughts of home and warmth and concentrate on survival. The snow was collecting in her dark hair. Her mind refused to function normally, to allow for the clear thought she so desperately needed. The wind whistled through the trees like the whine of an injured animal. Even the sound of the men and the dogs was now lost in the breeze. She could no longer hear them, but they were there. They would always be there, those who preyed on the weak.

How had she come to this place?

It had all started in southern Arkansas, in the place where the *trabajadores* gathered, the migrant workers. She had noticed the two men hanging around the migrant center, like vultures waiting for carrion. She knew that now, but not then.

The two men had been young, athletic-looking; one handsome in a rugged manner, the other seemingly sensitive to what the girls at the center had to say. *Attentive,* that was the word. Both had sympathized with the plight of those who had to be away from their homeland in order to earn a living. The handsome one spoke Spanish. Not well, but with an unusual accent that Gaby found charming. She had been enamored with the young man, and he had encouraged her. She had always known she was pretty, with her light olive complexion that was more reminiscent of the Mediterranean than eastern Mexico. Her dark eyes shone with a particular brilliance, marking not only her beauty but also her intelligence. She was larger than most girls her age, and with the size came an enhanced development. It all added up to her appearing older than she actually was, and she enjoyed the attention it brought her.

Twice she and a friend had sneaked off from the center, enjoying the freedom and company of the two young men. Her mother had cautioned her about the *Norte Americanos,* but she had not listened. After all, was she not mature enough to handle any situation? The young men certainly thought so.

Her mother's wisdom and warnings had proved prophetic. One night, a night she had chosen to be alone with the handsome one, it had happened.

It had started with a simple question: Would she like to go to Little Rock? It was only a few hours away in his car, and they could be back long before the sun was up and it was time to go to work. There were things to do there, places to see. Gaby had hesitated, remembering her mother's warnings, but had eventually given in to the young man's persistence and gentle cajoling. They had gone.

She had met the handsome young man after the rest of the family had gone to bed. They had driven east, heading for the Arkansas capital. The young man had brought a bottle of some type of liquor, clear like the tequila from Mexico. It had tasted of pure alcohol. One sip, no more. She was not a drinker. That had seemed to satisfy the young man, as she put the bottle to her lips. That was the last thing she remembered until she awoke in the strange place, her ankles and wrists bound by thick leather straps to some type of bed.

Terror had been instantaneous. A fear so profound she could actually *taste* it!

What had happened? A car wreck? Something terrible was taking place, but what? She couldn't remember. What about the young man? Had he been killed? Where was he? Where was she?

She didn't feel injured. There was no pain. As a matter of fact, she felt very little. The only sensation was the strange taste in her mouth.

She'd examined the room: white, antiseptic, unadorned. The

restraints on her wrists and ankles were formidable. She had tried to raise her head but could not.

She had been close to tears when the door to the room opened and a woman dressed as a nurse had come into the room. Behind her, a man in an expensive business suit, gray hair and beard, and mannerisms Gaby thought of as aristocratic, stepped into the room. And then, as if she was awakening from a dreadful nightmare, the handsome young man followed.

"She's been examined?" the man in the suit asked.

The nurse nodded. "She's in excellent health."

"What do you think?" the young man asked.

The man in the suit smiled. "You have done well, as usual. There will be a bonus in this for you."

Gaby had tried to speak, to halt the conversation that seemed to be going on without her, but her voice would not come. Had they done something to that, as well?

The young man smiled at what the man in the suit had said, all the time his eyes looking greedily at Gaby. It was then she realized she was being examined like one of the grass-starved beef cows her father used to herd between desert patches just outside their village.

"What about the family?" the man in the suit asked.

The young man smiled again and shook his head. "They will think like all the others. Just another Mexican girl who has run off for the better life in the states. The local police don't even take missing persons reports seriously. Provided the family files one, which is rare. And we have an added factor with this one. She told me none of the family has a green card. They skirted the border checkpoints in southern Texas, and the INS here in Arkansas hasn't caught them yet. The probability that the family will expose themselves by filing a report is almost nil."

The gray-haired man moved closer to the bed. Gaby recoiled at the look in his eyes. "Two," he told the nurse, his eyes never leaving Gaby. "No more than two. That's the rule, even for ones like her. Then get rid of her."

"Understood," the nurse replied. Her voice had been soft, the word barely audible, as if there were some compassion in her. Then the nurse had stepped nearer, a syringe in her right hand. She had plunged the needle deep into Gaby's arm with no regard for the pain she produced.

Gaby had wanted to scream, to force herself to wake from what was surely a nightmare. The strange taste had returned, only this time much stronger than when she had awakened. She had only time to register the foul taste when her eyes closed despite her efforts to keep them open. The next time she awoke, she was in the valley. At least that's what the other girls had called it, and so she called it that from that time on.

The valley was a place of terror. A place from which she had seen new friends come and go. Those who left never returned.

El valle. The place where she would have died, just like all the rest, had she not seized the opportunity to run. Even if she had to die in the cold whiteness of the Arkansas Ozarks, it would be better than the death that waited like a hungry demon to devour her in the valley.

She had waited, and when the opportunity came, she had escaped through an access door that, in God's providence, had been left open by an inattentive nurse. Out in the Arkansas winter, she had found a bleak grayness that offered as little hope as she had had in the house.

Gaby no longer had any sensation in her feet. The stinging pain was gone. In place of the pain was only blessed numbness. But that was just her feet. The rest of her continued to shiver in the cold. Her stomach was beginning to cramp. Odd waves of pain washed over her. Her head ached as it had never ached before. A strange sensation of sleep overtook her. She would have to get up, function, force herself to move if she was to stay alive.

The sound of the dogs swept over her like a warm Caribbean tide. How long had she been here? Too long, that much was obvious. The sounds were closer, much closer. She could make out random bits of conversation, disjointed phrases snatched from the speaker's mouth by an erratic wind. She could hear the heavy breathing of the dogs.

Would the snow make it more difficult for them to follow her? She
didn't know; she hoped so. But she had to keep moving. Which way
now? It didn't make much difference, she realized. Any direction
except the one the men and the dogs were coming from. She forced her
legs to react, to move, to take one step after the other until finally she
was running again.

Maybe she would find safety over the next mountain, in the next
valley. She would flee as long as her protesting limbs would allow,
then she would lie down and die. Somewhere, she'd heard that freezing to death was painless. She wasn't sure she believed that. After all,
wasn't she experiencing pain right now? The spasms that were beginning to twist her stomach into knots were almost debilitating. She
wanted to scream.

She stumbled up another rise and looked around. Another mountain loomed before her. As she started down into the tiny valley, she
heard a different sound. It was a humming or purring noise. Without
really thinking, Gaby changed direction, moving to her right, down the
mountain, toward the sound. As she drew closer, she sensed that the
sound offered the one thing she most wanted: escape.

She mouthed a silent prayer and moved toward the ever-
increasing noise.

CHAPTER TWO

The high-winged Cessna 185 bounced in a growing turbulence, like a straw tossed in a tornado.

"This is trouble," said David Michaels.

"It's building fast, out of the west," Dean Barber agreed. "We're going to have to get this thing on the ground, and soon."

David Michaels depressed the right rudder peddle and gently turned the yoke to the left. The small airplane twisted down and to the left, giving David a better view of the terrain below.

"What's down there?" asked Barber.

David thumbed the small intercom switch attached to the yoke, via the David Clark headset communication system. "Hills, trees, and snow. The same thing that was down there when we took off."

"Not exactly. When we took off, we didn't have that storm staring us in the face." Barber pointed through the windscreen. "I thought Harrison Flight Service said the weather was only overcast and ten miles."

David nodded. The Flight Service station in Harrison, Arkansas, monitored the weather for the Federal Aviation Administration.

"That's what they said. Obviously they made a mistake."

Dean Barber laughed, so loud that David heard it without the aid of the headsets.

"We'll never make it back to Clayton," David said seriously.

"You're going to log lots of hood time today, without the hood, I might add," Dean said.

"You said I was the best two-hundred-hour pilot you ever trained."

Ever since David had begun flying after retiring from the U.S. Navy, Dean Barber had been his flight instructor in the mountain burg of Clayton, Arkansas. When he was not attending to his duties as pastor of First Community Church, David could be found in the air, either in Barber's Cessna or his own Piper Super Cub. Today, the two men were aloft to train David for his instrument rating, which meant leaving the Cub in its hanger and flying the IFR-certified Cessna. Normally David would be flying "under the hood," a training device that allowed the student to view only the instrument panel. But with the storm building, there would be no need to don the hood. As the storm engulfed the Cessna, the instruments would be the two men's only salvation.

"I'm going to try Flight Service again," Barber said, as he dialed the radio to the correct frequency. Static crackled through the headsets. Barber punched in a second frequency and the noise was replaced by the clear tones of Little Rock Approach Control. He listened to the chatter between an inbound Southwest flight and the air traffic controllers.

"Radio's fine," Barber said.

"Yeah. Harrison is either off the air or the storm is blocking the transmissions."

Snow began to pepper the Cessna's windscreen; a north wind licked at the airplane's broad wings. Cold air slipped between a ragged door insulation strip next to David's left leg, and he shivered at the unwelcome intrusion. David checked the cabin heater switch; it was on full. The gasoline-powered heater was having trouble battling the intense cold.

Normally for David, the cabin of the Cessna or the Cub was a cozy refuge in a sea of disquiet—a good place to think. Lately, David's thoughts consistently centered on Cindy Tolbert, the Clayton County clerk. He had finally admitted to himself that she was the only girl he had ever loved. That love now expressed itself in quiet evenings together, rowdy church suppers, and intimate conversations about anything and everything.

At the moment, however, thoughts of Cindy were chased away by the storm bearing down on the tiny aircraft.

"Conway?" David asked.

The single-word question about the Arkansas city to the south was answered by a shake of Dean Barber's head. "Storm's already circled to the south. East too. Conway will be closed off. We'll have to find a field and put this thing down quick."

Quick. Dean Barber had a definite knack for understatement. David glanced out the side window again. The storm was moving like an avalanche toward them. David knew there would be one-hundred-mile-an-hour winds embedded in the mountain of clouds, carried along by the river of air called the jet stream.

David changed frequencies, this time to an en route flight controller at Little Rock's Adams Field.

"Little Rock, Cessna two-two-six-niner-niner, one hundred miles north at five thousand, preparing for an emergency landing," David radioed. As he spoke, he glanced in Dean Barber's direction. For the first time since he had known the flight instructor, he saw fear in the man's eyes. David found that disconcerting. "Remember, you said I was the best two-hundred-hour pilot you've ever seen," David reminded Barber.

The instructor smiled slowly. "Yeah, but you're still just a two-hundred-hour pilot. Don't ever overestimate your ability. I'll be on the controls when we make this landing, provided we find a place to land, that is."

David nodded, knowing Barber could land the plane in a cow pasture as easily as if it were the seven thousand feet of asphalt back at Clayton Municipal.

The headphones crackled. "Cessna two-two-six-niner-niner, Little Rock Control. Do I understand you are declaring an emergency, sir?"

David hesitated for only a second before replying. A declared emergency would activate the FAA emergency system. It would mean a mountain of paperwork, interviews with FAA officials, and tons of lost time, provided they lived to talk about it.

"Affirmative, Little Rock. Cessna two-two-six-niner-niner declaring an emergency. Two souls on board." The last phrase struck David with its significance. It had not been "two bodies" on board. It had not been "two men" on board, but "two souls," the standard nomenclature used by the FAA. For David, the phrase was particularly poignant.

When David had decided to take up flying, he'd sought out Dean as his instructor. He knew the man had flown F-4 Phantoms in Vietnam and came highly recommended. What David had not counted on was the man's animosity toward religion, any kind of religion. The ground rules had been set early on: "No talk of God—yours or anyone else's—while flight instruction is going on," Dean had said tersely. David had reluctantly abided by Dean's decree for the last year. David had hoped his lifestyle might have some impact, but the presence of a former chaplain and current pastor did not seem to curb Barber's tendencies toward rough talk. For David, it was more evidence that "lifestyle evangelism" lacked the impact he originally thought.

"Cessna six-niner-niner, squawk seven-seven-zero-zero and ident," the Little Rock controller radioed, jerking David's thoughts back to the storm. He had to concentrate.

"Got it," Barber said, tuning the encoding transponder to the emergency frequency and pushing the tiny ident button that would make the Cessna appear brighter on the controller's radar screen.

"Cessna six-niner-niner, I have you one hundred three miles north of Adams Field on the three-two-seven radial. What are your intentions, sir?"

"We're going to put down in a pasture to avoid an incoming storm," David immediately radioed. "If we bend the plane, the ELT will activate."

"Understood. Good luck, sir."

"To the right," Dean Barber said, pointing through the windscreen. "That looks like about two thousand feet down there. Must be a pasture."

David banked to the right, reduced power, and let the nose of the 185 drop slightly. Barber was right, there was a pasture about two miles east. A gust of wind sniped at the Cessna, seeking the underside of the high-wing aircraft, trying to flip the plane. David corrected for the gust, leveled the wings, and let the nose drop a little more. Instantly the airspeed indicator began to climb in response to the change in attitude. The quicker they could get on the ground, the better David would like it.

"Is this where God takes over?" asked Barber without looking at David.

David chanced a look at the man in the right seat beside him. In all the time they had spent together, this was the first time he had had any indication that Dean Barber even thought about God. Maybe, thought David, something *had* rubbed off on the man.

David trimmed the Cessna in its current attitude and thumbed the mike button. "I thought religion and God were off-limits."

"Just curious," the instructor replied. "This seems to be a situation where prayer would be a standard response. For the religious types, I mean. How come you're not praying?"

"I am. I've been praying since that storm blew up."

Barber looked at David. "I haven't heard a word come out of you except to talk to Little Rock. What do you mean, you've been praying?"

David smiled to himself. He knew what was happening. This was another version of the "foxhole prayer." He'd seen it before, from young, tough marines who were literally brought to their knees in prayer at the thought of impending death. And while death was not a given in their situation, it was interesting and heartening to see the Holy Spirit still worked on men such as Dean Barber.

David adjusted the trim tab once again to relieve the back pressure he had been holding on the yoke, pulled off more power, and corrected the flight path of the Cessna slightly to the right. Then he said, "Prayer is not something you have to do out loud. God hears us even when we think He doesn't or can't."

With those words, David remembered an earlier conversation he'd had with an FBI agent about the same subject. The agent had eventually accepted Jesus Christ as the only path to heaven. David hoped for the same result here, but he would have to let it be on Dean's initiative. The worst thing he could do would be to press the man. Besides, that was not his style.

"Yeah, well, if we get this plane on the ground in one piece, I might just want to talk about that."

David was elated. "Then let's get this thing down," he said.

David had been alternating his attention between the approaching storm and the Cessna's instruments as he continued the long approach into the pasture. Already snow and ice were beginning to accumulate on the leading edge of the wings. The Cessna was not equipped with deicing boots, and even a small amount of ice on the wings could be a real problem. Control had already diminished as the ice disrupted the clean airflow over the wings.

"You on?" David asked without looking to see whether Barber had taken control of the plane from the right seat.

"I've got the plane," Barber said.

David released his grip on the yoke and let the instructor fly the plane.

"Good setup," said Barber. "Correct attitude, good speed, touchdown point pegged. I should let you land this thing. I couldn't have done better myself."

David felt an immediate sense of pride, but he knew that his two hundred flight hours equaled maybe 1 percent of Barber's total hours in the air. It would have been the height of lunacy to land the Cessna himself.

Barber had the plane nose down, headed for the pasture. David watched as he pulled on ten degrees of flap, ran through the "before landing checklist," and cinched up his shoulder harness and seat belt. David followed suit.

"Looks pretty smooth, but there's no telling what's beneath the snow. Be ready to cut the master and get out of this thing in a hurry if something goes wrong."

"I'll keep praying," David answered.

"Lack of tenacity is not one of your faults."

David smiled. It was a beginning.

Barber allowed the Cessna's nose to drop slightly, picking up a few knots of airspeed. The wind was coming in hard and fast from the northwest. Luckily the pasture was oriented from the southeast to the northwest, negating much of the wind's effect. At least they would not have to deal with a hazardous crosswind on landing.

"I couldn't have set this pasture up better for an airstrip if I had tried," Barber said.

"I know what you mean. Almost made to order."

The white terrain rushed up in the windscreen as the plane descended rapidly. David glanced at the airspeed indicator. Barber was carrying more speed into the landing than was called for under normal circumstances. It was a prudent move, given the ice buildup and the increasing winds.

The plane's fixed landing gear touched the snow in a gentle caress. A blinding spray of snow, driven by the propeller wash, shot past the side windows. The plane settled; the tail wheel came down with a gentle thud, and Barber kept the aircraft straight down the pasture as the speed bled off rapidly. He ignored the toe brakes situated just above the rudder peddles, knowing any application of brakes might cause a disaster. There was plenty of room. Better to let the plane coast to a stop on its own.

The storm broke on top of the small plane even before the "after landing checklist" was completed. Snow and sleet pelted the plane. The wind picked up and the Cessna rocked in the buffeting tempest.

"There are some tie-downs and stakes in the cargo compartment. Clothing too. Let's get this thing tied down before it flies away on its own," Barber yelled above the noise of the building wind.

Both men were out of the plane in seconds. They retrieved the tie-downs and the clothing and in minutes were back in the plane's cabin, the plane secure and the clothing wrapped tightly around them.

"This will blow over in a few minutes," Barber said. "When it does, we get back on the radio and let Little Rock know we got down all right. Even then, we'll still have to fill out a ton of paperwork."

"I know," said David. "My first emergency landing. What about you?"

Barber grinned. "My second in thirty years, not counting Vietnam."

"What happened?"

As the wind howled outside the plane, Dean Barber told the story.

"Not much, really. I was flying a Piper Tri-Pacer. Sort of a nose gear version of your Cub. I thought I was switching fuel tanks and I inadvertently closed off the fuel. A Tri-Pacer flies like a brick without power. I had to put it down on a country road. When I discovered what I had done, I turned the fuel back on, cranked her up, and took off. I never even told anyone. Don't know why I'm telling you now."

"I'll keep the confidence," David assured the instructor, a wide grin splitting his face.

The Cessna shook as the wind built on the incoming tide of the storm. The plane struggled against the tie-downs. The snow increased along with the wind, producing whiteout conditions outside the small plane's cabin.

Then, as if a switch had been thrown, the wind subsided. The swirling snow settled to the ground, and the sun began to peek through broken clouds.

"Incredible," Barber observed.

"Almost as if there was a God in heaven looking down on us," David Michaels said.

Barber turned to David. "All right. We talk about it when we get back. Satisfied?"

"Deal," David agreed.

"Try the radio," Barber suggested. "The way this storm blew through here, we might be able to contact Harrison or Little Rock and cancel the emergency landing."

David twisted the master switch to "on" and activated the radios. Sure enough, he was able to contact Little Rock on the first attempt. He canceled the emergency and switched off the master.

"We'll have to wait until the sun melts the snow and ice on the wings," Dean Barber said. "Shouldn't take too long. In the meantime, let's do a little exploring. I'm curious about something."

"About what?"

Barber held up a single finger and waved it at David. "Not until I'm sure. I've already told you about the Tri-Pacer landing. I make it a rule not to make a fool of myself more than once a day. Let's go."

David climbed out of the Cessna. Barber was already striding toward the far end of the open pasture. David followed him, his curiosity building with every step.

Barber stopped his rapid pacing and scanned the ground. David caught up to him.

"What are you looking for?" he asked, crouching down beside Barber.

"I'm not sure. When the 185 touched down, I just thought the landing was a little too smooth."

"I thought that was due to experience. That was one heck of a good landing."

"Exactly. Too good. No stick-ups, no bumps. The ground is smooth, as if it's been graded. The orientation is perfect. I suspect it even drains during heavy rains. Too perfect for a cow pasture."

David stood up and looked around. What had looked like nothing more than two thousand feet of fortuitous pasture from the air now looked more like three thousand feet. The surrounding trees had been cut back more than two hundred yards. A strange layout for a pasture—long and narrow. More like an airstrip than a pasture, David realized.

"You see it, don't you?" Barber asked, standing up.

"Looks more like a private field than a pasture."

"That's the way it looks to me. Why would anyone clear out more than half a mile of strip in the middle of nowhere?"

"We're only guessing."

"Huh uh. Take a look around. There's not even the beginning of growth along the entire area. Someone is maintaining this strip in top condition. A good pilot could get a twin down easily. My bet is that when this snow melts, there's a grade-A, number one grass strip here. No foreign objects either. Might even get a Cessna Citation down here."

David could see what Barber was saying was true. It had to be an airstrip. Nothing else made much sense, but then an airport in the middle of the Ozarks, miles from the nearest town, didn't make a whole lot of sense either. Especially an airstrip like Barber was describing. It took men and equipment to maintain a good grass strip. Where were they? Who were they? With every question, the whole thing made less and less sense.

"The chart," David said.

"Don't bother," Barber said quietly, knowing what David was getting at. "It's not on any sectional chart I've ever seen. I've been flying these mountains for ten years, and this is the first time I've run across this place."

"How's that possible? This much clear space in the middle of nowhere is not exactly obscure. Someone would have noticed it."

Barber nodded agreement, then said, "Oh, it's not invisible. Quite the contrary. But its location makes it invisible. No houses, no structures of any kind. Nothing to tie it to aircraft. No hangers, no maintenance buildings, nothing. Anyone overflying this place would think the same thing we did—pasture, pure and simple. And I think we will find that it's not located on any regular flight path. You have to be coming here to find it. What we have here is a covert airfield. It's hidden so well the whole world can see it, and no one has any idea what it is."

"That's hard to believe. If it really is an airport, then what's the destination? There nothing around here."

"We can check that out later. Just so you won't have any doubts about what this place is, there's something else you need to see. Take a look over here," Barber said, pointing upward toward the tip of what looked like a limbless tree.

David followed Barber's direction. What appeared to be a tree without limbs was actually an airport windsock. The fabric hung limply in the wake of the storm. A pilot would have to know it was there and still use a good set of binoculars to view the sock from the air.

"One more thing, and this is the real clincher," Barber added, as he bent down. "Look at this and you tell me what it is."

David moved closer as Dean Barber swept away a small snowdrift. Beneath the snow was a small metal box no larger than an enlarged shoe box. The box was painted with random patterns of browns and earth tones. In a word, camouflage paint. David recognized the device instantly.

Three small windows were located in the end of the box, the same size as the cross section of the box. David could clearly see the red, amber, and green lenses. It was a VASI, a Variable Approach Slope Indicator, one of the simplest and surest approach instruments for assisted landings. A weatherproof conduit was connected at the rear of the box and buried in the ground. A few feet away, painted in the same camouflage colors, was a simple solar cell secured to a short post that would easily pass as a small sapling. Another box was attached to the same post just below the cells. David walked over to it and opened the waterproof lid. Inside were three rechargeable batteries, the power for the VASI. A small solid-state panel rested next to the batteries. A short antenna was attached to the circuit board and hung loosely from the bottom of the battery box.

"It's activated by an aircraft's radio, just like the runway lights back at Clayton Municipal. Five to seven rapid clicks on a predetermined frequency, and you have your own instrument landing system," Barber said.

David nodded and looked around the area. The only questions now were why was the airstrip here and who had built it? David was not sure he wanted to know.

CHAPTER THREE

When the storm finally broke, Gaby was dazed, confused, and dis-oriented. Had she heard the sound or only imagined it? Had it come from her right or her left? She could no longer be certain.

There had been snow and sleet, but the worst by far had been the wind. It had been relentless, persistent, painful. She'd sought shelter near a large tree whose trunk seemed as large as a car, and for a time it had protected her. But the wind had wended its way around the tree, seeking her like an unrelenting stalker. In the end, it had found her and chilled her to the bone. She was too weak to run now. Too weak to escape, to evade the men and dogs she knew were still in the forest.

But even in her semicomatose state, she was certain she had heard it. The sound was imprinted on her brain. It had been a different sound, not that of the men and dogs. Something different. A sound with the promise of hope. She had altered her course toward the sound, hadn't she?

But the suddenness and ferocity of the storm had finished her. The sound was no longer there, and with its demise had gone her hope. Now, as hypothermia set in, she felt a pleasant warmth coursing through her body. She rolled to her right, allowing the warmth to seep deeper into her inner self, and then she saw it.

The brilliant flash of blue caught her attention. A bright blue accented by the harsh whiteness of the freshly fallen snow. Her gaze left the small patch of blue, drawn to movement just beyond the color.

Movement!

Men!

Two men!

A racking sob caught in Gaby's throat. They had found her, the hunters. She had failed and now she would die in her failure.

But there was something different about the men in the valley below. They were not the men she knew. Not the men who ogled the girls at night, abusing them when they thought no one was watching. These two were different. Still, it was possible that these two were in some way connected to the valley. She had to be careful.

The warmth that had flowed through her was replaced by a surge of energy. The warmth was still there, lurking somewhere in the background, ready to return should she call on it, but she knew she would not. Not now. Now there was hope of deliverance, and that hope was rooted in the patch of blue she now recognized as a small airplane.

Gaby rose from her place beneath the tree, stumbling as the effects of the cold and fatigue overwhelmed her once again. Salvation was only yards away. The plane would carry her from the valley, from the mountains, from the horror. But she had to reach it first.

She moved with all the speed her quickly deteriorating physical condition allowed. As she dropped down into the gently sloping valley where the plane rested, the fuselage came between her and the two men, who appeared to be examining an object near the edge of the pasture. Gaby could see the aircraft easily now. The doors were closed, but there was some sort of compartment beneath the aircraft. She could make out an open hatch hanging loosely, revealing the dark inner space of the compartment. That was her goal, that small space. All she had to do was get there.

The sun was coming out, forcing the last remnants of the storm to the east. As she emerged from the forest, the sun lifted her spirits. She no longer felt the cold, the pain, or the wet. Freedom lay within reach. Even if she died in the belly of the plane, it would be better than death in the freezing mountains or capture by the men and the dogs. Death, so long as it was death outside the hideous valley, was acceptable.

Gaby moved cautiously, keeping the bulk of the plane between her and the two men, using the aircraft as a shield. She could hear their voices now, low and distorted. She could not understand the words. She spoke a little English, but the words that drifted to her over the frozen landscape were meaningless.

She staggered on, suddenly aware of her error. She had abandoned the protection of the forest, the relative security offered by conceal- ment. Gaby quickly glanced behind her. The ferocity of the storm had been a blessing in disguise. It had snowed heavily, but the wind had piled the snow into high drifts against stationary objects. The flat ground of the pasture was clear of snow. As she made her way toward the airplane, she left no telltale footprints. Had God provided her with this blessing? She didn't remember praying, but maybe she had. Maybe her subconscious had unknowingly lifted a petition toward heaven, and here was an answer.

Gaby picked up the movement of the two men at the edge of the pasture. They were standing up, preparing to return, she knew. She would have to hurry. Sixty seconds. That was all she needed to reach the beckoning door of the cargo space beneath the plane.

With no more than ten feet remaining, Gaby could almost feel the sanctuary the blessed darkness offered. She crossed the distance, peered into the storage compartment, and quickly forced her freezing body through the opening. It was a tight squeeze, much tighter than she had thought, but there was sufficient room, because the compartment was also deeper than she'd imagined. It was the dimensions that restricted her movement. Once in, it would be difficult for her to turn around so her head would be facing forward. No matter, she was inside, and that counted much more than comfort. She pressed her body into the rear portion of the compartment. She could hear footsteps crossing the frozen ground. She managed to turn around within the tiny space, her freezing muscles protesting at each movement. Now she faced forward. The light flooding through the open hatch seemed almost too brilliant to look at.

Footsteps echoed within the small enclosure. The two men were almost at the plane. What would they do now? Would they check the compartment? If they did, they would surely find her. What then? What if they were affiliated with the men who were chasing her? And if they weren't, could she convince them to take her with them?

The footsteps stopped. From her vantage point, she could see the legs of one of the men. They were talking. Again, she did not understand the words.

Then, as if all her questions were answered, the man tossed two heavy jackets into the compartment. Several metal objects and lengths of rope followed. In seconds, the compartment door was shut. Gaby gathered the two jackets around herself. Residual warmth from the men still clung to them, and it felt good. The warmth she'd noticed earlier was back; she was tired and sleepy. She no longer had the strength to hold her eyes open. As she allowed her eyelids to close slowly, she thought the feeling was the sweetest she had ever experienced in all of her fourteen years. Or was it fifteen? Sixteen? It didn't matter.

Gaby Ibarra slipped down into a darkness more profound than that of the small compartment, a darkness that threatened to claim her life.

CHAPTER
FOUR

Cole Branscum and Billy Bob Campbell stumbled along the wooded crest of the ridge. They were cold and angry. Their own responsibility for their current sad state of affairs only exacerbated their foul moods.

"Where are the dogs?" Billy Bob snarled as he grasped at tree limbs to keep from falling. His feet slid out from under him again, and he hit the rough ridge top with a heavy thud. He cursed.

Cole stopped on a small rise and looked back. His first inclination was to laugh, but Billy Bob Campbell was mean, and given their present situation, he knew Billy Bob's temper was no laughing matter.

"I heard them take off to the east," Cole answered. "I ain't sure where they think they're headed. None of the other *señoritas* ever took off that direction."

"Don't matter," said Billy Bob as he dusted off the snow from his camouflage overalls. "She's just like the others. None of them know where they're going cause they don't know where they are. She just knows less. You better get on them dogs. We ain't gonna find the girl without them," Billy Bob said, his voice rising.

"Don't holler at me, man. You supposed to be in charge, remember? We lose this one, ain't gonna be kickin' Cole around. They gonna want a piece of your hide, man."

Billy Bob edged menacingly closer to Cole. He knew he needed Cole and the dogs to find the girl, but he wasn't going to put up with any of Cole's mouth either.

"Listen up real good, Cole. We lose this one, we're both gonna be in hot water. I told you not to be messin' with the girls, but you don't listen. If Swann finds out what you been doin', you're as good as dead." Billy Bob moved closer, until he was chest to chest with his shorter partner. "And chances are I'd be the one to have to 'do' you. Now, you're a friend, but I'd still have to do it. So don't start with me about who's gonna be in hot water."

Cole Branscum took a quick step back. "It wasn't my fault this time," he said. "That stupid nurse left the door open. I didn't have nothin' to do with it."

"Yeah, well that may not be the way the nurse sees it. Let's get this girl and get back to the valley. I got a date tonight. Gonna take her to the VFW for some drinks and fun, so let's get this over with."

Cole nodded. "East. The dogs are headed east, toward the airstrip. Ain't nothin' in that direction for miles. They should run her down within an hour."

Billy Bob pushed Cole ahead of him. "C'mon, let's get going." With any luck, they would have the girl back in the valley in a couple of hours, and Billy Bob could take off for the small trailer he rented just outside of Benning, Arkansas.

Dogs barking in the distance echoed through the pine trees. Both men craned their heads in that direction.

"See. I told you. East," Cole smiled, revealing a set of crooked, tobacco-stained teeth.

"Let's move," Billy Bob ordered.

Both men moved out at a gentle trot, homing in on the sound of the dogs.

"That was Juniper," Cole said, identifying the howling dog. "He's onto something."

"Check your gun. We don't need snow jammin' the barrels if we need them."

The going was difficult, even though both men had spent most of their lives in these mountains. They had hunted, fished, and camped in the forest for years, but in all their experience, neither had seen weather like this.

Snow was rare in Arkansas, and the two men grumbled and cursed as they struggled through drifts and stumbled over downed branches. The storms that had been moving across the southern states with clockwork precision would make finding the girl difficult, even with the dogs.

Neither man spoke of the consequences, but each was aware of the price for failure. The other two escapees had taken a combined total of thirty minutes to capture and haul back to the house in the valley. But this one was different. She was either luckier or more determined. Cole and Billy Bob had already been in the woods for three hours. When the big wind had come up, they had sought protection underneath a rock-face outcropping. It had been barely adequate, and both men were tempted to abandon the hunt. Unless Juniper was actually following the girl's trail, they could well be out in the elements for another three hours. Billy Bob did not like that idea one bit.

The two men worked their way toward the barking. It sounded as though the dog had the scent. If that were the case, Billy Bob thought, he might make it to the VFW after all. But they would have to get to the girl before the dog, or there wouldn't be enough left of her to carry back. To Billy Bob, it really didn't make that much difference. He didn't like these foreigners anyway. Not like Cole did. But if the dogs got to her, Swann might want more than just a simple explanation, and that would take time. They needed to find her quickly.

Cole tripped on a tree root and went down hard. Billy Bob pulled up short, waiting for his partner to get up. He did not offer to help.

"It oughta be easier than this," Cole wheezed. "I'm freezing. Ground's frozen too."

"Can that dog track a dead girl?" Billy Bob asked.

Cole looked back at the larger man. "What're you talkin' about?"

Billy Bob sighed. Sometimes Cole's stupidity was too much. "The girl might already be frozen to death out here. Can the dogs trace her in that case?"

"If she's dead, we got no problem, right?"

Billy Bob shook his head at his buddy's stupidity. They had been together in high school, in the army, and afterwards, and Cole had never seemed so thick. Billy Bob wondered what he'd seen in the man to make him want to team with him.

"If she's dead, and those dogs of yours can't track her, we're gonna' be out here the rest of the night. We have to find the body. Can't afford to have someone else find her and start asking questions. Somethin' like that will bring every lawman from miles around. Swann won't like it. The Doc won't like it, and, more importantly, Memphis won't like it."

Billy Bob watched Cole's face reflect fear at the mention of Memphis. Swann and Doc could be handled; they'd done it before. But Memphis was a different situation. Those men were not the kind of people to put up with this type of failure. Truthfully, they were not the kind of men to accept *any* type of failure. They had to find the girl, dead or alive.

"The dogs will find her," Cole said morosely.

"Yeah, well, they better."

"Don't threaten me, man."

Billy Bob Campbell again moved close to Cole. "Those dogs don't find her, I'm gonna' sic 'em on you. And that's a promise."

"They'll find her," Cole snapped.

A dog bayed in the distance, followed seconds later by a second, distinctively different howl.

"Cutter's on her too," Cole exclaimed. "Juniper and Cutter both found her. We'll get her now."

Both men began running toward the sound of the animals. The dogs were good. Billy Bob would give him that much. But he had to keep Cole on his toes, and threats were the only thing that seemed to work.

From the sounds of the dogs, they were no more than half a mile away. With luck, they would have the girl in tow in less than an hour and be on their way back to the valley. Then a new fear struck Billy Bob. The same thought hit Cole at the same time, and both men looked at each other with renewed fear in their eyes.

"The airstrip," each man said simultaneously. They bounded through the woods.

As they ran, a familiar sound reverberated through the forest. It took a full ten seconds for the significance to register. Someone had landed in the "pasture." Someone unauthorized. And now they were about to take off. The gradual acceleration of an aircraft engine was unmistakable.

Was it possible? Billy Bob asked himself. Was this an organized effort to save this one girl? It didn't seem possible. Such a rescue would require split-second timing, but the girl's escape had been random, accidental. It couldn't have been planned. It had to be something else. But what could explain an unknown plane in the pasture? Billy Bob Campbell did not believe in miracles.

The increased pitch of the engine energized both men. They raced toward the airfield. An air of doom began to descend on them as the penetrating sound reached take-off intensity.

CHAPTER FIVE

With the walk-around done, and the tie-downs and jackets stowed in the belly storage compartment, David Michaels and Dean Barber strapped themselves into the seats of the Cessna 185. The Continental engine was ticking over with a steady beat.

The two men were silent. David ran through the take-off checklist, finally turning his attention to the small instrument attached to the center of the yoke by a small length of Velcro. It was no larger than two packs of cigarettes tied together end-to-end and weighed only a few ounces. He had ignored the instrument during the emergency landing, but now, as it stared back at him, an idea hit him.

David depressed the power switch in the lower right corner of the Lowrance AirMap GPS. The power came up, illuminating the screen covering the top half of the small instrument.

Dean Barber glanced in David's direction. "Good idea," was all he said.

In a few seconds, David stored the information he wanted. When he was finished, the exact location of the strange airfield was recorded in the memory of the Lowrance Global Positioning System. To return would be a simple matter of calling up the information for the stored waypoint and following the instructions displayed on the screen.

The GPS was a miracle of modern military technology that had finally spilled over into the world of civil aviation and outdoor recreation. The small instrument used a series of twelve satellites positioned eleven thousand miles above the earth to locate any position on the face of the earth within thirty feet. The truth was that the satellites were even more accurate than that, but the civilian versions of the GPS had yet to attain the accuracy of the military's.

The great thing about the AirMap was that it was portable, handheld, and battery operated. It could be used in an aircraft, an automobile, or hiking through the forest. David knew that only a fool could get lost using the diminutive piece of equipment. Removal from the Cessna was a simple matter of ripping the Velcro fastener loose and putting the instrument in one's pocket. He could attach the AirMap to his own Piper Cub or hand carry it if he decided to hike back to the strange airfield.

"Got it?" Dean asked.

"Got it," David affirmed.

"Okay. Let's get out of here. There's something very spooky about this place."

David smiled. "You're beginning to see ghosts behind every tree."

"Uh-huh. David, you know as well as I do that this airfield is in a place where no airstrip should be. That's strange enough. But the fact that it's also being maintained means someone is using it. Which raises two questions: Who? and Why? Don't tell me you're not thinking the same thing. Why else did you enter the coordinates in the GPS?"

"Maybe I'm just curious. Might make a good spot for a picnic. I'll bring Cindy up here someday maybe. Pack the stuff in the Cub and take off for the day."

"I'll believe that when I see it," Barber said. "In the meantime, let's get out of here. And while you're at it, crank in some more flaps and try to get this thing up before we're even with that large cedar tree on the left."

David located the tree in question. "I make it about a thousand feet."

"More like eight hundred. Short-field configuration. You get this thing up before the tree, and I'll buy the steaks."

"And if I don't."

"I like mine medium well," Dean grinned.

"Piece of cake, Barber. Get your money ready."

"I thought you didn't gamble."

David glanced sideways at his friend and instructor. "This isn't gambling," he smiled. "Don't forget, this thing is equipped with an STOL package."

"I haven't forgotten. But don't let your confidence overwhelm your logic. Now get this thing in the air before I change my mind."

David checked the instruments one last time, smiling to himself now. This was Dean Barber's standard method. It was one of the things David enjoyed about flying with him. He made learning fun and almost adventurous, without allowing it to become dangerous. With the Short-Takeoff-and-Landing system installed on the Cessna, the eight-hundred-foot takeoff roll in cold air would be a snap. But it was Dean's way of testing David under controlled circumstances. With almost three thousand feet of runway, there was plenty of space to err and recover.

"Rolling," David said. "And not to worry."

"Overconfidence has put many an aircraft on the ground when it should have been in the air. You're the best two-hundred-hour pilot I've ever flown with, but . . ."

". . . but I'm still just a two-hundred-hour pilot," David completed

Dean Barber's thought, as the Cessna rumbled and shook. He brought the engine to full power. "Let's get this crate off the ground."

It was always the same between the two. The same friendly banter, an outgrowth of the two men's time in the military and the genuine respect each felt for the other. Since the day David had walked onto the tarmac at Clayton Municipal Airport that glorious spring day more than a year ago, the friendship had flourished.

Upon retiring from the U.S. Navy, David had returned to his boyhood hometown of Clayton, Arkansas, to become pastor of First Community Church. The return had been bittersweet, occasioned by the death of his younger brother, Jimmy. The memories still haunted David during long nights when sleep was elusive. Those nights seemed to be coming more and more frequently.

Jimmy had been killed in a fall from the three-hundred-foot cooling tower of Arkansas Nuclear Three and Four, no more than a half hour away from First Community. It had been murder, and the fact that David had been instrumental in bringing the killers to justice had assuaged the empty feeling for a short time.

Between his preaching and pastoral duties, David had found it necessary to occupy his mind in another undertaking. Flying had seemed the perfect solution, and when he allowed himself to think about it, the plan had worked to an amazing degree. When he was flying, he found he could block out the memories that at other times seemed to flood his mind. He had soloed in less than twelve hours, had his private license in less than forty, had logged double-digit hours in multiengine aircraft, and was now working on his instrument rating.

But flying only moderated the hurt for those few hours he was able to steal from his weekly duties. The rest of the time his mind was occupied by thoughts of Jimmy, his father, James, and more often than not, Cindy Tolbert, the Clayton County clerk and David's romantic interest.

Cindy had been a pleasant surprise for him. At one point, more than a year ago, the pert, green-eyed woman had admitted to an infatuation with David way back in high school. It had come as a shock, and it had precipitated what David thought was only a minor romance. Now, as he looked back on events, it was difficult to pinpoint the exact moment when the romance had gone from minor to major. He and Cindy had been dating for the last year, and it was pretty much assumed in the community that they would eventually marry. He'd been a confirmed bachelor, and the thought of sharing the remainder of his life with Cindy Tolbert was both exciting and unsettling.

David felt a gentle tap on his shoulder. Dean Barber had the friendly grin on his face that had become so familiar to David.

"You're dreaming again. I've told you before to forget everything else when you're flying. Now get this crate off the ground."

David turned his attention to the instrument panel in front of him and the takeoff specifics of a short-field takeoff.

"Mags check, RPMs on the nose, instruments set and in the green, flaps and trim set," David recited the litany as much to himself as to Barber. "We're ready to roll."

David's hand was on the throttle, just about to push the control to the firewall when a tap on the shoulder stopped him. Dean was looking through the windscreen, off in the distance. David followed his friend's gaze.

"What do you make of that?" Barber asked over the intercom system.

Two men emerged from the tree line off to the left. They jogged in the direction of the plane, frantically waving their arms.

David removed his hand from the throttle, "I guess we wait and find out."

"Shut it down," said Barber.

David pulled the mixture control and waited for the engine to die, then flicked the master switch to off. Dean Barber already had his headset off and was unbuckling his seat belt and shoulder harness. David followed suit, and both men stepped down from the plane.

The two men from the woods were almost even with the plane as Dean skirted the tail of the Cessna.

In the aftermath of the storm, the air was crisp and cold. David entertained the thought of retrieving the jackets from the Cessna's storage compartment, but quickly dismissed the idea when he saw that the two men were armed. He fleetingly wondered if it had been a mistake to get out of the Cessna.

Even David's 6'2" frame seemed slight compared to one of the men. He had to be at least 6'7" and well over 250 pounds, and he looked dangerous. The smaller man seemed subdued. David did not like the feeling he got as the two men eyed the Cessna.

"Where'd you guys come from?" the larger man asked without preamble.

David returned the man's direct gaze. A feeling he'd almost forgotten returned in a flash. It was the same impression of unmitigated, unbounded evil he had last confronted over a year ago in the streets of Little Rock.

"The storm forced us down. We were lucky to find this pasture when we did. We were just about to leave," David said. Dean Barber quickly picked up the story line.

"Yeah," he added, "we were lucky the cows were gone, or we'd be buying beef for the next year."

"You guys hunting?" David asked, hoping to change the subject.

For a brief moment, confusion showed on both men's faces, then the larger man said, "Sure. You guys seen anything around here?"

Dean shook his head. "If there was anything around, we probably scared it off when we cranked this thing up. These Cessnas aren't known for being quiet."

The smaller man laughed. "I don't 'spose so."

"Nothing at all?" the larger man asked.

David had the feeling the man was not talking about animals.

"Not even a rabbit," David answered. "What are you hunting?"

"Wolf," the larger man answered. "Messed up some milk cows and chickens over to the west. Thinkin' their den is around in this area somewhere."

The smaller man had separated himself from the small group and was slowly walking around the Cessna. David followed the movement with a slight movement of his head.

"Cole won't hurt nothin'. Just looking at your plane," the large man said.

"No problem," Dean said.

David couldn't shake the sense of foreboding, even evil, that accompanied the two hunters. He had met guys like these during his military career—small-minded thugs who seemed to enjoy inflicting pain and misery on others. David didn't know exactly why he automatically classified the hunters this way, but he was certain the assessment was correct. He glanced again at the big man's weapon.

"Maybe you guys seen something from the air," Billy Bob Campbell said.

"Wolf pack? Can't say that we have," David answered.

"Or anything else?"

"Such as?" said Dean.

"Nothin' in particular. Just anything out of the ordinary."

"What's out of the ordinary in these parts? Other than that storm that blew through here, that is," David offered.

Cole finished his tour around the plane and came back to stand next to Billy Bob. Neither had made a threatening move, but David had the feeling they were more than capable of using the rifles they carried. He could tell the larger man was weighing his words carefully.

"There's all sorts of game in these woods. You might have seen movement."

"Nope. Nothing," David answered quickly.

"Better get moving," Dean Barber suggested to David.

"Seen any dogs?" the smaller man asked.

Barber and David looked at each other. Dogs were used to hunt deer and raccoon, but neither was in season at the moment. And any man who would pit hunting dogs against a wolf pack was insane.

"No dogs, either," David answered. "Now we've got to get this plane in the air. If you gentlemen will excuse us." With that David climbed into the Cessna as Dean walked around the other side. The two hunters stood still until David shouted, "Clear," and started the Cessna's engine, then they stepped away.

David once again ran through the checklist, set flaps and trim, and shoved the throttle to the firewall.

"Short-field," Dean reminded David.

"Have no fear. I want to get this thing in the air as quickly as possible."

"I know what you mean. Those guys are a little scary."

David didn't answer as the Cessna accelerated over the frozen ground. David watched the airspeed indicator, and when the correct speed was reached, he hauled back on the yoke and the blue Cessna leaped into the air like a thoroughbred. David re-trimmed and held a constant airspeed as they climbed. He retracted the flaps and banked left, circling the pasture. The two men were still standing there, gazing up into the sky. David leveled off and headed for Clayton Municipal Airport.

"Okay, what is it?" Barber asked. He had flown with David enough to know when something was bothering the pastor.

"Not counting the heavy trim?"

"What are you talking about?"

"The plane is heavy toward the rear. Look at the trim tab. I didn't have to run it as far to relieve back pressure on climb out, and it's not in the normal position for level flight either. Something happened."

Barber noted the trim tab settings and shook his head. "I'll have the A & P mechanic check the trim when we get back. But that's not what I'm talking about. Those guys back there shook you up, and that's not like you. What's the story?"

"Those two good ol' boys?"

Dean laughed at the remark. "They were quite a pair."

"You were military. Didn't you notice anything strange?"

"I flew F-4Es in the Air Force. I never got closer than a few thousand yards to ground troops, if that's what you mean. But I did notice the M-16s those guys carried. Interesting choice for a hunter."

David nodded. "Pretty good, except they weren't 16s. They were AR-18s. The latest version of the Armalite rifles. Five point five six millimeters. Eight hundred rounds per minute. Fully automatic. I'd say that was overkill."

"You don't buy the wolf story?"

David set the Cessna up for level flight and let the plane fly itself, his left hand only lightly touching the yoke.

"When was the last time you heard of wolves going after cattle in these parts?"

"I can't remember ever hearing that, but that doesn't mean it didn't happen."

"I don't buy it. Those men were hunting something else."

"Then why the wolf story?"

"The only explanation would be that they were hunting something totally illegal, and the wolf story is to hide that."

"Like what?"

"I don't know. There are still some black bear up here. Or maybe they're after deer out of season. Who knows? I just have the feeling the wolf story is a cover." David reached for his number one communications radio and tuned it to the unicom frequency used by Clayton Municipal Airport.

Clayton Municipal was not a controlled airport, lacking an FAA control tower. Pilots who utilized the airport were required to tune to a common frequency and talk among themselves to provide some sort of traffic control when landing or taking off. There was no chatter on the unicom frequency, which meant no one was taking off or entering the landing pattern at Clayton. David radioed his intentions, "In the clear." There was no answer.

"So you're maybe thinking 'survivalist'?" Barber asked over the communication headset.

"I'm not thinking anything," David answered. "It's just curious."

The remainder of the flight was made in silence, and in just over an hour, Clayton Municipal Airport appeared on the horizon, five miles to the southeast. David pointed through the windscreen. It was always like a homecoming to see the seven-thousand-foot asphalt strip appear among the trees and mountains. David checked his altitude and airspeed. He would overfly the airport to get a good look at the windsock which hung from a mast on one of the hangers.

The windsock indicated no wind of any significance, and David chose to make his approach to runway seventeen, taking him over low trees at the north end of the airport, rather than fly the "river approach" from the south.

At thirteen hundred feet, David banked into his downwind leg, adjusting his trim and speed as he went. Seconds later he turned a steep crosswind leg into a final approach.

"Don't do that on an instrument check ride," Dean advised.

"Have no fear. But I want to get this crate on the ground and check out some stuff with my favorite local government official," David replied, his eyes never leaving the white-stripped threshold of the approaching runway.

"That would be Miss Cynthia Tolbert. Where does she figure into this?"

David reached between the seat one last time to adjust the trim tab. "I'm not really certain. Just a thought. Now let me land this thing."

The large numbers marking the threshold were beginning to fill the windscreen. David alternated his scan between the instruments and the approaching asphalt.

"Threshold's pegged," Dean said softly, realizing David knew it anyway, but allowing the instructor in him to come out. "Just hold what you've got."

Suddenly, as if the whole world had exploded, a sudden and persistent banging reverberated through the airframe. David's first thought was that the engine had come apart in flight. His hands involuntarily grasped the yoke in a death grip. Sweat broke out on his forehead, and his heart pounded. He hazarded a glance at Dean Barber. By the look on the instructor's face, he was having the same experience.

"What the . . . ?" Dean began.

"She's still flying. Instruments all in the green," David said matter-of-factly. "Check outside, see if we hit something."

Barber popped the side window of the Cessna. Freezing air instantly filled the cabin. It did nothing to alleviate the perspiration pouring down David Michaels's back. Dean craned his neck as far out as he could, examining first forward then aft. He could see nothing.

Then, as suddenly as it had begun, the banging stopped. The absence of the noise was as disturbing as the onset had been.

"What the . . . ?" Dean began again. Before he got the words out of his mouth, the reverberations again assailed the small plane.

"We're almost on the ground," David heard himself shouting over the roar of the Continental engine and wind noise from the open window, ignoring the communications system.

"Fly the plane!" Dean yelled back.

The threshold was approaching at an alarming rate. David checked his airspeed. Too fast! He'd dropped the nose in the confusion and the airspeed had built up accordingly. David gently hauled back on the yoke, restoring the correct attitude just before the balloon tires of the Cessna touched the cold asphalt. He'd carried too much speed into the landing and the plane bounced once, seeking the sky on the rebound.

David held back pressure and allowed the excess airspeed to bleed off. The aircraft settled back to earth. This time, when the tires contacted the ground, they stayed put with a tiny squeal.

The reverberations had subsided, but the effect on David and Dean had only just begun.

David taxied the plane to the nearest hanger, ignored the shutdown procedures, pulled the mixture control, and waited until the prop stopped spinning.

Dean Barber was already out the passenger side door, quickly examining every inch of the Cessna's outer skin.

David snapped the master switch off and climbed out, joining Dean just aft of the left wing.

"Nothing out here," Dean said, shaking his head in disbelief.

"It sounded like it was coming from below, maybe the storage compartment. I would swear I didn't throw anything in there that could have done that," David said.

Brian Connelly, the airframe and power-plant mechanic who owned the hanger where David had parked the plane, walked out of the hanger wiping oil from his hands with a towel. "What's up?" he asked David and Dean.

"Plane's coming apart on us," Dean Barber said. "And it's only fifty hours out of annual. If you messed up my 185, Brian, I'm gonna beat you to within an inch of your life."

"Sure, Dean," Brian Connelly said amicably.

Connelly was at least as large as the side of his hanger, out-weighed Dean Barber by a hundred pounds, and still rode bulls in the local county fairs around the state. Most folks felt sorry for any bull Connelly drew. Dean Barber would have had about as much chance with Brian Connelly as a kitten attacking a pit bull.

"Besides, there's not a thing wrong with this plane, unless you bent it with that crazy landing you just made."

David gritted his teeth at the remark.

"There's some kind of pounding coming from the storage compartment," Barber informed Connelly. "Take a look."

Brian Connelly bent down and unsnapped the fasteners on the compartment, lowered the cover, and looked inside.

"Well, I found your knock, but you're not gonna like it," Connelly said.

"What are you talking about?" Dean demanded.

Brian Connelly reached into the compartment and carefully removed two jackets. He cradled the jackets as if he were holding a baby. David and Dean moved in closer. The face of a young girl was the only thing showing from the bundle of coats.

"Looks like she used her last strength to pound some of those tie-down stakes against the floor. From the looks of her, she may not last to tell us how she got there or where she came from," the mechanic said.

"The 'how' she got there is in question," David said. "The 'where' we know exactly."

"Better get an ambulance here fast. I'd say we're looking at advanced hypothermia," Connelly said.

"Put her in my car," David said. "It will be quicker than calling an ambulance. Call the hospital, Dean, and tell them I'm on my way. Get in touch with the sheriff, too, and tell her to meet me at the hospital. And tell whoever answers the phone at the hospital to get on the horn to Children's in Little Rock and get their helicopter down here now. Unless I miss my guess, our rural hospital isn't going to be equipped to deal with this."

Brian Connelly, carrying the girl as if she were a doll, sprinted for David's car, climbed into the rear seat, and settled in. "I'm going too. I can hold her. You might do more damage just letting her lie here."

"Thanks, Brian." David twisted the key, threw the car into gear, and sprayed loose gravel over the parking area as he raced for the airport exit.

What in the world is going on here? David asked himself as he spun his tires on the slick surface of the blacktop. *Is this girl going to die? How did she end up in the cargo hold?* The questions filtered through David's mind as he drove.

In less than five minutes, he barreled up to Clayton Memorial Hospital's emergency entrance. Three nurses, two EMTs, and the emergency room doctor stood just inside an enclosure as the car approached. They gently took the young girl from Brian's arms and rushed her inside.

As David and Brian watched the emergency team disappear with the almost frozen body, David felt a small prayer escape from his lips. He immediately berated himself for waiting so long to pray.

As he walked into the hospital to wait for news on the girl's condition, David suddenly saw the faces of the two "hunters" in his mind's eye. He had sensed evil in that desolate place, and now he knew for certain he would face it again.

CHAPTER
SIX

After the blue Cessna took off, Cole Branscum walked back into the woods to find his dogs. Billy Bob Campbell walked around the area where the airplane had been parked, searching the ground. Both men knew they could not face Jason Swann without finding the girl, but it was beginning to look like that was exactly what they would have to do. Billy Bob halfheartedly examined the ground, not certain what he was looking for.

When Cole returned with both dogs, they began baying as soon as they got close to Billy Bob. Juniper began snuffling in circles around where the blue airplane had been parked, while Cutter traced an invisible line back toward a thicket at the edge of the airstrip. In a moment, he was back and joined Juniper's excited exploration of the spot vacated by the Cessna. Billy Bob looked bewildered for a moment, but

Cole knew exactly what he was seeing—the dogs had come to the end of the trail.

Billy Bob and Cole were about as cold as they had ever been in their lives. But what they saw now made their blood run even colder. Billy Bob reached down toward a patch of dark ground amidst the blown snow. But instead of a patch of ground, his hand rested on a cloth slipper, the kind the girls were issued back in the valley. The girl had been here. She was on that plane!

Billy Bob cursed as he realized the hunt had come to an end, but a plausible story was already taking shape in his mind.

Cole finally quieted the dogs and walked over to where Billy Bob was standing.

"It's the girl's," Billy Bob said, holding up the slipper.

"What're we gonna' do?" shouted Cole.

Billy Bob smiled. "How's this? We were tracking the girl. Your dogs was doin' good. We almost had her in the pasture, when a blue and white airplane came out of nowhere, scooped her up, and was gone. A rescue, plain and simple. Nothin' we could do 'bout it neither. These guys were professionals. But we was lucky. We got the number on the airplane. We can give that to Swann. He can relay that up the line, and maybe, just maybe, we'll get out of this thing, and maybe have a little fun on the side too."

"What kind of fun you talkin' 'bout?" Cole asked.

"Look stupid. Can't nobody get on us for losin' the girl when it was a rescue attempt. Shucks, that means it got set up from the inside. We shore ain't had nothin' to do with that. Them stupid nurses are responsible for that sort of stuff. Girl got to a phone when they wasn't watchin'. So we're in the clear." Billy Bob paused, liking the story more and more as he went along. "The next thing is that someone's got to go after the girl and the airplane. That means those two pilots too. I don't know where that girl was, but she was sure 'nuff in that plane. Even if this weren't no rescue, they gonna' know something funny is goin' on around here when they get to where they're goin'. So somebody's got to shut them up. That could be us, if we play this thing right. We kill all three, get in good with Memphis, and maybe make a bundle of money on the side."

"How much?" Cole asked, hearing nothing but the part about the money.

"Who knows, man? We might get five, ten thousand for the whole shootin' match. Maybe more. Let's get back to the valley. The sooner we get this thing out of the way, the better I'll like it."

The men began retracing their steps back toward the valley. As they walked, Cole said, "What about that number on the plane? I didn't pay no attention to that. Shoot, I don't guess I even knew airplanes had numbers."

Billy Bob continued walking and smiled. "You're lucky, Cole, that you got ol' Billy Bob to watch out for ya'll. Number was two two six nine nine. Adds up to your IQ. That's how come I can remember it so easy. Now let's get back and tell Swann."

The two men broke into a slow jog, being careful not to slip as they moved through the forest. The dogs followed. In less than an hour, they would be back in the valley. With any luck at all, their arrival would be the beginning of the end of the three in the blue and white airplane.

CHAPTER SEVEN

Thomas Morris Fenwick ignored the reports scattered across his desk. They were suddenly nothing more than numbers strung together to form statistics. At one time, they had had a life of their own, representing years of hard work and dedication. But Thomas Fenwick's life had come crashing down around him in just the last ten minutes. The numbers were now meaningless.

He leaned back in his heavy, leather chair and wondered what he'd done to deserve such agony. He'd been a good father and husband. Maybe he worked too hard at times, but he had never forgotten what he was working for. His family had always been uppermost in his mind. They were the force that drove him, the force that had sustained him over the years. Now, just as he was about to achieve his ultimate success, a three-minute phone call threatened to destroy everything.

At sixty-three, Fenwick had a head full of white hair, a deep tan that defied the seasons, and a presence, enhanced by his sturdy six-foot, 230-pound frame that often placed him in the limelight.

Fenwick had begun in 1951. At sixteen, he'd lied about his age to join the army and had fought in Korea as an enlisted soldier. But a soldier's pay, he quickly learned, was not enough to care for his mother and two sisters back in Arkansas. His father had never returned from the Pacific in World War II, and the task of supporting the family had fallen to him, as the only male in the household.

When it became glaringly apparent that the army was not the answer, young Thomas had confessed his sin to the company commander, was discharged, and put aboard a U.S. Navy battleship bound stateside. En route, young Fenwick made a startling discovery: The navy sold cigarettes on board their ships at a price well below the market. There was a limit, but Fenwick learned to skirt the restriction by having nonsmokers aboard purchase their limit for him. When he walked down the gangplank in San Diego a month later, he carried several duffel bags of tobacco for which he had paid a pittance. The entire stock had lasted only as long as it took for word to spread that his cut-rate cigarettes were for sale.

It had not been an enormous cache from which to begin, but it had been enough. And it had proven to a young Thomas Fenwick that there was opportunity to be had for the taking, if only a little ingenuity, coupled with some quick capital, could be put to good use.

Fenwick was not certain when he began thinking of money as "capital." He'd had no formal education in the ways of business, but that didn't matter. One bought low and sold high. The difference was profit. The concept seemed simple enough. The challenge was to find *something* you could buy low that *others* were willing to purchase at a higher price. Fenwick soon discovered that people were willing to buy *anything,* so long as they thought they were getting a good deal. And a good deal was anything that sold for less than what they had to pay elsewhere.

In a word, Thomas Fenwick had discovered that discounts, or at least perceived discounts, sold goods quicker than he could purchase them.

His first enterprise had competed directly with the five-and-dime stores of the day and had been an instant success. From that early store, it had been a simple leap to start another in a neighboring town, and on and on. In less than five years, he had opened a dozen stores which kept him on the road day and night. The economic climate was ripe for just such an endeavor, and the stores continued to prosper and multiply.

Before he knew it, FenMark was born. "Fen" for Fenwick, and "Mark" for market. The name had come from his youngest sister, and he had embraced the name and the concept.

The concept that meant more than anything was family. Since Korea, Thomas Fenwick had had an inordinate orientation toward his family. He had made his mother and two sisters wealthy. He had married late and had made his wife of thirty years wealthy as well. His single area of failure—and that's how he looked at it—was his failure to have children.

The solution had been simple: adoption. But for Thomas Fenwick, there could be no loose ends, especially in the intricate details of legal adoption. He was already a millionaire many times over by the time the adoption question came up, and protection of his family's wealth was uppermost in his mind. That meant the adoption would have to remain secret. As far as the outside world was concerned, the son would be his natural offspring. That would eliminate the possibility of anyone outside the family laying claim to a portion of the FenMark empire. Not even his son would know about the adoption. It would be a closely held secret.

For the last twenty-eight years, the secret had been kept as religiously as any corporate secret could be. The only people aware that young Donald Fenwick was not the natural child of Martha and Thomas Fenwick were the family members and the doctor who had arranged the adoption.

A trusted confidant had recommended the doctor as a "miracle worker." As far as that person was concerned, the miracle had transpired, and Donald had been born. The truth was somewhat different, and it was this truth that current economic conditions forced Thomas Fenwick to conceal.

Donald had been brought into the family company, given responsibility commensurate with his name, and eventually named as CEO. At twenty-eight, it was an awesome responsibility, but one young Donald had been groomed for from the beginning.

Now, with the company expanding by leaps and bounds, the decision had been made to take FenMark public. Up to now, it had been a closely held, family-run business. But the rate of expansion had dictated an infusion of capital into the corporation to maintain its growth.

Initial public offerings of stock were delicate in many ways. The careful scrutiny of every detail by the underwriter risked exposure of Donald Fenwick's adoption. Such a discovery was untenable considering the current stages of negotiations.

But the phone call came. The voice had been specific, almost robotic.

Thomas Fenwick took a deep breath and picked up the phone at his right elbow. He spoke softly into the receiver.

"Agnes, have my son come in here, please." It was time to tell the truth. Or at least, part of it.

CHAPTER EIGHT

Helicopter N497CH touched down precisely on the red cross marker outside the emergency room of Clayton Memorial Hospital. The crew of the large Sikorsky helicopter had been lucky, skirting one of the worst snowstorms ever to hit central Arkansas. Senior Pilot Pete O'Neill could only hope he would be as lucky on the return trip. Though the weather in Clayton seemed to be clearing, he knew the storm was moving south, toward Little Rock and the Arkansas Children's Hospital.

O'Neill watched from his pilot's seat as Senior Flight Nurse Pam Herron raced for the emergency room door along with EMT Thomas Abbot. Between them they carried the flight gurney.

"What about the return?"

The question came from his copilot, John Leonard. It was the same question O'Neill had been asking himself since they had skirted the storm by detouring to the west after leaving Children's.

"If that front goes stationary, we could be headed right back into it," Leonard added matter-of-factly.

"If it goes stationary, we'll find a way. If this girl is as bad as I think, we may be her only chance. We'll get through, God willing."

John Leonard glanced at his friend. The *God willing* told anyone who cared to listen more about Peter O'Neill's character than any hundred words could. Leonard knew that O'Neill believed in the will of an omnipotent God. It was an idea the pilot had been drumming into Leonard for the year they had been flying together. Leonard would not admit it to O'Neill, but the persistence was beginning to have an effect on him. He'd seen things that did not make logical sense. Not really miracles, he had decided, but *things* that just did not seem to add up in a totally humanistic world.

Today might be one more case. It would take a miracle to get back to Children's in one piece.

The emergency room door burst open as Herron, Abbot, and four others came out carrying the flight gurney with a small body strapped to it. The patient was near death from hypothermia, and the gurney looked like a giant brown bear with all the blankets piled on and around the tiny figure. But it would take more than blankets, Leonard knew, to save the girl if her core temperature had dropped too low.

The paramedics yanked the helicopter door open, secured the gurney, and Herron and Abbot scrambled aboard, leaving the other four to head for cover as O'Neill twisted the handle of the collective, kicking up loose snow in the rotor's wake.

In seconds, helicopter N497CH was airborne. One of the last things John Leonard saw as O'Neill aimed the Sikorsky south was the arrival of a Clayton County sheriff's car on the blacktop below. He saw what looked like two women get out of the car, and then his attention was drawn back to the flight and the weather system that looked like an impenetrable barrier to the southeast.

"How is she?" O'Neill asked Herron.

Pam Herron looked up. "If we don't get her to Children's in twenty minutes, she doesn't have a chance," he told O'Neill.

O'Neill nodded silently, applied light pressure to the left pedal and redirected the helicopter's flight path directly into the storm wall.

John Leonard unconsciously tightened his seat belt and shoulder harness.

■　■　■

Clayton County Sheriff Janice Morgan watched the white helicopter disappear in the distance. Standing beside her was Cynthia Tolbert, the Clayton County clerk. The two women struck a delicate contrast. Morgan, a tall, almost aristocratic blonde, was the antithesis of Cindy Tolbert's petite, green-eyed countenance. The two had been friends for years, ever since they met at the Clayton County Courthouse where they both had offices.

When the call had come in about a nearly frozen girl being transported to Clayton County Memorial Hospital, Janice had stopped by Cindy's office to see if she would like to ride along.

Cindy had abandoned the real estate abstract she was working on and joined Janice.

Janice Morgan had been Clayton County sheriff for just over a year, ever since Tom Frazier had resigned the position. It was still not clear to Janice exactly what had happened with Frazier, but rumor had it he was an undercover special agent connected somehow with the White House. Janice now knew that the rumors were true, and she also knew that Tom Frazier had been one of the best men she'd ever worked for. Upon his resignation, a special election had been held, and Janice, with Frazier's endorsement, had been elected by an overwhelming margin.

Clayton County, Arkansas, was not the hotbed of crime that Memphis, or even Little Rock was, but the rural county had enough bootleggers and marijuana growers to keep her and her small contingent of deputies busy. Life was manageable in Clayton, and Janice liked it that way just fine. But once in a while something strange came along to remind her that, even in Clayton, evil still dwelled close to the surface.

"There's David," Cindy Tolbert said to Janice Morgan.

Janice watched the last glimpse of the helicopter disappear, then turned to see David Michaels approaching. For an instant, she felt a very slight pang of jealousy. At six feet two, and just over two hundred pounds, David Michaels was a handsome man in a rugged sort of way. At forty-eight, his hair was mostly gray. A year ago it had been cut to meet Marine Corps standards. Now, although it was slightly longer, it still reflected David's military preferences. There was no evidence of a midlife bulge around his waist. She and David had been contemporaries at Clayton High School and had even gone to their senior prom together. Cindy Tolbert was younger, and Janice had to admit, still quite a beauty.

Cindy and David had been dating since David's return just over a year ago. Janice was happy for Cindy, but she also recognized a certain stirring within herself when David was around. She shrugged off the feeling and met David as he approached.

"What's the story?" asked Janice.

David Michaels shook his head. "I'm not really sure, Janice," he began. "Dean and I were flying and were forced down by the storm . . ."

"David!" Cindy exclaimed.

"Easy, Cindy," David said, throwing his arm around the shoulders of the dark-haired county clerk. "We had to land in a pasture north of here and let the storm pass. We weren't in any real danger."

Cindy looked up at David, not sure she believed what he said about the danger. "God was looking out for you," she said.

David smiled easily. That was Cindy. At times he was humbled by her simple faith in God. It was one of the things that had drawn him to her, and that had carried him through the bad times after his brother died. Jimmy's murder had tested David's belief in a loving and compassionate God, which for a military chaplain was a crisis of faith that had almost ended his career. Since his retirement from the navy and his return to Clayton to become the pastor of First Community Church, his faith had been rekindled, largely due to Cindy's example and the weekly devotional times they shared at his father's house.

David had since moved out of his father's spare bedroom into a long-abandoned house on a rural road just outside of Clayton. He was in the process of renovating the house, which he had discovered was an early nineteenth-century log home when he stripped off the horizontal siding. In his new home, David was as settled as he had ever been in his life, but as he looked at Janice Morgan, he had the distinct feeling that life was about to become very unsettled once again.

"What about the girl?" Janice asked, jarring David from his reverie.

David felt Cindy's arm go around him, reminding him that she was there to support him yet again. "That's really the strange part, Janice. We landed in the pasture, tied the Cessna down, and waited out the storm. After the storm passed, Dean and I explored the place, and I guess the girl must have crawled into the storage compartment during that time. I have no idea where she came from. We were out in the middle of nowhere. Then when we landed back here in Clayton, there she was, almost frozen to death."

Janice Morgan had taken out a small notebook and was making notes as David spoke. Now she looked up and said, "You say you were exploring the pasture. Why was that?"

David was uncomfortable. Janice was a friend, but she was also the sheriff. It was a simple question, and he had nothing to hide, but he felt a vague uneasiness.

"Dean thought there was something strange about the pasture. Out in the middle of nowhere, oriented the way it was, and such. And he was right. We found evidence that the pasture was really a clandestine airstrip."

Janice Morgan stopped writing and looked up. "You mean you found a secret airport out in the middle of the Ozarks?"

David felt himself blush. It *did* sound crazy when you thought about it. But he also knew what they had found. "Exactly. There was a battered windsock attached to a camouflaged pole, made to resemble a tree. The pasture was short, as if it was maintained for that purpose."

"Was it on your sectional?" Janice asked.

The question reminded David that Janice Morgan was more than a pretty face. Janice Morgan was not a pilot, but she knew about flying, and the question about the sectional chart proved it.

"I'm not sure. Dean and I were going to check it out when we got back, but when we discovered the girl, our priorities obviously changed. We can go to the airport and pull out a sectional and look, but according to what Dean said, we're not going to find it on any map."

"You don't think perhaps it might have been an older strip, and now it's just abandoned? After all, this is winter. The grass could have just died."

"No way. We found one other thing up there—a VASI."

"A what?" Cindy asked, confused by the cryptic flying jargon.

David looked down at the woman by his side, and said, "A VASI. A Variable Approach Slope Indicator."

"It's used to aid in visual approaches," Janice Morgan added quickly.

David was impressed. "How do you know about that?" he asked Janice.

She smiled as she tapped her temple with her right index finger. "Never underestimate the mind of a law enforcement officer. Besides, I was out at Clayton Municipal the day they installed them out there."

"Janice is right," David continued, explaining the instrument to Cindy. "It uses three different colored lights to help in landings."

"And I don't suppose the VASI you discovered was old and rusted?" Janice asked.

"Not even close. As a matter of fact, it was attached to a state-of-the-art solar cell and a series of rechargeable batteries. The latest stuff. Someone is using that place for an airport."

"Can you find your way back?"

David remembered programming his GPS. "I can't, but Lowrance can."

"Who's Lowrance?"

"My GPS AirMap. What do you know about those?"

Janice Morgan smiled guardedly. "Enough to know that if you got that GPS programmed, it will take us back to the exact spot within thirty feet."

"Provided we want to go back," David added.

"Exactly. In the meantime, I'm going to check with Dean Barber and go over a sectional chart of that area. Where do you think you were?"

"It was a little confusing in the storm. Dean thinks maybe Benning County, and I agree. We can check that out on the AirMap. It's got a moving map using Jeppesen software."

"Are you saying you're going to fly back to that . . . 'pasture'?" Cindy asked.

David met Cindy's gaze, then glanced at Janice Morgan. "Not if I don't have to."

Janice nodded. "I'll check out the location and the girl. Wade Larsen is the Benning County sheriff. I'll give him a call too. I know I don't have to worry about you going anywhere," she said to David, "but I may need to ask you some more questions in the next couple of days, so don't start a vacation or anything."

"Don't worry. But I am thinking of going down to Little Rock a little later," David said.

"To check on the girl?" Cindy asked, looking up at David.

"Yeah. I'm worried about her. I've never seen anyone looking as frail as she did."

"I'll contact Arkansas Human Services," Janice said, "then I'll probably be down there too. First I want to see Barber."

"I'll ride back to the office with David," Cindy told Janice.

"One more thing, Janice," David began. "There were two men out there in the forest . . . and they were armed."

Janice Morgan nodded. "Lots of folks up here carry guns in the woods. You know that."

"I do. But not these kind. They were carrying AR-18s. Latest version if I'm right."

Janice scribbled a note before saying, "Armalites? That's a lot of firepower for a walk in the forest. They offer any explanation?"

"Yeah. Said they were hunting a wolf pack that attacked some cattle."

"I haven't heard of any attacks, but I'll check that with Larsen too." Janice Morgan turned on her heel, got back in her car, and drove away.

"Let's go," David said to Cindy. "I'll get you back to the courthouse."

"When are you going to Little Rock?"

"After I go back to the airport and get my gear and the AirMap. Maybe an hour."

"Come by the courthouse and pick me up. I'll ride along. You may need my company and I need the break."

David laughed. "You're probably right." He reached down and kissed Cindy lightly on the forehead. "Let's go."

■   ■   ■

Janice Morgan leafed through the reports on her desk. The events of the last few hours were disturbing, especially in light of the restricted-distribution bulletin she had received a few weeks ago. She had placed a low priority on it at the time, but now, as she read the information again, a shiver ran up her spine. *It's happening all over again,* she thought. *And it's happening to David Michaels. Incredible! Absolutely incredible!*

She dialed the number listed on the bulletin. Somebody might want to know about the two men carrying AR-18s in a rural valley in central Arkansas.

CHAPTER NINE

Snow had piled up against the tall white columns of the house in the valley, partially concealing the structure at different points. To Billy Bob Campbell and Cole Branscum, it looked like a large igloo in the middle of nowhere as they emerged from the forest.

When the two men stepped inside, they were quickly ushered into an oppressively hot room on the first floor of the house.

Jason Swann angrily paced the floor as the two men sat down on a sofa along the back wall. Swann was a small man, to the eternal embarrassment of his father, who believed that intelligence was directly proportional to height. Jason Swann had proven him wrong, but that had done nothing to heighten Swann's own self-esteem.

Swann's pallid white skin—he called it ivory—and mouse-brown hair added nothing to his overall appearance. When he was angry, as he was now, his normally light complexion turned a florid crimson. At that moment, his face was somewhere between ruby and deep scarlet.

"This sounds like one of your schemes, Campbell," Swann hissed accusingly. "Tell me again what happened to the girl."

Billy Bob squirmed on the sofa. He hated Swann. He hated the oversized office. He hated the way he felt when Swann spoke to him in this manner, especially in front of Cole. And he hated that he let Swann intimidate him. Billy Bob knew he could easily crush Jason Swann like a water beetle, but he also knew he dared not. Jason Swann never let him forget who was in control.

Billy Bob swiped a sleeve across his face to mop the rapidly forming sweat. "It's like we said, Mr. Swann. That airplane was there waiting on her. She had to have set it up somehow. Maybe used a phone when them nurses weren't watchin'."

Cole nodded his agreement, which drew Swann's attention.

"That the facts, Cole?" Swann asked. He knew both men despised him for his superior intelligence and position, and he knew they would rather lie to him than face his wrath.

Cole nodded, amazed that his mouth could be so dry when sweat was rolling down his back in rivulets.

"And you're positive the girl got in the airplane?"

"Yes, sir, Mr. Swann," Billy Bob interjected, then remembered the slipper he'd found at the site. He pulled it from his jacket pocket and handed it to Swann. "Here's the proof. I found this right where that plane was sittin'," he said hurriedly. "Ain't that right, Cole?" He looked furtively at his buddy, seeking support. "Even the dogs couldn't track no further than where the plane was sittin'. That's got to be proof, Mr. Swann."

"Billy Bob's tellin' the truth, Mr. Swann. Them dogs just stopped right there where that airplane was sittin' and started howlin' like banshees," Cole said.

Swann stopped pacing and stared at Billy Bob. He'd been listening to the same story for the last half hour, and there was something that didn't quite mesh. With Cole and Billy Bob, that was no surprise. Neither man knew how to tell the truth, and every time they lied— which was often—they stuck their feet knee-deep into their mouths. But he had to have proof before he could do anything else.

That's got to be proof, Billy Bob had just said. Up to this point, it had sounded as if the two had seen every aspect of the alleged escape and had only narrowly failed to prevent it. Now, with that one statement, Swann knew once again that the two were covering up something. He would get to the truth, but he would have to do it quickly. If the girl had been on that airplane, it had probably already reached its destination, which meant the authorities were probably already involved.

Except for one thing, thought Swann.

If Cole and Billy Bob were telling the truth, which was unlikely, and this had been a planned escape, why weren't the authorities already knocking at the door? Wouldn't that make more sense? If the two men in the plane knew about the valley, why would they attempt a risky and uncertain rescue instead of sending the police to storm the valley and free all the girls at once? Billy Bob and Cole had to be lying. The escape could not have been planned.

But even if the gestapo wouldn't be invading the valley any time soon, the girl's escape represented a very real danger. If the girl was on that plane, both she and the two men Billy Bob Campbell had described would have to be dealt with, and dealt with rapidly. The only way that Jason Swann would mitigate the damage was to place a call to Memphis. The men in Memphis did not tolerate failure, and their means of dealing with failure was sometimes extremely drastic.

Swann jammed his hand into his pocket. He let his mind wander for the moment, seeking a solution that seemed elusive. He must distance himself from the girl's escape, but that would be difficult. When he had been assigned to the valley, he'd understood that he was totally responsible for whatever took place. It was to be his own world, and he had the power of life and death.

It had taken years for him to work his way up through the ranks of the organization known as *Die Gruppe*—The Group. It had taken guts, stamina, and no small amount of deception. But he had been chosen for the valley assignment, and he had done it successfully. In the past, there had been some minor setbacks, but nothing like this. There had been escapes, too, but Billy Bob and Cole had always brought them back to the house. The recoveries had prevented his having to inform Memphis of the escapes, and as far as he knew, they had never been discovered. But now that had all changed. If he could not recover the girl, he would have to report the escape to Memphis. And even if Campbell and Branscum could find her, he would still have to deal with the men in the aircraft.

Swann thought for a moment, then turned to Billy Bob and Cole. He had a plan that, if successful, would place him forever in the good graces of The Group.

Jason Swann would orchestrate the recovery of the girl and eliminate the two men in the airplane. Should anyone else be involved, he would see to them too. It would take a little luck, but he was capable of handling the hillbilly hicks found in the Arkansas sticks.

Swann dialed a local number. While he waited for the phone to be answered, he fixed his gaze on Billy Bob and Cole.

With his hand over the mouthpiece, Swann said, "I've got a job for you two, so don't go anywhere. Now get out of here while I take care of your carelessness."

Billy Bob and Cole rose from their seats, only too happy to get out of the overheated room and away from the insufferable Jason Swann. Were it not for the money, Billy Bob thought, as he closed the office door behind him, he would have been gone a long time ago.

"Is he in?" Swann said into the phone as the two men left the room. Swann waited for a moment, then, when his party answered, said into the instrument, "I've got a problem. I need to know where an airplane with the number, two two six nine nine, is based."

As he listened to the response, Swann turned red once again, and he was glad that the other party could not see his involuntary response. "Okay, but get back to me as quickly as you can, or we're both going to be in hot water."

Swann replaced the receiver. He would have his answers within the hour. In the meantime, he would brief Campbell and Branscum about what they could do to rectify their blunder.

■　■　■

Donald Fenwick leaned back in his plush leather chair. The conversation he'd had with his father earlier haunted him. Still reeling from the revelation that he was adopted, he forced his mind back to the issue at hand. His father, Thomas, was concerned that if Donald's adoption came to light it would adversely affect FenMark's initial public offering. Donald could see it happening. The world economic community, for all its power, revolved as much around public opinion as it did profit and loss ratios, currency fluctuations, and leveraged buyouts. But there was a solution to the problem—a starting point, at least—and Donald knew what he had to do.

Having made his decision, Donald Fenwick felt relieved of a grievous burden. He would inform his father when the time was right.

CHAPTER TEN

Copilot John Leonard swallowed the lump in his throat as the Sikorsky helicopter jerked and bounced through the storm. He checked the digital clock on the control panel, then his eyes went to the aviator's chronometer strapped to his wrist, as if one or the other might be wrong.

The hundred-mile flight from Clayton Memorial Hospital to the Arkansas Children's Hospital should have taken no more than thirty minutes under ideal conditions. But these were not ideal conditions.

The flight was now into its forty-first minute, and Leonard could tell that Peter O'Neill was worried. O'Neill was as cool a pilot as Leonard had ever seen. Three tours with the First Air Cavalry in Vietnam had seasoned him, and later he had been one of the first army pilots to transition from the UH-1 Huey into the UH-60 Blackhawk.

Flying the Sikorsky after flying the Huey was like driving a Cadillac after learning on Grandpa's pickup.

As O'Neill battled the raging storm, Leonard monitored the instruments, watching closely for any sign of overstress within the helicopter's complex systems.

"We're losing her!" Senior Flight Nurse Pam Herron called from the rear of the helicopter.

Leonard glanced back to where Herron and EMT Thomas Abbot were feverishly working over the small girl in the rear of the helicopter.

"Five minutes, no more," Leonard said into his flight communications headset.

Herron looked up, meeting Leonard's gaze, and nodded. "Any longer," she said, "and we lose her."

"Eighth and Marshall coming up now," Peter O'Neill said.

John Leonard peered out the perspex of the Sikorsky. Sure enough, he could just make out the large red *H* marking the landing pad at Children's Hospital at the corner of Little Rock's Eighth and Marshall Streets.

"Get on the radio," O'Neill said.

Leonard thumbed the radio button and spoke to Adam Field Approach. He calmly recited the chopper's position and intentions and waited for an "all OK" message to come back.

The wind suddenly shifted, and O'Neill began to circle in from the southeast to approach the pad from downwind. The helicopter was being buffeted and slammed by winds well outside the Sikorsky's operating envelope. Operating temperatures were already soaring in response to O'Neill's out-of-sync inputs, but they were necessary to bring the helicopter down in such conditions.

"She's arresting!" Herron called from the back. "Have a crash cart waiting when we land!"

Leonard radioed the message, then without thinking, uttered the small prayer that had been forming in his mind for the last fifteen minutes. He was not a religious man, but for all his disbelief, the prayer was sincere.

As O'Neill brought the helicopter down on a steep approach, the airframe shook and bucked. His eyes were locked on the red *H*. To Leonard, it felt as if the helicopter was falling out from under him. His hand involuntarily went to the cyclic, but he quickly pulled it away. One thing they didn't need right now was two pilots trying to land the same machine.

O'Neill had the Sikorsky pegged to the target as if on a string. The undercarriage came down, and the wheels thumped into the concrete pad with enough force to rattle Leonard's teeth. He could only imagine what was going on in the rear with the small girl.

Even before Leonard could get his shoulder harness and seat belt off, the rear doors flew open, and a crash cart team, along with Herron and Abbot, pulled the gurney from the helicopter. The crash team immediately went to work as the gurney was hauled into the Cecil and Alice Pearson Emergency Center.

"God be with her," Leonard said, then blushed when he realized he'd said it aloud.

Peter O'Neill turned to his copilot. "Made it," he grinned.

"I was beginning to wonder," John Leonard said, beginning the shutdown procedures from the checklist. "That's one heck of a storm."

"That it is," O'Neill agreed. "But I wasn't talking about the storm. I was talking about you. You probably don't know it, but you were praying in my ear the whole time. Not bad for an atheist, or is it agnostic?"

"What are you talking about?"

"I'm talking about the prayer you started praying when we left Clayton and kept on praying the whole time we were in the air. You probably thought you were just thinking it in your head, but there were three of us on board who know exactly what you said."

John Leonard looked away, fixing his gaze out the windscreen of the helicopter on the dark clouds that seemed to surround them. Had he done that? Had he actually prayed aloud the entire way? Had he crossed that threshold he'd heard O'Neill talk about so many times. He *was* certain that whatever he'd said up there had been straight from his heart. And he knew, beyond a shadow of a doubt, that the One to whom he had said it actually existed.

"You want to talk about it?" Pete O'Neill asked gently.

John Leonard swallowed the lump that had formed in his throat. This time the lump was not due to fear. He *had* prayed the whole time. And not only had he prayed, but he had prayed *believing* that what he was asking would come true. And the proof, as his mother used to say, was in the pudding. The helicopter had arrived safely. Now, he thought, if the girl could only make it, he would be batting a thousand.

A small tear trickled down John Leonard's cheek, and he reached up to brush it away, but he felt no shame.

"How about a cup of coffee in the lounge?" Pete O'Neill suggested.

Leonard nodded as he finished recording his time in his flight log. This was one flight he would remember for the rest of his life.

"Let's check on the kid first," he said. "I'm worried about her."

As the girl was pushed into an emergency treatment room, Pam Herron motioned to the doctor who was about to treat the young patient.

"I think we have more of a problem than just the hypothermia," Herron told the doctor.

"Frostbite?"

"That too. But that's not the biggest problem. This girl is about four months pregnant."

Dr. Francis Boliver glanced at the girl on the gurney. "How old you think? Fifteen, sixteen?"

"No more than that," Herron answered.

"When will it end?" Boliver said as she and her trauma team went to work to save two lives instead of one.

CHAPTER ELEVEN

The call came just as Stacii Barrett stepped from the shower. It had been a long night and an even longer morning, but the midday shower had done wonders for her outlook on life. She needed some rejuvenation after last night's pretrial interview and this morning's meeting with her boss at the Arkansas Department of Human Services. He had called her into his office to hear the good news that he was increasing her caseload but reducing her budget. On top of that, a snowstorm had decided to sit on top of Little Rock, causing traffic snarls and delayed travel. All-in-all, it had not been a good twenty-four hours.

Stacii had come to the Department of Human Services out of the University of Arkansas at Fayetteville, where she had graduated with a Masters in Sociology and Early Childhood Development. By pure chance she had seen a notice on her dorm's bulletin board about State of Arkansas job interviews. She had gone and was surprised to see several hundred applicants milling around the interview area. She had filled out the forms and promptly forgot them. Two weeks later, she'd received a call from the State Director of Employment Security, and the rest, as they say, is history. After starting with the Employment Security Division, she had transferred to Human Services a couple of years later and had been there ever since.

It didn't seem possible that fifteen years had gone by, but now that she was the senior case worker for the department, her father had finally quit asking her what she was going to do with a degree in sociology.

Stacii lifted the receiver with one hand as she dried her short, brown hair with a towel. The apartment floor was cold, and she absently wondered what she'd done with her slippers.

"Stace?" the voice inquired from the other end of the line.

Stacii recognized the voice immediately. There was only one person in the office who called her "Stace."

"Yeah, Jerry. I'm just getting out of the shower. What's up?"

"Boy, I wish I had a job where I could take a shower this time of day. Some folks have all the luck," he said sarcastically.

Stacii bit her tongue. Jerry Allison was new to Human Services and still thought that his degree was more important than experience. It was no secret that he thought he should have Stacii's job instead of her, even though he had exactly one year and three days of experience behind a desk at Human Services. Stacii chose to ignore his frequent jibes. Along with most of the other case workers, she took Jerry Allison and his misplaced attitude of superiority with a very large grain of salt. Today, however, was worse than usual.

"What have you got, Jerry?" Stacii asked, not bothering to mask her annoyance. She was cold. The heat in the apartment was off again, she realized.

"Just got a call from Children's. They got a battered child case, they think. Morrison wants somebody over there ASAP."

Great, thought Stacii. She had already seen Kelsey Morrison once this morning when he'd told her about the budget cuts. Now he was adding insult to injury by assigning her a new case. What number was this? Two hundred ninety? Three hundred?

She reminded herself that Kelsey Morrison was one of the good guys. The Director of Human Services genuinely cared about his people. He always reminded everyone that the cases were not just numbers, but human beings. Kelsey Morrison was caught in the middle with the rest of the department.

"What's the initial evaluation?" Stacii asked.

"Nothing yet. That's up to you. We just got the call a few minutes ago. Seems some guys up in hillbilly country came across a girl, fifteen, maybe sixteen, half frozen to death. Said she looks like a wetback and they think she may be pregnant."

Stacii Barrett cringed at Jerry Allison's ethnic slurs. In two sentences, he'd managed to denigrate the inhabitants of the Ozarks and Mexico. He had all the sensitivity of a boulder rolling downhill. The man was ignorant. Not stupid, but ignorant. One day, Stacii thought, she would make an effort to educate Jerry Allison. In the meantime, she had to get to Children's Hospital.

"Tell Kelsey I'm on my way. It might take me awhile. The storm seems to have settled in here. Give me an hour."

"I'll tell him and I'll call Children's. You run into trouble, don't call me, I'll call you," Jerry said as he hung up the phone.

Stacii stared at the dead instrument in her hand and shook her head. Maybe she'd have to begin on Jerry Allison's education sooner than she had planned.

Stacii padded back into the bathroom, replaced the towel, then headed for her bedroom. She pulled slacks and a heavy sweater from her closet and shrugged into them. Combination leather and rubber mini-boots, along with her single heavy coat, completed the outfit. She examined herself in the mirror attached to the back of the bedroom door. *Nice,* she thought—*if you like looking like a giant brown bear.*

She smiled at the thought, and then dismissed it. Her short, bobbed brown hair complemented a face that required no makeup and the athletic figure she had as a result of her obsession with racquetball. A sprinkling of freckles across her nose gave her a slight tomboyish look that she liked.

Stacii stuffed a small purse in the pocket of her coat, picked up her keys, and was out the door. She would have to make a note to tell the building manager about the heat.

The drive to the hospital took longer than she'd expected. She had listened to the traffic reports on the radio and had tried to avoid the trouble spots by staying off the interstate system. For the most part, she'd been successful, but a fender bender at the corner of University and Markham had stalled her for a half hour. She'd taken University to I-630, hoping to make up the lost time.

Now, as she turned onto the Woodrow Street exit, she wondered what she was going to find at Children's. Jerry Allison had said a girl of fifteen or sixteen, probably Hispanic, and almost certainly pregnant. It was not a good combination.

She turned into the parking lot at Maryland Street and parked in an open space just outside the Pearson Emergency Center. The sliding glass doors of the center opened as she approached. She stepped through the metal detector just to the right of the guard station, shaking her head at the necessity for such precautions. It was a sad commentary on the state of humanity.

"I'm Stacii Barrett from Human Services," she told the nurse at the desk. "I'm here about the young Hispanic girl brought in this morning."

The nurse checked Stacii's credentials, then nodded. "Doctor Boliver is treating her," she told Stacii. "If you'll wait a moment, I'll see if she's available."

Stacii replaced her ID card and glanced around the waiting room. It was almost empty. Most people, *normal* people, she corrected herself, stayed in on days like this. *It's only us crazy Human Services case workers, nurses, and doctors who venture out,* she thought.

In moments the nurse returned. She was followed by a doctor whose name tag read "F. Boliver."

"Hi, Francis," Stacii greeted the doctor.

"Stacii. I thought Morrison might assign you to this case."

Francis Boliver and Stacii Barrett had worked together many times before, usually on cases like this one. Francis was married to a surgeon who practiced at Saint Vincents Doctor's Hospital on University Avenue, but Stacii had never met him.

"What's the story?" Stacii asked as she followed Dr. Boliver back into the treatment area.

"Life flight brought the girl in a couple of hours ago. The story I got is that a couple of pilots were forced down in the Ozarks when this storm raced through up there. When they got back to the airport in Clayton . . . "

"Clayton?" Stacii asked, surprised.

"Yeah. Clayton Municipal Airport. Why?"

"Nothing. I've got a good friend up there is all. Excuse the interruption. Please, go on."

"Anyway, when these two guys got back to Clayton, they found the girl in the storage compartment of the airplane, nearly frozen to death. They transported her to Clayton Memorial and called us. None too soon either."

Dr. Boliver led the way into a treatment room.

"The girl's core temperature was eighty-seven when they got her here. She was in the middle of cardiac arrest, but the team got her back."

"She's got heart problems at that age?" Stacii asked, confused.

Francis Boliver shook her head. "No. But when the super-cooled blood from the extremities reaches the heart, it can arrest. One of our problems in hypothermia cases is keeping the blood from the limbs from reaching the heart. We almost lost the girl. Right now, her temperature is back up to ninety-two and climbing. I think we may be out of the woods on this one, but we'll have to keep a close eye on her. Especially in her condition."

Stacii was taking notes as Dr. Boliver spoke. Now she stopped and looked at the doctor. "What *is* her condition?"

"The best we can tell right now is she's about four months pregnant. All indications are that the baby is all right for the time being. There's no way to know right now whether the hypothermia has done any damage to the child. We're scheduling some tests and we're about to run a sonogram. That should tell us something."

Stacii closed her small notebook and jammed it into her coat pocket. It never seemed to get any easier, but she had learned over the years to set aside her natural inclination toward empathy by concentrating on the facts of a case. But it was difficult, especially in these types of cases. She wanted to take the young girls in her arms and tell them everything would be all right, that she could make the hurt go away, and temper the anger that so many of them carried with them. But she'd learned she couldn't do that, and it had taken her a long time to work through what she considered to be failure on her part.

"Doctor?" a nurse was saying from the treatment room.

Francis Boliver nodded. "Come on, let's see what's happening."

Stacii followed Dr. Boliver into the treatment room. The girl on the gurney appeared small in the midst of the array of equipment. A member of the medical team looked up as they entered and stepped away from the head of the small patient.

Dr. Boliver moved closer; Stacii followed. The girl's eyes were open and looking around the room, as if she'd awakened from a long sleep like Snow White. Stacii recognized the fear in her eyes.

"*¿Donde estoy?*" the girl said in a weak voice.

Most of the team looked around at each other, wondering what she had said. One team member said, "She wants to know where she is," he said.

"Ask her if she speaks English," Francis Boliver directed.

"*¿Hablas ingles?*" the team member asked gently, using the informal case to ease the girl's fears.

Gaby Ibarra shook her head. Then she raised her hand, her thumb and forefinger close to each other, to indicate she did speak a little English.

"What's your name?" Boliver asked.

Gaby looked at the doctor; tears began to spring from her eyes. "Gaby Ibarra," she answered in a low voice.

"Well, Gaby," Boliver began slowly, "you are in a hospital, and we are going to take care of you. Do you understand?"

Gaby nodded her head. "Hospital?"

"That's right. In Little Rock, Arkansas."

"¿No en el valle?"

Francis Boliver looked up as if she had not understood the reference.

"No, not the valley," Stacii interjected. She had no idea what the valley was, but it was clearly a place the young girl did not want to be.

"Gracias a Dios," she said as her eyes closed from exhaustion.

"She said, 'Thank God'," the interpreter said.

"What is going on here?" Stacii Barrett said in a quiet voice. This case was already far different from any other she had handled.

CHAPTER TWELVE

Billy Bob looked up from a studious examination of his fingernails and tuned in to the telephone conversation that Jason Swann was engaged in across the room. Swann had summoned Billy Bob and Cole back into his overheated office and had barely begun to outline a new assignment for them when the phone rang.

He had been on the phone for ten minutes, but the tenor of the conversation had suddenly changed and Billy Bob sensed it. Even though he could only hear Swann's end of the conversation, he began to piece together that he and Cole would likely be hunting again soon, only this time the target list would be expanded to include the two men in the blue and white airplane, as well as the girl. Billy Bob felt a tingle of anticipation run through him.

While he and Cole were waiting for Swann to complete the call,

Billy Bob leaned back in his seat and began to think about the hunt.

He had killed before, numerous times. The first few times had been sanctioned by the government. For some, war was obscene. For Billy Bob Campbell, it was like a shot of whiskey poured directly into his veins. He loved it. It was not the killing itself he enjoyed, but the power he held over someone else's destiny. Power and control were mighty intoxicating, and it appeared that he and Cole were about to partake once again.

Jason Swann crisply hung up the phone, rose from his desk and handed Billy Bob a piece of paper. "That's the name of the man who owns that plane you saw. He's a flight instructor over in Clayton County. The other guy was probably one of his students. I don't know where the girl is yet, but we're working on that. The two of you get over to the Clayton airport, and see what you can find out."

"We'll need the truck, Swann," Billy Bob said. "The roads are gonna' be slick."

"Take it, just get over there and take care of those two. Check in with me when you get to Clayton. I should have the location of the girl by then. Do this right, and there will be a bonus for both of you."

"Let's get this straight," Billy Bob said. "This guy owns the plane. We find out who the second guy is, and we do away with them. In the meantime, you'll get the location of the girl, and then we do the same with her. Is that what you mean?"

Jason Swann sighed audibly. "That's exactly what I mean, Campbell. Kill them. All three of them. That's about as plain as I can make it."

"Yes, sir. That's plain enough," Billy Bob smiled. He read the name on the paper once again, then tucked it in his shirt pocket. Dean Barber was target number one. It would take at least four hours to get to Clayton. Billy Bob checked his watch and said, "Let's go, Cole." He headed for the office door. "We got work to do."

Jason Swann watched the two men leave. He had some misgivings about Billy Bob and Cole, but they were all he had right now. And if he wanted to rectify his own problems without involving Memphis, he had to use what he had.

He had no doubt the two men could complete the task. Both men were mean and tough. They weren't the smartest guys in the world, but that was not what he needed at the moment; he needed mean.

■　■　■

The old man replaced the receiver with concentrated exactness, not bothering to look up for the moment. When he did, he met the combined gazes of the other men in the room. Without exception, they were all old men. The youngest was in his mid-seventies, the oldest pushing ninety. They sat around a dark-stained oak table, polished to a deep brilliance. In the beginning, there had been seven of them, but the years had dwindled their number to five.

"Mr. Swann has failed us," he said in heavily accented English.

"Was ist los?" the oldest man asked impatiently.

"Speak English, please," another man said.

"To answer our companion's question," the man said, "That was our contact in Benning," continued the man who had spoken on the phone. "It seems another girl has escaped, and two strangers have become involved, quite inadvertently, in our affairs."

"Then we will have to deal with Mr. Swann," another of the old men said.

"That is understood," the first man agreed. "Might I suggest, however, we wait for the moment. Swann, it seems, has once again overstepped his bounds, but he might just solve our problem for us."

"Explain, please," another man said.

The first man cleared his throat, took a sip of water, and continued. "Swann has initiated actions to correct the current situation. I suggest we monitor his actions with an eye toward allowing him to take the full responsibility and blame for the results."

"What if his actions lead others to us?" another asked.

"If Mr. Swann were allowed to live, that might be possible. We will see to it that he does not."

Every man nodded in agreement. Swann would be allowed to clean up his mess, and then he himself would be "cleaned up."

"Then the project is still viable?" the oldest man asked.

"It is," the first man answered. "Great strides have been made, and we continue to improve our techniques, medical as well as political. The real hope still lies in the socialization techniques, though. We are close to the realization of our early vision."

Again each man nodded.

The first man rose from his place and walked to the window overlooking Memphis, Tennessee. From where he stood, he could see the Mississippi River and the Hernando-Desoto Bridge which formed a rounded *M* just to the west of the Memphis Pyramid.

The protocol worked. That much had been proven, but it was taking longer than originally planned. Years had been spent to this point perfecting the techniques, years that the men in the room no longer had. It was time to turn over control to another group of faithful. The newer members had already been chosen, their backgrounds investigated and verified, their loyalties examined. Those men would be the second generation, the men who would see the culmination of the project.

Those men would form the new group—the renewal of *Die Gruppe.*

CHAPTER THIRTEEN

As the weather continued to worsen, Kenneth Blair wondered for at least the tenth time whether he'd made the right decision. His wife, Susan, had an appointment at the Phelps Clinic on Germantown Parkway. From where his Jeep Cherokee was stuck in traffic, he could just see the high-rises of downtown Memphis, and he was not sure they could make the appointed time.

"Don't worry," Susan said, sensing her husband's uneasiness. "Dr. Phelps understands when we're late because of weather like this."

Kenneth grunted. "He can afford to be, with the prices he's charging."

Susan remained quiet, not rising to the bait. It was not the first time her husband had made such a remark. Not that it bothered her any more. It was his way of dealing with frustration, and there had been a lot of that lately.

Traffic was moving now, and Kenneth guided the Cherokee around the fender bender that had caused the delay. Germantown police were working the accident, their blue lights flashing in the growing gloom.

The weather front reflected his own mood, Kenneth Blair thought. Gray, low-hanging clouds obscured the sky completely. Earlier signs of clearing had given way to thicker, darker clouds, and the National Weather Service was now saying that the cold front had stalled. Conflicting weather reports called for everything from freezing rain, sleet, or snow, to a combination of all three. *So much for modern forecasting technology,* Kenneth thought.

Modern reproductive technology was failing them as well. They had been going to the Phelps Clinic for close to four years now, and they seemed no closer to having a baby. Their inability to produce a grandchild for Susan's parents was becoming the topic of some behind-the-back whispers in Tennessee society. Susan was the daughter of Joseph Harding Collins, president of one of the largest mortgage banks in the mid-south, and socialite Gwendolyn Southwick Collins. The guest list at Kenneth and Susan's wedding had included the then governor of Tennessee, both senators, and the vice-president of the United States.

Kenneth himself had risen to prominence as founder, CEO, and resident genius of New Days Technologies. His multiple-data encryption program for the Internet, which cost the user pennies yet offered total data security, had catapulted his company to the forefront of the Internet server industry. On paper at least, Kenneth was a multi-millionaire, and the couple had poured tens of thousands of their collective fortune into the Phelps Reproductive Clinic.

Kenneth and Susan had planned to have children immediately, and when a baby was not forthcoming soon after their wedding, Susan's father had recommended Dr. Phelps. After a couple of years with no success, Kenneth had begun to urge Susan to look for another doctor, but she always replied that "Daddy has the utmost respect for Dr. Phelps," and she had been reluctant to make a change. Now, after several rounds of arguments, they had agreed to consult with Dr. Phelps one more time before seeking a second opinion.

As they approached the clinic, Kenneth was once again struck by the impression that the Phelps building looked like a large granite mausoleum rising from the flat Mississippi River delta. Even though the weather was as nasty as Kenneth could remember, the parking lot was almost half full, a testimony to Dr. Phelps's reputation.

Kenneth felt Susan's hand resting on his arm. He glanced over at his wife. As always, she looked radiant. "It's going to be all right, darling," she said in her soft southern twang.

"I know it is," Kenneth said as he switched off the ignition. "I was just thinking about the surrogate program again."

"We've talked about that and you know how I feel," Susan said gently. "When we've exhausted all other options, then we can look into that. But don't forget, you're the one who has been pushing me to see another doctor."

"I know I have, and I still think that's the right way to go, for now," Kenneth replied.

Susan reached for the door handle. "Let's go see what Dr. Phelps has to say today."

■ ■ ■

Inside the clinic, Dr. Henry Phelps Jr. picked up the patient chart lying on his desk and thumbed through it without reading the contents. It wasn't necessary; he knew the file by heart. Already the number of patients in the program numbered in the thousands, and there were definite signs that a small percentage of the "placements," as he liked to call them, were beginning to pay dividends.

He glanced at the doorway and his eyes fell on the brushed gold nameplate on his door, which read, "Dr. Henry Phelps Jr., Director of Reproductive Endocrinology." He realized that the title was a bit grandiose, given the true nature of the clinic that his father, Dr. Henry Phelps Sr., had founded. Despite all the couples who had been legitimately helped during the past thirty years, the Phelps Clinic was not a benevolent service for the community. Its single purpose was far more sinister and cloaked in secrecy.

Dr. Phelps ran a large hand through his thick shock of fading blond hair. His features, particularly his nose and chin, were as severe as the pale blue eyes whose piercing gaze was only slightly softened by the steel-rimmed glasses he wore. At fifty-three, Dr. Phelps retained the physique of a man half his age, and his two-hour daily exercise regimen was almost as sacred to him as the work he did.

He had never married. There had never been time and even less opportunity. It was just as well. His work consumed most of his time. When he wasn't in the clinic or in his private gym at his Germantown home, he was usually overseeing the operation of Mid-South Obstetrics Management Services (MOMS), the management group that provided administrative support to the Phelps Clinic and numerous others in the mid-south region.

To the public, the group of clinics managed by MOMS appeared to be independent operations, but in truth, each clinic had been founded by MOMS for a specific purpose, a destiny. That destiny had been determined years ago, in another place and time, and it was now in the process of coming to fruition.

Dr. Phelps set the Blairs' file back on his desk. It was time to guide another young couple to the next step of the Lazarus Project.

CHAPTER FOURTEEN

"You've got that look again," Cindy Tolbert said.

David Michaels turned to meet her gaze. A hint of a smile crossed his face as he asked innocently, "What *look?*"

"*That* look," she answered quickly. "The one that says you're about to do something to follow your conscience that I'll think is crazy."

David laughed. "How is it you have learned so much about me in just over a year?"

"I'm a quick study, remember? And besides, it's more than just a year. You keep forgetting the crush I had on you in high school."

David Michaels and Cindy Tolbert were sitting in her office in the Clayton County courthouse. A fine snow was beginning to drift down, obscuring the sky once again. As David looked absently out the window, the wind began to gust, blowing sharp, icy snowflakes against the glass. He thought back to the calm-clear morning when he and Dean had flown back from the remote pasture in the Ozarks. It seemed as if God had provided a window of opportunity, just enough time to get the blue and white Cessna off the ground and back to the Clayton airport. He silently thanked God for using them to rescue the small girl.

At least she was in good hands now. David's mind kept drifting back to the circumstances that had landed the girl in the emergency room: the raging storm, the pasture that was really a secret airport, and two mean-looking "hunters" carrying automatic weapons in the middle of an Arkansas forest.

Cindy was right. He *did* have that look. It was the look that said his military training was overriding his all too brief civilian experience, and he was going to get to the bottom of it all.

". . . going to Little Rock?" Cindy was saying.

"I'm sorry," David said, as Cindy's words pulled him back to the present. "What was that?"

"I said, when are you thinking about going to Little Rock? To Children's Hospital?"

"I guess you *do* know me better than I thought," David smiled. "The sooner the better."

Cindy looked into David's eyes, and asked, "Is this the look of a pastor concerned about the well-being of a little girl or a career military man who doesn't know when to let go?"

David watched the small snowflakes begin to fall in larger clusters; thick, wet flakes that clung to the concrete sill outside the window.

"I'm going to Children's. I've got time and that girl may need someone to talk to," David said.

"I heard what you told Janice about the two men in the woods," Cindy replied quietly, avoiding David's gaze.

For a moment David said nothing. It was snowing heavily now. What he had told Sheriff Janice Morgan had been his first impressions, his gut reaction to the two armed men. He had tried to downplay the extraordinary weapons the two men in the pasture had carried, but he had seen the startled look on Janice's face.

"They were strange," David finally said. "Man, it's really starting to snow."

"Don't change the subject, David," Cindy said. "What about those rifles you were telling Janice about?"

David detected the alarm in her voice. "I probably overreacted on that one," David said. "Rifles are commonplace in Arkansas, you know that."

"You said they were Armalites, like that was something really unusual."

"I could have been mistaken. With all the copies of different weapons available here in the states, those could have been hunting rifles that just looked different." David hoped he sounded convincing.

Cindy glared at him and her anger flared. "I know you better than that, David Michaels. You spent too much time in the military to make a mistake like that. You were a penguin."

"A SEAL," growled David, smiling nevertheless.

"Whatever. And you told Janice those were Armalite weapons. Automatic ones, at that. I thought they were supposed to be illegal."

David pursed his lips. How could he tell Cindy it had finally hit him that the men in the forest had been hunting not a "what" but a "who"? He was convinced the two men had been after the small girl who had ended up in the belly storage compartment of Dean Barber's Cessna. *That* was what he wanted to check out, and the only source of information was the girl who was now at the Arkansas Children's Hospital in Little Rock.

But he would not tell Cindy. He did not want her worrying about him, and that was her nature. But he had to admit to himself, he sort of enjoyed the attention she showered on him.

Cindy had helped him work through Jimmy's death. Her prayers and concern had eased the pain, and in the end, he had realized that he was in love with her. He gently placed his arm around her and pulled her to him.

Cindy resisted for a moment. "Not here in the courthouse," she whispered.

David looked into her eyes. "There's no one in this whole county who doesn't know how I feel about you. This will not come as a surprise to them."

Cindy squirmed out of his grasp. "That's not the point," she responded, her hands on her hips. "You're a pastor. You're supposed to set an example."

David grinned widely. "I thought I was," he quipped, reaching for Cindy once again.

"Stop it," she said, swatting at David, this time with a smile of her own. "I know and you know you're going to Children's to see what you can find out about those two men, and whatever else you think you might have found out there in the jungle. You're going and I'm going with you. And you better call your father. You were supposed to go over there tonight, unless you've forgotten."

David had forgotten. Since moving out of his father's house and into his own, he'd made it a point to spend at least one night a week with James Michaels. He and his father were close. Even more so since David's brother, Jimmy, had died. Jean Michaels, Jimmy's widow, usually joined them on these family nights, and Cindy had been included as well. The weekly nights had helped all of them get past the stinging pain of Jimmy's death. Now they served as a touchstone for one another, keeping them in contact with each other. David had never realized how much he missed just being part of a family until he'd returned to Clayton. Now it was a part of his life he cherished.

"I did almost forget," David said. "I'll call him now."

"This storm is sitting on top of us, and it's snowing pretty good, now. We better take my car," said Cindy.

David feigned a look of hurt. "You mean you don't think mine will make it to Little Rock and back, don't you?"

Cindy smiled, reached up, and kissed David on the cheek, and said, "Just take the keys. That old Studebaker of yours is better off in a museum."

David took the keys. "Careful with that show of emotion. You're a pastor's girlfriend. You're supposed to set an example."

Cindy slapped playfully at David as he turned and scooted out the door. She followed him as they continued out into the gloom of the gray skies.

Once outside, the lightheartedness evaporated. David was worried. He *was* concerned about the two men and the AR-18 Armalite weapons they had been carrying. Maybe there was a logical explanation. If so, the starting place was with the almost-frozen girl now lying in Children's Hospital.

CHAPTER
FIFTEEN

"Looks like another hick town to me," Cole Branscum told Billy Bob Campbell, as they drove down the mountain and into Clayton.

"Shut up, Cole," Billy Bob snapped. He'd been driving for the last five hours, and in that time, he had had to listen to Cole's mindless banter like an endless mountain creek. He was tired, had a headache, and Billy Bob Campbell didn't like anyone when he was this tired, especially Cole Branscum.

The two had left Benning earlier in the day. The drive had taken them around one of the largest lakes in north central Arkansas. Normally the drive was gorgeous, but the weather had quickly gone from bad to atrocious. The radio reports emphasized the danger of the storm system that was sitting atop Arkansas at the moment. Snow had fallen continuously throughout the drive, forcing Billy Bob to concentrate on the road to keep from sliding off. Thus the headache. The combination of lousy weather and the thoughts about what they had to do weighed on Billy Bob, just like every other mission had prior to this one.

A mission. That's how Billy Bob thought of it. It was like being back in the army, preparing for one of the search and destroy missions he loved so much. But this one was different. Jason Swann had made that much abundantly clear. The two men in the airplane and the escaped girl had to be eliminated, and it had to be done—how was it Swann put it?—expeditiously. Billy Bob had never heard the word before, and he hated the way Swann spoke down to him, but he had understood the gist, and that was all that counted.

The road was slick as Billy Bob maneuvered the car down the long, winding approach into Clayton. He had been in the Ozark mountain town only once before, and that had been years ago. He would have to stop and ask directions to the municipal airport, the logical starting point.

Since he'd been in Clayton, the state had constructed a bypass around the town, and fast-food chains lined the highway like so many cheap beads on a necklace.

Billy Bob pulled into one of the fast-food restaurants, knowing it would be safer. Locals would constitute the labor force, but they would be used to seeing strange faces come and go. The highway was a main artery connecting southern Missouri and central and northern Arkansas. Anonymity was the overriding concern here. In a local restaurant, his face might easily be remembered if the police ever got around to forging a link between what was about to happen and any strangers in town during that same time. The fast-food chain would be safer.

Billy Bob parked the car and exhaled a sigh of relief. The tension in his shoulders and back was almost unbearable. The drive had taken more out of him than he'd realized.

"Coffee's gonna be good," Cole said, reaching for the door handle.

Billy Bob grabbed Cole's arm before he could get out of the car.

"Just keep your mouth shut, and let me ask the questions. We don't want to appear too curious. Might arouse suspicions."

"No problem, man," Cole answered. "Just let me get some coffee. This weather's the pits."

Billy Bob released Cole and watched as he scurried into the restaurant. Billy Bob shook his head, then followed. He was not absolutely comfortable with Cole on this job. He could not pinpoint what it was that bothered him, but there was something.

Inside the restaurant, Billy Bob and Cole each ordered coffee and hamburgers, accepted them from the delivery counter and selected a table near a front window where they could see the traffic on the highway. The gloom of the storm system had darkened the sky to almost night proportions, and every automobile that passed had its lights on.

"What's the plan?" Cole asked, munching on the assembly line burger.

"Ask about the airport, find that blue plane, and find this guy named Barber. Once we find him, we'll get the name of the other guy who was with him, and we'll go from there."

"This ain't a very large place. What happens if we run into one of those guys? They're sure to remember us. Could cause problems."

Billy Bob nodded. For once, Cole was right. They needed to get in and out of Clayton as quickly as possible. The longer they stayed, the greater the risk.

"Yeah, there's a chance. Wait here," Billy Bob said, and got up and strolled to the order counter.

"Yes, sir?" the girl at the counter asked.

"You got an airport around here, right?"

"Yes, sir. Just over the north bridge going out of town. Take a right just over the bridge and another right when you see the hangars. You can't miss it. But it's just a small airport. No commercial flights or anything like that," the girl added.

"No problem. We were just looking for a flight instructor," Billy Bob said, wondering why he'd said that. It was that kind of statement that could nail them if this girl happened to remember them later on.

"That would be Dean Barber. He's the only one out there. Ask at the first hangar. Brian Connelly is the owner and the mechanic out there. He's usually around. Big guy, about your size. He'll know where Mr. Barber is."

"You seem to know a lot about what goes on around here," Billy Bob said.

The girl smiled. "It's a small town. Everybody knows what goes on."

"Right," Billy Bob answered. He would have to remember that. That was the reason for his discomfort. Everyone *did* know what went on in a small town, and Clayton was the epitome of the rural small town. It was the same reason he was certain he knew who Jason Swann had called to get the information on the airplane. It would have taken someone with a little pull and access to FCC records, at least in a semiofficial capacity. Given that, Billy Bob was certain the information had come out of the Benning County sheriff's department. It was a thought worth hanging onto. One never knew when such information might come in handy.

Back at the table, Cole had finished his burger and was watching the sparse traffic ply the snow-covered road outside.

"Airport's just north of here. Let's go," Billy Bob ordered.

In minutes Billy Bob was once again behind the wheel of the car and headed north out of town. He had no trouble finding the road the girl had told him about and then the hangars off to the right. He turned down a double lane road leading toward the hangars and in seconds was parking the car in a snow-covered parking lot that crunched under the car's tires.

There was only one other car in the lot; Billy Bob figured it probably belonged to the mechanic, the man named Connelly.

"Stay in the car," Billy Bob told Cole, as he got out. The parking lot was slick. Billy Bob could see several airplanes parked on the tarmac. Each was tied down, and the snow accumulated on the upper surfaces of the wings told him that none had been flown recently. There was no single-engine blue Cessna in sight.

A small office extension was attached to the nearest hangar with a sign that read "Connelly Aviation" painted on the upper glass portion.

Billy Bob walked to the door and tried the knob. It turned without resistance, and a voice from inside boomed, "Come on in."

Billy Bob had no choice but to continue. If Dean Barber was in the office, he was caught. No doubt the flight instructor would remember him as one of the men he'd met in the forest, and if there was anyone with him, he would have to kill them both. This job was getting messy very quickly, Billy Bob thought.

The voice had come from a man sitting behind a scarred oak desk. Oil stains covered the portions of the desk Billy Bob could see. The rest of the desk was covered with odd forms and papers stacked in neat piles at each corner. Three mismatched filing cabinets were located against the wall behind the desk. A large map of the United States hung on the facing wall. The map was scribed with concentric circles with Clayton at the epicenter. A long string was thumbtacked to the side of the map with a shiny bolt tied to it to serve as a weight. Billy Bob wondered what the string was for.

The most impressive item in the office was the man sitting behind the desk. Billy Bob could see the man was easily as large as he was, and maybe larger. Billy Bob was relieved; the man was alone. He would be Brian Connelly, the owner of Connelly Aviation.

"Lousy weather to be out in," Connelly said, not bothering to get up from his chair behind the desk.

"Yeah. You got that right," Billy Bob answered back. "Didn't really think about it until I got here, and then it was too late."

"What can I do for you?" Connelly asked.

"Well, I know this is gonna' sound strange, but I was looking for a flight instructor. Name's Barber."

"That'd be Dean Barber," Connelly said warily, looking up at the big man who'd just entered his office. "He's not here right now."

"No wonder with this weather. Just thought I'd stop by and say hi. We go way back."

"Military?"

Billy Bob looked quizzically at the mechanic sitting behind the desk. "Military?"

"You guys in the military together?" Connelly clarified.

"Oh, that. Naw. Just friends. Told me the next time I was close to drop in. I should've known he wouldn't be flying in this weather."

"He's supposed to fly up to Springfield in the morning and pick up some clients to fish the White River. Trout. The way this weather's settin' in, he may have to cancel."

"Tomorrow? It would probably be just as easy for me to meet him here in the morning. I've got some other business to take care of, and I can come back through here then. What time is he going to be back?"

Brian Connelly shuffled through some papers on his desk. "Here's his note," he said, pulling a scrap from the pile. "He wants to take off at nine in the morning. But, like I said, with this weather, he might have to cancel. Just have to wait and see what it does. Dean doesn't like to fly when it's like this. He's pretty careful."

Billy Bob thought for a moment, then said, "But Dean's the one who saved that little girl, right? I thought I'd congratulate him on a job well done."

Brian Connelly looked at Billy Bob and smiled. "You heard about that, already, huh?"

"Girl over at the restaurant said something about it," Billy Bob lied.

"That little girl was half frozen when I fished her out of that storage compartment," Connelly said.

"So she was in the belly storage compartment of the plane?"

"Yeah. Neither Barber nor Michaels seem to know how she got there. It was weird."

"Michaels?" Billy Bob repeated with interest.

"David Michaels. He was the other guy in the airplane. Actually, he's one of Barber's students. Already got his license. Preacher's working on his instrument rating now."

"Preacher?"

"Yeah. David Michaels. I call him Preacher. He's the pastor of the First Community Church here in town. He's the one who took her to the hospital."

Billy Bob felt his spirits rise. He now had the name and occupation of the second man involved and the location of the escaped girl. There couldn't be more than one hospital in a hick town like Clayton. Things were looking much brighter despite the weather just outside the office window.

"Course, the girl's not at Memorial any more."

For a moment Billy Bob did not understand the statement. Then he felt his spirit drop at what he was being told. "The girl's gone?"

"Yeah. Helicopter from Children's Hospital came down from Little Rock and picked her up. Those guys flying that thing were either the bravest guys in the world or the craziest. Everybody in town's talking about them. Last word I heard was she's in bad shape. Might not make it."

Once again Billy Bob's spirits soared. Not only did he know who the two men in the forest were, but now there was a chance he and Cole wouldn't even have to kill the girl. *Shucks,* Billy Bob thought, *she's probably already dead.*

The phone on the oil-stained desk jangled. Brian Connelly picked up the instrument and listened for a long minute, then responded, "Sure. It'll be ready," before replacing the phone.

"You're in luck. That was Dean on the phone. He's still going to Springfield in the morning at nine. Sorry, I should have told him you were looking for him. I can call him back right now."

Billy Bob stopped Connelly with a quick wave of his hand. He had already pressed his luck far beyond what he should have. "Don't do that. He's busy and I have to get back on the road. I'll be back out here in the morning. I can talk to him then. In the meantime, I've got other things to do. Tomorrow will be fine."

"OK. If you say so. I've got to get the Cessna ready for Dean."

"The plane's here?"

"Sure. In the hangar. Dean doesn't like it to be out in the weather, so he rents a corner of my hangar. He wants me to go over it for tomorrow's flight. It'll be IFR all the way, and he wants to be sure everything's working."

"IFR?"

"Instrument Flight Rules. In this weather, he'll be flying on instruments most of the way tomorrow."

"Nine o'clock, you say?" Billy Bob asked.

"On the dot. Dean will file an IFR flight plan with the Flight Service Station in Little Rock. You can be sure he'll hold to that nine o'clock takeoff time."

For Billy Bob Campbell, it was almost too good to be true. He already had a plan for getting rid of Dean Barber. Now all he had to do was come up with one to rid the world of one more pesky preacher, and his job would be done. The girl was probably already dead. It was turning out to be a much better day than Billy Bob had anticipated.

"What about that preacher. David Michaels, you say?" Billy Bob asked, trying to be nonchalant.

"What about him?" Connelly asked.

"He live around here?"

"If you mean in Clayton, I guess technically the answer is yes. He's got a log cabin he's renovating about two miles out of town to the south. When he's not flying or preaching, he's usually at the cabin. Either there or with his girlfriend, Cindy Tolbert. She's the Clayton County clerk down at the courthouse."

"Thanks," Billy Bob told Brian Connelly. He knew he was pushing his luck with the big mechanic. There was no doubt that Connelly would remember him if questions ever arose about how Dean Barber or David Michaels died. That meant he would have to come back and kill Brian Connelly as well. He could not take the risk of leaving the mechanic alive to identify him at a later date. But that would come later. Right now he had another priority. He wanted to find David Michaels.

Michaels. What a twist of fate. Nothing more than a country preacher. What could be easier? Killing the preacher would be almost boring, Billy Bob thought. It would be easy money, and he could stand some easy money for a change.

Billy Bob Campbell bid farewell to Brian Connelly and walked out the office door humming to himself. Fate had finally smiled on him.

Now all he had to do was find David Michaels.

■ ■ ■

Brian Connelly made a mental note to remember the man who'd just left his office. There was something strange about the man, Connelly thought, but he couldn't quite put his finger on it.

CHAPTER
SIXTEEN

The old man rose shakily from his knees, the strain showing on his face. His prayers had long ago been directed to a being other than the God of Creation. Somehow, he found a perverse logic in that.

He looked around the room; it was sparsely furnished, just the way he liked it. At least, the way he liked this specific room. The rest of the house was much more elaborate, an eclectic mix of old and new. The furnishings reflected his own thought processes. There were things from the past that needed to be preserved, but there were also things of the present that had to be incorporated into his way of life.

The old man walked to the door. Outside this room he felt a certain vulnerability. He had no explanation for the security that seemed to permeate his being when he was in his prayer room, but it existed, against all logic.

How long had he been in this house? Fifteen years? Longer? It had been in 1979, hadn't it? Nineteen years; almost twenty, now. That had been the last time he was in Brazil. What had been the name of that beach? His memory seemed to be failing him these days. Bertioga. That was it. Bertioga Beach, just two hours south of São Paulo.

It had been January, the old man remembered. The sweltering heat of the Brazilian summer had been tormenting. It had been the perfect time to die. He had wanted that, then, to die. Life had not been kind to him in those years. São Paulo had been a nightmare. He had been alone, his concentration fading, his resolve faltering. The loneliness had been an almost unbearable burden. But it had been the loneliness which had rekindled his desires, his passions.

In times like those, his mind reverted to the familiar, the understandable. He had recalled his reason for living: the project.

Not that he had ever really forgotten it. The project had been the reason for his life. *His* purpose. He could remember that day in Lorient as if it were yesterday. He had watched his friend board the U-boat, *Eins Zwei Drei,* beginning the long journey to the United States. His own journey had taken longer and had required several detours, but he had finally made it.

The old man tugged absentmindedly at his full mustache. His hand then went to the thin scar at his forehead, the result of an earlier failed plastic surgery. The surgery had been an ill-fated attempt to change his appearance, to hide from the world. The scar still itched at the most inappropriate times. He would wait until the sensation went away before he joined the other men.

The other men.

The old men.

Die Gruppe.

They waited even now in the library in the adjoining wing. There were decisions to be made, plans to finalize. He was the head, the leader. He had always known it would come to this, even when he'd been living in São Paulo and Buenos Aires. Before then, even. His life was too important to be wasted. He'd known that, *sensed* it as if by some strange providence.

To that end, it had been the sacrifice of another which had allowed for his own immigration to the United States. With his previous identity dead and buried in a hillside grave in Embu, Brazil, his life had taken on a new and more important role.

He gently rubbed the scar once again, letting his fingertips trace the thin line, then waited again for the tingling to subside. He was ready.

He exited the small prayer room with the confidence of the god he believed himself to be. Only a god could have accomplished what he had. Only a god could now be living among the enemy in such splendor and comfort and still be in a position to affect the world in the manner in which he could.

But the time had come for him to step down, to abdicate the throne, so to speak. All of the old men would eventually pass this way, he told himself. There were four others like him. They had done all they could. Their most important contribution would now be the passing of the project to others. The foundation had been established, the cornerstone laid.

The library was just off the main corridor, near the front of the house.

The house. He wondered what people of this affluent East Memphis neighborhood would think if they knew who their neighbor really was. Would they rebel? Cry for justice? Demand penitence? He doubted it. The world was too blasé, too indifferent to the plight of others. It had not always been so, and it had been that attitude of universal justice which had almost put an end to his life's work. But times do, and did, change. It was now a world which wanted good only if that good was not inconvenient, if it cost nothing.

The old man smiled as he placed his hand on the polished brass of the door knob. In only minutes, the transition would be made. The reigns of a world gone mad would be turned over to another generation of zealots. A generation born and bred for only one purpose, for one end. For the project was everything.

"Gentlemen," the old man spoke as he entered the library. "The time has come," he said, taking the seat nearest the glowing embers in the massive stone fireplace. He retrieved a package of cigarettes and lit one. He filled his lungs with the smoke, allowing a renewed sense of invulnerability to infuse his spirit.

The four men who had been waiting for the old man had stood as he had entered. They now took their respective seats, turning their full attention to their leader.

"The men, the *patriots,*" the old man whispered, "who are about to take our place are here in this house. It is our duty to transfer the power and the direction of *Die Gruppe* into the hands of these men."

Each of the old men in the room nodded at the statement. None spoke. They were all tired; wasted men who needed the time left to them to die with dignity. But in their dying, a flame would be rekindled. The new members of *Die Gruppe* would carry on, like a rising phoenix in a barren land. And they would carry on with a new vigor and strength unavailable to this older group of men.

"The time is right," one of them said. The others again acknowledged the truth.

"Yes, my friend, the time is right." The old man turned to the single nonmember in the room, his servant and constant companion through the years. "Would you show the gentlemen in, please."

The servant clicked his heels together lightly and nodded.

The door opened; seven men filed into the room. No one said a word. A strange reverence was present in the library, a feeling of unworthiness. Every man knew why he was here; everyone felt the weight of responsibility the ceremony carried with it.

With quick movements that belied his age, the old man went from man to man, pinning each lapel with a small medal hanging from a blood-red ribbon trimmed in white. No one spoke.

With the medals bestowed, the old man stepped back, raised his hand sharply, and saluted the seven men.

Each man in turn saluted the old man.

"Gentlemen," the old man began, "you have been chosen for your skill, your loyalty, and your courage. We in this room will support your decisions as if they were our own, for in a very real sense, they are just that. Never hesitate to do what you think correct. Never try to justify your actions before the world. Never acquiesce to the mediocre. Never compromise. Never seek consensus, for in consensus is found weakness. It is with honor and pride I bestow upon each of you the medal which you now wear." The old man stopped, his breath coming in short gasps as he spoke. He waited until he could again speak.

Again, no one uttered a sound.

"More importantly," the old man continued, "you have been entrusted with the plan of the ages, the blueprint for a new world. Never forget that. For you are now the men of *Die Gruppe*. You are the men of the future."

Later, as the old man relaxed by a newly rekindled fire, a snifter of brandy in his hand, he thought of the new men who would carry on the project. They would have hard decisions to make very soon. The first would deal with the problem which had presented itself in the form of Jason Swann and his decision to kill three people. The decision, in and of itself, was not a bad one. But it was one that should have come from him. Swann had overstepped his bounds. For that, Jason Swann would have to die.

The old man sipped the brandy. He extracted another cigarette from the package, lit it, and rested his head on the back of the chair. Exhaustion seemed to come more easily these days, and his pleasures were fewer.

The old man—the man known to the members of *Die Gruppe* only as Lazarus—closed his eyes and savored the aroma of the liquor as it mixed with the rising smoke from the cigarette he held in his left hand. The dreams returned.

CHAPTER
SEVENTEEN

Jason Swann strolled down the upstairs corridor of the house in the valley with a feeling of elation. He had just gotten off the phone with Billy Bob Campbell. Campbell had told him about finding the flight instructor, or at least his plane. He had also told him of the flight instructor's plan to fly to Springfield, Missouri, the following day and of his plans to eliminate the man. But the best news had come in the form of a name. David Michaels was the name of the second man in the airplane, and according to Campbell, the mechanic in Clayton had confirmed the rescue of Gaby Ibarra. Ibarra had been airlifted to Children's Hospital in critical condition. There was a good chance the escaped girl was already dead. The pieces of the puzzle were quickly falling into place.

David Michaels.

That was the second man's name, and the really good news was that the man was nothing more than a simple country preacher. The news could not have been better, as far as Swann was concerned.

Swann chuckled to himself as he headed for the primary nurses' station. He wanted to check on the nine "patients" still under his supervision. Seven of them were due to deliver babies at various times. Two were awaiting implantation as soon as arrangements were made. The arrangements were complicated and time-consuming, but Swann was amazingly patient, even in his current state of mind. Each successful implantation resulted in a bonus well into five figures. Each functional entity, as the newborns were termed upon birth, resulted in another bonus. With seven about to be born, and two more on the implantation list, life was beginning to look good.

Even the loss of Gaby Ibarra could be accepted within the context of a business misfortune. True, Swann thought, the loss of the four-month-old baby the girl was carrying presented more of a problem than the loss of the girl herself. The baby had already been contracted for. The delivery date had been set, and the receiving family was to have been notified in only days by a MOMS affiliate.

According to his information, the family which was to have received the Ibarra child would have made an excellent addition to the Project Matrix. All the parameters had been in place. An excellent family, young and vigorous, with unlimited potential. The wife had been convinced she was unable to bear children but, nevertheless, wanted them desperately. The husband was well-known, a potential political power broker, with money to back such an endeavor. They were perfect candidates for the project.

Swann stopped at the nurses' station and leaned on the chest-high counter. Two nurses were always on duty. One, Barbara Lomax, was busy writing in charts. The other, Daniel Montgomery, was somewhere on the floor, checking on the girls.

One of the two nurses was always a man. Female nurses had better rapport with the girls, but a man was needed for security purposes, in addition to the other security personnel. Obviously, something had gone wrong, and Swann wanted to find out what the problem was. How had Ibarra escaped? That was his overriding concern at the present.

With Campbell and Branscum in Clayton, the two pilots identified, and the location of the girl established, he was feeling more or less in control of his situation. But he knew he still had a problem where the men in Memphis were concerned. The men would want answers. He needed to mitigate the ramifications coming out of Memphis, if at all possible. The deaths of the pilot, the preacher, and the girl were a good start. Now he needed to assure those men that his operation was secure. It was not beyond the realm of possibility that his own initiative would be looked on with favor, and perhaps even another bonus.

"Where's the Ibarra chart?" Swann asked nurse Lomax.

"Right here, Mr. Swann," the nurse answered, handing Swann the color-coded folder.

Swann flipped through the folder, noting the times of medications and exercise. Each girl was on a strict regimen of daily supervised exercise and nutrition. Never were two girls allowed to exercise together, and never were they allowed more than an hour a day together in the common room.

The upper floor of the house was a well-concealed, high-security prison, as well as a fully equipped, ultramodern maternity ward. How Gaby Ibarra had escaped was beyond Jason Swann's imagination.

He continued to thumb through the chart, noting exercise times. He had already turned a page when a thought struck him. He flipped back two or three pages and read an entry with interest.

"What is this?" he asked the nurse, pointing to an entry in the chart.

Barbara Lomax took the chart and read the entry. "It appears the girl complained of problems with the plumbing in her bathroom."

"What kind of problem?"

"It doesn't say here, Mr. Swann."

"What's the procedure when this happens?" Swann was familiar with almost every situation imaginable, but for the life of him, he couldn't remember if the complaint of a plumbing problem carried with it a specific set of procedures to be followed.

"We call Johnny, and he comes up and checks it out," the nurse answered.

Johnny Carter was the on-site maintenance man. He was the only one at the house, and for good reason. Already, the staff was edging toward unwieldy. The more people who knew what went on at the house, the better chance of it getting out, and that could not be allowed. Carter, like the rest of the staff, was well paid and highly motivated to maintain the secrets of the house. Motivation, for most of the staff, also came in the form of police records and, at times, even outstanding arrest warrants.

But the single greatest motivation for every staff member was the pledge each had signed promising unflagging loyalty to *Die Gruppe*. Each knew the penalty for revealing the secrets of the valley. Rewards were great; penalties severe. In truth, to the person, none of the staff ever even spoke about the house outside the confines of the valley. It had been done only once, and the speaker had never again been heard from.

Loyalty was not the problem, Swann knew. Stupidity might well be another matter altogether. One could mandate adherence to certain standards. No one could mandate intelligence.

Swann looked at the chart, not seeing the words. "When Carter was checking on the girl's bathroom, where was the girl?"

"In the common room, Mr. Swann."

"Alone?"

"I believe so, sir," Lomax answered nervously, knowing that leaving a girl alone was strictly against regulations.

Swann tossed the chart onto the nurse's desk and headed for the common room at the end of the corridor. He pushed through the double swinging doors and entered the room.

The room was a combination of two rooms, actually, with a center wall knocked out to enlarge the area. Swann glanced around, taking in the amenities. The first thing that caught his eye was a door in the far corner. The door had been added for safety but was kept locked for security reasons. Swann walked over to it and checked the locking mechanism. It was locked; the knob would not turn.

Swann turned to leave, then another thought struck him. He walked back to the door, checked the knob once again, then pushed on the closed door. It opened easily. A small Band-Aid was affixed to the locking mechanism, rendering it ineffective.

That was how she had gotten out. Gaby Ibarra had somehow opened the door, affixed the Band-Aid to it, and then gone back to her room. When the time was right, she had slipped out of the room, out the door, and into the Arkansas forest.

Jason Swann cursed under his breath. Someone's head was going to roll for this, and he'd be sure it wasn't his.

But knowing how the girl had gotten out brought a certain amount of closure to the situation. Another question had been answered. For that, he was thankful. Now it was time to close the door on the pilot and the preacher. Campbell could check on the girl after those two were out of the way.

Swann almost giggled to himself as he walked back down the corridor, down the stairs, and to his office. A pilot and a preacher. A *preacher.* What could be easier?

■　■　■

Billy Bob Campbell tossed his meager belongings on the bed. Cole Branscum did the same on the other bed. The two men had checked into one of the newer motels just south of town, using fictitious names. They were lucky to get a room at all. The storm was worsening, and travelers were flocking to all the motels in the area, trying to find some respite from the storm.

Billy Bob worried that the storm would delay Dean Barber's flight to Springfield tomorrow. He hoped not. His plan for doing away with Barber depended on the man's taking off on time tomorrow morning.

As for the plan to kill the preacher, David Michaels, Billy Bob had not come up with what he considered an acceptable scheme as yet. He would work on that while he watched some cable TV and checked out the Clayton, Arkansas, phone book.

"What's with the phone book?" Cole asked, flopping down on the bed.

Billy Bob smiled. That was Cole. No imagination. A local phone book was the single best source of information on any person in any community. It was so common, it was usually overlooked.

Cole didn't wait for an answer before flipping on the TV with the remote. He tried the all-sports channel first. It was showing a rerun of a golf tournament.

"Golf," Cole muttered. "What a waste," then flipped through more channels before settling on an all-pro wrestling match.

Billy Bob ran his finger down the listing in the phone book until he found the name Michaels. There were three listings: James Michaels, Jimmy Michaels, and David Michaels.

David. That was the one. Billy Bob picked up the phone and dialed the number. He let it ring a dozen times before hanging up.

"Not home," he announced.

"Who?"

"The preacher," Billy Bob told Cole.

"Don't worry 'bout no preacher, man. We do the pilot in the morning, then we find the preacher, do him, and we're out of here. No problem."

Billy Bob liked the sound of it. Simple and quick. Two for the price of one. But somewhere, in the back of his mind, a little voice was nagging at him. What was it? The pilot, for sure. There was no way it could be the preacher.

Billy Bob tossed the phone book on the credenza which held the TV and flopped down on the other bed. A little sleep would be good. What with the snow and gloom, this was perfect sleeping weather. Tomorrow was the day. After tomorrow, Swann would owe him big time, and he was going to see that the little man paid.

In less than two minutes, Billy Bob Campbell was snoring louder than the cacophony issuing forth from the cage-match on the television.

Cole Branscum watched with unabated interest as the eight men in the wrestling ring beat up on one another.

CHAPTER EIGHTEEN

David Michaels took the Woodrow Street exit and headed for Twelfth Street. He turned onto Battery, moving slowly on the icy streets toward the Arkansas Children's Hospital. The drive to Little Rock had taken almost twice as long as normal due to the road conditions. The Arkansas Highway Department had graded and salted the roads, but the going had still been arduous.

"What are you thinking?" Cindy Tolbert asked, looking at the man she loved.

David didn't answer immediately. There was a throbbing just behind his eyes, put there by his overconcentration while driving in the slush and mire.

"Is it the girl?" Cindy asked gently.

David nodded. "I keep wondering how she got into the belly of that airplane. We were in the middle of nowhere, in some of the worst weather I've ever seen. It just doesn't make a lot of sense."

Cindy didn't respond to David's musings. She'd been hearing the same thing since they had left Clayton, hours earlier. The total content of David Michaels's conversation had consisted of wondering about how the girl had gotten in the Cessna and whether she would be all right.

"And those two men showed up out of nowhere too," David continued, talking almost to himself. "That was strange too. Way too coincidental."

"Maybe they really were hunting wolves, like they said," Cindy said.

The car began to slide as David rounded a corner. He twisted the steering wheel in the direction of the slide, and the car recovered.

"Careful. This is the only car I've got, and it's not paid for," Cindy chastised.

"Sorry," David responded. "Good thing we took yours. Mine would never have made it, I'm afraid."

Cindy Tolbert laughed. "Yours won't make it out of your yard. When are you going to buy a decent car?"

The switch in the conversation from the girl to David's car lightened the mood.

"Come on. Give me a break. I like old things. And it's a Studebaker Lark. If you really had a crush on me in high school, like you said, you would remember I had one of those back then."

Cindy peered straight ahead. "The only thing I really remember from back then was how much I thought I loved you."

"Thought?"

"Yes, *thought.* I'm beginning to think I must have been crazy. There's really nothing very special about you, you know. Maybe I need to reevaluate my thinking."

David glanced out of the corner of his eye at Cindy. She was still looking straight ahead, but a grin had appeared, and from what David could see, her green eyes were sparkling with delight. He could feel the affection he had for her well up inside him like an Ozark Mountain spring about to overflow.

Cindy was always there for him when he needed her most. It had been Cindy who had first mentioned that the Reverend Glen Shackleford was about to retire from the pulpit of First Community Church, and it had been Cindy who had suggested to David that he would be perfect for that position.

More importantly, it had been Cindy Tolbert who had reminded David of his own belief in God and his responsibility as a minister of the gospel. That had been something he had been trying to run away from, David realized now. He'd been a military chaplain then, and for him, it had been the farthest thing from the pastorate he could find. It was true that some chaplains saw themselves in a pastoral role, but he never had. He had seen himself as a warrior. A modern-day King David, he remembered thinking, wryly. It had taken tragedy, death, and Cindy to make him see what it was God had called him to do.

Now, after more than a year, David knew he was on the verge of asking Cindy Tolbert to marry him. He had to admit to a potpourri of feelings concerning Cindy. In the first place, he really had no place to take a wife. The house he'd found a few miles out of town was in the early stages of renovation. Just like the Studebaker he loved so much. Cindy owned her own house and he knew she would have no problem with him moving in with her after they were married. But David was old-fashioned; he wanted to provide for his wife.

Cindy would jokingly call his attitude chauvinistic, but he knew better. He had been taught Southern manners from an early age by a father whom he loved and respected. He still remembered the love and warmth that seemed to permeate every room of the house where he and Jimmy grew up. Those had been good days, loving days, and he could envision them happening again with Cindy.

The huge bulk of the Arkansas Children's Hospital drew David's thoughts back to the present. He felt Cindy's hand reach out and touch his right forearm. He kept his left hand on the wheel and reached for her hand. Somehow, she had felt the fear he was feeling. Again, as always, she was with him. And despite his efforts, his thoughts immediately returned to her.

It had been Cindy who had really taught him to be a pastor and not just a preacher. Coming out of the military, David had recognized his lack of interpersonal skills, especially within the context of a quickly changing civilian world. It had been, and still was, a strange sensation for him. He had come a long way in the last year, but he was far from being the perfect pastoral type.

The situation into which he was about to be thrust was the perfect example. In the military, he could have followed an expected pattern and been done with it. He would have been expected to show up, say a few comforting words, recite a short prayer, and be gone. It would have been easy, impersonal.

But that was not the way it was now, and a certain part of him was grateful for that. His emotions had been reawakened, ignited by caring and love. And as always, it had been Cindy who was responsible.

David squeezed Cindy's hand just before turning onto Marshall Street. They had arrived. David parked the car just down from the helicopter pad.

"Let's try the ER," Cindy suggested.

David followed Cindy out of the car and toward the emergency room. "I've never been very good at this kind of stuff," David said, walking beside Cindy toward the glass doors.

"You will be. You'll see. You care. That's what's important. That and being there. You don't really have to say a whole lot in these situations. Trust me."

David smiled. That was Cindy, directing him once again through a tough time. His arm went around her as they made their way to the ER door.

Inside, they looked around. There was a nurses' station facing them. They had to pass between a metal detector before reaching the station. To David, it was a telling indictment on the condition of today's society. There should have been no need for such security measures, especially in a hospital designed for the care of children. But here it was, and David felt a pang of remorse because of it.

They walked to the nurses' station. There were two white-clad nurses, working on computers behind the waist-high counter.

"Excuse me," Cindy began. "We're from Clayton. Your helicopter brought in a young girl a few hours ago from there. Can you tell us anything about her condition?"

The nurse, somewhere between forty and fifty, David guessed, looked up from the computer screen and smiled. It was the kind of smile that put a person at instant ease. He immediately envied the nurse.

"I can't say anything about that. I'm sorry."

David stepped up. "Is there any way we can find out about her? I'm her pastor."

Cindy glanced sideways at David and grinned. It was not exactly the truth, but then it was not exactly a lie either.

"I'm sorry . . . ," the nurse began.

"Reverend David Michaels," David supplied.

Cindy's grin widened. It was the first time she had ever heard David refer to himself as "Reverend."

"Well, Reverend Michaels, I can tell you the name of the Human Services representative on the case. As far as I know, she's still in the hospital. Maybe that would help."

"That would be a great help. Thanks."

The nurse tapped on the computer keyboard, waited a second, then said, "Her name is Ms. Barrett. I can have her paged for you."

"Thanks. If you don't mind," David added, as he felt Cindy's hand on his forearm once again.

"It's Stacii," Cindy said in an excited whisper.

"What are you talking about?"

"I'll bet you Sunday dinner that the Ms. Barrett the nurse is talking about is Stacii."

Somehow, David felt as if he had missed part of the conversation. "Who is Stacii?"

"That's what I'm trying to tell you. I think Ms. Barrett is Stacii Barrett. I went to school with her. She works for Human Services as a case worker."

"Cindy!" a voice called from behind them.

Cindy and David turned just as a young woman ran into Cindy's arms. "It is you," Cindy exclaimed. "I was telling David it had to be."

"David?"

"David Michaels, Ms. Barrett," David introduced himself, holding out his hand.

Stacii Barrett shook David's hand, then took a step back and examined the two carefully. "Is there something special going on here?" she asked.

Cindy blushed for a moment. "David and I have been seeing each other for about a year. If you kept in touch, you would know about it," Cindy scolded.

"And if he was so important, you would have called me," Stacii responded, her face lighting up with a warm smile.

"I think she's got you there, Cindy," David interjected.

"Maybe," Cindy conceded.

"But old-home week is not why you're here, is it?" Stacii asked.

"It's about the girl who was brought in earlier. The nurse told us you had been assigned to the case. We thought it was just a medical situation."

"Right," David said. "What's Human Services got to do with this?"

"Normally nothing. But this isn't a normal case. The girl appears to be about fifteen or sixteen. Speaks a little English, but mostly Spanish. She's been able to answer a few questions so far, but she's far too weak to be interrogated. The hospital called us when they discovered the girl was pregnant."

"Pregnant?" David exclaimed. "How . . . ?"

Stacii held up her hand. "I know all the questions, but we don't have any of the answers yet. That will come in time. The girl did mention something about an airplane. Rumor is that two men saved her life. You wouldn't happen to know the men, would you?" Stacii addressed David.

"I was one of them. The other was my flight instructor, Dean Barber."

"I had a feeling," Stacii Barrett smiled. Just as quickly as it had come, the smile left her face. "Tell me what happened."

"Let's sit down," Cindy suggested; the trio moved to the waiting area chairs.

David began with the storm and told Stacii the story, up to where the Children's Hospital helicopter took off from Clayton Memorial Hospital. It was the first time Cindy had heard the encounter from start to finish without interruption.

"That kid is lucky," Stacii said quietly, after David had finished. "There are a lot of questions that don't have answers at this point."

"One of which is, how did she get into that airplane storage compartment in the first place?" David said.

"And how did she get pregnant?" Stacii added.

"And will she live?" Cindy said.

Both David and Stacii turned to Cindy. Her question was the one each had been afraid to voice, but now it was out in the open, and it was the question that dwarfed all the others.

"Rumor has it that one of the pilots was a preacher. That's you, right?"

"That's me," David acknowledged. "I didn't know it showed. The preacher part, I mean."

"It doesn't. Just a good guess."

"Don't depend on him being the stereotypical preacher, though," Cindy added, grinning. "He came out of the military, and I'm still trying to orient him to civilian life. I'm not sure how well I'm doing."

Stacii Barrett laughed lightly. It was a pleasant laugh. "Well, to tell the truth, I'm not that religious, anyway."

"Do you believe in God?" David asked.

"In my line of work, it's easier to believe in the existence of the devil," Stacii replied. "Or at least to believe in evil."

"That's a start," David said.

"We have staff here who speak Spanish," Stacii continued. "The girl said some strange things, and then she clammed up, as if she was afraid something might happen if she kept talking," Stacii turned to David. "What, if anything, do you know about a valley near where she was found?"

David thought for a moment. A valley? What valley? Every mountain had a valley. There were thousands. What was that? The girl had been in the Ozarks; there were valleys everywhere. Was it near where he and Dean Barber had landed? It would have to be, or the girl would have died of exposure. Was there something going on in that part of the Ozarks that needed to be exposed? Had evil once again invaded the place he loved?

David shook his head. "Nothing. Did she give any indication where this valley might be? Any directions?"

Cindy Tolbert looked into David Michaels's eyes and said, "Before, I was afraid you were going to do something pastoral. Now I'm afraid you're about to do something very unpastoral."

David returned Cindy's gaze, a quiet hardness behind his eyes.

■　■　■

Janice Morgan sat in her office, staring at the phone as if it were an alien being. She'd called the Benning County sheriff's office, trying to find out anything she could about the nearly dead girl David Michaels and Dean Barber had unknowingly transported into all their lives.

The conversation had been bizarre, bordering on the ludicrous. She had known Sheriff Wade Larsen for several years. They had first met when Janice was a new dispatcher for Clayton County. Last year, when she had been elected sheriff, she had seen him at the Arkansas sheriff's convention in Little Rock. He had been cordial, but just barely. It was apparent to Janice that Larsen was from the old school of law enforcement, the one which mandated a sheriff could only be male. Of all the law enforcement officers in the northern part of Arkansas, Larsen was by far the least accommodating.

She had not really expected much from the call, but Larsen had brushed her off with not even a hint of professional courtesy.

As she sat reflecting on the conversation, she realized he had at least had the courtesy to take her call until she had mentioned the strange girl and the airplane on which she had arrived in Clayton County. With that, Larsen had become almost antagonizing, insinuating that there were cases better left to the real professionals. Janice had let her temper get the best of her, and she had told Larsen just exactly what she thought a professional law enforcement officer was and that her description did not include him.

Now, as she thought about it, she smiled to herself. She had said some things that would have been better left unsaid as far as inter-agency cooperation was concerned, but she had to admit that what she had said made her feel a whole lot better.

And Larsen's attitude had sparked an interest in the strange girl's appearance. It had almost sounded as if the Benning County sheriff knew what was going on. If that was the case, she was going to find out.

Janice picked up the phone and dialed a number in the 212 area code. Earlier she had made the report about the two men carrying the AR-18s Armalites. This time she was going to add her own spin on the events that were unfolding in northern Arkansas, and she was also going to ask some very pointed questions. The chance of getting direct answers to those questions was remote, but she would press the issue, if it came to that. From her perspective, lives might depend on the answers she received.

CHAPTER NINETEEN

"What kind of preacher lives in a place like this?" Cole Branscum asked.

Billy Bob and Cole had been surprised when they had first come upon David Michaels's home. After checking into one of the motels south of Clayton and taking a short nap, they had stopped at a combination self-service gas station and convenience store. While Cole filled the tank on the truck, Billy Bob went in and bought his usual assortment of junk food to take back to the motel room. He had asked the girl behind the counter about the pastor of the First Community Church. Didn't he live south somewhere? The girl had been cooperative and knowledgeable, telling Billy Bob how to get to David Michaels's house. As it turned out, just about everyone knew where the preacher lived. It was sort of an ongoing, good-natured joke, the way the Reverend David Michaels was fixing up the old house by himself.

Billy Bob had paid for the food and the gas, and he and Cole had followed the simple directions, turning off the road which led west for a couple of miles. The road was hazardous, slick with snow and ice, and Billy Bob had had to be particularly careful.

The house had not been difficult to find; it sat back from the secondary road a good quarter of a mile, but could easily be seen from the turnoff that led to the house.

Billy Bob had turned into the drive. Cole had been horrified.

"What if someone's home?" he whined.

"Then we do him right here and now, and be done with it," Billy Bob had answered. "He ain't nothin' but a preacher, and I hate preachers, anyway. Ain't never found one worth his salt."

But there had been no one home. The house itself was obviously in a state of renovation, just as they had heard. Heavily chinked logs were exposed on the outside. A stack of siding had been piled to one side and covered with clear plastic. A small garage sat to one side of the house, with no connection to the house itself. The entire area was surrounded by tall pine trees, with an opening that looked down on the approaching county road. Should they have to return here to kill the problematic preacher, they would have to be careful on the approach. A man inside the house could easily see anyone approaching from the drive.

Billy Bob got out of the truck; Cole followed. The two walked up to the front porch. The porch was the old-fashioned type that went across the entire front of the house. *It would be a nice place to spend a fall afternoon guzzling beer and shooting the empty bottles,* Billy Bob thought. Maybe, after he killed the preacher, the place would be put up for sale, and he just might buy it. That would certainly be the ultimate joke, Billy Bob thought.

"What's under the plastic over there?" Cole asked, moving toward yet another covering. This one was next to the garage and totally obscured by a darker plastic covering. Unlike the plastic which covered the siding, this cover had obviously been placed over its object with care.

Billy Bob plowed through the deep snow to where Cole was. Cole had raised the corner of the plastic and was peering beneath it.

"It's an old car," Cole said. "Don't this guy own anything new?"

Billy Bob yanked the plastic from the car. "Studebaker Lark," he told Cole. "Pretty good shape too."

Cole said, "Never heard of it."

"You're too young. This one looks like about a sixty model. Company didn't last too long after that. This Michaels fellow must have a thing about old stuff. Renovating this junk of a house and probably doing the same thing with the Lark."

"Let's check out the house," Cole suggested.

"Good idea."

The two climbed the wooden steps to the porch. There was a slight hollow sound as their boots echoed off the log walls and the space beneath the porch.

"Preacher might have left a key close by," Cole said.

"Might not have even locked the door," Billy Bob countered. "In places like this, there's still some trust."

Cole laughed. "Yeah. Trust. What a joke."

Billy Bob tried the doorknob, and the door opened. The elusive commodity of trust seemed to still be intact in Clayton, Arkansas.

The interior of the house was dark. The windows were small in a style from an earlier period, when heat needed to be conserved at all cost. The cloudy weather conditions coupled with the small windows gave the interior a rather dreary feeling.

"You go that way," Billy Bob told Cole. Each man explored the house on his own.

A central fireplace separated the main floor. On one side was the living room, on the other a dining area and kitchen. The living area was more-or-less serviceable; but the dining area and kitchen appeared as if an Arkansas tornado had struck. Boxes and paraphernalia lay everywhere. There was no sink or faucets in the kitchen. A small refrigerator sat in the middle of the floor, humming quietly.

Wrapped around the stone fireplace was a staircase leading to an upper loft area. Billy Bob climbed the stairs and peered into the loft.

"This is the bedroom, up here," he yelled back to Cole.

Cole followed Billy Bob and the two examined the sleeping quarters.

In sharp contrast to the downstairs, particularly the kitchen area, the loft bedroom was immaculate. It was larger than it first appeared, and Cole and Billy Bob each explored separate corners. Cole took the closets and before long called to Billy Bob.

"Take a look at this," Cole said, holding up a clothes hanger.

Billy Bob walked over and took the hanger from Cole. "I'll be a son of a gun. The preacher was a soldier."

"Marine," Cole corrected.

"Well, to be honest about it, not even a marine. The uniform is a marine uniform, but the insignias are navy. The preacher was a squid."

"Does that make a difference?" Cole asked.

"Not to me. A preacher's still a preacher, and this one ain't gonna cause us any problems." Billy Bob hung the uniform back in the closet without noticing the trident insignia above the left breast pocket. The insignia of a U.S. Navy SEAL.

"Yeah, well, let's get out of here. We know where he lives, and we can take care of him whenever we want," Cole said.

"Yeah. Provided we find him. Everyone seems to know where he should be, but we still haven't found him yet."

"Maybe he's at the church."

Billy Bob laughed aloud. "That's the first smart thing you've come up with today, Cole. Let's go find that church."

The two left the house and climbed back into the truck. Billy Bob gunned his way back down the drive, tires spinning and slipping on the frozen, snow-covered earth, heading for the First Community Church.

■   ■   ■

There had been a call on the answering machine when Kenneth and Susan Blair had entered their Germantown home. It had been from Dr. Henry Phelps Jr. with a message to please call the Phelps clinic and to speak to no one but Dr. Phelps himself.

As they stood listening to the tape, Kenneth felt his wife snuggle into his arms and embrace him. A small, almost undetectable shudder went through her body, and Kenneth pulled her closer, hoping to allay any fears the message might have caused.

"I'll call him," Kenneth said.

"What if it's about the baby?" Susan asked fearfully.

"Let's wait and see," Kenneth suggested, as he picked up the phone.

The earlier visit with Dr. Henry Phelps had given each of them new life. Adoption had been one of the possibilities and now seemed to be the only one. There was a chance of a child matching all the pertinent criteria becoming available within the next several months. Kenneth had not asked how it was possible. He had not wanted to know. He only knew he and Susan might have the child they had wanted, and that, at this point, had been enough. They had left the Phelps clinic in a state of euphoria. Now, for some reason, Kenneth Blair felt threatened.

He picked up the phone and dialed the clinic. His pulse began to race.

■   ■   ■

The old man slumped back in his chair. He had been completely updated on the goings-on in Arkansas. Not only had he received news from the Benning County sheriff's department and Jason Swann, but from Dr. Henry Phelps Jr., as well.

He turned to the other man in the room. Despite having turned over the reins of control to a younger group, old habits died hard, and the men of *Die Gruppe* still looked to him for guidance. He'd known it would be that way, even after the ceremony transferring power from the older men to the younger, and he relished the unspoken respect associated with the informal liaison.

"Your son just called," the old man said to the other man.

Dr. Henry Phelps Sr. nodded his understanding. The Phelps Clinic had been started by the senior physician and turned over to Henry Phelps Jr. when the time was right.

The clinic on Germantown Parkway was one of the primary institutions for the completion of the Lazarus Project. The overall coordination of the project was handled through the Mid-South Obstetrical Management Services offices in downtown Memphis. Ninety-nine percent of what MOMS handled was legitimate. The one percent in question dealt directly with the project.

That one percent was the principal reason a Cray-2 supercomputer rested in the basement offices of MOMS Computer Services Division. The Cray was required to amass the information needed to ensure quality within the project. DNA sequencing required massive amounts of computer memory and power, which could be had only through the use of the outrageously expensive machine.

It was that one percent which Dr. Henry Phelps Sr. and the old man, known only as Lazarus, were about to discuss.

CHAPTER
TWENTY

The weather had only marginally improved when Dean Barber arrived at the Clayton Municipal Airport the next morning. Brian Connelly was already in his hangar, waiting for the pilot.

"You're really going?" Connelly asked his friend.

Barber joined Connelly near the blue Cessna where the mechanic had been going over the plane in preparation for the flight. The interior of the hangar was warm compared to the temperature outside. Several large infrared heaters hanging from the metal rafters were operating full blast. Barber always kept the Cessna in the hangar during bad weather, particularly during the winter, to prevent problems.

"I called Flight Service a half hour ago. Ceiling's eight hundred and visibility is three miles. No turbulence to speak of. And it's only a couple of hours to Springfield. I'm not about to lose this charter. Couple of guys want to come back to the White River for some trout fishing. If they're game enough to fish in this weather, I'm game enough to fly them in. Besides, it looks worse than it is."

Connelly said, "The plane's in good shape, but you'll find that out when you do your preflight. Good thing it's in the hangar. With the temperature the way it is today, it probably wouldn't have even turned over if it had spent the night outside."

"Thanks, Brian," Barber said, as he began the preflight ritual. As he walked around the aircraft, he asked Connelly, "Heard anything about the girl?"

"Nope. I heard David went down to the hospital yesterday. I haven't heard if he came back or not. Probably spent the night down there. The return trip would have been a nightmare over those roads. Maybe we'll find out something when he gets back."

"Maybe," Barber said, inspecting the small pins connecting the control rod to the elevator assembly. "Sounds like David, though. If there's anything he can do to help, he'll do it." Barber made his way toward the right wing, drawing some fuel from the tiny inspection valve beneath the wing with a clear plastic vial and examining the fuel for traces of water. There were none. He thought about David Michaels and his evident concern for other people. *If there's anything he can do to help, he'll do it.* It was true, Dean realized, far beyond what he had ever seen from any other person. He had commented once to David, who had simply smiled and said, "That's a pale reflection of God's concern for every person." Dean had bristled at the remark at the time—in fact, that had been the beginning of their agreement to leave religion out of their conversations—but now Dean wanted to know more. Dean recognized a peace, a certain stability, in David Michaels that he himself had never known; suddenly he longed for that peace.

Dean turned his attention back to his aircraft.

"I heard some stuff about David," Brian said cautiously, not really sure how to bring up the subject. "I've never asked him, but you might know."

"Know what?" Dean asked, turning from the plane.

"Last year I heard he's the one who took out those guys in Little Rock. The ones with Collins Construction. You know, the Nuclear Three and Four thing and his brother? Heard he shot them in the middle of the street in downtown Little Rock, like at the OK Corral."

Dean finished his preflight check and turned to face his friend. "Wrong. Those guys ran up against Tom Frazier."

"The sheriff?"

"Ex-sheriff. Turned out he was a special agent working for the White House. Long story. I'll tell you when I get back. Now help me roll this thing outside."

The two men rolled the Cessna out of the hangar, and Dean Barber climbed into the left seat. "Remind me to enlighten you when I get back," he said, then closed the door.

Brian Connelly stood in the hangar doorway while Dean quickly went through the prestart list, cranked the engine, and taxied out to the runway. Then he closed the large sliding doors and went into his office, musing about David Michaels and Tom Frazier.

Brian checked his watch: three minutes until nine. Barber would be in the air by nine and opening his flight plan with Little Rock Flight Service right on schedule. *He's nothing,* thought Connelly, *if not punctual.*

■   ■   ■

Dean Barber did a run-up, checked the magnetos for the last time, and reset his instruments. The engine indicators had taken a little longer than normal to climb into the green because of the cold weather, but they were all within operating parameters now.

After a quick call over the Clayton unicom frequency, Dean Barber shoved the throttle to the firewall. The Cessna accelerated rapidly. With only one person in the craft, even carrying a full load of fuel, the acceleration pinned Dean against the seat.

He always enjoyed flying in cold weather, despite the occasional problems that plagued the plane's heating system. In the heavier cold air, the plane literally jumped from the runway when rotated.

Today was no different. At the appropriate speed, Dean gently pulled back on the yoke, and the plane leapt from the ground. The vertical speed indicator immediately registered more than an eight-hundred-feet-per-minute climb.

Barber had taken off from runway three-five, which put him almost immediately on the course he would follow all the way into Missouri.

Barber thumbed the microphone button under his left hand and radioed Brian Connelly on the airport's unicom frequency just to say good-bye. Then he punched the first button of his number one radio, switching to the Little Rock Flight Service Frequency to open his IFR flight plan with the FAA.

Before he could transmit, he felt a slight thump, which was magnified in the cold still air. Another thump followed the first in quick succession.

Barber's eyes flew to his instruments. They were all still in the green.

Another thump.

What's going on? Barber wondered, slightly flustered. Finding the girl in the belly compartment yesterday had been a terrifying ordeal in itself. Now, it seemed, history was about to repeat itself. He was within a few hundred feet of punching into the heavy cloud layer overhanging the airport. If there was a problem, it would be better to stay beneath the cloud base where at least he could see clearly.

Barber reached for the trim tab wheel, rotated it to relieve the pressure on the yoke, and adjusted the Cessna to level flight, just beneath the clouds.

Another thump vibrated through the airframe, and Barber felt his earlier concern rise to a full panic. It was the same feeling he'd had when his F-4 Phantom had taken triple-A fire over North Vietnam—an almost debilitating urge to throw up, coupled with stomach cramps and the impulse to jump from the plane. His thoughts went almost immediately to the short conversation he'd had with David Michaels and his own earlier thoughts back in the hangar. If God really existed—and at a time like this, he was inclined to believe He did—then maybe a miracle was in order. Dean prayed a short prayer, almost an involuntary reflex prayer, but a prayer nonetheless. For some reason, it eased his anxiety.

He scanned the instruments once again, then checked the parts of the aircraft he could see from the cockpit.

In the gray, half-light of the day, he could see nothing. Again his thoughts ran to yesterday morning's landing. He had told David that he was open to talking about God. Now, as yet another thump vibrated through the airframe, he found himself wishing that conversation had taken place.

Fly the plane. His military training brought his attention back to the present moment. *Fly the plane.* That was always the overriding directive in these situations.

Another thump, this one seemingly closer than the rest, but coming from a different part of the airplane than the others. What was going on?

He scanned the instruments again. There was the natural tendency to want to get the airplane on the ground, but without a clear indication of a problem, Dean was reluctant to turn back to Clayton.

Then suddenly, as his eyes registered the reading of his tachometer and manifold pressure gauge, he realized there was a big problem. As if to confirm his conclusion, the engine coughed, shaking the entire aircraft like a bear with a freshly caught trout.

For a second the engine smoothed out, then coughed several times in quick succession. Barber watched with horror as the propeller stopped spinning. It was like the ending of a particularly hideous nightmare, only this one was real.

He checked his altimeter; it read thirteen hundred feet. That put him at a real altitude above ground of only eight hundred feet. Not enough to complete a turn and put the Cessna back on the runway at

Clayton. He berated himself for not immediately beginning the turn, which would have at least given him a chance to reach the threshold.

There was not much time left. The Cessna was falling from the sky at an alarming rate. Barber reached for the trim control and trimmed the airplane for its lowest rate of descent without power. Distance was unimportant; there was nowhere to land the plane safely. Nothing but treetops appeared below the falling plane's wings.

Dean Barber thumbed the microphone button and spoke into the microphone attached to his headset. He was amazed at how calm he sounded. "Little Rock Flight Service, Cessna two two six niner niner going down north of Clayton Municipal Airport. Repeat, Cessna six niner niner declaring an emergency, going down north of Clayton Municipal Airport."

The words were barely out of his mouth when the blue Cessna clipped the top of the first tree. The force threw the airplane into a sideways skid, forcing the plane to drop even more quickly than before.

The last thing Dean Barber recognized before the aircraft slammed to a halt against the trunk of a massive pine tree was the tachometer pegged to zero. His last thought was of his conversation with David Michaels, and he wondered whether God would take his willingness to discuss Him into consideration when he reached the gates of heaven.

■ ■ ■

Billy Bob Campbell heard the splintering sound of the Cessna as it plowed into the pine forest just north of where he stood holding his AR-18 rifle. He waited expectantly for the explosion which was sure to follow, but it never came.

What happened? he wondered. *It should have exploded on impact and should be burning at this very moment.* He had depended on a fire to erase the signs of the .223 caliber bullets he had pumped into the fuselage.

At first, he was not sure he had done any damage at all or if he was even hitting the aircraft. He had loosed several shots at the broad wings of the Cessna, thinking it would explode instantly. When that did not happen, Billy Bob had aimed for the engine compartment and fired several rounds at the quickly disappearing airplane. For a fleeting moment, he thought he had missed the blue craft entirely. It just seemed to fly on and on, and then he had heard the first sputter and the engine quit.

It had all taken place in a matter of seconds, and the plane had quickly flown out of sight. The crashing sound had carried on the cold air all the way to where Billy Bob was positioned. But the explosion never came.

His first impulse had been to race for the plane, to be certain Dean Barber was dead. But Billy Bob knew it would not be long before others would arrive, and he could not afford to be connected to the crash. Even if the plane did not burn and the bullet holes were discovered, it would be a colder day than this before the ballistics could be traced back to him.

Billy Bob checked the small, fire-retardant bag attached to the ejection chamber of the rifle. Satisfied that it had collected all the brass casings, he hurried through the forest to where he had parked Jason Swann's truck. He would head back to the end of runway one-seven and pick up Cole.

The plan had come to him after he had talked to the mechanic yesterday. Most pilots, he'd discovered, used runway three-five when they could, so he'd positioned himself just off the end of the strip, hidden in the trees, and waited.

Barber had been right on time. The blue Cessna had passed overhead at one minute after nine, and Billy Bob had unloaded an entire clip from his Armalite into the plane. It had worked. Cole had been at the end of the other runway, just in case, but he had not been needed.

Now all he had to do was find the pesky preacher, do him in, and head back to the valley and a well-deserved bonus.

As Billy Bob climbed into the truck, he slid the rifle into a holder behind the truck's seat. In the process, the small bag containing the brass shell casings scraped against the doorjamb of the pickup. A single brass shell fell unnoticed and lay bright against the frozen surface of the snow.

CHAPTER TWENTY-ONE

When he thought about it later, David Michaels would recognize his second visit to the Arkansas Children's Hospital as a major turning point in the life of Gaby Ibarra and his own spiritual sojourn.

The previous day's visit had proved fruitless. David and Cindy had arrived at Children's, met Stacii Barrett from Human Services, and waited for information about the condition of the small Hispanic stowaway. The only word from the doctors was that the girl was stable, but she might lose the baby.

David and Cindy had sat in the waiting room for a few hours while Stacii tried to speak to the girl through an interpreter. But, after uttering a few phrases, the girl had refused to say any more.

"It's like she's terrified of something or someone," Stacii told David and Cindy.

"Or some place," David added.

Both Cindy and Stacii looked at him with surprise.

"The valley," David said. "You told us she said something about a valley. Maybe that's what scares her. Maybe whatever goes on there, wherever it is, is what terrifies her."

Stacii Barrett nodded. "You may be right. It was the very first thing she said."

When it had become clear that they would not be able to see the girl that day and the snow had begun to fall outside once again, David said, "I hope we can find a couple of motel rooms at this hour."

Stacii quickly replied, "Well, you'll only need one, because Cindy's staying with me. We've got some catching up to do. I'd offer you a place as well, but my apartment isn't big enough."

"Besides," Cindy had said, turning to David with her green eyes sparkling, "I know exactly what she wants to know, and you would only be a hindrance to the conversation."

David had been puzzled as the two women stood there smiling at him, but he had gone along with the plan. Two hours later, he had found a motel room west of the hospital off Interstate 30. The National Weather Service had issued another severe winter storm warning, and weary travelers were flocking to every available motel as the snow began to pile up on the roadways again.

David was exhausted from the drive from Clayton. He turned on the TV to catch the latest weather report, but he was fast asleep before the news came on.

The next morning, later than he'd planned, he awoke to the sounds of children's cartoons on the television. The storm had continued all night, and the roads were now snarled as the underequipped Arkansas Highway Department struggled to remove the snow. The trip from the motel to the hospital was going to take longer than David had planned. He had told Cindy and Stacii he would meet them around nine o'clock, but when he checked his watch as he waited for an orange dump truck to spread salt on the roadway, it was already 9:03.

He was late, but he knew the women would understand, if they were even at the hospital themselves.

David briefly contemplated flicking on the radio but decided against it. He was soon lost in thought about a terrified young woman and a mysterious valley in the Ozarks.

The snow equipment was moving now, clearing a path as it went, and David followed behind a few cars making their way east. He checked the time once again, calculating it would take him another hour to reach the hospital at the rate he was going.

His thoughts shifted to Cindy Tolbert and Stacii Barrett. He remembered the gleam in their eyes when they had parted last night, but he had been so preoccupied that he hadn't realized until this very moment that the reason for that gleam was him. The two women had spent the evening talking about *him.* A narrow grin spread over David's face as he maneuvered the car along the slick streets. For some inexplicable reason, he enjoyed the thought of two attractive women discussing him, but it caused him to blush uncontrollably.

Traffic, what there was of it, was moving slowly but steadily. David could see Children's Hospital in the distance as he crept along. He hoped that Cindy and Stacii would already be there.

David turned into the same parking lot he'd used the day before. There were only a handful of cars in the lot, and David realized he did not know what kind of car Stacii Barrett owned. He would have to wait until he was inside to see if they had made it.

Sure enough, the two women were waiting inside the main entrance. David felt his heart leap at the sight of Cindy, and it was at once the most wonderful and frightening feeling he had ever had.

As David walked through the automatic doors into the hospital, he noticed a strange expression on Cindy's face. Stacii looked grim and avoided eye contact with him. His emotions immediately did a nose-dive. Had the girl died?

Cindy ran into David's arms as he got closer.

"I'm sorry, David," she sobbed.

David was perplexed. He pushed Cindy away, holding onto her shoulders at arm's length.

Cindy looked at David and said, "You don't know, do you?"

"Know what?" David asked.

Stacii Barrett walked over and put her hand on Cindy's shoulder. "About what happened in Clayton a few hours ago."

"What are you two talking about?"

"It was just on the news," Stacii said, as Cindy once again clung to David.

David wrapped his arms around Cindy and stared at Stacii over Cindy's head.

"What happened?"

Stacii continued, "A small plane crashed this morning just after takeoff."

David felt as if he had been punched in the stomach. A cold dread filled him. "A small plane?"

"It was Dean's," Cindy said, increasing her grip on David. "It was on the radio just before we arrived."

David stood stunned for a moment, not willing to believe what he was hearing.

After a short moment, he said, "Dean?"

"He was alive at last report," Stacii said. "He was taken to Clayton Memorial. The doctors there wanted to airlift him to Little Rock Doctor's Hospital, but nothing is flying today. At least not in this direction. There was talk of an airlift to Springfield. The weather is a little better up there, but not much. That's all we know right now."

"How . . . why . . . ?" David could not get the words out.

"The NTSB and the FAA are up there right now. Apparently there's an NTSB member who lives in Clayton."

David nodded. "Marshall Schaal. Good man. He's visiting his parents. They live just outside of Clayton."

"That's the name," Stacii acknowledged. "Anyway, he's on the scene, and he put in a call for an FAA investigator too. And *that* really is all we know at this point."

David thought for a moment. Marshall Schaal *was* a good man. Rumor had it he was in line to become chairman of the NTSB. He was well respected, and his experience was unequaled.

But why, David wondered, *did he request an FAA investigator?* The NTSB and the FAA were not the best of friends when it came to jurisdiction of the nation's airspace. The NTSB clearly retained jurisdiction for aircraft accident investigations. Marshall Schaal was one of the NTSB's senior investigators, and he had the power to do whatever necessary at a crash site. Normally, a small plane crash would not turn any heads at NTSB or FAA headquarters in Washington D.C. An investigator would be assigned certainly, but nothing more. Schaal's presence in Clayton was perhaps providential, but only something unusual would precipitate a request for an FAA investigator.

"How's the girl?" David asked, when his thoughts finally returned to the point at hand.

"Sleeping," Stacii answered. "And her name is Gaby."

"She's so sweet," Cindy added, coming out of David's arms, wiping her emerald eyes with a tissue.

"You've seen her?" David asked Cindy.

Cindy nodded. "Stacii got me in. They're pretty protective here, but Stacii has some pull."

"We won't know anything for a while. The doctor wants her to rest for a couple of days before we start asking her questions again," Stacii said. "Her condition should be stabilized by then, and the baby will be out of danger too."

"It doesn't make any sense at all. What was a young girl, pregnant to boot, doing in those mountains in this weather?"

Cindy stared into David's eyes. "When are you going?" she asked.

"Where?" David responded.

"To the valley, wherever it is."

"What makes you think . . ."

"Don't start with me, David Michaels. I know exactly what you've got on your mind. You're going back to wherever you made that landing. You can't stand not knowing and you want to answer all those questions you just asked. So when are you going?"

David shrugged. He had learned it was impossible to hide his intentions from Cindy. Call it woman's intuition, insight, or anything else, she always seemed to know his mind—at times, even before he did.

"I've got to get back to Clayton and check on Dean. Then I'll think about what I'm going to do from there."

"The way you described the place you landed, do you think you can find it again?" Stacii asked.

"You're going to use your magic wand. Right?" added Cindy.

"Magic wand?"

"You told Janice about your AirMap, remember?"

David smiled sheepishly. He would have to be more careful if he wanted to protect information from Cindy. He'd forgotten she'd over-heard his explanation of the AirMap to the Clayton County sheriff. In any case, he was much too preoccupied now to go into detail.

"I'll find the place," David said. He walked purposefully toward the exit, pausing as he reached the automatic sliding glass doors. "Are you coming with me?" he asked Cindy.

CHAPTER TWENTY-TWO

The sparkling white blanket of fresh snow glistened in sharp contrast to the evil that had long ago overtaken the tiny, hidden valley.

Sheriff Wade Larsen turned onto a narrow road, which led off the pavement and into the heart of the valley. Had he not known the route existed, he would have easily passed it by without a sideways glance. But he had traveled the path many times before. Each time, he felt as if he were traveling the road to perdition, with no hope of return. The valley seemed to have a temperament all its own, as if it were not just an elongated depression in the earth, but a spiritual being of some sort. A place with its own personality, one of death and corruption.

Larsen was not a religious man. Far from it. It had been his sins that had compromised his position as sheriff and now ensured his continued loyalty to men he knew nothing about but who paid him well for his protection and, far more importantly, his silence.

Larsen had been Benning County sheriff for more than thirty years, and now, at age sixty-one, he was beginning to feel the cumulative effects and stress inherent in the job. At slightly under six feet tall but considerably more than 230 pounds, Larsen's face was continually florid from the effort needed to move about. His nightly conversation with a bottle of bourbon, which he kept by the old recliner in his TV room, only made matters worse.

But eating and drinking always took the edge off the stress that accompanied protecting the secret of the valley.

Usually everything went like clockwork. There had been other escapes, but they had been taken care of by Billy Bob Campbell and Cole Branscum, the two "good ol' boys" hired for security purposes. No one outside the valley had ever found out about those escapes, and as long as no one found out, Wade Larsen could pretend he did not know about them either.

Even the semipunctual planes that landed in a pasture just to the west of the valley did not raise many eyebrows. Had there been any curiosity about the landings, something would have had to be done, but there had not been so much as a single phone call to the sheriff's office concerning them. All in all, things went smoothly where the valley was concerned. Until today. The phone call from Clayton County Sheriff Janice Morgan was beginning to wear on him. Wade Larsen did not like Janice Morgan. As a woman, he had to admit, she was a looker, but in Larsen's mind, women had no place in law enforcement, particularly in rural Arkansas.

Under different circumstances, he might have pursued a relationship with her, but even as he considered such a liaison, he knew it would never work. Janice Morgan was what Larsen's father—the previous Benning County sheriff—termed a "highbrow." She was educated, intelligent, and sensitive. All traits Larsen considered detrimental to the performance of a rural county sheriff.

Larsen's car skidded on the newly fallen snow as he made his way deeper into the valley. The tire chains he'd installed on the rear tires bit into the slick surface. The car recovered quickly; the snow had not yet turned to ice on the roadway.

The lane he was traveling began to narrow, and Larsen had to concentrate on his driving to keep the police cruiser in the center of the road.

Even with the whiteness surrounding him, Larsen had the feeling he was headed into the heart of overwhelming perversity, almost as if he were being swallowed by a huge dragon. He stopped the car for a second and looked around. The whiteness, even beneath the gray sky, was almost blinding. But even amidst the undefiled landscape, the feeling of darkness seemed irrepressibly omnipotent.

Larsen's thoughts reverted to the conversation he'd had with Janice Morgan. She had come right out and asked what he knew about a Hispanic girl who had been found in the woods in Benning County. Had anyone filed a missing person report? Was there a Hispanic family living in the western portion of the county to whom the girl might belong? Could he make inquiries and get back to her within forty-eight hours?

The questions had irritated Larsen, not so much because of their content but because of their origin. He hated being put on the spot by a woman.

Larsen thought about his father as he threaded his car through a particularly constricted area. *What would Dad have said or done about the people in the valley?* he mused to himself. But he knew that even if the old sheriff were still alive, he could never ask him.

Tom Larsen had been sheriff in Benning County long before Wade was born and probably would have held the office longer had he not died of a sudden heart attack. Wade had been his chief deputy at the time, and the office had fallen to him much the way inheritances do within families.

Tom Larsen had been an honest man, a man of morals, values, and honor, despite his provincial view of women in law enforcement.

Unfortunately, morals, values, and honor were three characteristics that Wade Larsen no longer possessed.

The sheriff slowed his cruiser as he neared a rock face off to his left. He never went beyond this point. Always there was someone to meet him near the promontory. Even in the modern-day world of electronics and instantaneous communications, some conversations could not be trusted to spurious electronic signals.

A small man stepped away from a nearby tree, and Larsen stopped the car. He got out as the man approached the squad car.

"What is it, Larsen?" Jason Swann demanded.

Larsen had long ago discovered he did not like Swann. But Swann was the conduit through whom cash payments flowed, and Larsen would never do anything to jeopardize the money he had become accustomed to.

The sheriff waited until Swann drew nearer, then said, "I got a call from the Clayton County sheriff a few hours ago. She was asking about some Hispanic girl that was picked up near here. What do you know about it?"

Swann laughed, a vile sound that reverberated off the rock face. "That's none of your business, Larsen," Swann said. "It's all been taken care of."

Larsen bristled at Swann's response. Normally he would have ignored the disparaging tone in Swann's voice but not today.

"You fool," Larsen answered between clenched teeth, "do you know what's going on right now? Do you have a clue?" Larsen spat out the words as if particularly distasteful. He could feel his blood pressure rising and knew his face was turning that shade of red that made him look like an overripe tomato. That fact only served to aggravate the situation.

Jason Swann was taken aback by the outburst, but he recovered quickly. He was, after all, the representative of *Die Gruppe* and, as such, the overall controlling power where the valley was concerned.

"You listen, you fool . . . ," Swann began. He never got even the beginning of the second sentence out before Larsen's huge fist caught him beneath the chin, sending him sprawling into the snow.

"No, you listen, idiot," Larsen snarled, now standing over the supine Swann. "You are about to blow this whole thing wide open. This is not the first time something like this has happened. We both know what's going on in this valley, and it's pretty clear you don't have a handle on things. Your boss needs to know he has a fool in charge over here in Arkansas. That fool is you, Swann," Larsen said, pointing with a stubby finger.

Jason Swann scrambled to his feet and moved several feet back from Wade Larsen. He had misjudged the Benning County sheriff. He would not make the same mistake twice.

"Take it easy, Wade," Swann said, holding his hands up in front of him in a conciliatory gesture. "We can work this out. I've already taken care of most of it. The girl is dead, and one of the pilots who flew her out of here just crashed his plane over in Clayton. The only other person who has any idea about what happened is some preacher, and I'll deal with him too."

Larsen seemed to relax for a moment, leaned up against the front fender of his car and crossed his arms over his barrel chest.

"That's what you think, is it?" Larsen asked.

Jason Swann felt an instant of uneasiness.

Larsen continued, "Morgan says the girl is in Children's Hospital down in Little Rock, and she's alive. She's being treated for hypothermia. She's liable to live, Swann. As for the plane crash, I heard about that too. I don't know what or how you did that, but it had better be undetectable. There's a representative of the National Transportation Safety Board already in town. Seems his parents live in Clayton, and he was at the scene in under an hour. Lousy timing, huh?"

Once again, Jason Swann felt fear beginning to build in him. The girl was alive! The plane crash engineered to kill one of the pilots had taken place, but had the man died? Of all places in the United States for an NTSB investigator to be visiting, it had to be tiny Clayton, Arkansas. What else could go wrong?

"What about this preacher?" Larsen asked Swann.

Swann shrugged as his hand went to his chin to rub the spot where Larsen's fist had connected. "That's all I know. There were two men in the plane. The one that just crashed and some preacher. Fellow named Michaels. David Michaels. I've got men looking for him right now."

Wade Larsen snorted. "Men? *Men?* You mean Campbell and Branscum? They are as likely to mess this whole thing up as not." Larsen stopped for a moment, thinking. "Are they the ones who caused the plane crash?" Larsen asked suspiciously.

"What if they are?" Swann asked defensively.

Larsen allowed a wide grin to spread across his face. "Then you got more problems than you know. Those two couldn't pour water out of a boot with the instructions on the heel. If you think they can engineer a plane crash without leaving a trace, you got another thing coming. But that's your worry, not mine."

Swann again felt fear coming to a boil in his gut. The consequences of such an error in judgment were frightening. The consequences of *Die Gruppe* discovering his error was cause for further concern, and the repercussions if Lazarus himself disapproved were positively nauseating.

Larsen returned to his cruiser. Swann stood in a daze as the Benning County sheriff turned his car around and headed out of the valley.

Larsen breathed a sigh of relief when his tires were once again on asphalt. He was always happy to get away from the valley. It felt as if a dark and pernicious cloud were lifted from him as he drove back toward town.

Jason Swann watched the car as it disappeared from sight, wondering for the first time if he should have chosen a different course. Maybe he could mitigate the inevitable. He could always say that

Campbell and Branscum had gone out on their own in an attempt to rectify the problems they themselves had caused. That was it! That would be his story to *Die Gruppe* and to the man he knew only by the code name Lazarus.

Swann felt better, almost euphoric, as he climbed into his vehicle, which had been concealed in the forest, and started back for the house deep in the valley.

He had some things that needed tending to. Files he had to review, to update, to ensure his own survival. Larsen thought he was a fool, but Swann was nobody's patsy. And the files hidden in his office confirmed his shrewdness. He had compiled enough information over the years not only to implicate the men in Memphis, but—and this was speculation on his part—to reveal the identity of Lazarus. It was this last file that always sent chills down his spine. He was certain he knew who Lazarus was. If he was right, it would be a revelation to shock every moral thinking person on the face of the earth. But this information could also get him killed very quickly, if not used in the correct manner.

■   ■   ■

Lazarus rose from his knees again. It seemed he had been in that position more often than normal, but he needed to communicate his feelings, his thoughts, to a power greater than himself.

When he had finished, he was not certain that the prayer had helped. He was not even sure he had prayed a prayer. Had the words actually escaped his lips, or had they been confined to his thoughts, never to have been heard by the power to which he prayed?

He could remember praying the same way many years ago. Then, he had been certain he prayed to the God of Creation. After all, wasn't he creating life in a manner of speaking? Was it so hard to believe that God could be in what he was doing then as well as now?

Lazarus walked slowly from the room, looking back at the makeshift altar he had long ago fabricated. In the back of his mind, he knew the power that inhabited his prayer room was the same power that reigned over the valley in Arkansas, and other similar valleys shrouded in secret, and that power was not the God of Moses, and not the God of Abraham nor Isaac, but a malicious, dangerous power which had no concern other than the destruction of mankind. But, he told himself, one man's destruction is another man's creation, and in that he knew his project would go forward.

CHAPTER TWENTY-THREE

As soon as he slid behind the wheel of Cindy's car, David's thoughts went to Dean Barber and the airplane crash. He flicked on the radio, and between the music and the weather, the story of the small plane crashing in Clayton was the number one story. There were no new details, but David kept the station tuned in, hoping to learn whatever he could.

"They haven't said he's dead," Cindy said. To David, it seemed as if she were reading his mind.

"They said they can't airlift him out either," David added. "Clayton Memorial is all right for some things, but if there's a real problem, Dean needs to be down here, or at least in Springfield."

"I know," Cindy agreed. "But the weather is worsening from the south. It's almost like it's following us as we go."

David knew the storm was just that: a storm. It was not an outward expression of God's disapproval or wrath. But it didn't make the trip any easier.

He knew it was virtually impossible to get Dean Barber out of Clayton at the moment. Air travel was completely shut down and travel by road was increasingly difficult. David was not even certain he could get himself and Cindy back to Clayton. He knew that once he left Interstate 40 the highway leading north would be in worse condition than the one they now traveled. The Arkansas Highway Department would have its hands full just trying to keep the main thoroughfares open.

After two and a half hours, the exit leading north appeared. The trip from Little Rock, which normally took an hour, had almost tripled. The prospect of the last seventy or so miles to Clayton was not a trip David relished.

"You think we'll make it?" Cindy asked pensively.

"If we're lucky," David answered.

"You know this has nothing to do with luck. Prayer is the key here. Prayer and careful driving."

David smiled. Prayer solved everything for Cindy. This time she had at least included a practical aspect, but he knew better. Not every prayer was answered in quite the manner she asked it, but he had to admit that she had a better concept of answered prayer than he did. Even when no answer came, that seemed to suffice for Cindy. It was one of the things that irritated him about her. Her solution to any problem was prayer and even a no answer was an answer. David envied Cindy's simple faith. He sometimes wished he had the same outlook, but he was too pragmatic. He had seen too much of the real world, too much of the carnage of war, the devastation wrought by man's solutions.

True, David realized, his own faith had grown immeasurably since he left the military, but he knew he still had a lot to learn about the way things were done in a constantly changing civilian world. Though Cindy was a good teacher, David knew he still had the tendency to fall back into his old military patterns, which usually included overt action to the exclusion of covert prayer. He would have to begin uniting the two more often. Right now, he knew it was prayer that he needed most, not for himself, but for Dean Barber.

As David's thoughts returned to his injured friend, a growing uneasiness and a sense of failure clawed at his insides.

What if Dean died today? Had he, David Michaels, the pastor and spiritual leader of First Community Church, done all he could to see to it that Dean Barber had come to know and accept Jesus Christ as Lord and Savior? Had he even provided a faithful witness, allowing Dean to make his own informed decision? And if he had, would Dean Barber have made the decision to end up in heaven if he died today?

The answers were elusive and painful for David.

"What is it?" Cindy asked. She sensed that more than the snowstorm had enveloped David.

"Nothing," David murmured. He tried to erase the images of flying with Dean all those hours. The opportunities had been there, and despite the agreement he had made with his friend, he knew now he should have pressed the issue of salvation. That was what bothered him most. He had had the opportunity to tell Dean about Jesus, and each time he had found a way not to do it. His timidity now haunted him.

As he had feared, the state highway leading north from I-40 toward Clayton was much worse than the interstate. *Three more hours to Clayton is a conservative estimate,* thought David. He glanced over at Cindy. She had leaned her head back against the headrest, and her eyes were closed. David felt an instant of overwhelming love. He would have to remember to tell her how much he loved her.

■　■　■

Kenneth Blair felt his wife's small hand on his shoulder, and he placed the newspaper he was reading on the table next to his chair.

Susan Blair had quietly entered the den, but there was purpose written all over her face. When Kenneth looked into his wife's eyes, he knew she had made a decision.

"I want to look for a new doctor," Susan said.

Kenneth rose from his chair and embraced Susan. "Are you sure?" he asked.

"Positive."

"What about what Dr. Phelps said. About not being able to have a child, I mean?"

"I was so wrapped up in myself, I think I may have overlooked the obvious. Besides, it never hurts to have a second opinion. Right?"

Kenneth Blair tightened his embrace. "No, it never hurts. Do you have someone in mind?"

Susan Blair nodded. "Catherine Thompson told me about another doctor. I thought I'd give her a try."

"Her?"

"Dr. Elaine Miller. She teaches at the University of Tennessee Medical School."

"Sounds good to me," Kenneth said. "When do we go?"

"Tomorrow at ten. And I'm quitting the medication Dr. Phelps prescribed until I've talked with Dr. Miller."

"Better take the medication with you. She will probably want to know what you've been taking."

"You're right."

Kenneth Blair said nothing more. He kissed his wife, then held her for a long moment. He had a funny feeling that tomorrow they were going to learn something new.

■　■　■

Stacii Barrett faced her dilemma head on.

She had been happy, almost ecstatic, to see Cindy Tolbert again. The night before had been a collage of memories and good times. It had been years since the two college mates had seen each other, and they had stayed awake exchanging stories until neither one could hold her eyes open.

Cindy had gone to bed, and Stacii had stayed up a few more minutes to complete a report on the rescued girl at Children's Hospital. What the report did not contain, and what Stacii had not told Cindy or David Michaels, was the name of a person that a hospital orderly had passed to her.

The girl had been in the ER when Stacii arrived, and as the trauma team examined her, an orderly had stepped into the corridor where Stacii waited. When Stacii had asked about the girl, the young man had handed her a small yellow sheet, one of those self-stick notes, which he said he had found in one of the young girl's pockets.

"You may be the right person to take a look at this," the orderly had said.

Stacii took the note and read the cryptic message. Not really a message, but a name. She decided not to include the name in her report. She wanted some time to check it out, to determine how, if at all, this person figured into the unfolding saga of Gaby Ibarra.

As Stacii folded the note to return it to the small notebook she carried, she reread it one more time. It was simple, to-the-point: Wade Larsen, Benning County Sheriff.

Why was the sheriff's name on a piece of note paper stuffed into the pocket of a half-frozen stowaway?

Stacii had no answers, only more questions, but now she had a lead to follow. She made a quick phone call to secure a four-wheel drive vehicle from the Arkansas Department of Human Service's fleet.

The weather was worsening, but she figured that the sport utility vehicle would be able to negotiate the slick, winding roads over to Benning County.

CHAPTER TWENTY-FOUR

The voice was there, deep in the background, cajoling, urging, whispering, *demanding.* It was the voice that had conceived the project, the voice that had given him the strength needed at the outset. It was the voice of atrocity, of fear, of terror—the omnipresent voice that directed everything.

Lazarus settled back in his chair and allowed his mind to drift back more than fifty years to a swampy valley an hour outside of Krakow, Poland. Was that when he had first heard the voice? He couldn't remember. Maybe it had been when his son was born. Maybe even earlier, when he'd first married in 1938, sixty years ago. Whenever it had begun, Lazarus had followed the voice for virtually all of his adult life. And the voice was responsible for his success.

Success? Lazarus smiled wryly at the thought. His definition of success was far different from anyone else's. But that had been the story his entire life. He had always been different, one step ahead of the masses, *enlightened.* That was the word: *enlightened.*

The door to the study opened and a butler entered carrying a small silver tray with a single glass on it. Lazarus checked the wall clock above the mantle; it was time for his afternoon drink and, in typical German fashion, his servant was right on time.

"Perhaps you might throw another log on the fire while you are here," Lazarus shivered slightly.

The young man placed the small tray on the end table just to the right of where Lazarus sat, retrieved a log from near the large, stone fireplace, and carefully placed it on the blazing fire. It was strange, he thought, that his master seemed to be experiencing some sort of chill lately. The fire was roaring, and the single oak log quickly caught, emptying its heat out into the room. Already the temperature was in the high eighties, but it never seemed to be enough.

"Thank you," Lazarus said, lifting the snifter of brandy and swirling the dark liquid around the sides to better distribute its calming aroma. He lit a cigarette.

"Of course, sir," the butler replied, then quietly exited the room.

Flames leapt in the fireplace, sending their scorching heat out into every corner of the library. Lazarus sat watching the fire and sipping his brandy. Neither seemed able to warm him outwardly or inwardly. It was as if a cold, dark cloud had invaded the room.

His thoughts drifted back to the voice. In the beginning he had not been certain he was really hearing a voice. At first the words, the ideas, the concepts had come at odd moments, moments of reflection, moments of deep thought. They were his own thoughts, he had assumed at the time, but they had been so profound, so intellectual, so *penetrating,* that he had attributed them to another power outside himself. Such thoughts could have and would have only come from God.

But he had been wrong, he now knew.

During those first years in South America, the voice had deserted him. It had been with him in Germany, in the early years. But after the war, corresponding to the time of his escape from Europe, the voice had disappeared. The direction, the instructions had failed to come to him in their normal manner. The *enlightenment* had ceased during those years.

And then suddenly the voice had returned. And it had conceived the idea of his simulated death by drowning on the beach at Bertioga, Brazil. The voice had suggested the man to be used as his surrogate in the drowning. And the voice had suggested when the time was right for his immigration to the United States to take personal charge of the project.

And Lazarus had obeyed the voice.

From his chair near the fireplace, Lazarus could see the snow beginning to accumulate into wispy drifts near the house and up against the stone fence surrounding the property. He shivered again, wondering whether the reaction was from the chill in the room or just his advanced age.

Perhaps, Lazarus conceded, the chill he felt was due to the loneliness that always surrounded him these days. He knew that his son, Rolf, was in Switzerland, along with his grandchildren, but it was information of little value. He could not afford to expose himself, despite his belief that those who had sought him so many years ago had long since abandoned the search.

He could still remember the good times they had had skiing in the mountains and the occasional field trips into the countryside. The most memorable excursions had come during his leave times and official furloughs when he could get away from his work and from the voice.

The doorbell rang, and Lazarus waited for the butler to announce the visitor. The door to the library opened slowly.

"Dr. Phelps is here to see you, sir," said the butler.

"Do not let our friend wait. Please, show him in," Lazarus said with a grand wave of his hand.

Dr. Henry Phelps Sr. strode into the room with the ease of

familiarity, although the east Memphis house, and particularly the library, still produced a strange sense of disquiet in him.

Phelps was a large man, much larger than Lazarus, with a full head of white hair. Unlike Lazarus, Phelps was clean-shaven. At one time he had worn a mustache much like his host, but he had shaved it off years earlier and had never regrown it. His blue eyes had a penetrating quality about them that seemed to look through a man rather than at him. In his later years, the doctor had gained weight that had settled around his middle. In all, Dr. Henry Phelps Sr. looked like the consummate grandfather, although he was not and probably never would be. His son had never married. There were always other priorities.

Phelps dropped into a chair across from Lazarus. Instantly he began to sweat in the heat of the library. It was one of the things he did not like about visiting his old friend. Today was worse than normal.

"You are roasting, my friend," Phelps said.

Lazarus allowed a thin smile to crease his lips. He rubbed at the scar on his forehead. The heat made it itch. From the table next to his chair, he retrieved a package of cigarettes and lit one.

"You should have stopped that a long time ago. As a doctor, you know the dangers as well as I do," Phelps continued.

Lazarus inhaled the smoke and let it out slowly, directing it toward the fireplace so the draft could carry the smoke up and out.

"You are correct, my friend," Lazarus agreed. "But it has been too long, and I am too old to deprive myself of what few joys I still have."

"Perhaps you are right. It just seems to be a contradiction."

"Maybe a contradiction in this world, but not in the afterlife."

"So, we are back to that, are we?"

Lazarus nodded. "The voice has returned."

Phelps stared at his longtime friend in disbelief. He had heard of the voice before but had always dismissed it as an eccentricity.

"We have turned over control too quickly," Lazarus continued.

"Control?"

"Die Gruppe."

Phelps rose from his chair. The heat really was unbearable, and he removed his coat. "We are old men, my friend. It was time."

"It was too soon. There are problems. The voice has told me so."

"In the valley, you mean," Phelps added.

"In the valley," Lazarus repeated as affirmation. "With Swann and others. The valley is in danger, which puts our plans in jeopardy too. We cannot risk exposure. Swann has assumed too much responsibility. He has placed the project in jeopardy."

"Could that not work to our advantage?"

Lazarus swallowed the last of the brandy. "It could, but it won't."

"You sound certain."

"I am."

"The voice again?"

"It has instructed me on what to do. The first is to reassume control of *Die Gruppe,* at least for the time being."

"Henry will look on that as an intrusion."

"It has to be done. We, the old ones, are the only ones who have the original fire still burning. We are the ones who know what has happened and why. We are the ones with the drive, the vision."

"A vision controlled by the voice?" Phelps asked with a tinge of disgust.

"Yes, my friend. A vision of what could be, what *should* be."

Phelps rose from his chair. The heat seemed to have abated despite the roaring fire. There was a chill in the air. He retrieved his coat and put it on.

"This is ludicrous. We are talking about the rantings of old men."

"We were once young men, and we thought in the same fashion."

"That is true. But that was many years ago. Things have changed."

Lazarus leapt from his chair, passion ignited in his eyes. "Changed? Nothing has changed. The world is still in need of our wisdom, our knowledge, our foresight. *That* has not changed. There are still those who do not belong. They have always been with us, and unless we can reverse that, they always will be."

Phelps was shocked at the vehemence spewing from his friend's mouth. The room was colder now than he could remember. Two logs burned in two, and fell into a deep bed of ashes, spreading glowing coals over the hearth. With such a fire, the room should still be as hot as it was when he arrived, but it was much colder now. What was going on? he wondered.

"You are right, of course," Phelps told Lazarus. "Let me think on it for a while. I will call you later."

Lazarus watched as his friend left the room. He shivered as the cold invaded his being. Why could he not warm this room?

■   ■   ■

There were always options, choices, thought Jason Swann as he leafed through the contents of the file folder on his desk. The problem had never been finding those options; the problem had always been which of the various alternatives to choose.

As the strange conversation with Sheriff Larsen coursed through his mind, Jason Swann was becoming painfully aware that his options had been reduced to a bare minimum. The girl those two idiots had let escape from the valley was alive and well and in the Arkansas Children's Hospital in Little Rock. One of the men from the plane, along with the plane, had crashed, but there was no definitive information on the pilot. He, too, could still be alive, if Branscum and Campbell had fouled that up as well.

Billy Bob and Cole. They were the source of all his problems. If they had done what they should have, none of this would have happened, and he, Jason Swann, would be sitting pretty, just waiting for more bonus money to roll in. Waiting for the inevitable to occur on the upper floors of the house.

But they had fouled up and, in the process, had implicated him. At least that's what Larsen had led him to believe, and the latest information from Memphis seemed to confirm that fear. If this thing exploded onto the national scene, or even the regional scene, he knew he would be thrown to the wolves without delay. He had always known that. That was the nature of the business he was in. What he also knew was that someone in his position needed a fallback position, one which offered explanations and alternatives. What he had in front of him at this very minute were the alternatives.

Swann stopped flipping the pages of the file and began to read. He had worked on the file for more than three years, when he first realized he would need something to protect himself. The file would not exonerate him from his own deeds, but it would certainly focus attention away from him and onto those who were really responsible for the goings-on in the valley. And now it looked as if he would have to use it.

Swann closed the file and locked it away in his desk drawer. He wanted to make his rounds, to review the facility one last time. Then he would take the file and some other pertinent information and leave the valley forever. Let them discover what went on here. It would make no difference to him. Jason Swann would be long gone, and in the process, he would cast the blame on the man who really was responsible for the valley. The man he knew as Lazarus.

■   ■   ■

Billy Bob Campbell and Cole Branscum could wait no longer. They needed to get rid of the preacher, David Michaels, and get out of Clayton County. Billy Bob had counted on a fire to hide the evidence of why the plane went down, and he was smart enough to know that it would not take a nuclear physicist to figure out what had caused the crash. He and Cole needed to be long gone.

But first they had to kill David Michaels. And to do that, they had to find him.

"Get up, Cole," Billy Bob called to his partner.

"It's cold, man."

"We got work to do. We're goin' out to the preacher's house and stake it out. He's bound to show up sooner or later. Nobody gets too far from home in this kind of weather."

Cole mumbled a few words and turned over in the motel bed, pulling the covers with him.

Billy Bob strode from the bathroom, jerked the covers off Cole, and kicked at him.

Cole was too quick. He avoided the blow and darted into the bathroom out of Billy Bob's reach. He wasn't sure what it was, but Billy Bob Campbell was getting edgy and mean. More so than normal. Must be the weather, Cole thought, as he locked the door and twisted the shower on.

"Five minutes, man," Cole shouted from the bathroom.

Billy Bob Campbell stood fuming outside the locked door. Maybe, when this was all over, and the preacher was dead, he just might have to "do" Cole. After all, the police would need someone to blame for the murders and Billy Bob couldn't see any reason why that person should not be his best friend, Cole Branscum.

■　　■　　■

Dr. Henry Phelps Jr. examined the single filing cabinet that represented the bulk of his involvement with the Lazarus Project. The files contained almost fifty years of research and experimentation. Experimentation which he could not allow to come to light.

Phelps's father had instilled in him the importance of certain values, which from his youth Henry Jr. had never questioned. Now the theories espoused in the files were beginning to bear fruit. With MOMS using the Cray supercomputer for the DNA sequencing, results would be more predictable.

The files represented research dating back more than fifty years, research which had begun in the marshlands of southern Poland on the banks of the Vistula River. It wasn't as controlled or as scientifically relative as he would have liked, but it had been a start. The process had become more and more sophisticated after his father brought the research to the United States in 1944, and Henry Jr. had continued the refinements when the research was passed on to him.

The phone on his desk jangled, and Phelps picked it up. It was his father. He listened for a moment, his brow furrowed. Without saying a word, he replaced the receiver and returned to the filing cabinet. He pulled open the top drawer and extracted a file, placed it on his desk, and sat down to examine it. The file was the single nonmedical file in the cabinet, and Henry Phelps Jr. had hoped he would never have to use it. That hope had just been shattered by his father's phone call.

The file was indexed by a single name on the folder's tab: Lazarus.

CHAPTER TWENTY-FIVE

When David Michaels and Cindy Tolbert finally drove into Clayton, David had a headache to match the weather. And all accounts on the radio indicated the storm was not likely to move in the near future. A low pressure system on the Louisiana Gulf coast was pumping moisture over the top of a high pressure dome that was hovering over Arkansas like an avenging angel. The combination made for the fiercest winter storm to hit the state in recent history.

"Home or the office?" David asked Cindy as they entered the city limits.

"The office. I better check on what's going on there first. Probably not much in this weather, but better safe than sorry. What about you? Where are you going?"

"I thought I would drive on out to the airport and then maybe stop by the hospital, see what I can find out about Dean."

Cindy could feel the emotional strain that David was under. She sensed that in addition to his concern about Dean Barber, David was battling with guilt too. Why the guilt she was not sure, but knowing David as she did, it was possible that he was blaming himself for the crash. It made no sense, but that was David's way. And while it sometimes created a burden for him, it also was one of the things that made him a much better pastor than he would admit. The people of Clayton knew the Reverend David Michaels cared, even about those who were not part of his congregation.

"Let me ask in the office first. Might save you a trip. Surely Janice knows something."

David shook his head. "Forget it. I want to see where the plane went down, anyway. Better for me just to go on out and see what's what."

David pulled into the center of town and parked the car near the courthouse. The snow was deep along the sidewalk, and the two had to hold on to each other to keep from slipping. Once inside, David stopped.

"You go on," Cindy said. "Call me before you head back this direction."

"Will do," David assured her, then turned and was out the door.

Cindy stood for a moment in the cold corridor, muttering a prayer for David. Whatever it was that was bothering him, she prayed it would soon be resolved. The last time she had seen him like this was when his brother had been murdered. Cindy repeated the prayer as she headed for the far end of the corridor and her office.

■   ■   ■

David Michaels carefully pulled the car out of the parking area, smiling to himself as he remembered he was not in his old Studebaker, but in Cindy's Taurus, and that she had not said a word to him about taking her car. He had just assumed she would let him, and that was the way it had turned out. He would have to be more thoughtful in the future. He was beginning to take Cindy for granted, and that would never do. He loved her too much for that. The frank admission of his affection momentarily took him by surprise. It was time he gave more thought to the type of relationship he really wanted. That relationship, he knew, included marriage.

As he drove across the river bridge out toward the airport on the north side of town, David made up his mind that as soon as this latest crisis was over, he would ask Cindy to marry him. With that decision suddenly made, David found it amazingly simple to concentrate on the task at hand: finding out what had happened to Dean Barber.

David turned into the road leading to Brian Connelly's hangar. Despite the weather, there were three cars in the parking area. David parked and headed for the office.

Brian Connelly sat at his desk, his feet, as usual, resting on the oil-stained desktop. Two other men were in the office, drinking coffee. David recognized Marshall Schaal, the NTSB investigator whose parents lived in Clayton. The other man he did not know.

"David," Marshall Schaal said, his hand outstretched. "It's good to see you."

David shook Schaal's hand as the other man rose from where he'd been sitting.

"David Michaels, meet Phillip Cowens with the FAA."

"Mr. Cowens," David said, shaking the man's hand.

"Phil, please. I've heard of you, Reverend Michaels."

David smiled. "Forgive me. I'm still getting used to the 'Reverend' bit."

"That's right," Cowens said. "You were military all the way, weren't you?"

"Twenty years. I was more accustomed to 'Commander' than 'Reverend'. How 'bout just plain David."

"David it is, then," Cowens agreed.

David liked the FAA inspector instantly. He turned back to Marshall Schaal. "What about Dean?"

"In the hospital. Broken leg, collarbone, and ribs. The yoke caught him when the plane went in. Luckily he had his harness cinched up pretty tight. Comes from being a fighter pilot, I suppose. Whatever it was, it saved his life. Doctors thought he had some internal injuries and wanted to airlift him out to Little Rock or Springfield, but they changed their minds. The x-rays and tests came out pretty good, but he's still pretty rocky. The doctors are keeping him sedated to reduce movement and allow those ribs to heal. He's going to be sore for a few months."

David felt an overwhelming sense of relief at the report. He would have a chance to talk to Dean Barber, and this time, nothing would dissuade him.

"The plane?"

Marshall Schaal glanced over at Philip Cowens, then said, "That's another story altogether. Phil and I were just going over the findings, trying to figure out how to break the news. I haven't even called the chairman yet," Schaal said.

"By that, I gather the crash was not weather related?" David asked.

Again Schaal and Cowens exchanged glances. This time neither said a thing for a long moment. Then it was Phil Cowens who spoke.

"Maybe you should come with us. We've got the crash site cordoned off. We're using county sheriff personnel for that. You knew Dean Barber as well, if not better, than anyone around here. There's something out there we want you to see. We could use your input into this, if you're game, that is."

"When do we leave?" David asked.

"Borrow a coat from Brian, and we'll get started," Schaal said.

The trip to the crash site should have taken no more than ten minutes, but with the snow, it took David, Marshall Schaal, and Phil Cowens almost an hour to reach the spot where Dean Barber's plane had gone down. The route took them north, away from the airport, then via a small county road which would not see a snow plow for the duration of the winter. Finally they had had to walk the last quarter mile or so into the crash site.

The blue Cessna was crumpled almost beyond recognition. The wings had struck surrounding trees and had folded back on the fuselage, much like a U.S. Navy airplane whose wings were designed to fold to facilitate aircraft carrier storage. The fuselage itself was bent and twisted at its midpoint, forming an inverted "V." The cabin of the plane rested nose down at nearly ninety degrees. The entire craft occupied no more space than a compact car might have in similar circumstances. It was a miracle, David thought, that Dean Barber was still alive. He smiled to himself when he realized that is exactly what miracles were all about.

The three men approached the aircraft, and for the first time David saw several uniformed Clayton County deputies surrounding the plane. Yellow police barrier tape was strung from trees to cordon off the site.

Without a word, Marshall Schaal stooped low beneath the yellow tape and walked toward the aircraft. David and Phil Cowens followed.

David broke the silence. "How did Dean get out of this thing?"

"Folks from a nearby house heard the plane go down and rushed out to see what was going on," Marshall Schaal answered.

"Why the plane did not burn is beyond me," Phil Cowens said. "You can see where the fuel spilled out on the ground. There, where the snow is discolored and melted."

"Maybe the snow had something to do with that," David suggested.

"We thought about that," Schaal said. "But that's really not the answer. Come over here," he said, motioning for David to walk around to where the wings had folded back onto the fuselage.

David followed Schaal's directions.

"See anything unusual?" Schaal asked.

David examined the aircraft, looking for the anomaly to which Schaal was referring. He heard Cowens's footstep crunch in the frozen snow as the FAA inspector drew nearer. All David could see was the mangled metal of what used to be the airplane.

"I don't really know what I'm looking for," David told the two men who now stood by him.

"There," Cowens said, pointing to a portion of the folded wing. "Near the wing root."

David looked closely at where Cowens pointed. A shudder ran through his body at what he saw. The cold seemed suddenly more intense; the coat he'd borrowed from Brian Connelly did nothing to warm him. When he finally spoke, it was only slightly above a whisper.

"It looks like a bullet hole," David said.

"Keep looking," Schaal said.

Now that he knew what he was looking for, David could see numerous holes in the left wing, the wing nearest the pilot. On the sections he could see clearly, the bullet holes had gone completely through the wing.

"By all rights, the plane should have exploded. That had to have been the plan. We were not supposed to see these holes, just a burned and twisted aircraft," Phil Cowens told David.

"Janice Morgan said something about you and Dean meeting up with a couple of guys during an emergency landing," Marshall Schaal began. "Something about weapons."

David continued examining the wreckage, then turned to Schaal and Cowens.

"They were carrying Armalites," David told Schall and Cowens. "The size of the bullet holes in the wings will probably match. The bullets are only slightly larger than a .22 caliber rifle. But that doesn't explain why the plane went down. A few holes in the wing wouldn't do it, unless, as you say, it exploded. Which it obviously didn't do."

"You're right about that," Schaal agreed. "Take a look at this," he said, directing David toward the crumpled engine compartment. The NTSB investigator pointed to a single small hole just behind where the crankcase breather tube exited the cowling.

David bent down to examine the hole more closely. "Another bullet hole, I'd guess."

"That's what brought the plane down," Cowens said. "The holes in the wing would have done it eventually, when the fuel finally drained out, but that would have taken quite a while. There would have been plenty of time for Barber to realize what was happening, turn back for the airport, and land. But it looks like a single bullet entered the lower cowling, struck the magnetos, and brought the plane down."

"Dumb luck, on the part of the shooter," Marshall Schaal muttered.

"Not so lucky for Dean Barber," Cowens said.

"Whoever was shooting at the plane didn't know much about aircraft," Schaal continued. "It was only by chance that the bullet caught the one part in the engine compartment that would bring it down."

"With no magnetos, the spark plugs don't fire, and the engine quits. It's as simple as that," the FAA investigator said.

David Michaels addressed the two investigators. "And you brought me out here because you think there's a connection between the two men we met in that pasture and this crash?"

"We're grasping at straws here," Schaal said. "This has turned into a police matter with those bullet holes. Janice Morgan has already called in the state police. We're bringing in a specialist from Washington. But all that's not going to do any good without an idea of who would have a reason to shoot down this airplane. That brings us back to the only connection we have at the moment. Your two men out in some secluded pasture carrying weapons that just happen to use what we think is the correct size ammo. It might just be coincidence, but it would be a mighty strange one. Unless, of course, we can think of someone else who would want to blow Dean Barber from the sky."

David Michaels listened to the logic. With a dead certainty, he knew that the two men in the pasture were the ones responsible for the crash. But it was not a certainty he could officially share. He needed more proof. He needed those two men. And David Michaels knew he had the ability to track them down.

■ ■ ■

Thirty miles north of the I-40 interchange, the state highway forks and heads west through some of the most beautiful landscape in northern Arkansas. Though scenic, the route is also treacherous, especially when visibility is hampered by driving snow and the roadway is slick and icy. Nevertheless, the highway was the most direct route from Little Rock to the Ozark mountain town of Benning, Arkansas, so Stacii Barrett made the turnoff and drove cautiously toward the west.

The yellow self-stick note she had been handed by the hospital orderly was the only lead she had concerning the young lady at Arkansas Children's Hospital. Normally, she thought, she would not be as tenacious as this, but there was something about this case that drove her.

It had taken all her persuasive powers to get authorization for the trip, especially under the current weather conditions. Now, as she wound her way slowly through the pine and hardwood forest, she was wondering if perhaps she had been too hasty in her decision to go to Benning.

The state's snow removal efforts had not yet made it as far as the Benning highway. A thick cover of snow blanketed the roadway, and Stacii reduced her speed to little more than ten miles an hour. At this rate, she would be lucky to reach Benning by nightfall, and being stranded on the highway was quickly becoming a possibility. The cell phone she carried offered only slight comfort. She would be able to tell someone about her plight, but with travel increasingly difficult, it might be impossible for anyone to reach her. Fear welled up inside her, but Stacii forced it back down and kept driving.

The next road sign indicated that Benning was another twenty-seven miles. Not so far, she thought. Stacii checked the lighted clock on the dashboard, calculated the distance versus her speed, and figured she would roll into Benning about eight o'clock in the evening. She had called a motel in Benning and guaranteed her arrival with a credit card, so at least she would have a room, provided she could keep the car from sliding into a ditch for the next two and a half hours.

■   ■   ■

Tia Trevilla strained against the padded restraints as the brutal stab of pain subsided. Sweat formed on her forehead, and the muscles in her back and lower abdomen coiled in rebellion at the waves of contractions that now came more and more often.

She glanced furtively at the empty bed across the room. That had been Gaby's bed, and Gaby had been her friend. Tia hoped beyond hope that Gaby had made it out of the house, out of the valley, away from the pain and agony that she was now experiencing.

This would be her first child, but it was not supposed to happen this way. This was not her child. Tia Trevilla was only seventeen years old and had never been married.

Tia prayed silently, asking for remission of a sin she was not certain she had committed. Was it a sin to have a child in this manner? After all, she had had no control over the process. Her body was being used without her permission. She had been kidnapped, just like Gaby.

A wave of pain and nausea swept over her once again, and she tried to scream, but nothing came. No sound, no moan, no indication that she had any control of her body.

A sound came from the far side of the room, and the nurse appeared, along with another person. Both were clad in white, their faces obscured, their eyes—unkind and uncaring—were the only indication that the figures had any interest in her at all.

Tia closed her eyes against the inevitable horror.

CHAPTER
TWENTY-
SIX

David Michaels kicked off his snow-sodden boot as he pushed through the front door of his half-restored log home. After the time spent with Marshall Schaal of the NTSB and Phil Cowens of the FAA, David had called Cindy to tell her he was on his way to pick her up. She had already arranged to ride home with a friend who worked in the courthouse, and she encouraged David to stop by to check on Dean Barber. At the hospital, he had been unable to see his friend, but he had been assured by the doctor on duty that Dean was doing quite well, considering the circumstances. He would not be up flying in the next two or three weeks, but the next two or three months were not out of the question. The good news was also a reprieve of sorts for David. It was late afternoon when he finally turned into his snow-covered drive and parked near the tarpaulin-draped Studebaker Lark.

The sight of the old car buoyed his spirits, and the thought of tooling around the mountains when the weather cleared gave him a sense of delight. He had owned a similar car when he was growing up, and it was those memories he relished most.

He recalled driving through mountains on fire with changing autumn leaves, cool breeze blowing in the windows, and the fresh smell of the air as it made its way down from Canada. Those memories tied in with the beginning of football season and the approach of Halloween and Thanksgiving, which he always enjoyed.

But those memories, like most, were bittersweet. Most of the things he'd done had included his younger brother, and now Jimmy was dead. David knew he would see his brother again in heaven, but that thought did not assuage the feelings of loss and deprivation. A blunt stab of pain still plagued him when he thought of Jimmy.

Despite his sadness, David knew they had been good years, good times, and the mere thought of the old Studebaker Lark nestled under the protective cover gave his soul reason to rejoice. It represented a physical connection with the past and a lot of good memories.

David closed the door behind him, shrugged out of the coat he'd borrowed from Brian Connelly, and switched on the nearest table lamp. The old log cabin did not have wall switches or overhead lighting. That was one of the things he was planning for the coming year. Until then, he made do with table lamps precariously placed around the house.

Thoughts of the Studebaker were replaced by a vision of Dean Barber's blue Cessna crumpled into a heap north of the airport. The bullet holes in the wings were as clear in his mind as if he were standing next to the airplane. Anger welled up in his heart.

Someone had tried to kill his friend, and they had come very close to succeeding. He was angry at the sniper, but he was also angry with himself for feeling relieved when he was unable to see Dean at the hospital. As a pastor, it was part of his role to offer consolation, but he had felt somehow unable to comfort Dean, and he was mad at himself for that.

David reached for a second lamp as he went into the kitchen planning to fix himself something to eat and review the events of the past couple of days. He was beginning to feel as if he were right back in the middle of Jimmy's murder case.

In the half-light offered by the lamp, David pulled a can from an overhead cabinet, opened it, and dumped the contents into a saucepan. He lit the gas stove and placed the pan over the flame. It was not until the aroma began to fill the air that he realized he'd opened a can of chili.

His mind, he realized, was somewhere else.

David stirred the chili, reduced the flame, and went into the living room to build a fire. He had installed a wall-mounted gas heater in the cabin but still preferred the sight and sound of a log fire. The fireplace was actually a structural component of the cabin, acting as the center support for the one-and-a-half story building.

The first floor contained the living room, a small dining area, and the kitchen. A narrow staircase led to an upper loft area which served as the cabin's solitary bedroom. David had installed a small bathroom with a shower stall in part of the upper loft. He had plans to add on to the cabin changing its basic rectangular shape into a T by adding another, larger bedroom and full bath at the rear of the house. He would need the extra room if he were going to ask Cindy Tolbert to marry him. He would need a suitable home for his bride. So far, he had not made much progress on the renovation, and the cabin was livable only for an ex-military man accustomed to roughing it.

David laid the elements of the fire: pine kindling atop old newspaper resting on andirons, with split red oak logs above. He touched a match to the newspaper, and in less than three minutes, the pine was crackling, and flames were licking at the dried oak. David smiled at the sound of the fire.

With the fire going, he returned to the kitchen. His thoughts turned to the girl in the belly compartment of Dean's Cessna. How had she gotten there? Who were the men who had appeared in the forest carrying Armalite rifles? Had they tried to kill Dean Barber? They were all questions needing answers—answers he didn't have. He suspected the answers lay somewhere to the north, near the pasture where he and Dean had made their emergency landing.

He had the exact location of the pasture stored away in his portable Lowrance AirMap. The Global Positioning System would return him to the exact location, whether he flew in or hiked in. But would such a trip be worth the effort? Was he jumping to conclusions where the two men were concerned? Where Dean Barber was concerned? Certainly, someone had shot down the plane, but there was no proof it had been those men.

The bubbling chili brought David out of his reverie. He shut off the burner, spooned the chili into a bowl, retrieved some bread from another cabinet, and headed for the rocking chair in front of the fireplace.

He was barely in the chair, the chili bowl balanced in his hand, when the window to the right of the front door exploded inward, spraying shards of glass over a hundred square feet of cabin floor. An all too familiar cacophony of sound filled the room: the sound of automatic weapons.

■　■　■

Billy Bob Campbell felt as alive as he ever had in his entire life. The AR-18 Armalite vibrated in his hands as he gently squeezed off multiple three-round bursts from the rifle. Just to his left, he could hear Cole's Armalite firing away. In the leafless cold of the Ozarks, the two weapons sounded more like miniature explosions of fireworks than deadly rifle fire.

"I got him," Cole called over the rattle of the automatic weapons.

"I saw him," Billy Bob called back. He went down when I fired through the window. *I* got him."

"Dream on, man," Cole yelled back.

Both men emptied their twenty-round magazines into the log house, jammed another into their weapons, and continued to fire. Wood splinters and glass exploded from the structure. After the fourth magazine, David Michaels's log home looked as if vehement wood-peckers had assaulted it. All the windows along the front were blown away and glass shards littered the front porch.

"What do you think, man?" Cole called to Billy Bob.

"Let's wait a couple of minutes," Campbell said.

Both men cleared their weapons, inserted another magazine into the rifles, and waited.

■ ■ ■

David Michaels crouched behind the wall where he had taken cover from the barrage of bullets. Every window had exploded. A small gash dripped blood where a shard of glass had slashed him across his forehead. As for the rest of the house, the areas accessible from the windows were devastated. Pictures on the far walls were pockmarked by bullets. Items that had been sitting on various tables had been blown to the floor, and now littered the small area rugs like so many pieces of confetti.

The shooting had ceased, but David remained behind the wall. His questions about the two men in the pasture had been answered, and his heart was pounding a staccato rhythm against the walls of his chest. His breathing came in short intakes of the chilled, mountain air which now poured into the cabin through the destroyed windows. David tried to regulate his breathing and in the process slow his hammering heart. The sudden assault had sent a surge of adrenaline coursing through his body, and he knew from experience that his heart rate would not return to normal for several hours. He knew the symptoms. It had happened before in Vietnam and Saudi Arabia.

To help himself think clearly, he turned his attention to the weapons used in the assault. They had been firing 5.56 mm ammunition; he knew the sound of that particular caliber by heart. When the weapons had opened fire, his first thought had been that the assailants were using AR-15s. But the rate of fire had been too great. Given the events of the past seventy-two hours, David was sure the salvos were coming from the muzzles of AR-18 Armalites. And whoever was doing the firing knew what they were doing. There had been only controlled, three-round bursts which were more accurate than longer, sustained fire.

David scanned the room quickly. His only weapons, a Remington 12-gauge shotgun he used for bird hunting and a Browning Hi-Power 9mm automatic pistol, were both upstairs in the loft bedroom. Any attempt to retrieve the weapons would mean climbing the open staircase to the loft, which would put him directly in the line of fire of at least one of the blown-out windows. That would almost certainly mean a quick and violent death.

Still, it might be a risk he would have to take. If the two killers decided to enter the house, he would be utterly defenseless. The thick logs and heavy chinking of the house had saved his life. Although the damage appeared devastating, it was only superficial. David doubted that even a .50 caliber sniper rifle could penetrate the heavy wooden structure, and the thought provided him some comfort as he tried to decide what to do next.

He could wait. The men might think they had killed him already. Out of instinct, he had dropped to the floor when the attack began, rolling quickly perpendicular to the assault, seeking protection behind the log wall.

But waiting would mean he was only delaying the inevitable. If the killers were as well trained as he believed, they would not be content to remain outside, hoping that they had killed their quarry. They would want to confirm the kill, and to do that, they would have to enter the house.

David thanked God that in the first moments of the attack, bullets had shattered both lamps he had switched on earlier, plunging the interior of the cabin into near blackness. If he made a move to secure the weapons in the loft, at least he would not be backlit.

But there was still the problem of motion. Motion was the one thing most evident in low-light situations. So even with the lamps out, movement was risky.

Silence prevailed. David cocked his ear toward the nearest open window, just above and to his left. The ground outside was snow-covered and frozen, offering him the advantage of hearing anyone who might try to sneak up on the house. Any footsteps would echo in the cold like the snap of broken branches in a forest.

David realized his eyes had already adjusted to the darkness. He had one more chance, he realized. If he could move enough to draw fire from the killers while they were still at a distance, he could effectively negate their night vision, giving him a chance to reach the shotgun and the automatic pistol.

It was a gamble, one he would have to take in the next thirty seconds before the men outside decided to enter the cabin.

There were two shooters, David knew. He had identified their positions by sound. If he were lucky, the two men were far enough away from each other that the flash suppressers on their weapons would be of no use to each other. Flash suppressers worked well for the person firing the weapon, but they did not suppress the actual flash. Anyone not directly behind the weapon would be affected by the muzzle flash. David knew if he could get both men to fire again, their night vision would be ruined by the flash of each other's gunfire. It takes at least one minute for night vision to return under such circumstances. Sixty seconds was all David would need to be up the stairs.

David looked around quickly. There were several objects well within reach, and he chose one of the lamps which had been snuffed out by the initial gunfire. He took a deep breath, moved nearer the window, and held up the lamp. Gunfire immediately erupted, catching the lamp with at least one bullet from the burst. The lamp was wrenched from his hand leaving two fingers numb.

Had both men fired? He couldn't be sure.

David convinced himself that reflexes would have surely taken over, and each man would have fired almost involuntarily. It might be his only chance, and he had less than fifteen seconds left to take advantage of it.

Suddenly, a sound swelled and penetrated the forest around the house, at once familiar but unexpected.

A car was coming up the road leading to the house!

■   ■   ■

Both Billy Bob Campbell and Cole Branscum had reacted to the slight movement in the blown-out window to the right of the entrance door. Whatever it had been had been blown to bits by the almost instantaneous firing of both men.

"Was that him?" Cole asked, after the firing had ceased.

"Had to be," Billy Bob answered. "We got him for sure that time."

"Then let's get out of here," Cole said, standing up. He was wet and cold from lying on the snow-covered ground, and he was ready to get out of Clayton County as quickly as possible.

Billy Bob stood, shaking the frozen moisture from his clothes. He, too, was cold but knew the kill had to be confirmed.

"You stay here. Keep your gun on that window. I'm going to confirm the kill," Billy Bob ordered.

"Come on, man. We got him. Let's get out of here."

"After I check it out and not before."

The sound of tires on a snowy road froze both men in their places. Someone was coming! Lights from a vehicle were coming up the drive leading to the house.

Billy Bob had parked their vehicle out along the county road, and he and Cole had made their way through the forest. It had been a stroke of genius, Billy Bob told himself. Besides, had there been a car within sight of the house when the preacher had arrived, it might have aroused suspicion. Now, with another car approaching, his foresight was their salvation.

"Let's get out of here," Cole urged, his voice carrying the unmistakable tone of panic.

"Let's go," Billy Bob finally agreed.

"Besides, we saw him fall that second time. He's dead."

"That's the story we tell Swann too," Billy Bob said, as he and Cole made their way down a gentle slope toward the wall of trees into which they would disappear. "We get our money, and we get out of the state. I have a feeling this thing is about to come down around somebody's head, and it ain't gonna be mine."

The two killers wound their way through the forest, found the car where they had left it, and scurried like pack rats out of Clayton County.

■ ■ ■

To Janice Morgan, as the headlights of her patrol car washed over the front of David Michaels's log house, it appeared as if a war had been waged, and the house had been the first fatality.

She braked to a sliding halt, slammed the transmission into park, leaping from her police cruiser, and crouched low as she made her way around the car, using it for protection. The odor of smokeless gunpowder still hung in the air.

"David!" Janice yelled toward the house. With the heavy clouds, there was no moon, no light.

"David Michaels!" Janice Morgan yelled again. "Are you in there?" She felt a sense of urgency, but she could not take the chance that whoever was responsible for the shooting might be in the house, waiting.

"Be careful," came David's reply from within the house. "They were out front, just down from the shallow drop-off."

As her vision adjusted to the low light, Janice Morgan could see the slight depression David was talking about. There was no one there. "Five minutes," she yelled back at David, knowing he would understand her cryptic message. She checked her watch, all the time keeping watch for the shooters. It was the longest five minutes she could remember.

"Nothing?" David called from within the house.

"Nothing," Janice answered, feeling more freedom now to exchange information with David. "If they were in the shallow depression, they are long gone. You armed?"

"Shotgun and pistol," David called back.

"You know what to do. I'll take this side."

The darkness was profound, an inky blackness only barely illuminated by the whiteness of the snow cover. Now was the time to move.

David slipped out the back door, skirting the rear of the cabin, coming up on the area where the shooters had been. He could make out the shadowy figure of Janice Morgan already standing at the area. He crunched through snow to join her.

"Someone doesn't like you," Janice said as David approached.

When David drew near, Janice Morgan's mouth fell open. "You said you were armed. Where's the shotgun and pistol?"

"Upstairs," David said sheepishly. "I couldn't get to them for the gunfire, but I didn't want whoever was out here to know that."

"Whew," the sheriff exhaled, "I'm glad they're gone, then."

"You and me both," David said, bending down to examine a depression obviously formed by a human body.

"That's where one of them was," Janice said. "The other one was just over there. There's enough brass on the ground to make a boat anchor."

David retrieved one of the shells and examined it. "Let's get in the house. I want to see these casings in the light."

The two walked to the cabin, separately for safety, looking around as they moved. It was an uneasy feeling knowing that men capable of such terror had been in this forest only minutes earlier. Both knew they could return at any time.

Inside the house, David switched on a single light, being sure that neither he nor Janice were in line between a window and the light source.

"I think they're gone," David commented, returning his attention to the brass shell.

"How can you be certain?"

"They would have opened up on us by now. This was a hit-and-run operation."

"Any idea who tried to kill you?"

"A very good idea, but if I were to say it, it would sound stupid."

"The two men you told me about at the hospital?"

"The same ones who shot down Dean Barber's plane with him in it. Take a look at this brass casing," David said, handing the brass shell to Janice Morgan.

"Five point five six millimeters. High-velocity. The same type of ammo used by the Armalites the two men in the pasture carried."

"Right. And I don't have any reason to believe someone else with this type of weaponry is after both Dean Barber and me. Coincidence has come to a halt right here and now."

"I agree. I can also tell when you have something on your mind. What is it?"

David looked around the room. It was quiet now, almost tranquil. Anger welled in him once again, this time directed at the men who had invaded his life.

"I'm going back to that pasture. Correction, to that secret airport. That's where all this began, and I have an idea that's where I'm going to find some answers." David remembered what the Hispanic girl had said. *El valle.* The valley. Somewhere near that airport was a valley that someone seemed to think required AR-18 protection. He would find it.

"What do you want from me?" Janice Morgan asked.

■　　■　　■

Sheriff Wade Larsen corked the bottle sitting on his desk and stared at the photographs adorning the wall of his office. The Wall of Fame, he called it. The photos were of every sheriff who had served Benning County in the past. They had been men of principle and men whose standards and convictions had been beyond reproach. Men who believed not only in the law, but in justice, which was the ultimate end of all law.

Larsen gulped down his whiskey, letting the liquid burn in his throat and warm his stomach. Then he uncorked the bottle and splashed another shot into his glass.

He was not yet drunk, but he had a good start on it, and there was no reason he could see for stopping.

Drunk was the only way he could deal with the Wall of Fame as it stared back at him from the dirty, cream-colored office wall. His photo might appear on the wall one day, but when the good citizens of Benning County learned the truth, he had no doubt the photo would be removed. Having his own photo next to his father's was a shame he was not certain he could live with anyway.

The alternative was to right the wrongs he had done. He had been, on the whole, a good sheriff for the county, but that would be forgotten when the truth was known. Maybe there was still time to correct the egregious harm he had done. Nothing could bring back the lives he had helped to ruin, but he could prevent further damage.

Wade Larsen jammed the cork back in the bottle of sour mash bourbon, swiveled his chair around to face the single filing cabinet at his back, unlocked the bottom drawer and pulled out a thick file folder. He began reading through the file, his stomach now churning, not so much from the whiskey, but from the unforgiving data that confirmed the depths to which he had sunk.

CHAPTER TWENTY-SEVEN

Stacii Barrett was beginning to think she had made a drastic error. The drive to Benning had been a nightmare, but she had arrived. After an uncomfortable night in the local motel, she had gone to see the sheriff.

He was not in the office, but she interrogated several deputies, all of whom professed total ignorance of a missing Hispanic girl. In fact, they had looked at Stacii as if she were slightly mentally unbalanced.

The rest of the day had been frustrating. She had slogged through wet, cold snow, asking questions door-to-door in Benning. Nobody knew anything about the young girl. Now Stacii was cold, her feet were wet, and she could feel the beginning of a fever creeping into her system. The chill she had felt earlier had taken on a slightly different character. Not the time to come down with the flu, she thought.

She decided to call it quits for the time being, get out of her wet clothing, and soak in a warm bath back at the motel. The warm water might head off whatever bug it was that was trying to gain a foothold in her system.

She drove to the motel and parked the sports utility vehicle. She had been told at several stops during the day that it was not necessary to lock doors in Benning, as if the town still possessed the righteous morals and mores of times past, when people were honest, and vigilance was not the standard of operation. Nevertheless, Stacii locked the doors.

Pulling her keys out, she entered her motel room with little on her mind but a relaxing hot bath.

The sight that greeted her made her breath catch in her throat.

The room had been ransacked. Her clothes, along with the few furnishings in the room, had been strewn about. Her single suitcase lay open against the far wall, its lining ripped out. Pillows had been ripped open, adding their feathers to the disarray. The mattress lay askew across the bed, its covering cut and torn as if some great monster with huge claws had ripped at it. The sight was frightening, and Stacii began to panic.

Before she could react further to the destruction, a sickly sweet smell assailed her nostrils. The presence of the odor did not register at first, and when it did, it was too late.

She sensed rather than saw the movement behind her. A strong hand holding a small yellow washcloth clasped the fabric over her nose. Another arm was around her waist, holding her fast. She struggled against the superior force, but to no avail. At one point, she felt the heel of her boot connect with the shin of the man holding her, evoking nothing more than a small grunt.

The room began to spin as she breathed in the sweet smell. Colors collided, walls washed into themselves, and the light rotated on its axis, like a globe out of control. Then there was nothing but blackness.

■   ■   ■

Billy Bob Campbell concentrated on the task at hand—getting out of town as quickly as possible. As he drove, he reviewed the happenings of the past thirty-six hours.

Things had not gone exactly as planned, and he muttered to himself about loose ends. If only that car hadn't shown up. Not being able to confirm that the preacher was dead nagged at him as much as his failure to completely destroy the blue Cessna. In both cases he had been close, but he wasn't absolutely certain he had finished either job. Of course, when he reported to Jason Swann he would tell him that both deaths were confirmed, but that would only serve to buy himself enough time to get out of Arkansas.

Billy Bob stole a quick glance at Cole Branscum, huddled fast asleep with his head wedged between the back of the seat and the car door. It was just as well, Billy Bob thought. He needed time to think, and with Cole awake and jabbering at him, it would have been impossible.

Billy Bob reached for the radio and flicked it on. It seemed the weather was getting worse instead of better. Normally, an Arkansas winter storm lasted twenty-four hours at the most, but this one lingered on. He wanted to hear the forecast, which could have a bearing on how and when he was going to get out of state.

Billy Bob punched the "search" button until the radio stopped on an all-news station. A wrap-up of the weather was on and he listened with interest. The front that had brought the storm to Arkansas was stalled and looked as if it would persist at least through the next twenty-four to forty-eight hours. *Perfect timing,* Billy Bob thought.

He was about to punch in a country and western station when the announcer's voice stopped him.

". . . of an apparent hunting accident," the voice was saying. "Repeating. The Reverend David Michaels of Clayton died today of wounds received in an apparent hunting accident near his home in Clayton County. Mr. Michaels had been the pastor of First Community Church, Clayton, Arkansas, for the past year. Funeral arrangements have not yet been set by the family. Moving on to other items . . ."

Billy felt his heart leap with joy as he punched the "search" button again. The radio settled on a station playing country music. The day had suddenly brightened. He glanced over at Cole again. He was still asleep. He had not heard the announcement. All the better, thought Billy Bob. Now he could complete the plans which had been festering in the back of his mind, plans that did not include Cole Branscum or Jason Swann.

■　　■　　■

With her shock of unruly, flame-red hair, Dr. Elaine Miller had years ago opted to keep the thick mass cropped as closely as possible while still preserving a feminine appearance. As a 5'11" high school girl—and basketball player—she had endured the taunts and jeers of fellow classmates who couldn't decide whether to call her "stringbean" or "carrot," so they settled on "veggie." The experience had instilled in her an inordinate amount of caring and compassion. In her second year at the University of Tennessee Medical School, she had won the Miss Tennessee title and gone on to represent the state in the Miss America pageant, which had provided a modest measure of retribution.

Now, after several successful years of private practice as a nationally recognized expert in reproductive endocrinology, Dr. Elaine Miller possessed a unique mixture of understanding and absolute mastery of her chosen profession that made her one of the most sought after experts in the United States.

Kenneth and Susan Blair had not previously considered Dr. Miller as an alternative because of the reputation of the Phelps Clinic.

But that was now in the past, and as the Blairs sat in Dr. Miller's office, waiting for the doctor to finish evaluating Susan's test results, both wondered privately why they had waited so long to consider alternatives to Dr. Phelps.

Compared to the Phelps Clinic, Dr. Miller's office was surprisingly stark. Located in a quiet section of Germantown, just east of the parkway on Poplar Avenue, the Reproductive Clinic of Memphis disdained the crass commercialism that seemed to be taking over other medical practices. One would never see an advertisement for the Reproductive Clinic of Memphis splashed across the broad sheet of the *Commercial Appeal,* the mainstay Memphis newspaper.

The RCM quietly went about its business of providing solutions to human reproductive puzzles. Dr. Elaine Miller did her own thing. Years earlier, she had told Mid-South Obstetrical Management Services to take a hike, which had not endeared her to many of her colleagues who saw MOMS as a savior for overworked medical office staff. But that was Elaine Miller's decision, and she had no regrets.

Kenneth and Susan Blair were relaxed as they waited for the test results, and they had a renewed confidence that a satisfactory resolution could be reached.

Dr. Miller entered the office carrying a stack of test results in her left hand. She wore an expression that reminded Kenneth Blair of the face of a child who had just been caught with his hand in the proverbial cookie jar. It was an expression of confusion mixed with self-doubt, as if to say, "I understand what has happened, but I don't know how it happened."

Elaine Miller sat in a third chair, not behind her desk. "Kenneth and Susan," Elaine Miller began, using the technique of calling all her patients by their first names and thus putting them at ease. "I have the results of your test, and I must say they are very confusing, given what you have told me."

Kenneth started to say something but was cut short by Dr. Miller's upraised hand.

"Let me continue, please. As I was saying, I'm slightly confused at the test results in light of what you have told me about your inability to have a child. I am not, however, surprised at your actual inability to conceive. While those might sound like contradictions, I assure you, they are not."

"I don't understand," Susan Blair said.

"You began going to the Phelps Clinic early in your marriage. Your progress has been monitored by the clinic since not long after your wedding. Is that correct?"

Kenneth Blair said, "We thought we should go ahead and establish a relationship with a good doctor because we wanted to begin a family immediately."

"And I commend you for that step. Unfortunately, some actions were taken that—how shall I put this?—were not in your best interest."

Kenneth Blair sat forward in his chair and asked, "What kind of actions, Dr. Miller?"

"When you first came in, your wife handed me a bottle of pills, which she said had been prescribed by the Phelps Clinic. Is that true?"

"You know it is. You have the pills."

"Those pills serve one purpose, and one purpose only," Elaine Miller said quietly.

Now both Susan and Kenneth were on the edge of their chairs. Neither spoke.

"Susan," Dr. Miller said, "those pills will not help you conceive a child. Those pills are used exclusively to prevent conception. They are a very powerful and rarely prescribed form of birth control."

■   ■   ■

"Are you sure?" Janice Morgan spoke into the phone.

"Positive," came the reply from the other end.

"Then it's legal, as far as it concerns David?"

"As legal as if you or I were doing it," the voice answered. "As of this day, Commander David Michaels is reactivated into the military service of his country and assigned as special liaison to the office of the president of the United States."

"And he will know nothing about it?" the sheriff pressed.

"Nothing, unless you choose to tell him, which I would advise against at this point. What you have already done, and what he is about to do, will easily be covered under the auspices of the position, but Commander Michaels will be better off kept in the dark. We wouldn't want him to throw caution to the wind. That could be dangerous. For him as well as others."

Janice Morgan thought about what she was being told. The theory was valid, of course. Too much authority under these circumstances could be deadly.

"I won't tell him, provided I even see him again," Janice Morgan said. "He's preparing at this very minute. From what he told me, it sounds like he's planning a military operation. I think I will check on him one last time."

"He may have finished as a chaplain, but he was a SEAL. If there's something to find in those north woods, he'll find it," the sheriff's contact assured her.

"I just hope finding it doesn't come at too high a price," Janice said.

"You and me both."

Janice Morgan hung up the phone as she reached for the phone book. She needed to call David to at least tell him good-bye. She hoped it wouldn't be for the last time.

■   ■   ■

Had she not spoken with Janice Morgan earlier, the radio announcement would have devastated Cindy Tolbert. As it was, listening to the false radio announcement that David Michaels had been killed in a hunting accident had been difficult.

Now she sat in her living room, hunched down in her grandfather's old rocking chair. Her knees were tucked up under her chin, her arms encircling them in an attempt to quell the shaking that coursed through her body. She glanced quickly at the telephone sitting on a small table across the room. Normally, she would have called Jean Michaels, David's sister-in-law and Jimmy Michaels's widow, but Jean had taken her two boys to Springfield, Missouri, to visit her parents. Cindy felt abandoned.

She relaxed for a moment and picked up the Bible lying next to her chair. The rocker was a place of refuge, and the well-worn Bible was always close by.

Cindy flipped through the well-marked pages until she came to
1 Peter 5:7. She read the short passage out loud, "Casting all your care
upon him, for he careth for you." She closed her eyes and let the
meaning sweep over her, and for a brief instant she felt the love and
compassion of God flow through her.

Her shaking had stopped, but a nagging worry still flickered in the
depths of her mind. What David was doing was dangerous. Despite the
assurances she'd received from Janice Morgan, she knew that David
was in danger.

Danger seemed to be part of David Michaels's makeup, almost a
necessary ingredient for his survival. She had lost one husband years
ago, and she did not want to lose another. Although David had not for-
mally proposed, she knew it was only a matter of time. David was now
an important elements in the fabric of her life, and she would cling
tenaciously to those all-important pieces.

As she put the Bible down, she wondered if just being a pastor and
husband would ever be enough for a man like David. He'd made the
military his life for twenty years, and it was certainly understandable
if he missed the action and excitement that came with such a life.
Perhaps he would even miss the hardships too. That life could not be
duplicated at First Community Church.

Cindy rose and the old rocking chair creaked. She went to the
phone and dialed. It was answered on the second ring.

"Mr. Michaels, this is Cindy. I need to talk to you."

When David's father told her to come right over, Cindy grabbed her
coat and headed out the door. At least now she had someone to talk to,
someone who might be able to explain the actions of the man she loved.

The winter air was bone chilling, but the walk was not long, and
the route was familiar. She'd taken it hundreds of time before, beginning in high school when she'd first had a crush on David. He'd never
paid much attention to her, but that had been all right. Just being near
him had been enough in those days. When David had returned for his
brother Jimmy's funeral, she'd told him about the crush. She had been

amused by his reaction, a combination of embarrassment and surprise. Since that time, she and David had fallen deeply in love. For her, it had been a dream come true. But now that dream was threatened. Maybe David's father knew what was going on.

Cindy rounded the corner at Vine and Caldwell Streets. She could see the lights burning in the front room. James Michaels was waiting for her.

Suddenly headlights appeared behind her. Her first thought was that David had followed her and was about to surprise her, but that thought was quickly dispelled as a green Mercedes sedan pulled up beside her. The driver rolled down the passenger side window and leaned toward her.

From what she could see, the man was extremely handsome in a rugged manner.

"Excuse me," he said.

Cindy walked to the open window. "Can I help you?"

"I'm looking for Cross and School Street. I think I made a wrong turn somewhere."

The request was innocuous enough. Cross and School were several blocks back from where the man had come. It didn't seem likely that he could have missed them, but anything was possible, Cindy knew. She was about to point out the directions, when the man grabbed her right arm through the open window. She started to scream; she felt a sharp sting, and the words froze in her throat. Blackness instantly overtook her.

■   ■   ■

"Please, Doctor," the member of *Die Gruppe* said, "give us your personal assessment of the situation as it now stands."

Dr. Henry Phelps Sr. cleared his throat. He was reluctant to reveal what he now knew about the man known as Lazarus.

"I have met with him. I can tell you unequivocally that the man is in the early stages of a total mental breakdown. I can't explain it, but

something has happened to push him over the edge. He is not thinking clearly at this point and could cause problems."

"That would be unfortunate, Doctor," the same man responded.
"Lazarus has always been the inspiration behind the project. It was his
idea, his strength, which set it in motion, his resilience that kept it going."

Dr. Henry Phelps Jr. rose from his chair at the head of the long
table. "My father has pointed out the danger we find ourselves in
at the moment. Unfortunately, it is not a danger from outside our
organization. As judicious as our strategy has been up to now, we
must continually evaluate our objectives in light of our resources
and abilities." He paused for effect, scanning the men at the table,
the men of *Die Gruppe,* who now controlled the project with all its
ramifications.

"If I may," Dr. Phelps Sr. interjected.

"Please, father, continue."

"I need to make this perfectly clear. I do not know what has happened to precipitate the actions by Lazarus at this time, but I believe it
to be some form of outside force, or perceived force, which has caused
him to react in the manner in which he has."

"I don't understand what you are saying, Doctor," another group
member responded.

"Simply put, and I was never one to believe in such things, but it
would seem Lazarus is *possessed* of ideas and beliefs that are not his
own. Or at least, I have never known them to be his."

"Are you telling us you think Lazarus is possessed by some sort of
demon?" another member snorted in disbelief.

"I'm telling you that Lazarus is not himself, for whatever reason.
Possessed may be too strong a word. *Influenced* might better describe
the current situation."

"*Possessed* or *influenced.* The semantics are irrelevant," the same
member continued. "You are telling us Lazarus is not in his right mind."

Henry Phelps Sr. sighed and reluctantly nodded his head in agreement. "It would appear so," he concluded.

"Doctor, if you would," the first member to speak began, "explain what you know has occurred in the last few hours."

"As I said, I spoke with Lazarus a few hours ago. He seemingly has no memory of turning over leadership of *Die Gruppe* to this body. In his mind, he is still the leader and spiritual head of *Die Gruppe*. As such, he sees himself as—how shall I put this?—as the *Führer* of the organization."

There was a general stirring around the table as what Phelps was telling them sank in. Men, powerful men, looked into one another's eyes, and what they saw there was fear.

"Continue, Doctor."

"A representative from the Arkansas Department of Human Services arrived last night in Benning. I was informed of this only a few hours ago through our normal channels. She has been asking questions about the young girl who escaped."

A voice, strident and angry, asked, "How did she know to go to Benning?"

"I have no idea. Nor does my contact, but the crux of the matter is that she is there."

"She won't learn anything," another member chimed in.

"That is not the point," Phelps Jr. said.

"How so?" the member asked.

Henry Phelps Sr. continued. "The social worker has disappeared."

"Then that problem is solved," said the second member to the left.

"No. It is just beginning. We think she has been kidnapped and that the Benning County sheriff's department is responsible, acting under orders issued by Lazarus. It appears that our founder has not yet released the reins of control."

This time the room came alive with the angry voices of the members of *Die Gruppe,* making a continuation of the discussion impossible.

"This is outrageous. . . ."

"Insane . . . "

"The man is crazy. . . "

Dr. Phelps Sr. held his hands over his head, palms out, arms spread. "Please, gentlemen. Let me finish."

The raucous outburst slowly subsided; order was restored.

Dr. Phelps Sr. continued. "We do not know the location of the social worker." Phelps consulted a notepad on the table in front of him. "Her name is Stacii Barrett. Possibly she is being held some place nearby. Possibly even in the Benning County jail. That is not of concern for the moment."

Again an outburst erupted, silenced quickly by the senior Phelps.

"To what end?" another member demanded.

"I don't know at this point. Perhaps she was getting too close."

"And Lazarus and those fools in Benning County think that the disappearance of a state worker will not provoke further investigation? Insane!"

"I agree," Phelps Sr. said. "But we have a greater priority for the moment. A radio broadcast from Clayton County picked up by the wire services announced the death of the Reverend David Michaels about an hour ago. Michaels was one of the men in the plane who began all of this. The plane itself crashed the other morning on takeoff at the Clayton airport. It seems Lazarus or Jason Swann or both have been busy. Out of sanction, I might add."

This time the assemblage was quiet. A sense of foreboding infused the room.

"What else?" a member asked quietly.

"It appears Lazarus may have ordered Damon to kidnap this preacher's girlfriend," Phelps replied in almost a whisper, "at about the same time he was reported killed. We don't know why. We think the woman is being transported here to Memphis."

"The man has truly lost his mind," someone added. The general agreement was affirmed with nods from all those present. "And now Damon has reappeared."

"Possibly. *Probably,* to both statements. At this point, Lazarus wants to show that he is in charge. Bringing the woman here would serve to bolster that image, as would the involvement of Damon."

The room had gone from riotous to restrained in a matter of seconds. The implications could be catastrophic. Such actions could easily spell the end of the project and *Die Gruppe.*

"He began this whole thing," one member offered, his voice subdued.

Dr. Phelps Sr. nodded once again. "You all know how I got here, how I was saved the embarrassment and the humiliation of the postwar trials at Nuremberg. How I escaped long before escape was even seen to be necessary. I have had a good life here. Together, and that refers to this group as well as to Lazarus, we have built an empire whose power lies in the subtle exercise of influence. It has been successful far beyond what anyone could have envisioned. Anyone that is, except the man whose dream it was: Lazarus. But even conceding that, the time has come to understand that what is best for Lazarus is no longer best for *Die Gruppe.*"

"Suggestions," Henry Phelps Jr. said, directing his question to the rest of the group.

The men in the room were contemplative for a moment. The decision, as definitive as it was, was not an easy one to make.

"He must die," one man finally said.

A chorus of nods confirmed the verdict.

"It will not be easy," Henry Phelps Sr. said. "I don't know how to say this, but he seems to know everything that is happening, almost as if he were sitting in this very room."

"But there are no guards?"

"Just the housekeeper and the butler. And, of course, Damon."

"We don't know that for certain," a member said.

"It's logical."

Again, all nodded in agreement.

"None should present a problem, even if the girlfriend from Clayton is there when it happens. She might have to be sacrificed in order to neutralize Lazarus."

Dr. Henry Phelps Jr., the new chairman of *Die Gruppe,* said, "Sacrifices have been made up to this point. One more should not be a problem."

PART II
THE VALLEY

CHAPTER TWENTY-EIGHT

David Michaels punched the power button on the small cellular phone and tested the battery charge. Satisfied, he turned the phone off and gently stuffed the small instrument into the heavily laden backpack at his feet.

He retrieved a list from his shirt pocket and quickly reviewed it. It was all here, from the small white-gas stove to the bottled water and the Garuda Kusala backpack tent. The tent, a two-man structure, weighed slightly more than five pounds, which aside from the bottled water he'd packed, was the heaviest item in the pack. The entire list, now carefully sorted and arranged in the internal frame pack, weighed in at a few ounces over fifty pounds, a hefty haul by any measure, but still less than the eighty-pound packs he was accustomed to in the military.

After informing Janice Morgan of his plans, David had pulled together all his outdoor gear, along with his camping supplies, making sure he had what he would need to survive in the snow-covered reaches of the Ozark Mountains. It had taken most of the night but he had tested all the equipment. It would have been utter foolishness to venture out into the winter landscape with a stove not functioning or a rip in the tent's single-wall fabric.

He had called Brian Connelly to enlist his help, but it had taken some persuasion to get Brian to go along with him. Not that he was reluctant to help, but Brian knew that what David proposed verged on insanity. Reluctantly, he had agreed to fly David to a fixed point in Northern Arkansas, the point known only to David's Lowrance AirMap as "UNKNWN1."

"You're sure about this?" Brian Connelly asked, coming out of the side office of the large hangar.

"As sure as I'll ever be," David Michaels answered, hefting the backpack at his feet.

"What's that thing weigh?" Connelly asked.

"Fifty pounds, more or less."

"Come on, Rev. No way you can carry that thing for any length of time."

David smiled. "That's why I'm getting you to chop off at least two days worth of hiking by flying me in, provided, of course, that Piper Cub of yours can get off the ground with the two of us and the pack."

"Don't start on my Cub. You've got one, too, and you know I'll get it in the air. Shucks, as cold as it is, I could take off sideways on this runway."

"But can you land it in the middle of a snow-covered pasture?"

Brian Connelly feigned a hurt look, then joked, "If you can shoot pool on it, I can land the Cub."

David laughed to conceal his nervousness.

"What's so funny?" Janice Morgan asked as she slid the giant hangar door shut.

"What are you doing here?" David asked.

"I'm hurt. I'm checking on the patient. Don't forget, there are only a handful of us who know that the radio announcement was fake and that the Right Reverend David Michaels is not dead. Not yet anyway. But it won't take long for the truth to get out. Cindy is particularly upset about the whole thing."

David nodded. "I know. I'm going to have some explaining to do when I get back."

"You got that right, buddy," Brian Connelly chimed in. "I, for one, want to know what's going on."

"You will, Brian, I promise. Right now, the fewer people who know, the better."

"But you've only got, at best, twenty-four hours, maybe thirty-six before the truth gets out," Janice said. "That's not a lot of time."

"Let's hope it's enough," David added. "And to be sure of that, we need to get that Cub in the air right now."

"She's ready anytime," Brian said.

"You got everything you need?" Janice asked.

"Including the cellular phone." David pointed to the pack lying on the hangar floor.

Janice Morgan walked over to a pile of miscellaneous paper and packing material strewn on the floor next to David's backpack.

"What's all that?"

"Exactly what it looks like," answered David. "Junk. Paper. The packaging I discarded from the foods I'm carrying. No need to pack in packaging when you can help it."

"Clothing?" Janice asked.

"The three *Ws*," David answered, hefting his backpack.

"Three *Ws*?"

"Wicking, warmth, and wind," David said. "Clothing next to the body wicks away the moisture. Next layer traps body warmth. Top layer is breathable and windproof. Basic cold-weather clothing."

"Sounds like you know a lot about that sort of stuff," Brian Connelly said.

"Don't forget our reverend here is ex-military," Janice Morgan told Connelly.

David grinned, but there was no humor in the expression. "I know enough to stay alive, I hope. Let's get in the air, Brian."

"Toss the pack in the plane and get the hangar door. I'll push her out."

David did as he was told, tossing the pack into the Cub, then sliding the large hangar door open. A cold blast of air shot into the hangar like an express train.

Brian Connelly and Janice Morgan pushed the small plane from the hangar as David closed the door behind them. Janice stood by the plane while Brian climbed in, ran a quick prestart checklist, and started the Cub's Lycoming engine.

David, his voice obscured by the ticking over engine, mouthed a "thank you" to Janice and climbed into the plane. He pulled the Lowrance AirMap from his jacket pocket and switched the small device on. Over the cabin communication headset, David said, "Heading is two-eight-eight."

"Two-eight-eight," repeated Connelly. "Let's go flying."

Connelly taxied the Cub out to the end of the runway, did a quick run-up, and shoved the throttle to full power. The Cub raced down the runway, its tail coming up quickly and lifting into the air as Connelly gently pulled back on the stick.

"Not bad," David offered.

"I had to dump some fuel. Sixty pounds, to be exact."

"Ten gallons. What's that leave? Twenty-five?"

"Twenty-six. Three hours at 75 percent power," Connelly answered over the headset.

"That's going to cut it pretty thin, Brian," David said.

"Yeah, but don't forget, I'm going to dump about two hundred and seventy-five pounds up in the north woods somewhere. That'll extend my time aloft on the trip back. Provided we don't waste any fuel getting to this pasture of yours."

"We won't. The AirMap will lead us right to it."

Connelly banked the plane, then leveled out on a heading of two-eight-eight. "What's the AirMap show as our ETA?"

David checked the device. "One hour, ten minutes at this speed."

"Yeah, I think we're picking up a slight head wind, and having to stay low because of the cloud cover isn't going to help."

"You should have an hour and forty, fifty minutes of fuel to get back on."

"Less the weight and a tailwind to boot. No problem," Brian said, turning his attention to flying the light aircraft. Then another thought entered his mind. He wasn't sure he should mention it, but now it suddenly seemed particularly important. "Rev," Connelly said.

"Yeah, Brian?"

"I got something to tell you. About a man who came into the office the day before Dean crashed."

David Michaels concentrated on Connelly's explanation and description of the man the mechanic talked to the day before Dean's crash. David felt his teeth grind in anger at the unknown man. When Connelly was finished, David said nothing.

As they flew on, David thought about what he was doing, about the strange sense of déjà vu that enveloped him. There had been no snow on the ground then, but the last time he had been in the forest of northern Arkansas was outside the sprawling Arkansas Three and Four nuclear power plant near Clayton.

Then, he had been trying to find out what had happened to his brother, Jimmy. He had not been alone. FBI Special Agent Morton Powell had been with him, and he wished the agent were with him now. Powell had become a close friend during the ordeal, and David had kept in touch, even after Powell had been transferred to the Indianapolis office.

The drone of the Cub began to work its magic on David. He had always been fascinated by flying. That fascination had led him to Dean Barber and had propelled him to his private license in record time.

As they flew, his mind drifted to the one thing he did not need to think about at this time: Cindy Tolbert.

He had purposely not talked to Cindy before he left. She might have tried to convince him to cancel the excursion back to the secret airfield. Just the sound of her voice would have been incentive enough not to go, to have remained warm and comfortable and within easy reach of the woman he loved.

The urge to tell Brian to turn the plane around and return to Clayton was overwhelming, and David forced the thoughts of Cindy from his mind, focusing once again on the monotonous drone of the craft's engine.

He had left it to Janice Morgan to explain to Cindy. David held no illusions. He would face an angry woman when he returned, but he would cross that bridge when he came to it.

"Time?" Brian Connelly asked.

David checked the AirMap. "Nineteen minutes. Come to heading two-eight-two."

"Got it. Wind's blowing more out of the west than I thought," said Connelly, then he lapsed back into silence.

David wondered what he would find in the woods. In nineteen minutes, he would be back in the pasture where he had seen the two men carrying Armalites. Back where a pregnant girl had climbed into the belly of a now-destroyed Cessna and had flown to freedom and safety, risking death from hypothermia in the process. And somewhere, less than an hour from where he now sat, there was a valley. A valley with a secret.

"I show five minutes," Brian Connelly said.

David checked the AirMap again. "Four minutes."

"No need to begin a letdown. We're not high enough to worry about descent time. And I think I see your pasture."

David craned his neck to see out the Cub's windscreen. "That must be it. Nothing else around it for miles, and the AirMap is showing arrival."

"Let's put her on the ground, then," Connelly said, beginning his prelanding checklist.

The Cub nosed down as Connelly headed for the open pasture area. The flaps-down stalling speed of the Cub was thirty-seven knots. David knew Connelly would have to hold some additional speed heading into the wind. A sudden lull in such a head wind could cause the Cub to stall and crash into the pine forest below.

But Brian Connelly was an experienced pilot, and the Cub flew as if on a wire, the wheels touching down on the first third of the open area.

As the Cub came to a halt, Connelly said, "This was too smooth to be a pasture, but that's all I'm going to say about it until you get back."

David Michaels climbed out of the aircraft and winked at Connelly. He grabbed his pack and shouldered it. With that and a thumbs-up, David scrambled away from the airplane as Brian Connelly swung the plane around and headed for the end of the pasture where he had just touched down. In a matter of minutes, the Piper Super Cub was only a small yellow dot in the winter sky.

David Michaels watched the plane disappear. He had never, in all his life, felt as alone as he did now. David recognized another aspect to the loneliness, and the realization made him shiver. It was the feeling of malignant evil, the same demonic presence he had encountered more than a year ago in the streets of Little Rock.

Although he recognized the evil, this time it seemed different. *Why is that?* he wondered.

■   ■   ■

Cindy Tolbert came awake slowly. The primary sensation was one of struggling to rise to the surface from a particularly deep, dark, watery abyss. But there was a secondary sensation that accompanied the first. It was one of elation and joy at the realization she was still alive.

She struggled to open her eyes, but there was nothing but blackness. She blinked into the purple depths, knowing her eyes were open but unable to dispel the darkness. Her hands went to her face, to her eyes. Yes, they were open, but all was darkness.

With the movement, she realized she had a headache. Her head felt as if it had swollen to twice its normal size. Her eyes burned, all the more so in the blackness. A surge of nausea swept over her, adding to her misery.

Cindy reached out to explore the dark surroundings and suddenly she remembered.

The small wooded area right before James Michaels's house! The man! He *had* been there! He had asked her a question, then the stinging sensation in her arm, and she had passed out. It was all real, and she had been certain she would die. But she was not dead, not yet anyway. That thought jolted her into a higher state of consciousness. She was alive! That was something.

She tried to shrug off the nausea and the headache as best she could. Another perception crowded in. She was moving! Not her, but wherever she was. Where was that? She reached out; her hand contacted a rigid object. She traced the object with her hand, first in front of her, then overhead, and finally beneath her. She was in a box! A moving box!

She felt the gentle flow of air over her face. She reached out again, tracing the air current from her face to its source. A small vent located in the corner of the box supplied the air. Fresh air. Why fresh air? What made it necessary to supply the box with air?

The movement continued, becoming more pronounced as time passed. The sensation of speed now accompanied the gently rocking motion. She was in a car, the car moving at moderate speed. But where? Why?

Terror began to overwhelm her senses. Even the nausea and headache gave way to an impending feeling of doom.

And then the realization of what was happening hit her. She had been kidnapped, drugged, and placed in a box in a vehicle. The box was special, with its own vented air supply to keep her alive. Whoever had done this to her had planned it, prepared for it, and executed it with flawless timing, all to spirit her away—alive.

That meant she was needed alive, at least temporarily. That thought did nothing to lessen the terror still building within her.

The vehicle bounced, throwing Cindy to the top of the box. She was not injured, but for the first time she realized the box was padded. Someone had gone to a great deal of trouble and expense.

With her hands she continued to explore her dungeon. She felt the junctions where the walls, floor, and top connected, seeking any weakness in the box's construction, an opening. There were none. The box was well-built, seamless to her prying fingers. There was no way out.

Again the car jostled her within the box, but gently, as if it traveled over a poorly maintained asphalt roadway. A state road, perhaps, or a primary rural county road.

Time lost its meaning. Cindy tried to focus on the luminous dial of her watch, but the glow had long since dissipated. She must have been in the box for a long time.

The nausea returned, and Cindy's hand shot to her mouth to stem the feeling. She pulled her knees to her chest, her arms encircling her legs in a fetal position. As she moved her arms, she struck something attached to the short wall of the padded box. She reached out and felt it. A plastic bottle! She explored it more closely. It was attached to the wall by what felt like a plastic strap. She felt around the bottle and the holding strap. Her hand settled on a small bulge. She pulled at it, and the bottle came loose in her hand. She found the bottle's top and twisted it. A small "crack" told her the bottle had been sealed. She smelled the contents. Nothing. She stuck her finger into the liquid. Water! Her captor had provided her with water. It was then she realized how thirsty she really was. But how could she know it was really water? What if she drank and lapsed back into the darkness from which she had emerged only minutes earlier. Minutes? Or had it been hours? She had no way of knowing.

She held the bottle in her hands, her fingers exploring the rounded ridges of the container. She brought the bottle to her nose again. Still no smell. She tested the liquid again with her finger. Water. No doubt. She put the bottle to her lips and allowed a few drops to trickle down her throat. She would test it slowly, deliberately, drops at a time until she was certain the bottle did not contain anything but water.

Her hand sought the bottle cap, and she replaced the cap to preserve its contents. She would wait, what? Five minutes? Ten? How would she know? Time and space melded into one, and before she realized it, Cindy Tolbert closed her eyes and slept.

Her last conscious thought came in the form of a short prayer. *Please, Lord, just let it be over.*

At that very moment, the driver of the car felt a stab of pain shoot through him like an arrow from a crossbow. The instant of pain subsided, but he knew what had caused it, and his anger flared. This time, he thought, the ending would be different. And the girl in the trunk of his Mercedes would make the difference.

CHAPTER TWENTY-NINE

The pain was instantaneous and piercing, but only fleeting in duration. It was bearable, but it was a warning.

Damon peered ahead intently as he drove, his neck muscles taut, shoulders aching. It had been a long night, but a profitable one. The girl had suspected nothing until it was too late. By then he had plunged the needle into her arm, and she had quickly fallen into unconsciousness. It had been a simple act, a violation of earthly law, but that did not trouble Damon. For him, it had been a delight, a pleasure to be remembered and savored.

The road ahead was covered with snow and the weather threatened to produce more later in the day. Another arctic cold front was forecast for the region, with promises of temperatures in the low teens. Another huge low pressure system along the Louisiana coast was pumping moisture into the central United States as far north as southern Illinois and Indiana. The weather would not clear for days. That suited Damon's purposes.

After rendering the girl unconscious, Damon had placed her in the car. Something had told him it would be better to wait until morning before heading back for Memphis, and he had waited. There had been no witnesses when he'd loaded her into the box in the trunk of the Mercedes in the early morning hours. He had driven out of Clayton using the less-traveled roads and bypassing the interstate. The back roads would be safer, less prone to detection.

The entire operation would have been easier had he used his powers. Damon did not like the restrictions of this physical domain, but for the time being he had to accept them.

A noise issued from the small radio on the seat beside him. A muffled, coughing sound that Damon recognized immediately. The girl had regained consciousness.

He smiled. It was evident that she was frightened, and although her feelings were of no real consequence to him, he took delight in his ability to instill fear and terror in the unsuspecting. He could detect the sounds of pending sickness, caused, he was sure, by the chemical he had injected. The thought gave him an inordinate amount of pleasure, until the girl had mouthed the obscene prayer, and the pain had shot through him like an assassin's bullet.

But the prayer had not lasted long. The girl had found the water bottle and had tested its contents. Damon had smiled at that too. It would taste like ordinary water, and after an entire night without liquid, the girl would probably drink greedily. The chemical in the water would then render her unconscious again.

If she found the water, she would also recognize the small vent which provided fresh air for her, but he was confident that she would not find the small microphone embedded in the wall of the box.

He listened to her movements for a while, heard the seal on the water bottle crack open, and grinned. It had taken longer than he'd anticipated, but eventually quiet returned to the box, the girl lapsing into unconsciousness again.

Damon checked the time. He had been on the road for two hours. Under normal circumstances, the trip from Clayton to Memphis would take no more than four hours, but the back roads were slick and snow-covered, and the only road-clearing efforts he had seen were a few feeble attempts by an occasional highway department dump truck to scatter sand and salt on the roadway.

He had seen few vehicles. Traveling was too dangerous, and the threatening sky precluded even the most daring from venturing outside. *Perfect conditions,* he reflected.

At the reduced speed he was now traveling, the trip would take another four or five hours. But time was irrelevant. Damon laughed at the thought. *Time?* He wondered what the world would say if they knew that time *really* did not exist. That it was an invented medium, spoken into existence by the enemy. Time was nothing more than a framework upon which hung the thoughts and dreams and disappointment of pathetic mortals. Mortals whom Damon hated.

One mortal in particular—U.S. Navy Commander (Ret) David Michaels, the military chaplain turned country preacher—now threatened to undo years, *eons,* of Damon's work.

Last year had been the first direct confrontation with the man, and it had not been pleasant. Damon had sent another to do battle, confident his surrogate would accomplish the task. But he had underestimated the preacher and the surrogate had been defeated in the streets of Little Rock, Arkansas. It was not the surrogate's defeat that bothered Damon. The underling had been rewarded for his failure, relegated to the darkest reaches of agony until Damon decided penance had been done. No, what bothered Damon was the strength of character and the deeper spiritual faith Michaels had acquired during the battle. Now defeat would be even more difficult, more elusive. But it was a battle which must be joined nonetheless.

The battle.

This time it would be different. There would be no surrogate, no stand-in, no marginally effective semi-demon waging ineffectual conflict. This time he, Damon, sublord of the netherworld, would be the soldier and the victor. He had worked long and hard for this, from the beginning of time, from the birth of those he despised and hated—the mortals of earth.

Success, this success, was his for the taking. The strategy had been envisioned earlier in the century, when the depravities and degradations of men aided in their own destruction. But the destruction had not been complete. Far from it. There had been no total capitulation by those he hated, but he had planted the seed which yet grew and blossomed. It had been his voice heard in those days, his suggestions to initiate what the mortals now under his control so aptly called the Lazarus Project.

Damon had laughed at the name—Lazarus. The man the Son had raised from the dead almost two thousand years ago. How appropriate to turn one of the greatest miracles of all time into a global strategy for the downfall of the very people whom the Son loved.

A sound penetrated Damon's thoughts, and he turned his attention to the small radio next to him. The girl had stirred, briefly, but now there was nothing.

It was the girl, Damon knew, who would be the leverage he needed to do battle with David Michaels. Not her as such, but just the thought of her, her perceived helplessness and the mortal's penchant for mercy. It would be all he needed.

Damon rubbed his shoulders. How he hated taking on the form of these despised humans. The frailty of their bodies was almost too much to bear, but it was necessary if he wanted to engage David Michaels. He had to take on the same form as his mortal enemy.

But there was an upside to it all. That was what he saw when he looked in the mirror. His face was what mortals termed "ruggedly handsome." His long hair was thick above intelligent brown eyes. The jaw was angular, but not so square as to put off the women. His muscular build was evident, even when he wore the expensive clothes he was partial to. In all, he was what most people thought of as sexy.

Sexy? He laughed at the thought as he slowed the Mercedes for an icy corner. It struck him as absurd that most humans thought of his kind as ugly, misshapen, deformed creatures, capable only of existence in the deepest regions of darkness. That simple belief accounted for more souls in the lower regions than almost any other strategy. Humans expected sin to be hideous, repulsive in the extreme. But that was not the case. Sin could be, and was, attractive, enchanting, even captivating, at least on the surface. It was not until one got to the root causes of sin that the realization of its depravity came to light, and when exposed to the light, sin could be seen for what it was. But few people wanted that exposure. And few today understood the degradation of sin. Most spoke of self-gratification, individual rights, and the belief that God existed to grant whatever wish a true believer requested. Few mentioned hell, the lower reaches, the place of darkness and agony. Fewer still believed in its existence, and that was just fine.

Earlier, in mid-decade, the "God is dead" movement had begun, but had quickly been extinguished. Now the "hell no longer exists" movement had caught on. The idea that any road to God was the right road was preached from pulpits. Ecumenicalism had become the latest catchphrase embraced by the masses.

But men like David Michaels could change that. The preacher knew the truth, and he preached it to whomever would listen. And his audience was growing. The fiasco in the streets of Little Rock last year had brought Michaels to the attention of the entire state. His messages were heard on the radio every Sunday, and several of the surrounding stations had picked up the broadcast. Now there was talk of his going national with his message of truth. That could not be allowed. It was time for the orchestrated downfall of the country preacher. Damon had done it before, to others, and he could do it again.

The Mercedes skidded momentarily, snatching Damon from his thoughts. He corrected, slowed the car, and continued. There was no sound from the box in the trunk. Cindy Tolbert was still unconscious.

Damon checked the time. Three hours, more or less, to Memphis. When he got there, he would talk with Lazarus, and the final conflict would begin. David Michaels, and his message, would die. It might mean the end of the project, but that was all right. The project, as well as the men of *Die Gruppe,* had served their purpose.

■ ■ ■

Lazarus stared into the roaring flames of the fireplace. He still could not understand what was happening. The more wood he threw on the fire, the colder the room got. Nothing seemed to be able to warm even the area nearest the blaze.

With shaking hands, he extracted a cigarette from a half-empty package and lit it. Holding the cigarette in the European style, he sucked deeply on it, letting the nicotine work its magic on his brain.

It was coming to culmination, he knew. The goal, his purpose in life, was close to fulfillment.

He had always known the purpose of his life. He had known early on that he was one of the enlightened ones, one of the seers. That purpose had been abridged more than fifty years ago—shortened, modified. But he had seen the change coming and had delayed the inevitable. It had been his foresight that had sent the men, the doctors, out of Germany to the farthest reaches of the earth. It had been his initiative that had formed *Die Gruppe.* It had been his zeal, his power, his ingenuity that had propelled the growth and influence of *Die Gruppe.* And it was his ability to see into the future that would continue to give him the advantage over others less gifted.

The young fools, the new order that nominally controlled *Die Gruppe,* had no concept of his power, his ability. When he dropped to his knees and bowed his head in his prayer room, the answers would come. The voice would return. Solutions were no farther away than his own subjection to a greater power. A power represented by the small voice that came to him at those quiet times.

It was the voice which had warned him of his death sentence ordered by the young men of *Die Gruppe*. And, he remembered, by his oldest friend in the world, Henry Phelps.

Lazarus snickered at their lack of imagination. Had they seriously thought that he, the man behind the project, had not recognized the signs of impending overthrow? Had they thought the tug of avarice and greed was unrecognizable to him?

Already he was in the process of retaining the true power, which he had been given so many years ago. While the men of *Die Gruppe* fumbled and floundered for answers, he had already put in motion the endgame. At this very moment, Damon, his secret weapon, was on his way to Memphis with the girl.

Damon had already sent two of his own men to the house in the valley. In a few days, there would be no house, no evidence of the procedures that had once been carried on there. No clues as to the nature of its purpose. Nothing to reveal the genius of the project. And with the absolute destruction of that place, the project would continue unabated at other locations. Success was near. Even now, placements were increasing. The strategy had worked, *was working*. It was becoming easier to find men susceptible to the project. Men and women of wealth and status whose primary focus was on maintaining their wealth and status at all cost.

Lazarus shivered. Perhaps a snifter of brandy would suppress the chill. Brandy and a few more logs on the fire. He would smoke one more cigarette, finish his drink, and go into his prayer room. In the midst of success, he could feel the cloud of doubt creeping over him. He needed reassurance, and he knew he would get it from the one who inhabited the tiny room.

■   ■   ■

"It'll cost you more'n 'at," Billy Bob Campbell told Jason Swann.

The two men were faced off in Swann's downstairs office in the white-columned house. Billy Bob had dropped Cole Branscum off by his battered house trailer before proceeding to Swann's office. He'd told Cole to get his gear together while he collected the money from Swann. What he hadn't told Cole was that as soon as he had collected the money, he was going to tip off Sheriff Wade Larsen and let Cole try to explain the murders over in Clayton County. He had no doubt that Cole would try to implicate him, but by then he planned to be several hundred miles west of Benning County.

But the culmination of his plan depended on collecting a tidy sum from Jason Swann, and Swann was balking at the figure Billy Bob had presented.

"That's the agreed-to amount. Now take it and get out," Swann ordered loudly.

Billy Bob sat back in the chair which fronted Swann's desk. "I don't think so, Swann. You got enough money stashed around this joint for both of us to retire, and I want my share. And I don't think you want me to start talkin' to the wrong people."

"That sounds like a threat," Swann said, his eyes squinting at the larger man.

"Pretty good. That's exactly what it is. So what're you gonna do about it?"

"You start talking to the authorities, and you and Cole are going to get that last needle in your arm. Don't forget Arkansas still has the death penalty."

"You're probably right about that, but I wasn't really thinkin' 'bout talkin' to the authorities. I was thinkin' more in the line of them folks in Memphis."

Jason Swann felt the color drain from his face; his breath caught in his throat; and despite the sudden chill in the room, small beads of sweat appeared on his forehead.

"I see you get the drift," Billy Bob smiled. "Now let's talk a little more about how much them jobs was worth."

Jason Swann fell back into his chair. He would have to comply for the time being, but his mind was again functioning, seeking a way out of the current predicament. It would mean having to do away with Billy Bob Campbell and Cole Branscum, but that could not be avoided. What he needed was time.

"Come back tomorrow morning. I'll have the money ready," Swann lied. "But once I get you what you want, you're going to get out of Arkansas. Somewhere where no one will find you and Cole. Is that understood?"

Billy Bob wrestled his body from the chair where he sat and smiled down at Jason Swann. "Of course, boss. You know me. Always willing to cooperate," Billy Bob said, turning to leave. "By the way, you did hear the news about the preacher gettin' killed in the huntin' accident?"

Swann nodded. "I heard it," he answered morosely.

"Yeah," Billy Bob slurred. "I thought you might'a heard. Till the morning, Swann. And don't try to stiff me and Cole. Got it?"

Swann nodded to the retreating back of Billy Bob, thinking, *You just made your last mistake, big man.* Swann picked up the phone, dialed, and waited for an answer. *By this time tomorrow, Billy Bob, my man, you will either be in jail or dead. And I don't really care which.*

■   ■   ■

Wade Larsen gulped down four aspirin and chased them with a slug of lukewarm water. He picked up the phone and punched the lighted button. He knew who it was, and he suspected what the man wanted. But he had made his own decision, which, when it came to light, would shock not only the man on the phone but other, more powerful men across the Mississippi River. It had not been an easy decision, but he was convinced it was the right one. Right or not, it was made, and he would live or die with it.

"Yeah, what is it?" Larsen said into the phone and then listened as Jason Swann droned on with his demands. As he listened, he felt as if a ton of dead weight were being lifted from his shoulders. The sound of Swann's voice validated his decision.

Wade Larsen waited until Swann had hung up, then reached over and thumbed the small button of the miniature tape recorder he had activated. He extracted the tiny tape cassette and locked it in his desk drawer; then he picked up the phone and dialed. It was time to start setting things right.

CHAPTER THIRTY

It was colder than David Michaels had first thought. The winter storm plaguing Arkansas had intensified in the last hours, making David glad he had taken the necessary precautions.

David stood in the northern Ozark pasture, alone in the midst of an unforgiving whiteness that seemed to close in on him from all sides. It was the solitude, he knew, that made him think of Cindy Tolbert. The thought of her short auburn hair, her gentle face, and her vivacious green eyes sparkling with laughter filled him with wonder. How could such a woman actually profess love for him? But she did. She had made that abundantly clear. The awareness of his feelings for her and the reassurance that his love was returned warmed his heart, if not his fingers and toes.

With that warmth surging through him, David headed for the far side of the pasture. He wanted to examine the Variable Approach Slope Indicator and the battery pack he and Dean Barber had discovered earlier.

The freshly fallen snow covered the instrument, but only barely. When he bent to examine the device more closely, David realized that only the instrument case was covered. The tricolored lens was free of snow, which indicated that someone had been in the pasture recently. A wariness settled over him. He would have to be cautious. This was not a military training exercise where you could make a mistake and learn from it. This was as real as the rice paddies of Vietnam or the barren wastelands of Desert Storm.

The question now was, which way from here?

David shrugged out of his pack and retrieved a plastic-coated topographical map he'd picked up from the local office of the Arkansas Land Management Services. A quick glance at the elevation lines on the map showed he was not in the most hospitable territory in northern Arkansas.

David examined the map for a moment. Using the AirMap, he cross-referenced the tiny computer map with the topographical map and pinpointed his location with ease. His map-reading skills were rusty, but they were more than adequate to verify his location.

The surrounding topography resembled much of the Ozark range with which David was familiar. Rounded, rolling hills covered in leafless hardwoods and blanched evergreens stretched out in every direction, rolling to the horizon in unbroken mounds. The forest floor was littered with decaying leaves showing through thin patches of icy snow. Snowdrifts mounded against every exposed obstacle. The sky and land seemed to meet at each mountaintop, neither claiming ownership nor relinquishing title to the other. It was a world wrapped in shades of gray, much like most of life, David thought. He thought once again of Cindy, and the grayness was replaced by a warmth that seemed to infuse every fiber of his being.

Nothing in sight offered any clue as to which way he should go. Neither he nor Dean Barber had seen the girl climb into the belly of the

Cessna, but they had seen the two men with the Armalite rifles standing on the far side of the clearing. That would be his initial direction. Which way had that been? David scanned the surroundings, orienting himself. The Cessna had ended up just to his right. That meant the two men had been . . . where? Just to the left of that tiny knoll. That would be his starting point.

David checked the map once again, noting the ground swells and valleys he would have to negotiate in that direction. Several valleys could possibly be the right one. He would have to check them all. The enormity of his task was becoming clear. It would take divine intervention to find the valley.

A cold wind forced its way between David's parka hood and the wool cap he wore. Cold needles stung his face, but that was all. He'd dressed for the weather; the multiple layers of clothing would do their job. His body would be warm. But his spirit suddenly registered a cold that seemed to come, not from the surrounding countryside, but from some other source, a source David recognized instantly: a deepening cloud of depravity.

David closed his eyes and bowed his head in response to the feeling. He prayed, his lips moving in the cold air, his petition forged upward and through the gray cloud mass above him, slicing the air like a bolt of lightning. He felt better.

David lifted the backpack, tugged the shoulder straps tight, fastened the waist belt, and adjusted it to transfer more of the weight onto his legs. He began to climb the gentle slope in front of him.

The weather seemed to grow bleaker as he went, but it was the ever-increasing feeling of spiritual heaviness that weighed David down. He found it difficult to ward off such feelings. The depression lingered longer than it should. It took real effort to work through such feelings.

Then in a flash he realized what was happening. He *was* headed in the right direction. The morbid atmosphere was proof enough of that. The closer he came to the hidden valley, the heavier and more despondent he felt. He was on the right trail, and his direction finder was no longer the Lowrance AirMap or the plastic-coated topographical map but the believer's heart within his chest.

David trudged up the first hill and down the back side. The snow was not as deep in the forest as it had been out in the pasture, but the going was nonetheless slow. Ice-coated tree roots made traveling slow and arduous. A single slip could easily break an ankle or even a leg. He was glad Janice Morgan had insisted on his packing the small cellular telephone. At the thought of the phone, he reached into the side pocket of his pack and extracted the tiny instrument. He powered up the phone and checked the signal indicator on the tiny screen. The signal was almost at the maximum. At least he had communications capabilities. He switched off the phone and replaced it.

Removing his right glove, David reached into his parka pocket and extracted a piece of hard candy. Both pockets were full of the sweet stuff. He popped the confection into his mouth and sucked on it as he moved through the trees. Most people paid little attention to their bodies in winter, but it was essential to recognize the danger signs that came with frigid weather. Hard candy was a way to keep the physiological fires stoked, and it was imperative to ward off even the slightest signs of hypothermia. Once begun, the effects were not easily reversed, especially in the Ozark woods in the dead of winter.

As he moved deeper into the timber, David thought of the times he and Jimmy had trudged through similar terrain, just outside Clayton. Those had been good times, fun times.

David looked around, taking in the rugged countryside, recognizing the intense beauty an Ozark winter painted over the surrounding landscape. It was like a watercolor painted in varying hues of blues and grays, interrupted by the dark siennas and burnt umbers of the timber. Sounds seemed to creep along the forest floor from great distances. It was an odd sensation, the intense quiet punctuated by a gentle drift of subdued reverberation.

As David's PAC boots crunched into the frozen snow-covered ground, his thoughts strayed to a forest almost thirty years ago, not more than three hours from where he now stood.

It had been a family day outing, or as much of one as he could remember. The three men of the Michaels family, his father, brother, and himself. The next-door neighbors, the Wallingfords, had been along. The small conclave had driven up into the northern Ozarks, near a small river that was scheduled to be dammed in a few years. David's father had gone there as a boy, and he wanted to see it once more before the engineers brought in the heavy equipment and destroyed the natural beauty of the meandering stream.

The Wallingfords had two sons about the same age as David and Jimmy. They had decided to play "war" on that day, a combination of hide-and-seek and "ambush," using fallen pine cones.

David and Jimmy had been the first team to be pursued, and David remembered vividly the trail they had taken out of the camp area. They had chosen a small bottleneck in the trail as their ambush site, and there they waited. They had waited until it was almost dark, but the Wallingford boys never showed up. David took Jimmy's hand and started back for camp. But along the way, he took the wrong fork in the trail, and darkness overtook them before they reached the warmth and safety of their father's arms. They had spent several hours wandering around in the half-light of dusk before they had been found. David had put up a brave front, mostly for his brother's sake, but he had been frightened. He had promised himself then and there he would never again allow the powers of nature to intimidate him in such a manner, and he never had.

Until now.

The sharp crunch of ice beneath his boots brought him back to reality. He stopped for a moment, checked his direction with a small compass, then scanned the trees in the distance.

Had it been his boot's contact with the icy surface of the forest floor that had brought him out of his reverie? Or had he heard another sound, a sound that soared on the cold air of the winter forest? A foreign sound, an alien sound. A sound made not by the creatures of the woods or the gently swaying trees of the forest. A distinctly man-made sound.

David stood still, barely breathing; he removed his parka hood and wool cap and listened intently for the unfamiliar, the unusual. There was nothing. Had he imagined it? Had it been part of his daydreaming?

The sun was getting lower behind the thick bank of gray clouds. The temperature had dropped in the past hour, and David knew there would be more snow tonight. He would have to choose his campsite carefully, staying out of the depressions and valleys where the cold air sank. A gently sloping hillside with an eastern exposure would keep him out of the coldest air and offer protection against the wind, which was beginning to pick up out of the west.

David found himself looking forward to unpacking his tiny stove and preparing some hot tea to warm him from the inside. Armed with a steaming cup of tea, he could prepare a meal and begin the ritual of settling in for the night.

A change into dry, warm clothes would be welcome too.

The emphasis went from searching for the hidden valley to locating an appropriate campsite.

David slipped momentarily, regained his balance, and started down the small slope in front of him. Then he heard it!

This time it was clear, the heavy winter air transmitting the sound like an expensive amplifier—clear and distinct. It was the sound of another person—and that person was in trouble.

■   ■   ■

The green Mercedes crept along the partially cleared streets of the expensive Memphis suburb. Snow machines and city crews were working at a feverish pace to clear the upscale neighborhood of the worrisome white stuff. Memphis Light, Gas, and Water vehicles worked on power lines downed in the storm. It had begun to snow again, and the battle to clear the streets was becoming futile.

Damon smiled as he passed the dump trucks filled with sand and salt, heavy snow-clearing blades attached to the fronts. He suspected other, less-affluent districts were having to accept the snow as a fluke of Mother Nature and live with it.

Damon's objective came into view down the street and to the right. The house was not massive, but it was nonetheless impressive, Damon had to admit.

Set back from the street a good hundred yards, the house was constructed of carefully quarried stone, the pieces fitted together with the precision of one of Switzerland's finest watchmakers. Over the years, the stone had darkened and molted, transforming the character of the house slowly, but inexorably, to match that of its present owner.

A curving drive with both east and west entrances terminated in a white gravel parking area directly in front of the main door. The landscaping was abundant but over-planted in a manner common to earlier years. The trees that filled the yard had been left to their own volition and had nearly obscured the house from the street. The trim was what most of the neighbors thought of as Bavarian, with geometrical white borders bright against the darkened stone.

Damon carefully turned the Mercedes into the west entrance and crept along the drive. Unlike the public streets, the approach to the house was covered by several inches of undisturbed snow.

The radio at his side crackled, and he turned his attention to it. The woman was awake. Perfect, he thought. It was time for her to discover her true destiny. A destiny which would end within the great stone house.

Damon braked and the car slid gently to a halt. He sat for a moment, ignoring all distractions. The final victory was within reach. He had planned for it, ached for it, and yes, even prayed for it. Prayer was a weapon in his arsenal, though the one he prayed to was the god of the netherworld.

The main door opened, drawing Damon's attention away from his thoughts. Lazarus stood in the doorway.

Damon felt an immediate loathing for the man, but he could discard the emotions for now. He still needed Lazarus, needed his evil. But once the coming battle was over, he would kill the old man, and he would enjoy doing it.

■   ■   ■

Like a window whose room-darkening shade had been suddenly and violently snapped open, Gaby Ibarra awoke. She looked around the room, trying to remember exactly what had happened. Months melted into seconds; memories flooded in.

The plane. The forest. The valley!

El valle!

It all came flooding back to her in an instant, the horror, the terror, and her absolute abhorrence of what went on in the valley. Tears welled up in her dark eyes as she remembered those whom she had left behind. They were her friends, especially Tía. What was happening to her? What had the evil in the valley done to her?

There was no other way to describe it. A corrupt darkness enveloped the valley. A choking atmosphere so heinous as to defy description.

Gaby looked around the room. Bright colors surrounded her, from the multicolored pastel walls to the brightly colored bedspread and broadly striped chair by her bed. There was a feeling of peace and comfort in the room. A feeling she had not experienced in months. A feeling of safety.

Gaby closed her eyes and let the tranquility of the room sweep over her. As she slipped into a therapeutic sleep, she mouthed a simple prayer for the safety of the other young girls still in the valley. Before she fell asleep again, a feeling of warmth and contentment infused her soul, and Gaby Ibarra knew that God was now in the process of answering her simple prayer.

■   ■   ■

The top of the enclosure flew open, and Cindy blinked at the sudden whiteness. Standing over her was the largest, most handsome man she had ever seen in her life. She had not imagined it back in Clayton. His hair, dark but streaked with lighter shades, flowed to his shoulders. His blue eyes were too pure, icy. His features were aristocratic, angular, emphasizing a jawline straight off the cover of a pulp-fiction novel. It was hard to estimate his height, but six foot six would not be far wrong. Even with the heavy coat he wore, Cindy recognized the bulk of hardened muscle beneath the fabric.

With an ease born of massive power, the man reached down and pulled Cindy from the hidden box and set her on her feet. She looked up at the massive stone facade of the house and shuddered, unable to move. She wanted to see David, to feel his arms around her, his strength and reassurance. Then the huge man plunged another needle into her arm and the whiteness faded to black in a matter of seconds.

■   ■   ■

Lazarus watched from an upstairs window as Damon carried the woman into the house. He should have rejoiced, but a nagging in the back of his mind told him he was no longer in control of his own destiny. He had officially turned over the reins of *Die Gruppe* to the new generation. That had been a mistake, he realized. He had called on Damon to resurrect his position of dominance. But something was terribly wrong. It seemed as if Damon himself had seized control of current events.

Lazarus pulled a package of cigarettes from his pocket and placed one in his mouth. He noticed a pronounced shaking as he tried to touch the tip of the match flame to the end of the cigarette. It was not a good sign.

Lazarus inhaled the smoke, coughed once, then headed for his prayer room. He needed to talk to his master. Something was not right.

■   ■   ■

At the same time Cindy Tolbert was being carried up the stairs of the Memphis house, Tom Frazier sat in his White House office and pondered his latest phone conversation with Janice Morgan.

It was unimaginable, *inconceivable.* "It" was the involvement of David Michaels in another situation so similar to one that had occurred a little more than a year ago, when Tom Frazier had been the sheriff and Janice Morgan had been his senior deputy.

Frazier reached for the phone on his desk and dialed. He needed to know he was on the correct course, that his actions would not result in the one thing he had managed to avoid a year ago—the death of David Michaels.

CHAPTER THIRTY-ONE

David Michaels stood his ground for a moment, concentrating on the direction of the sound. He focused not so much on the words but on the tenor. One man, almost certainly alone, and he did not sound like someone who was familiar with the forest, especially the forest in winter. David quickly ruled out the men who maintained the VASI equipment at the landing strip and the two men he'd seen with the rifles. This was someone else.

The sound was erratic, random snatches of words spoken in a panic, discordant voice pleading for rescue or for a quick end, whichever was the least painful.

David moved quietly but steadily toward the sound. He would be no good to anyone should he slip on an exposed tree root or rush headlong into overhanging branches, either of which could blow his cover and render him incapable of ministering to the hapless individual.

Ministering. Strange that he would think in those terms at this moment, but it was the correct perspective, he knew. *Ministry* was what he did. Not only to those in need but also to those with whom he would rather not associate. The dregs of humanity. The flotsam and jetsam that always seemed to rise to the top, never really very far away from his comfort zone, his haven.

David stepped over a fallen fence rail covered with snow. Had it been summer, he might have found a copperhead, a rattler, or a cottonmouth moccasin enjoying the cool shade along the fence row, waiting patiently for the unwary to set foot in its domain. Not unlike sin, David thought. But not today, not in the snow. Cold was not the domain of snakes, but, he corrected his metaphorical thinking, cold could spawn sin as easily as a summer day.

The sound was closer now but weaker and somehow more insistent in its frailty. David stopped to take another bearing on the sound. The winter forest could be tricky. He listened to the now muffled petitions floating through the unforgiving chill of the air. There was not much time.

David checked his bearings on the topo map and continued quickly, but cautiously, through the white woodland, his full attention focused on the ever-diminishing sounds. Based on the map, he expected to encounter a sharp drop-off just to the west of his present position. The next time he stopped to orient himself, he was struck by the eerie silence that now pervaded the forest. The noises had ceased.

Alarmed, David struggled through the pine and hardwood trees, throwing caution out the window, stumbling and slipping in the direction of where he had last heard the sound.

A feeling of overwhelming helplessness swept over him in a rush of raw emotion. It was the same feeling he had after explaining the basics of God's good news to an unbeliever and then watching that person walk away.

David quickened his pace. He was now slipping and sliding, forced to his knees as his boots skidded across hidden obstacles in his path.

He was only marginally aware of the cold and wet seeping into his body from his now damp outer shell.

He mouthed a silent prayer as he ran, entreating a benevolent God to give him time to reach whoever might be in trouble.

Suddenly the forest opened up onto a rocky crest overlooking the valley floor below. It was brighter here, because the snow had covered the clearing like a quilt. The stark whiteness seemed to provide its own light, in contrast to the shadowy gloom of the forest.

David stopped in his tracks and scanned the area. It was no more than twenty feet from side to side, a small, elliptical clearing, and the snow was undisturbed. Almost.

David now saw what he'd failed to notice in his cursory examination. *Footprints!*

David quickly shrugged out of his heavy pack and gingerly moved to the edge of the outcropping. The footprints led up to the edge before terminating in a deeper, wider indentation in the snow. A trough formed by what? A body slipping over the precipice? It fit.

David rushed back to his pack and extracted a hundred-foot climbing rope. He doubled the rope, looping it to a sturdy, skeletal oak, and hurried back to the edge, rope in hand. There was no time to fashion a climbing seat for himself. He had to get a look over the edge of the drop.

David quickly brought the rope around his left side, around his back and between his legs, forming a makeshift harness that would allow him to rappel down the rock face. He stepped backward onto the rim of the stone, carefully working his boots into the side of the cliff and hoping he would not slip into the yawning abyss below.

David craned his neck over his right shoulder, trying to catch a glimpse of whoever might be below. He saw no one. He worked his way downward, careful not to kick loose any rocks that might careen into the ravine.

Twenty feet down the rocky knob, another outcropping of rock extended out into the valley. To traverse this, David knew he would have to swing free and drop.

He took a deep breath, realizing for the first time that his heart was hammering in his ears and his pulse was racing beyond all reason. He'd not considered the consequences of his actions until this very moment. What happened if he were injured, if he were somehow disabled? Who would save him?

A portion of Isaiah 59:1 flitted through his mind. *The Lord's hand is not shortened, that it cannot save.* "I guess my faith works here, or it doesn't work at all," David said out loud, and he adjusted his grip on the rope.

With renewed confidence, David stepped from the edge, slowly feeding the rope through and around his body as he dropped into the open space. Just as he came even with the outermost section of the promontory, he saw a man wedged tightly in a small rift on the rock face. The man's face was almost as white as the surrounding snow. David could not tell whether the man was conscious, but something about the man's posture told David he was still alive.

David worked his way toward the man, being careful not to loosen any rocks. In seconds, he was within arm's length. The man's eyes were still tightly closed, and David had purposely not called out to the man for fear of creating an even graver situation.

Now, within feet of the man, David spoke softly, evenly.

"Come on. Wake up," he said.

The man's eyes flew open in an instant. Bloodshot, rabid eyes stared back at David Michaels, so crazed that David felt a sharp intake of cold air knife into the deepest reaches of his lungs.

As suddenly as the man's eyes had opened, they closed again, and he spoke slowly and weakly, "Thank God." A prayer had been answered, and this man clinging to the cold, unforgiving rock knew it.

"Let's get you down," David said easily, knowing the task was easier said than done.

The man did not move, did not reopen his eyes. He only nodded, almost imperceptibly.

David quickly reviewed the situation. He could tell that he did not have enough rope to reach the valley floor below, and he knew he could not haul this man up the face of the cliff.

For a brief moment, he wished for his brother. Jimmy had been the climber, the athlete. The maneuvers necessary to save this man would have come as second nature to Jimmy Michaels. David blinked away the tears that came suddenly and unexpectedly to his eyes and refocused his thoughts on the situation at hand.

He quickly recognized that there was really only one option; the two men must work their way down. He scanned the surrounding fissures and outcroppings, looking for an anchor point. Just to his right he saw it! A deep score in the rock, almost four inches deep at one point. It was their only hope.

David gingerly traversed the rock face, positioning himself just below the small fissure. This was it! From his belt pouch, David pulled out his SwissGear multitool, the closest thing to a weapon he had at hand, and began to pry loose a large rock. When the rock came loose after much chipping, prying, and scraping, David wedged it into the fissure. He found two narrow footholds just beneath him, and positioned his feet on them.

"Lord," he prayed, "let this hold me." With his feet in position, he tested the support, found it adequate, and pulled the doubled rope from around his body. Then he dropped one strand of the rope, leaving him holding only a single strand. He began to pull ever so gently. The rope pulled away from the tree around which David had looped it, coming free without a problem and dropping over the protruding cliff. With the rope now dangling below him, David fed the one end up and through the now closed fissure, much like threading a needle. The rock he had wedged into the fissure functioned perfectly, holding the rope as David fed it through. In minutes, the doubled rope hung below him and he could see where it reached the valley floor.

"You still with me?" David asked the almost frozen man.

Again an almost imperceptible nod acknowledged the question.

"This rope won't hold both our dead weights. We are going to have to use it as a support only. I will go first, and then you will have to move over and take it. We can work our way down this rock, but you will have to help. Can you do that?"

"I'll try," the man said weakly, without emotion.

"Good. Now move over and take the rope after I move down about five feet." David moved down, then motioned for the man to follow. At first, he was not certain the man could do it. But finally the stranger moved, grasping the rope with stiff hands. David moved downward, using the rock outcroppings to support his weight as best he could, not wanting to test the holding power of the wedged rock to its maximum.

Both men moved in cadence, slowly traversing the rock, moving ever closer to the valley floor and safety.

It seemed like an eternity before David felt the ground beneath his feet, but he made it. The man above him finally stepped onto solid ground seconds later.

The man turned to David, a smile on his blanched face. "Thank you," he said, before collapsing to the ground.

David quickly positioned the man on his back. He was breathing effortlessly, leading David to conclude that the stranger had fainted from sheer terror. As David tended to the man, making him as comfortable as possible, he realized that he recognized him. His face, despite the cold-induced whiteness, was familiar. Where had he seen him before? Then it struck him.

What in the world, David Michaels wondered, *is Donald Fenwick, CEO of the nation's largest retailer, doing in the Ozark wilderness in the middle of winter?*

■   ■   ■

It was their first time in this part of the country, and while the two men were uncomfortable with the alien surroundings, they were completely at ease with their assignment. Damon's instructions were always explicit and he always paid them well.

"Hick town," said the driver of the expensive sports utility vehicle.

The second man nodded as they swung through the county seat town of Benning, Arkansas.

"The road out to that valley is supposed to be on the other side of town. Shouldn't be too hard to find. Place ain't big enough to hide much," the driver continued.

Again the second man only nodded, but this time he pulled a map from the door pocket at his knee and unfolded it on his lap. Without a word he examined the colored lines on the map, grunted an affirmation that they were headed in the right direction, and returned the map to its place.

"This gonna be the biggest score yet," the talker said. "Ol' Damon's gonna have to dig deep in his wallet for this one. Yeah, boy. This is gonna be some fun."

The silent partner glanced at the driver. He gave no indication that he had heard what the man had said. Sometimes, he thought to himself, his driving partner was a little too exuberant.

He turned his thoughts to the man called Damon. *Man? Perhaps calling him a man is not even correct,* he mused. Not that Damon did not have the appearance of a human. Quite the contrary. Damon might well be the most well-developed human on the face of the earth. He had a handsome, athletic build, with a countenance that rivaled the most popular movie heroes. But there was something just slightly too perfect, too transcendent about Damon.

The scenery changed as the car passed out of Benning and into the countryside, and the quiet man turned his attention back to the upcoming job. He never enjoyed these reflections about his employer. Too much introspection was bad for business. Damon paid well and on time, and that was all that mattered.

"Turn's coming up," the driver announced.

The quiet partner glanced at the map, verifying the turn. He gave no outward indication that the driver was correct, but had he disagreed, he would have said so, and the driver knew it.

The utility vehicle slowed and turned onto the snow-coated country road that led into the deeper reaches of the Ozark Mountains. In less than an hour, the duo would swing into action, and another problem would be eliminated, another paycheck earned.

■   ■   ■

Exactly twenty-nine and a half miles from the turnoff taken by the two men in the sports utility vehicle, Jason Swann was in conference with Billy Bob Campbell.

"Those are unreasonable demands," Swann repeated for at least the fifth time in two minutes.

Billy Bob sat in the overstuffed chair in the far corner of Swann's office, his feet propped on the glass-topped coffee table. He had enjoyed the bent of the conversation to this point, but now he was getting tired, and he was ready to get out of the office, away from the whining Jason Swann and out of Arkansas.

"Git the money, Swann. Negotiations is over," Campbell interjected between Swann's protestations.

"You don't get it do you, you hillbilly clod—"

Billy Bob's hands were around Jason Swann's neck before the administrator could move an inch, his powerful grip holding Swann like an Arkansas chicken whose neck was about to be snapped.

"Time's up, smartmouth," Billy Bob whispered menacingly in Swann's face. "You got the money here, and I better git it right now or you'll end up like that preacher and airplane pilot. You ain't gonna see tomorrow's light. Got that?"

Swann tried to speak, but his throat was too constricted for speech. He had seen Billy Bob Campbell angry before, and he knew the big man lost all sense of reason when it happened. There would be no reasoning with the oversized hillbilly hick. Payment would have to be made—and swiftly.

He wriggled from Billy Bob's grasp, rubbing his damaged throat with his hands. "I got the money," Swann rasped, the words coming out in a hoarse cough.

"Git it."

Swann moved to the wall behind his desk, swung a poor reproduction of a John Singer Sargent watercolor landscape to the right,
revealing a small wall safe. As he spun the dial, he was trying to figure a way out of his current situation. He might have to kill Branscum
and Campbell. The thought gave him a surprising amount of pleasure.

■   ■   ■

Wade Larsen was standing outside the Mayflower Restaurant
when an unfamiliar four-wheel-drive vehicle carrying two men passed
through Benning. He recognized the type of men they were and immediately climbed in his police car to follow them at a distance. As they
had wound through the circuitous route leading to the valley, Larsen
had surmised their destination. He had backed off to a half mile, letting the two men slip from sight around the winding road. It was no
problem following them; he knew exactly where they would turn off
the main road.

Larsen slowed as he approached the narrow entry to the backwoods
road. He nodded grimly when he saw the tire tracks tracing the route to
the valley. He automatically reached down to touch the shotgun stored
under the seat and turned his cruiser into the snow-covered road.

He eased to a stop a hundred yards short of where the sports utility
vehicle was parked. The house in the valley was well out-of-sight. Larsen
got out of his car, pulling the shotgun from its soft carrier below the front
seat. He closed the door quietly and began moving through the woods.

It still amazed the sheriff that the true nature of the valley had
never been revealed. He felt a stabbing pang of guilt at the thought of
what went on within his jurisdiction.

But that has come to an end, he reminded himself. He would no
longer overlook the atrocities that occurred inside the mansion in the
valley. His nightly bourbon binge was unable to erase the truth, and
he knew it was time to put an end to the place.

He pressed his large frame into the side of a massive pine tree and
watched the SUV.

Soon the doors to the vehicle opened and the two men stepped out, each carrying an automatic weapon. There was no longer any doubt as to what was about to happen. The problem, as Wade Larsen saw it, was what he could do about it.

CHAPTER THIRTY-TWO

"What have you done with the girl?" Lazarus asked.

"That should be none of your concern. At least, not at this moment," Damon answered.

The two men were in the library of the Memphis house, seated within a few feet of each other and the huge fireplace. Empty brandy bottles littered the floor next to Lazarus's chair. The large, marble ashtray on the table at the old man's right elbow overflowed with cigarette butts and ashes. The typical Germanic order of the room had long been forgotten.

Damon smiled to himself as he kept his gaze fixed on Lazarus. It had been the same for all these years, he thought. The man had never realized what was happening to him and, in fact, had thought himself in control of his own destiny. He was about to learn the truth.

"This woman was about to disclose the secrets of *Die Gruppe* and the Ozark facility?" Lazarus continued in a worried voice.

Damon sat back in the deep wing chair and picked up the brandy snifter at his elbow. He sipped gently at the liquid, enjoying the word games with Lazarus as much as the fragrance of the dark elixir. The fire cast long shadows in the room; the heat seemed to be confined to an area no more than two feet outside the fireplace. Damon watched Lazarus shudder involuntarily as a draft of chilled air swept across the room.

"Her name is Cindy Tolbert, and she knows nothing about the valley operation. I need her for another reason. The woman is my concern, not yours. Her purpose is crucial to my own agenda," Damon said.

Lazarus sprang from where he sat. Anger flared. "You should not have brought her here. She will have to be eliminated."

"Eventually," Damon agreed easily. "But not now. I have a reason for what I have done. It does not concern you at this point."

Lazarus's eyes blazed as brightly as the fire. "You do not dictate strategy or tactics to me," Lazarus screamed. "This is my operation. *Mine.* Do you understand that? I will not have hirelings talking to me in this manner!"

Damon sat impassively in his chair, ignoring the old man's angry outburst. He had expected it. If he felt anything, it was contempt.

Lazarus stalked the room like a cornered animal. He threw his hands into the air and continued, "This is intolerable. You defy me. The men of *Die Gruppe* defy me—men who have neither the expertise nor the experience to deal with the project. My best friend, a man whose life I saved, put back on track, confided in, and supported, defies me before the very group I created. It is *intolerable! Unacceptable! Inexcusable!*"

Damon swallowed the last draught of the brandy, letting its fiery sweetness trickle down the back of his throat. There were some consolations to the human form, he thought. But the time had come to set the record straight.

"You use words such as *intolerable, unacceptable, inexcusable.*
These are words that reflect your personal feelings." Damon slowly
placed the brandy snifter on the table next to his chair, the gesture calling attention to itself by its very deliberateness. *"Your* feelings, *your*
directions are no longer acceptable. It is *you* who have become intolerable, unacceptable, and inexcusable."

Lazarus abruptly ceased his pacing. The fire in his eyes glowed
brighter, fiercer than it had only seconds earlier. A maniacal expression spread over his face. His mouth flew open, mouthing words that
never came.

"You dare to—?" was all he could manage.

Damon leaped from his chair and Lazarus recoiled.

"You dare to speak to *me* in such a manner?" Damon was in
Lazarus's face now, looking down on the old man, his long hair flowing like a mane. Lazarus seemed to shrink into himself. The room was
now colder than it had ever been, as if all sources of heat had been
sucked away. *"I* have been responsible for all your successes," Damon
roared. Do you truly believe you have the intellect, the farsightedness
to accomplish what you have over these past decades?" Damon turned
and stepped away from the old man. "You were chosen," Damon said,
wheeling around to face Lazarus again. *"I* chose *you. You* did not
choose *me,* old man."

Lazarus was surprised by the swiftness of the verbal assault, but
he recovered quickly. "What are you saying? Of course I chose you.
You were nothing when I found you years ago, and you are only of
value as your service relates to me," Lazarus argued. "You—"

Damon cut the old man off instantly. *"You?* There is no *you.* There
is no *Die Gruppe,* of which you are so proud. There is only *me.* And
my agenda is so far removed from yours, you have no concept of its
importance."

Damon stepped closer to Lazarus, gripping the old man by the
lapels of the heavy coat he wore to ward off the cold.

"I am the master of this house," Damon said through clenched teeth, "the master of your so-called *gruppe,* the master of all I touch. Do you understand what I am saying, old man?"

Lazarus squirmed free of Damon's grasp, his composure suddenly gone, a shrunken, defeated man. Replacing the fire in his eyes now was an expression of fear and loathing. Of the two emotions, fear was by far the more dominant, and Lazarus backed away.

Damon advanced on the terrified Lazarus, his own power now established, his dominance supreme.

"You actually believe it was you who directed the happenings in your homeland? You believe those men who were the leaders led by their own ingenuity, their own cunning?" Damon asked in a low voice. "You think such atrocities sprang from *your* vision, from the vision of *any* mortal?"

Lazarus regained his voice. The words came out in a high-pitched squeal. "Mortal? *Mortal?* What are you trying to say?"

Damon smiled expansively. "You are beginning to understand, I think. Allow me to expand." Damon walked to the sideboard situated against one wall and poured himself another snifter of brandy. He swirled the amber liquid around the bell of the glass, sniffing the aroma, then sipped gently. "We have been failed by your kind before," he continued. "You were chosen; *they* were chosen back then. All of you thought you were the masters, the omnipotent ones. You were wrong. *They* were wrong. It was only my foresight that kept you from the trial, from the hangman, and only because I considered you worthy of a further investment of my time. *I* was responsible for the Lazarus Project. *I* was responsible from the very beginning, from the days in France and Germany and Poland."

"But," the old man began, "you are not that old. You could not have been born yet."

Damon chuckled. "Yes, I can see where that is a problem for you, but you are constrained by the idea of time and place, and neither of those concepts applies to me. It was me who saved you then, again in Brazil, and finally brought you here. It will be me who saves you one last time too. But let me assure you, this will be the last time. Your use-fulness to me is quickly coming to an end. I would estimate you have no more than a few more years to live."

Lazarus sat heavily in his favorite chair. "That is no news. I am, as you say, an old man, and there is very little left to live for, if what you say is true. The body dies along with the dreams."

Damon laughed an ugly, deprecating laugh. "Spare me the maudlin sentiments, old man. You will live longer because I have need of you. Regardless of what you might think, you still have the power to direct, to lead *Die Gruppe* in the manner I desire. For that reason, and that reason alone, I will keep you alive."

Lazarus looked up at Damon, trying to fathom the depth of the man's power. "You have the power of life and death, then?"

"I have the power of life and death in the same way you did more than fifty years ago. It's a power I exercise with as little empathy for those involved as you did. You do remember, do you not?"

"I remember all too well," the old man agreed. "We were gods in those day," he continued, his zeal beginning to build again, his dignity restored, if only for a moment.

"Gods? Yes, you thought highly of yourselves in those days, in the days before Nuremberg. That was the one thing I could always use to my advantage—your pride. And it served both of us well. Now, in just a few more years, I will have what I set out to acquire so many years ago. I will be the ultimate master of all I can see. And you and yours will have helped me along the way. For that, you will be rewarded, but I think not in the way you envision. But that is for a later discussion. We still have work to do, and you will be instru-mental in that work."

"The woman?"

Damon rejoined a deflated Lazarus at the fireside chairs. "She will be killed, but first she has a function to perform. She is bait."

"Bait?"

"Another story. Only a tangent to what is really taking place, but an important one. She will be used to lure an old enemy into this place, and then I will kill him."

"The project is your path to total domination of the economic system of the United States and ultimately the world."

Damon sipped the brandy again, observing the old man over the rim of the glass. The fire had died down; the cold was more penetrating than ever, almost to the point of total discomfort. "As I said, you are beginning to understand. Power, real power, is a closely held commodity. Regardless of what people think, power flows along the same lines as finances. Control the men, you control the finances and ultimately the world's systems. And the United States is the center, the epicenter if you will, of that control. It is only necessary to appeal to the vanity of certain men, or threaten as the case may be. With the threat of exposure, loss of power, the threat of financial impotence comes capitulation," Damon expounded. "But you know that already, don't you, Doctor? You have seen these very things. You have watched mediocre men rise to greatness, or at least notoriety."

The old man started at the word *doctor;* the term was seldom used. Outside the windows of the house, snow was again falling. To the old man, it appeared as if the snow marked the end of the world as he knew it. What Damon was saying was all true, and looking back on it, the old man could pinpoint the times, the places, when and where he had chosen this life. While there may have been outside forces at work during those times, he knew the choices had been his and his alone. The path he had taken, albeit influenced by external factors as Damon suggested, had been his path, *his* choice.

"I can see by your expression, Doctor, that you finally realize what has happened to you. And you are correct in your thinking. All the choices, the decisions were yours. Again, it is no great feat to appeal to the vanities. That is all that is necessary."

Lazarus nodded involuntarily.

"There are still those in this world who seek you, Doctor. Men who would see you dead. And even your death would not be sufficient payment for the atrocities you committed, but death is the greatest payment which can be demanded of you. But they will never find you. I will see to that. I have need of you."

Lazarus buried his head in his hands, his thoughts returning to those divergent pathways. Yes, the choices had all been his, and he had made them with as little compunction as if he had been deciding what to have for lunch. There were men who searched for him, who would like to see him die. And he would defy them to his last dying breath. Contained within this newest decision, Lazarus realized he had made one last choice, and the choice was like all the others, life for himself at whatever the cost, and death to those who would have it otherwise.

"I can see you have decided. Good. We can now begin to exercise the power and influence necessary to accomplish our mutual goals. I will start by telling you that the members of *Die Gruppe,* the group you control, have voted to have you killed. They view you as a handicap. I will see to it that you are not the one who dies."

"Henry?"

"Dr. Henry Phelps Sr.? Your friend, the friend you saved all those many years ago, was instrumental in the decision to have you killed. You see, you cannot trust anyone now but me. Remember that, Doctor. And now I must end this assassination attempt before it disrupts my plans. Do excuse me for a few hours, Doctor," Damon said, rising from his chair. "I will return to take care of the girl, but only after she has served her purpose. Do nothing until then."

Lazarus watched as Damon walked from the room. With him seemed to go the last vestiges of comfort. The fire was now nothing more than smoldering embers, and the old man knew no amount of wood would warm the room ever again. It was his destiny, and he would live it out.

■　■　■

The room was dark and dreary, a perfect picture of what a dungeon should be, notwithstanding the expensive amenities, rich tapestries, and heavy fabrics.

Cindy Tolbert explored her richly appointed prison cell. Her head still ached from the chemically induced coma from which she had emerged less than an hour ago. A portion of her fear had now been replaced by anger. The fear was still there, but it was blunted by her growing hostility.

There was another sensation in the room, one of evil, an overwhelming sense of degradation and corruption. It was not the normal sense of evil as she had come to know it, but one that seemed to have its origins in another dimension and another time.

Cindy shuddered at a sudden draft of icy wind. She looked around her but could see no source for the breeze.

The room was large, larger certainly than any such room she had ever been in. There was an antique, four-poster bed of oversized proportions. The walls were covered with a heavy brocade wallpaper, the flocked pattern almost blood red over a warm beige background. The effect was that of blood streaming from the very walls. Table lamps provided scant illumination, as if the room itself absorbed the rays that attempted to brighten it.

The windows were reinforced with thick iron bars, but Cindy could see the snow falling outside. From the street, the bars appeared to be ornamental, in keeping with the architectural design of the house. The room had two doors, but both were made of thick oak slabs strong enough to defy all but the most powerful assault.

She was in jail, held against her will, and for what? She had no idea. She did not know the man who had abducted her, drugged her, and spirited her away in that awful coffin of a trunk. What was going on? Did it have anything to do with David's foray into the forest? Janice Morgan had told her to ignore the story of David's death and that David would explain when he returned. Was there a connection?

Another wave of cold swept over her, and Cindy felt as if the cold penetrated to her very core. For her, there was only one choice. She dropped to her knees and began to pray. She continued for more than an hour. When she stood up, a feeling of inner warmth comforted her, despite the cold. The evil she knew dwelt within the house no longer held sway over her inner being. She would continue to pray, but she would also add feet to her prayers by exploring the room. That was one of the things she had learned from David in the past year. Sometimes God really did expect action in association with prayer. For Cindy, the time for action was now.

■   ■   ■

"Communications have been positively established," Dr. Henry Phelps Jr. informed the men seated around the large conference table.

"How long will this take?" one man asked.

Phelps consulted his watch before answering. "The task is scheduled for completion within the hour. A successful outcome will be relayed directly here via a secure line. We need do nothing but wait for the communiqué."

"I still do not understand the purpose of this meeting," another man chimed in.

Phelps Jr. smiled condescendingly. "As I said earlier, this meeting is duly authorized and recorded in the corporate minutes, giving each of us an ironclad alibi. Should questions ever arise, we are all in the clear."

"What questions?" demanded yet a third member of *Die Gruppe.* "We are supposed to be beyond scrutiny."

"Insurance," Henry Phelps Jr. answered. "Where there is no need to take chances, we will not. Understood?"

All heads nodded in acknowledgment and obedience. Every man knew his role and every role was important.

"Very well. We will wait until we have confirmation. Coffee and refreshments are in the outer room. Please feel free to partake as you wish. After the notification that Lazarus is dead, we will dismiss. It will be to our mutual advantage not to meet for the next few months. I will notify you of the next time and place."

"Then you have assumed control?" the first man asked, a touch of animosity in his voice.

"Unless there are others who would aspire to this chair, yes. Do you have a problem with this?" Phelps asked, directing the question to the questioner. "Any of you?" he said, now addressing the entire group.

No one spoke. No one would aspire to control *Die Gruppe.* There was no opposition.

"Good. Then we wait."

■   ■   ■

Sheriff Wade Larsen peered cautiously from behind a large tree. The two men were studying a map which the driver had pulled from a door pocket. The taller of the two men, the "quiet one" Larsen had subconsciously dubbed the man in control, pointed in the direction of the valley.

Larsen watched as both men shouldered their automatic weapons and retrieved two packs from the interior of the SUV. The packs were obviously heavy, and the shorter of the men, the driver, had trouble hoisting his on his shoulders. He finally struggled into the straps and the two men started off through the trees.

Larsen felt his pulse quicken. He would follow the men at a distance, though it would be dangerous; the leafless trees and pristine snow offered almost no cover. If the two men ever looked back, there would be no place to hide.

Larsen checked his shotgun and the automatic pistol on his hip and waited until the two men were out of sight before following. At least he would not have to tail them closely. Their footprints in the snow would be easily followed. There was always the danger that the two might double back, but he would deal with that if it happened.

Larsen stepped from behind the tree and moved out in the direction the men had taken. His pulse still pounded in his ears.

■   ■   ■

Nothing but an old man, they had assured him. He had picked up the address, along with a floor plan of the house and a picture of the man, from a manila envelope in a rented locker at Memphis International Airport. They were right, the man was ancient, but despite the gray hair, full mustache, and clouded brown-green eyes, the face was familiar. Where had he seen it before? His recollection was of a much younger man, but the identity could not be concealed. He shoved the photo back into the envelope. Maybe the name would come to him before he killed the old man. Not that it mattered, but it would be nice to put a name to the face.

The man took the I-240 exit and headed for the address listed on the data sheet. He picked up the cellular phone he had also retrieved from the airport locker and checked the battery charge. The phone was his means of direct communication, and he had been assured the signal could not be intercepted by any scanner on the market today. It was a totally secure line, a one-time communication device, to be disposed of after its use.

As his car crawled along the snowy interstate, the man thought about the trip to Grand Cayman he had booked earlier. The money would be waiting in a numbered, offshore account in Georgetown. Despite the ice and snow that still gripped the city, flights were able to take off from the airport. All he had to do was finish one simple job and return to Memphis International for his flight to the Caribbean. Life was grand.

CHAPTER THIRTY-THREE

It's almost too easy, the man thought. The drive from the airport had taken much less time than he'd anticipated, which left him a half hour to scout the surrounding area, a nice, older, upscale neighborhood whose homes sat back from the road. Each house rested on a plot of land of two acres or more. The setback and lot size meant one thing— isolation. And isolation was an important factor in his work. Isolation meant anonymity. Anonymity meant safety. Safety meant innocence—not innocence in the technical sense of the word but innocence in the practical sense. The man adhered to the legal standard that stated a person was innocent until proven guilty. Given that parameter, to date, the man was guilty of nothing.

He parked the car in a lot he had noticed several blocks from the target and walked back to the house. The icy streets were deserted.

When he reached the house, he saw random lights on in the first and second story windows, but he detected no movement, no shadows passing in front of the backlit windows. The intelligence report stated unequivocally that the old man would be home. The old man was always home, the report said. Both the cook and the maid would have already gone home, and the only other servant, a male butler, had private quarters in the rear of the house. The old man would most likely be found in the downstairs library, just off the main corridor to the right of the entryway.

There were alarms, but they were only a slight inconvenience to a true professional. The man entered through the rear of the house in minutes. The butler was nowhere to be seen.

The man worked his way toward the front of the house, listening, moving catlike along the darkened corridors. He stopped, listening to the creak and moan of the structure itself. He shivered; the house was cold, almost unbearably so. How could the old man stand such intense cold? Most old people he knew kept their houses hot to scorching. But not this old man. Not this house. Something was different about this house.

The man began moving again, following the floor plan toward where he knew the old man would be. He pulled a small automatic pistol from his right coat pocket and a dark, cylindrical silencer from the other. He screwed the silencer onto the weapon as he moved closer to the front of the house.

He could see the door now, set in the wall to his left. A yellow light flickered from beneath the crack at the bottom of the door. Someone had a fire going in a fireplace. That explained the cold in the hallway. The old man was eccentric to the point of not allowing heat to be wasted on any room but the one he was in. But the cold seemed to increase in its intensity as he neared the warmed room.

It was cold and getting colder. He was now within an arm's length of the door, and the cold was so intense it was painful. How could it possibly be colder inside than out?

The man shivered inside his expensive wool topcoat. There was something very wrong here. He could sense it, *feel* it. Not only in the cold that seemed to bear down on him like a huge weight, but in a manner less tangible, less explicit.

The assassin reached for the doorknob and twisted it. It rotated quietly; the door opened. The man pushed inside.

The room was lit only by the flickering flames of the fireplace, but the light was sufficient. The light was accompanied by the hiss and roar of the oak logs being consumed in the yellow flames. Despite the fire, the room was even colder than the hallway. How was that possible?

Two leather wingback chairs faced the fireplace, and the killer immediately saw the old man sitting in one of them. The chair was canted toward the fireplace and the door, so that anyone sitting there could not only enjoy the view of the fire, but know when someone entered the room as well.

The man stepped further into the room, pistol poised.

The old man in the chair turned toward the killer. There was no emotion in the tired eyes, no spark that would suggest that any humanity existed within his being.

For a moment, the assassin forgot the nearly debilitating cold of the room. He raised the silenced weapon, aiming for the old man's forehead. He noticed the cigarette that dangled beneath the old man's full mustache, a gray ash precariously balanced from the glowing tip. The brief distraction was a split-second too long.

He saw the flash an instant before he felt a crushing pressure in his chest that forced the air from his lungs in a single, searing gasp. As he fell backward against the door frame, he saw the handsome young man who had shot him standing beside the other chair. As the wounded would-be assassin tried to raise his pistol to return fire, a second jacketed bullet hit him in the throat. The last earthly sight he saw was of his killer standing over him, smiling. The handsome face remained in view as the last flicker of life drained from his body. As the light in his eyes died, he felt a horror he would never have believed possible, and he knew that his ordeal had not ended with his death.

. . .

Damon stepped over the body, retrieved the small cellular phone from the man's coat pocket, and dialed a number. The phone rang only once before it was answered.

"Your man is dead," Damon said into the instrument, then punched the "end" button on the tiny keypad and smiled to himself.

. . .

Donald Fenwick! The CEO of FenMark and one of the richest men in the world! It was incredible, inconceivable! But true.

After Fenwick passed out, David gently placed him beneath a large pine whose expansive branches limited the amount of snow around its base. He checked the man's pulse and vital signs and determined that he had fainted from exhaustion and a very real case of fear.

David went through the man's pockets, extracting an expensive calfskin billfold. The driver's license confirmed Donald Fenwick's identity but offered no clue as to why the young millionaire was now sprawled on the frozen valley floor.

David turned his attention to retrieving his backpack, which was loaded with his supplies, tent, and sleeping bag. His pack and all his supplies were still on top of the rocky bluff. He would need them if the two of them were to survive the approaching night. He checked on the businessman one last time, then started hiking around the rock face to the east, skirting the sheer cliff, climbing at a leisurely pace to conserve energy along the more gently sloping lateral trails. It took him a half hour to reach his equipment and another twenty minutes to return by the same route. On the return trip, David worried that Donald Fenwick might have awakened and left or was in the early stages of hypothermia. Either was a possibility, and neither was acceptable under the circumstances.

But when he returned, he found Fenwick in the same spot, curled into a semifetal position. His initial concern left when he drew closer and heard a low snore escape from Fenwick's throat. Donald Fenwick had simply curled into a ball and gone to sleep. David had smiled at the sight, relief buoying his spirits for the moment.

The mystery of what one of the world's richest, most influential men was doing in the middle of this most inhospitable climate nagged at David. He had briefly scouted the area on top of and below the cliff and had found no pack, no tent, nor any semblance of camping paraphernalia other than his own. David pulled the plastic-coated map from his pack and examined it closely. He was pretty sure of his location, and if he was correct, there was no dwelling within miles of where they were.

David crouched beside the sleeping man and examined him more closely. Fenwick's garments were state-of-the-art cold-protection gear, a vital point David had overlooked earlier in his haste. His gloves were actually hyper-cold weather mittens, designed to allow one's hands freedom via concealed slots in the palms, but otherwise were the ultimate protection against the biting cold. Whatever Donald Fenwick was doing out here, he had more or less dressed for the weather. More or less, David thought, because there was no evidence of any other form of protection. The lack of a tent in the freezing cold might have been a fatal mistake. David again scouted the surrounding terrain for any supplies or provisions the retailer might have brought with him. He found nothing. Whatever Fenwick was doing, he'd planned on completing in a single day and then getting out of the forest. That much was clear. Either that or the man was a fool, a possibility David had not yet ruled out.

David set about erecting his Garuda Kusala tent. The tent was small, and its low tunnel design would make for a cozy night with two grown men inside, but there was little option. The sun was beginning to set; darkness would come very quickly at the end of this winter day, and with it a stinging, dangerous chill.

With the tent erected, the small stove set up, and snow melting for boiling water, David roused Donald Fenwick. He was amazed that he had been able to sleep through the last forty-five minutes as if he were in his own bedroom.

Fenwick came awake with a start, the same bloodshot, terror-stricken eyes gazing back at David. The fear subsided almost immediately and Fenwick sat up, his back supported by the trunk of the pine tree.

After almost thirty seconds, he spoke, "I owe you," he said to David Michaels in a low whisper.

David handed Fenwick a cup of steaming tea. "Drink this," he ordered gently. "It'll help."

Fenwick took the cup in mittened hands.

"Be careful," David warned. "It's hot."

Donald Fenwick blew on the liquid, then sipped at it hesitantly. After the first two sips, he downed the fluid in two great gulps, the contents having cooled in the chilled mountain air.

"Ginger tea," David told the rich entrepreneur. "It'll warm you from the inside out and won't dehydrate you like coffee or regular teas."

Fenwick looked up at David, stood up, and handed the cup back to him. "That's two I owe you. . . ."

"David Michaels. And I don't keep score."

"I do, David Michaels."

"Why?" David asked, returning to the small stove and preparing another cup of tea for himself. The darkness was quickly creeping across the forest floor. The snow was turning a deep shade of purple as long shadows moved to obscure the light. The clouds added to the deepening gloom, as if a curse had suddenly fallen over the forest.

Fenwick rose from where he was sitting. "That's the way I am. I don't like to owe anyone."

"That's a pretty cynical attitude. You're always going to owe someone something."

"Possibly. But I try to keep my outstanding debts to as few as possible."

"That's capitalism talking, Mr. Fenwick, not humanity."

Fenwick moved to where David was crouched in front of the stove. "How do you know who I am?"

David stood, the tea cup in his hand. He sipped the contents, his eyes looking over the cup's rim into those of Donald Fenwick. He lowered the cup, still holding Fenwick's gaze with his own.

"I would have to be blind not to recognize one of the richest men in America."

"Bill Gates is richer."

"I doubt there's a significant difference at your level."

Fenwick laughed. "I suppose you're right."

David finished the tea and went to his pack. "We'll need to get some food in us. In case you haven't noticed, it's already dark. We're going to have to spend the night here."

A sudden look of concern crossed Fenwick's face. David recognized the look. Not one of fear but merely concern. He wondered about it.

"You haven't asked me about getting stuck on that rock face."

David began unpacking the remainder of the supplies he would need for the evening meal. "If you want to tell me, that's up to you. If you don't, that's up to you too."

"That's a rather morbid lack of curiosity, wouldn't you say?"

"Maybe, but we aren't talking about my lack of curiosity; we're talking about you dangling from a rock cliff in the middle of the Ozarks. If you want to tell me, then tell me. You don't want to, don't."

"Morbid. Just like I said."

David chuckled as he began preparing the meal. He turned to Fenwick and said, "We got ourselves a basic problem, Mr. Fenwick. . . ."

"Donald."

"Donald, then. There's still the problem of sleeping arrangements."

"Yeah, I thought about that. I only meant to be out here for a few hours. That was before I got too close to that rock cliff."

"Well, this isn't Little America . . . "

"Little America?"

"Outpost at the South Pole," David explained. "But it's going to be cold tonight. I've got enough stuff in my backpack for both of us to survive the night, but it's not going to be comfortable. At least it's cloudy, and it's going to stay that way through the night."

"Why is that lucky?"

"Means the temperature will at least stay like it is right now. With a clear sky tonight, we'd be looking at temperatures near zero."

"Why are you doing this?" Fenwick asked.

"Doing what?"

"Helping me. You don't know me other than what you may have heard, and that probably isn't that great."

"More cynicism."

"Maybe. But most people would worry about themselves first."

David smiled. "What's makes you think I didn't?"

"Now who's being cynical?"

David went about completing the preparation for the meal. He'd extracted two packets of freeze-dried food and opened them and began melting snow for the boiling water he would need to rehydrate the food. Darkness was only a few minutes away when he finished. Donald Fenwick had remained next to the pine tree, saying nothing. When the food was ready, David motioned for the CEO of FenMark to join him. David bowed his head and said a quick prayer of thanks for the food and for the safety of the cynical Fenwick.

Fenwick waited until David finished, holding the hot food, then said, "You're what? A religious zealot? An overactive social worker?"

"Preacher," David answered, beginning to eat.

"I don't buy that. You move and act like some high-powered actor in one of those action movies that tries its best to blow up the world in two hours. Military, maybe. Preacher? No way."

"Eat," David commanded.

"That's what I'm talking about. Right there. You're someone used to giving orders, just like me. And you're used to being obeyed too.

Just like me." Fenwick stared at David in the dwindling light, slowly chewing his dinner.

"There's some bottled water in my pack to wash that down with. If it hasn't frozen solid."

"Where?"

"Down inside," David answered.

"Not the water. Where's your church?"

David finished off the food and reached into his outer pocket for some hard candy. Already he was feeling better, as long as he did not think about the reason he had come to the frozen forest. For a fleeting second, that reason seemed to overwhelm him like the darkness which had now settled in around the small camp, engulfing the two men.

"Clayton. A few hours south of here. We have a FenMark store, in case you're wondering. Everyone knows what you and your father look like. You can't miss the pictures on the wall when you pass through the checkout stands. That's how I knew who you were. Not counting the fact that you're an Arkansas favorite son."

David watched as Donald Fenwick's expression changed in the low, flat light of the nighttime woods. What had caused the change? The mention of Clayton? That seemed highly improbable. The mention of FenMark? The photos? Father? That was it, thought David. Nothing else could account for the reaction. Whatever was troubling Donald Fenwick, and there was something, David knew, it had to do with the senior Fenwick.

The darkness was almost complete now. The snow retained the strange quality of luminescence, filtering a small amount of light into the surrounding countryside. David went to his pack and pulled out a small, fuel-operated lantern. It would not provide a lot of light, but it would create a much more comfortable atmosphere. David had the feeling that Fenwick had come to these woods for much the same reason as he had. The idea was disturbing because David was not really sure *why* he was there himself.

"I'm ready. Maybe I should be telling this to a preacher anyway," Donald Fenwick began in a low voice.

"Ready?" David replied gently.

"It's a strange story. Convoluted. Circuitous."

"It's your story," David said.

"You're a strange sort of reverend, David Michaels."

"If you mean by that, that I haven't tried to force my religion on you yet, then you're right. I don't do that. That's not my job. I'll tell you the truth, about a man named Jesus Christ, but the decision after that is up to you, not me."

"You're not the snake-oil salesman type then. Is that it?"

David smiled at the portrayal. He didn't care too much for the "snake oil" approach to the gospel either.

Donald Fenwick moved closer to where David sat. The rays of the small lantern engulfed the two men in a small area of shimmering light. The wind had died down, and the snap and crackle of tree limbs freezing in the cold could be heard throughout the forest. Donald Fenwick took a deep breath, and began, "You're a preacher. You know the story of Lazarus," Fenwick stated factually. "There's another story of Lazarus you don't know," the man continued. "A much more frightening story."

■ ■ ■

Dr. Henry Phelps Jr. stared at the phone in his hand. The men of *Die Gruppe* around the conference table knew that the worst had happened.

Phelps replaced the receiver and sat heavily in the chair at the head of the long table. Words would not come. Explanations or excuses were meaningless.

■ ■ ■

Lying on the large bed located against one wall of the bedroom, Cindy Tolbert felt her fear magnified into a dread she had never before known. The sound of a firearm being discharged somewhere in the large house had filtered its way up the winding staircase.

She could feel tears begin to flow down her cheeks, and she wondered again what was going on. She and Stacii Barrett had argued about prayer only days earlier when she and David had been in Little Rock to check on the girl at the hospital. But no amount of semantics, theological discussion, or personal opinion to the contrary could change the fact that when she prayed she felt better. Only an hour earlier, prayer had been her companion. Now Cindy slid from the bed and knelt beside it. She put both hands together and buried her face in them, the words flowing as if she were talking to her best friend, which she was.

■   ■   ■

Wade Larsen quickly discovered that he had not come equipped for this type of tracking. With only his uniform boots and jacket for protection, he was beginning to see the error of his ways. His socks were soaked through and the cold added agony to every step. It was a dangerous situation, not so much because of what the cold might do, but simply because the discomfort took his mind off what was really important, and that was keeping the two men in sight.

Larsen held no illusions as to what the men were doing in the valley. That was self-evident. What he did not know was who had issued the orders. It was a question he knew he should have asked many years ago.

The two men stopped up ahead. Larsen ducked behind a long-dead cedar tree whose multiple branches looked like the backbone of a huge, permanently grounded fish.

The two men looked around, and Larsen did not move. There was little enough cover in the snow-covered forest as it was. He did not want to give himself away by unnecessary movement in the failing light.

The wind keening through the trees carried snatches of conversation back to where the sheriff huddled next to the cedar. The words, disjointed but audible, chilled Wade Larsen even more than the Ozark winter snow.

■   ■   ■

"You hear something?" the driver asked, checking the area where Wade Larsen pressed close to the dead cedar.

"You're getting the willies. Just keep your mind on the job. It's going to take some time to set these charges so the place goes up all at once."

"Won't there be an investigation?"

"So what?" the once quiet man said. "This is rural Arkansas. Who do you think is going to investigate? And don't forget, the local law is in on this. No, there won't be an investigation."

"What about all the bodies? I mean, there are supposed to be people in this place," the driver said with a trace of concern in his voice.

"It will all be buried when the place burns. As far as the locals are concerned, it will be just another abandoned house that burned in the backwoods," the bigger man said. "Now let's get moving. We need to be there before nightfall. We can do our best work during the night. By morning, there won't be anything left of the place to investigate."

The two men shouldered the heavy packs they had brought with them and moved deeper into the woods.

CHAPTER THIRTY-FOUR

A look of deep concern crossed Tom Frazier's face as he hung up the phone in his fourth-level basement office in the White House. It was a look the man sitting across from him could not ignore.

"That was the lady sheriff?" the guest said, more a statement than a real question.

Tom Frazier nodded at Julius Goldman. "There's been no contact with Michaels since the fake radio announcement of his death and his trip into that valley. His cell phone is still turned off."

"But my friend, there was to be no contact until he found something. Was that not the arrangement?"

Tom Frazier nodded again, slowly. Goldman was right, but that did not stop the agent from worrying about his friend. "You don't know Michaels, do you, Jules?" Frazier asked, using the Mossad agent's shortened first name. He and Goldman had been friends since Frazier's addition to the president's support staff several years ago. Frazier was not the normally high-profile person associated with the OOP. As a matter of fact, most people, even those closest to the president, did not really know what Tom Frazier did. And that was the way it was supposed to be.

Frazier did what others would not or could not do. He was the ultimate troubleshooter.

Goldman sipped at the cup of tea resting on Frazier's cluttered desk, and answered, "I've never met the man. I do know the stories circulating about the Collins Construction thing that happened last year. Sounds to me like a rather resourceful gentleman," Goldman concluded.

Tom Frazier smiled at the assessment. *Resourceful* was certainly a word to be applied to Commander David Michaels.

"But," Goldman continued, "it is difficult to imagine any preacher with the skills necessary to accomplish the task which might lie before him."

"*Preacher,*" Tom Frazier began, "does not fully convey Michaels's capabilities."

"So I have heard. Nevertheless, you can't seriously expect even a military preacher, chaplain I believe you call them, to effectively penetrate this organization?"

Frazier rose from his desk and moved around to a second chair facing the desk and Goldman. "Michaels might be the only hope we have at this point, given the restraints placed on this office. David Michaels may well be the catalyst."

Goldman smiled. "You are, of course, speaking of the laws of this land which seem to protect the guilty far beyond reason. In Israel, we would simply arrest the man under our terrorism statutes. No fuss, no bother."

"The 'fuss' you're speaking of is known as civil rights over here," Frazier shot back.

"Ah, yes. The catch-all phrase your ACLU survives on and which allows some of this country's worst criminal elements to remain free and unfettered. Wolves among unsuspecting sheep. I will never understand the theory behind it all."

Frazier reached for the cup of coffee he'd left on his desk. It was cold now, and the remnants of the powdered creamer floating on the surface made the substance utterly unpalatable. Frazier set the cup down and turned to Goldman again. "It's not difficult to understand. The laws we have enacted are in place to see to it that what happened to your people in Germany during the war does not happen here. What you get when you suspend human and civil rights is a Nazi Germany or a Stalinist Russia. No mystery to that."

"That is perhaps a point to be argued at some future date," Goldman smiled. "For now, we need to concentrate on the matter at hand."

Frazier bristled momentarily, then let the remark slide. After all, the man was right. David Michaels was the important focus for the moment. Frazier strode back to his desk chair, pushed it aside, and grabbed a file folder from amid the clutter.

The file folder was distinguished by the broken red border and the words "Top Secret" stamped across the face of it. The big difference from this folder and others Frazier had seen was that the words were all in Hebrew.

Frazier opened the folder, staring at the photograph for a long minute, taking in the brown-green eyes, the clean-shaven oval face, and the gray German uniform adorned with the insignia of the German SS on one collar tab and the three diamonds of a *Haupsturmführer* on the other. The presidential agent felt an involuntary chill race through him.

Frazier flipped the photograph over, revealing a more recent one. This time the photo showed a middle-aged man walking on a South American beach with family members. A paunch had begun to form around the man's middle, and he now sported a full, almost scraggly mustache. The hair was now gray, combed straight back.

Frazier looked over the folder to where Julius Goldman sat quietly. "You are certain about this?" he asked.

"There is no doubt, my friend," Goldman answered, his voice lowered as if he were speaking of some sacred holy man.

"The Bertioga drowning was just a ruse, then," Frazier said, almost to himself.

Goldman said nothing.

"And the exhumation in eighty-five?"

"Another ruse. Orchestrated by some friends. The subsequent autopsy was performed by men we now know were members of the inner circle. Men of *Die Gruppe*."

Frazier shook his head in disbelief. It did not seem possible, but the evidence lay before him.

"Let's go over it again, Jules."

"It is simple. The Mossad is asking for your cooperation in this matter. According to all other sources, all except that file you now hold, the man is dead. As you say here in America, all the "t's" have been crossed and all the "i's" dotted. Officially the man is dead. It is impossible to get a warrant or extradition papers for a man who is dead and buried in Sao Palo, Brazil. You can understand our dilemma."

Frazier understood. More than that, he believed Goldman. "And if you can't get warrants and extradition papers, it will be difficult to justify a full-scale investigation using conventional law-enforcement means."

"Exactly. Your laws, not ours," Goldman said.

"Exactly. So that leaves us with the Office of the President in general and this office in particular." Frazier sat down heavily. "I've already taken this to the boss. It's not unlike what happened last year with the Collins Construction thing you just mentioned. But you do understand that this office has no authority to arrest, only to investigate."

Goldman nodded grimly. "That is understood, my friend. But we need your influence and, quite frankly, the sway that can be exercised from within these walls. We have to prove this monster still lives. With that done, we will be able to obtain the necessary documents to take him back to Israel and stand trial for his war crimes."

"Okay, Jules. As of right now, Commander David Michaels is in the Ozark hills searching for a valley we know exists—"

"Thanks to our information," Goldman broke in.

"Yes, thanks to your information. As soon as he activates his cell phone and calls Janice Morgan at the Clayton County sheriff's office, we will set him onto our man here. You've verified the Memphis address?"

"Of course. We have the floor plan obtained from blueprints, the house staff, and the protective devices and their locations."

"What about the other man you told me about?"

Jules Goldman rose from his seat for the first time and began pacing the small office. "Therein lies the real problem. We do not know who he is. All our investigative efforts have revealed nothing. Every time in the past we got within range of our target, this man appears and we end up with nothing. It has taken us years to track him down, to find out about the Memphis address. We have had agents observing the place, quite clandestinely I assure you, and never on a continuous basis. Just enough to assure ourselves that this monster is still in place." Goldman ceased his pacing and turned to Tom Frazier. "Only yesterday, this other man reappears, this time with a girl we believe is a hostage. A woman. We are working to identify her right now. There is something strange going on. A climax in the making. We can't afford to lose this man again. Your Commander Michaels is the torch we need to smoke this creature out."

"And when 'my' Commander Michaels finds out I have used him again, he's liable to come in this office and smear me up against these boring walls," Frazier said.

Jules Goldman met Frazier's gaze across the desk. "A preacher?"

Frazier laughed. "I keep telling you, Michaels is not your standard, run-of-the-mill preacher. But you will learn that as we go along. One more thing, Jules. Tell me about the woman you mentioned. The kidnap victim."

∎ ∎ ∎

The room was warm and cozy, and Gaby Ibarra felt the warmth deep in her soul. It was not just the physical warmth, although that was part of it. It was the gentle spirit of the nurses and doctors who seemed to have taken an increased interest in her since she woke up.

A hospital chaplain had visited her only an hour earlier, and now as the dim winter light faded outside her window, she wondered about what the young woman had told her. It had not really been what Gaby thought of as a homily, as the priest from her village might have called it. It had been more of a question-and-answer period, with her asking the questions and the young chaplain answering them. The discussion was religious, in a manner of speaking, but not any religion she knew anything about. The chaplain had talked about friendships, relationships, and personal involvement. *Almost,* Gaby thought, *as if I myself had the ability to converse with God.*

The chaplain had spoken of a personal relationship with Jesus. She knew Him only as the Son of Mary, and all she could picture was Him hanging on a cross, bleeding out His life's blood. But the young lady had said the cross had been the beginning, not the end, and Gaby had understood.

And there had been no condemnation in the young chaplain's voice about the baby that Gaby carried. There had been only understanding and love and reassurances that whatever was necessary would be done to see that the baby had a good home. Until that moment, Gaby had not thought of the baby as part of her, but the realization was slowly dawning. It was her baby, part of her.

That was where the inner warmth had come from. They had prayed—in Spanish. The feeling of complete contentment had flowed into her almost immediately, like magic. But this feeling was honest, not like the temporary feeling she used to get by going to the priest's church on the village square.

Gaby snuggled into the warmth of the bed, letting her new contentment sweep over and through her in a wave of total exultation. She was going to be all right, she knew.

Her eyes closed and she slept the sleep of the forgiven.

■ ■ ■

Susan Blair waited impatiently for her husband to walk through the door. The news had come less than a half hour ago, and she was bursting at the seams to tell him. He would be shocked and pleased to learn that in less than nine months, they would become the parents they had always wanted to be.

For a split second, Susan Blair felt a residual shudder rush through her at the thought of what had been done to both of them at the Phelps Clinic. But that was over, and so was the feeling of frustration that had always accompanied their frequent visits to the Germantown clinic.

Kenneth Blair came into the room, and Susan rushed into his arms. *Today,* she thought, *our lives begin anew.*

■ ■ ■

Wade Larsen had no choice. He could not remain out in the cold. He was not dressed for it, and darkness was quickly falling.

He had followed the two men long enough to verify their destination and their intentions. He would go back to his office, round up his deputies, and return with the equipment and men he needed to stop what was about to happen in the Ozark valley.

This would be his last righteous act before resigning his position as sheriff. What would happen after that, he was not sure, but he would deal with that when it came. Right now, he calculated that he had only a couple of hours to prepare and get back to the valley before irreparable damage was done and innocent people died.

■ ■ ■

Less than two miles away, beneath Christmas Bluff, as the huge rock face was known locally, David Michaels listened to the end of Donald Fenwick's story.

When he finished, Fenwick sat back against the tree trunk he'd been using as a backrest. David sat near the small lamp, trying to understand what he'd just been told. He had no trouble believing the story; it was too demonic to be anything but the truth.

He felt his heart race within his chest. A year ago, he had faced similar circumstances, except that what he'd just been told was so demonic, so sadistic, that it would take all his abilities and all his faith to deal with it.

David Michaels was scared, and prayer was the best answer for his fear.

CHAPTER THIRTY-FIVE

The cold was miserable and wet. David Michaels and Donald Fenwick talked until the fuel in the small lantern had exhausted itself, and then they talked some more, their words floating in and out of the night chill like bats searching for a roost.

Donald Fenwick's voice was low, modulated, but utterly sincere. David asked questions, probing, searching. And when the two men finally finished, each had a greater understanding of the other, and each knew what the other was doing in the wintry forest.

David Michaels was horrified at what he had heard, but as a pastor he was not surprised.

They went to bed, cramming inside the small tent David had packed. They had divided the clothing and sleeping equipment as best they could. David gave the more substantial sleeping bag to Fenwick and saved the space-thermal blanket for himself. During the night, the sounds of the forest—the freezing and cracking of tree limbs, the low moan of the wind, and the occasional animal noise—could be heard.

But these were not what kept David awake. His mind was in turmoil, planning, reviewing, preparing.

David tried to roll over, his movement restricted in the small tent. He knew he had slept, but it had been fitful, unfullfilling.

The cold nipped at him, first at his extremities, then deeper inside, where he was not sure if it was really the cold or just the onset of advancing age.

He recalled the jungles of Panama and the Joint Operations Training Center located at Fort Sherman on the isthmus. The weather there had also been torturous. The only difference, David thought wryly, was a temperature variance of a hundred degrees.

David glanced over at the man snuggled down in the sleeping bag. His head was covered by a protective cap, and David was pleased to see that Fenwick had taken his advice and not tried to bury his face inside the sleeping bag. That simple act would have increased the relative humidity inside the bag, possibly freezing, making the bag useless for retaining body heat.

David struggled out of the tent, running his hand over his closely cropped gray hair. Small particles of ice came away in his hand. He shivered, his limbs ached. He was getting old, he told himself, but that was a malady he dearly hoped to hold at bay for as long as possible. He made a mental note to increase his daily exercise regimen when he got back home.

He fueled the small stove, gathered wood for a fire, and set about preparing the morning meal. It would not be much, certainly not as much as he had planned, not with Fenwick sharing it. But it was all they had, and it would have to do.

When David touched a waterproof match to the burner of the small stove, the roar sounded like a jet engine igniting. Fenwick's stirring within the tent brought a smile to his face.

"Breakfast in ten minutes," David called to the pulsating tent.

The movement in the tent ceased momentarily, then continued with renewed vigor. After a full two minutes of struggle within the tent, Fenwick called, "How do you get this stupid zipper open?"

David laughed and strode toward the tent. He had the businessman freed in seconds. Donald Fenwick looked like exactly what he was, a fish out of water.

But David had to give him some credit; at least the man had come to the real source of his problems. Fenwick was facing his adversity head on. David's mind returned to the night before and what he had learned from Fenwick. It didn't seem possible, not in a truly civilized society, but civility seemed to be up for grabs lately in the good old US of A.

David was tempted to power up the cell phone he had brought with him, call Janice Morgan at the Clayton County sheriff's department, and tell her the whole story. She would notify county, state, and federal authorities and be in the valley in a matter of hours. But before he called in a full frontal assault, David wanted to verify Fenwick's story. Then, when he knew the truth, he would contact Janice. He would preserve the battery power of the small phone until then.

Deep in his soul, he knew that what Fenwick had said was true, but the possibility that such a place existed sickened David at the very core of his being. Then he remembered the young girl who had taken refuge in the belly of their airplane, surviving only on desire and guts. The girl had been pregnant, which confirmed what Fenwick had said. But he needed to *see,* to *understand.*

"You're thinking about what I told you last night," Donald Fenwick intruded.

David blinked away a tear he had not realized had formed in the corner of his eye. "Yes. I was."

"You're having a problem with it. Believing it, perhaps."

David shook his head. "That's the problem I'm *not* having. If you had seen the evil I've seen, you wouldn't have any problem believing that this valley really exists."

"You want to see it."

"Exactly. As soon as we've eaten and packed up, we're heading for that valley."

"How far away do you figure?"

David had perused the map earlier. "Couple of miles, no more. If the location you gave me is accurate, there's only one valley with the topographical features you mentioned. The stream cinches it. Two miles northeast. Maybe an hour at most in the snow. Double that for an inspection sweep."

"Inspection sweep? What are you talking about?" Fenwick asked with a quizzical look.

"If this outfit is as tight as you say it is, there's bound to be some sort of security devices. Motion detectors, systemic detectors, cameras. That sort of thing."

"I don't think so. The place is so isolated they don't see the need. Besides, it's a good bet the local smokies are in on the whole thing."

"The sheriff?" David quizzed.

"Almost certainly. That's the way things are done in these rural counties."

David nodded again, this time in the affirmative. "I'm beginning to learn that. Okay, we still do a sweep for detection devices, but we won't overdo it."

The snow David had placed in the aluminum pot over the small camp stove was boiling. "Let's eat, get some tea in us, and get going."

"Agreed," Donald Fenwick said.

In less than ten minutes, the two men had consumed the food, downed two cups apiece of ginger tea, and had the camping gear stowed in David's backpack.

"You got the map," Fenwick said.

"Let's go."

The two men trudged through the gray landscape for more than forty-five minutes, their fogging breath the only indication of the effort each man was putting into the trek.

Twice they stopped as David checked the map and the compass. Satisfied with their direction, he plowed on, not wanting to ask Fenwick if he was tiring for fear the answer would mean a further delay in getting to the valley.

A sound from behind stopped David. He turned to see Donald Fenwick puffing up the slight rise he had just climbed.

"Like I said," a weary Fenwick offered, "you're more than just some ordinary preacher. You're going to have to confess before this day is over. You're not even breathing hard."

"Clean living," David shot back.

"Uh-huh. Don't give me that. Who are you?"

"The Lone Ranger?" David continued.

"*That,* I might be willing to believe," Fenwick huffed. "How much farther?"

"If my calculations are correct," David said, consulting the map, "the valley should be just over this rise. I hope we'll be at the far end, away from the house you told me about. Better to get an overall view."

Fenwick said nothing, his breath coming in rapid expulsions of foggy, frigid clouds.

The two moved on in silence.

David thought of Cindy as they moved deeper into the frozen forest. It was happening more and more these days. Out of the clear blue, his mind seemed to shift gears from whatever he was doing to the beauty of her green eyes and her acceptance and understanding of him. To David, Cindy was the epitome of love and generosity. She had also become a sounding board for him in times of trouble.

In the year since he had taken over the pastorate at First Community Church, he had faced situations and problems he could never have foreseen in a million years. David could still remember a statement he'd made to the previous pastor, Glen Shackleford, expressing his concern that military chaplaincy experience would not easily translate into a civilian context. He had been both right and wrong.

Situations *had* arisen. Some he had handled effectively, with caring and love and understanding. Some he had not been prepared to face, and it was those instances where he had, at appropriate times, confided in Cindy. Her insight and sensitivity—qualities he was still developing— had carried him through the maelstrom of pastoral indecision.

David smiled inwardly. Most people, particularly close-knit congregations like First Community, thought of the pastor as all-knowing, all-caring, all-understanding. As far as David knew, the only person who had ever possessed those qualities had been Jesus Christ. David confronted indecision, doubts, and lack of understanding every day of his life. He did not have all the answers, and knowing his limitations contributed to a reservoir of self-doubt that threatened to overwhelm him during critical times.

But through it all, there was Cindy, her green eyes reflecting her understanding of the agony he sometimes felt. At those times, when he was with her, just talking quietly, he was amazed at the feeling he had for her. It was love, he knew, but it was love that seemed to transcend any love he had ever experienced. There was a physical attraction, of course. That could not be denied. But his feeling for her was so much more that sometimes the depth of it frightened him.

A hand on his shoulder jarred him from his daydream. He had been trudging through the forest snow, his head in the clouds, and now, as he returned his attention to the present moment, he saw the valley.

"That's it," Donald Fenwick said.

David scanned the terrain. It was beautiful, but there was no denying the sense of foreboding, the impression of unabated evil that now sent a shudder through his body.

David's map reading had been perfect; he had brought them into the valley at the far end, the point furthermost from the house Fenwick had described last night.

The valley lay on a long axis away from them. Snow-covered mountains rose on both sides. A river cut the depression into two equal parts. Pine trees, more brown than green, pushed up to the sky, sparse hardwoods making their presence known only by the starkness of their leafless branches.

Were it not for the staggering feeling of oppression, the valley would have been a dream come true to anyone who loved nature.

"The house is at the far end, near the bend in the river," Fenwick said.

"I make it about a mile and a half," David calculated. Another hour, he knew, taking it easy, watching for detection devices and maybe even hired guns.

As if he had read David Michaels's mind, Donald Fenwick said, "There won't be any guards. Not on the outside, at least. That's part of the lure of this location. It's so remote, not many people even know about this valley."

"We're still going to take it slow and easy, just to be on the safe side. What you described to me last night is an organization that doesn't take chances. We won't either."

The morning sun had crested the horizon somewhere behind the thick bank of snow clouds. It had been dark when they had broken camp and hiked the two miles to the entrance of the valley. Now, despite the clouds, there would be enough light to be seen should anyone be watching.

"We'll stay just inside the tree line to the right. Walking down the middle of the valley would be an invitation to get ourselves killed," David told Fenwick.

"Like I said, you're more than a simple preacher."

"Let's go," David ordered in a low voice, ignoring Fenwick's remark.

The two men cut to the right, keeping to the incline formed by the mountains on their right. The trees were thick, but not so thick as to impede their progress to any great degree.

The cold and the snow were obstacles, but even they were not David's greatest concern. He could not tell whether Donald Fenwick felt the oppressive spirit, but David recognized the growing power of an unknown evil as the two pushed deeper into the valley, closer to the house.

The two men worked their way along the ridge in silence. The only sound was the crunch of snow beneath their boots and Donald Fenwick's labored breathing. It took another hour to reach the point David had selected on his map. He stopped abruptly and Fenwick almost bumped into him. The businessman had been walking behind, tracing David's steps in the snow, his head down. He pulled up just short of David and his head came up.

David pointed down to the valley floor, where the house was now clearly visible. To David, it looked like the White House in miniature. Great white columns rose from a marble portico. Twin wings stretched out on each side, expanding the visual effect. Even at this early hour, lights burned on the first two floors. Whatever activity was taking place within the edifice was off to an early start.

Then, as David scanned the surrounding area, his eye caught movement off to his left, below him, but still above the level of the house itself. David raised his hand, a warning to Donald Fenwick to remain quiet. The movement was gone for only a moment, and then returned. Someone was moving through the tree line below them. The trees blocked the movement, affording David the flickering effect of movement which had caught his eye only seconds earlier.

There they were! Not one, but two!

David motioned Fenwick to crouch where he was, as he did, lowering his outline, reducing his visibility.

The two men below carried packs similar to David's. They moved cautiously, carefully, taking in the view below them but totally oblivious to what was above them.

Police? was David's first thought. But what happened next answered that question.

The two men stopped and unslung their packs. One of the men began rummaging through his pack and pulled out several blocks wrapped in brown paper.

David's blood ran cold at the sight. He had seen it before, many times, enough C-4 plastic explosives to level the white house in the valley.

■　■　■

Right or wrong, Wade Larsen was going through with his plan. He'd watched the two men yesterday shoulder packs and start for the only place in the valley of any significance.

Knowing he could not do anything himself, he'd quickly returned to Benning and set about mustering all the deputies he could. He had broken out the automatic weapons, tear gas canisters, and what body armor the Benning County sheriff's office owned. It had taken him the better part of the night, and it was nearly dawn before the small force returned to the valley and made their way to within a quarter-mile of the house.

Some of the deputies, the newer ones, had no idea what was taking place. Most had never been to the valley before. Others, the more seasoned, the more trusted, knew exactly what was taking place. For some of them, the house had been a secondary source of income for more years than they could count. Whatever was about to take place, they knew the money was about to cease.

Larsen spread his forces out on a line paralleling the river, which twisted around the back side of the house. He decided their best angle of approach would be from the far side of the house, from the opposite ridge. With his men placed along the river, they were out of sight, their presence shielded by the mass of the house.

Now there was nothing to do but wait.

■　■　■

The only light burning in Tom Frazier's office was the single-bulb lamp on the corner of his desk. It had been a long night, and the disarray showed it. Jules Goldman sat quietly in the same chair he'd occupied less than twenty-four hours earlier.

"It's confirmed, then," said Frazier.

Goldman remained quiet. It was not the time to speak.

"The man named Damon has Cindy Tolbert, and it's pretty apparent the reason is to get Michaels to come after her."

Again Goldman said nothing.

Tom Frazier cursed, his voice low, but nonetheless vehement in its exclamation.

"It has to be this way," Goldman said finally.

"But I don't have to like it," Frazier replied angrily.

"No, you don't."

"Michaels is confirmed in the valley. An aircraft mechanic and pilot confirmed dropping him off in the pasture."

Goldman sat up, his attention piqued.

"The pilot, a guy named Brian Connelly, said Michaels took him straight to the place using a GPS."

Goldman whistled. "I'm beginning to believe you're right about this Michaels. He's not your ordinary preacher."

Tom Frazier met Jules Goldman's gaze. "Not ordinary at all," he said, then fell silent.

■   ■   ■

Billy Bob Campbell and Cole Branscum waited while Jason Swann opened the small wall safe. Billy Bob had left Swann in his office yesterday late with the understanding he would be back for payment before dawn. When Billy Bob had arrived home, Cole had been waiting for him. There had been nothing to do but tell Cole of the arrangements and bring him along for the payoff.

Billy Bob fully intended to dump Cole on the roadside somewhere between Benning and the Missouri border. But first he wanted the money he knew Swann kept in the safe.

"That's enough," Billy Bob said as soon as Swann swung the safe door open.

"Enough what?" Swann challenged.

"Enough of you, that's what. Step away from the safe. I'll think I'll just pay myself for services rendered," Billy Bob said.

"What . . .?"

"Step away," Billy Bob ordered in a low voice.

Swann stepped back. Billy Bob Campbell was holding an automatic pistol in his right hand, and Swann was too smart and too frightened to do otherwise.

Billy Bob went to the safe and looked inside. He reached in and pulled out a cloth money bag. He opened it, whistled, and looked up at Swann.

"How much have you stolen? A hundred grand? More?"

"There's two hundred and fifty thousand in that bag. Take what I owe you, and get out," Swann said, trying to sound menacing and failing.

Billy Bob laughed. "I think we'll just take it all. After all, who you gonna call? The cops?"

"Take the money and let's get out of here," Cole said, a trace of worry in his voice. He'd seen the same look on Billy Bob's face before, and somebody usually died soon after.

"I got it. Don't worry. A few hours and we're out of this place, and we're rich."

CHAPTER
THIRTY-SIX

The quiet one called the driver "Pete;" Pete called the quiet man "Marvin." The two had learned the value of an alias from working for the man they knew as Damon. Damon was probably not the man's real name, either, but neither would have ever raised the question. Most people naturally feared Pete and Marvin. Not Damon. Damon elicited an inordinate amount of fear from the two men. There was something very special about him, but they would never raise that question either.

The pair had done a lot of work for Damon. Mostly the work was the same as what they were now doing, correcting mistakes which could only be rectified in a very specific manner. That usually meant someone had to die.

Pete and Marvin had arrived in the valley just as daylight was fading, which gave them an opportunity to observe the house for a few hours. The activity seemed to be concentrated on the upper floors.

Through the upstairs windows, they had seen shadows moving to and fro, coming and going. Together they had counted at least half a dozen different shapes moving in the upstairs corridors and rooms. From the activity, it was also apparent that there were others residing in the upper rooms, others they could not see.

Not that it made a difference to Pete and Marvin. Their job was to reduce the white house to smoldering rubble.

The two men had watched the house until almost eleven o'clock, when the lights went out in most areas of the house. Most, but not all. There remained two lights burning upstairs and two downstairs, but the activity had been reduced to a minimum. It was time to act.

Pete had carried the heavier of the two packs, and both men set about removing the contents, sorting the various components, and assembling them.

When they were finished, eight two-kilogram blocks of C-4 plastic explosives, complete with detonators and timers, lay on the ground in front of them. Close to twenty pounds of explosives were ready to be attached at various points around the house.

Each man had taken four blocks and quietly worked his way around the perimeter, searching for vulnerable points. Blocks of C-4 were attached to supporting columns and structural features. One block was reserved for the spot where a one-inch propane line entered the house near a thousand-gallon storage tank. That one charge alone, combined with the fire that would follow, would probably destroy the house completely. With seven other charges strategically placed, the house would be reduced to rubble within seconds of detonation.

Once the explosives were set around the house, the two men hiked to the edge of the valley, where the coverage of trees was thicker, to set up camp for the night. At first light they would affix additional charges to the telephone lines to cut off communication in case something went wrong with the explosives at the house.

The two slept for almost five hours, undisturbed by either the winter cold or the task ahead.

Marvin awoke first, ambled over to Pete's tent, and kicked at it with a snow-encrusted boot. "Up and at 'em," he said quietly. "Time to finish this and get out of here."

Pete crawled from his tent, hair disheveled, eyes bloodshot and narrow. He was about to reply when both men's attention was drawn to a new sound.

The two eased away from their campsite in time to see a pickup truck drive up to the white house. Two men climbed from the cab and entered the house. Lights came on in a downstairs corner room and they could see figures moving. About the same time, the upstairs sprang to life, slowly at first, but more rapidly as shadowy figures made their way down the corridors, flipping on lights.

"This place starts early," Pete whispered to Marvin.

Marvin did not reply. Pete understood. They needed to set the last of their charges and get out of the valley. Pete pulled the pack containing the C-4 toward him and began removing the last blocks of explosive. The quicker they finished, the better. Besides, Pete reminded himself, he had a date tonight with a particularly cute blonde back in Little Rock, and he didn't want to be late.

The two killers divided the remaining blocks of C-4 between themselves. One man started for the back of the house, the other for the farthest utility pole he could see.

Each man carried a MAC-10 automatic weapon. One could never tell when it might be needed.

■   ■   ■

Wade Larsen had a sinking feeling that he'd made another mistake.

He'd gotten his small team of deputies into the valley unobserved, but he had no idea where the two men he'd followed the day before were located. Not knowing could prove very costly. Now, as he and his men hunkered down to the rear of the house near the river bend, he became acutely aware of another problem.

None of his men, including himself, was accustomed to working outdoors in the harshness of the Ozark winter, at least not for extended periods. The temperature had fallen during the night. Not drastically, but enough to make their current situation extremely uncomfortable. The cold was slowly invading even the insulated clothing each man wore.

From their place of concealment, the lawmen could see the lights start winking on in the house. They had seen Billy Bob Campbell and Cole Branscum drive up twenty minutes ago. What exactly those two hicks were doing out here at this hour was just another quirk thrown into the equation that the Benning County sheriff was trying to solve.

The lights in Jason Swann's office had come on a few seconds after Billy Bob and Cole entered. Now, the upper-floor lights were coming on, signaling the start of a new day for the staff and the young girls on that floor. He had never confirmed it, but Larsen thought he knew what was happening in those second-story rooms. But what was happening on the first floor and out here in the forest was a more immediate concern.

A slight movement to his right caught Larsen's eye. Out of the semidarkness, a deputy appeared. "Lot's going on up there, Wade," Gary Hantz said in a whisper.

Larsen nodded to the young deputy. Hantz was one of the "new generation" deputies, as Larsen called them. Highly educated, intelligent, intuitive. Hantz was also one who knew nothing about what went on in the valley. Larsen was acutely aware of the disappointment he knew the young deputy would feel when he discovered the truth.

"We'll wait," Larsen whispered back. "The two men I told you about are here somewhere." With no further explanation, Larsen fell silent, and Hantz moved back to his previous position.

The knot in the pit of his stomach tightened, and Wade Larsen decided he'd made a grave error by even showing up in the valley this day. Maybe it would have been better just to let the men do what they had come to do, and with any luck, all his problems concerning the valley would be eliminated.

Another movement caught his eye, this time in the distance, along the lower part of the ridge that paralleled the valley.

Two men, moving slowly and quietly, appeared in the growing light. Billy Bob and Cole were still in the house, along with Jason Swann, Larsen was certain. Almost every light on the upper floor glowed in the flat, gray morning light.

The two men moved with purpose, one toward the house, the other back down the road, and Larsen could see each man carried bundles. Hantz was back; this time his whisper carried a note of urgency.

"They've got MAC-10s, boss," the young deputy exclaimed. "Who are these guys?"

Larsen put a finger to his lips. "Later," he told the young man in a low voice. "Get your guys up along the riverbank and come in behind them. I'll take my men around the rear, using the house as cover. Keep it down. Sound travels a long way in this cold."

Hantz moved off, motioning to the two deputies on his team. Larsen motioned to the remaining three men, and they began working their way around the rear of the house.

Larsen and his group had just taken cover behind the corner of the house, one deputy almost tripping over the one-inch propane line that fueled the house, when a shot rang out, piercing the tranquillity of the valley.

■　　■　　■

To David Michaels, it was the worst sound he had ever heard. Donald Fenwick, moving behind David, reacted immediately, the fear on his face reflected in the bleak dawn light. The CEO started to speak, but David stopped him with a hand signal. Fenwick moved closer to David and followed the commander's gaze down into the valley.

"The two men with the MACs didn't do it," he whispered to Fenwick. "That shot came from inside the house."

Movement further on, near the river bend now caught David's eye. Two . . . no . . . three men were moving along the riverbank, mirroring the movements of the second man who had headed down the road, away from the house. With the sound of the shot still hanging in the air, the three men along the riverbank and the man on the road with the MAC-10 froze in place. All eyes were fixed on the white house.

David shifted his attention to the other man. The one who had been heading toward the house had dropped to the ground, his MAC-10 aimed and ready to fire.

"What the heck is going on?" Donald Fenwick whispered urgently.

"I don't know. There are a bunch of guys down there now, and I don't think they like each other very much. I can see uniforms on the three at the riverbank. The law must have gotten in on this."

"The law in Benning County *is part of this*," Fenwick shot back, fear now evident in his whisper. *"I told* you *that."*

"Yeah. So you said. But something is coming apart at the seams, and I have the feeling we may be the only ones who can stop it."

"We?" Fenwick said in a panic. "You know why I'm up here, and it's not because I have a death wish."

"Me, then," David said, not taking his eyes off the activity below. The shot had frozen the action below, throwing time into slow motion. David had the same feeling he had experienced more than a year ago in the streets of Little Rock, except now he found himself trapped in the cold of an Ozark winter. As the last sound waves dissipated among the hills and trees, movement returned to the valley.

Shadows in the corner room on the bottom floor washed over the window, chaotic, disjointed. *That* was where the shot had come from, not from outside, but inside the house.

"Stay here," David ordered Fenwick.

"Where're you going?" the businessman asked. Fear showed in his voice.

"Down there," was all David Michaels answered, moving down the slope, toward the house and the valley.

*   *   *

Cindy Tolbert was familiar with fear. Certainly in the past several hours she had faced her share of it. The uncertainty of what was going on, the mystery of her kidnapping, the house where she was held captive all elevated her anxiety to new heights. But there was something else now. She'd had the feeling before, last year when she first learned that David Michaels and an FBI agent were heading for Little Rock to confront the evil that had gripped Collins Construction International. Once again, she sensed that David was in trouble, and that meant she had only one course of action.

Cindy dropped down beside the bed and began praying. For a short moment, she wondered whether this is what it had been like for Paul when he prayed in prison. She squinted her eyes tighter, hoping to focus on the face of the man she loved. It worked, and the sharper the focus became, the harder she prayed.

Whatever the problem was, she knew prayer could change the outcome. With that realization, she strengthened her petition, realizing as she prayed just how much she really loved David Michaels.

CHAPTER THIRTY-SEVEN

This is absolutely incredible, David Michaels thought, as he scrambled from the vantage point he'd shared with Donald Fenwick, stumbling over snow-covered timber and the uneven terrain. His attention was riveted on the single man with the MAC-10 who had started down the road away from the house. Now, as he moved closer, he could make out the three men along the riverbank. They were wearing the uniforms of the Benning County sheriff's department. One of the deputies, his young face almost glowing in the predawn light, rose from his position of concealment.

David wanted to scream at the young deputy but knew it was too late. The MAC-10 barked sharply, spewing three evenly spaced shots across the valley. The deputy was thrown backward, almost into the river.

David felt his heart sink, and then anger welled up inside him. He was sickened by the shooting of the deputy, but anger was by far the stronger of the two emotions and it propelled him into action.

His Navy SEAL training took over.

Act; *react!*

React; *move!*

Move; *attack!*

Turn disadvantage into advantage; do the unexpected, the *unexplainable!*

Suddenly, David's boots skittered along an ice-covered flat rock; he lost his balance, tumbling down the steep incline, his momentum carrying him directly into the path of the killer. David felt has body rolling and tumbling like a circus acrobat, his surprise gone, his advantage lost. He saw the man turn, reacting to the sound; the obscene MAC-10 swiveled toward him.

Deputy Gary Hantz watched as the department's newest recruit was blown back almost to the river's edge by the deadly burst of the MAC-10 fired by the man on the road. Before he could react, he saw another man come out of nowhere, racing down the mountainside above them, moving like an avatar from a horror film. Just then, the man slipped on something and plunged headlong down the hillside.

The shooter turned in response to the sound above him. He raised the MAC-10, swinging the short, deadly weapon in the direction of the tumbling specter.

Deputy Hantz had never pulled his weapon on another human being. Not that he hadn't been trained, or that, given the appropriate circumstance, he wouldn't. It was just that he'd never been put in that position. Until now.

He yanked the 9mm Beretta automatic from his holster. There was no time to aim; it was either instinct and training or nothing.

Hantz felt the Beretta buck in his hands. Both eyes remained fixed on the man in the road. Later, the young deputy would swear he saw every bullet as it exited the barrel of the black automatic.

The first shot struck Marvin just below the right shoulder blade, the force of the 9mm slug twisting the killer away from the sliding David Michaels. The second and third bullets hit Marvin in the chest, throwing him backwards. He was dead before the MAC-10 was ripped from his hands by a fourth bullet.

David Michaels heard the sound of the Beretta. He had almost arrested his headlong slide down the mountainside when he saw the man below him spun around by the force of the first bullet. His attention was drawn back to the riverbank, where he could now see two uniformed men, one with a black handgun leveled at the man on the road. Three more successive flashes burst from the muzzle of the pistol. The man on the road was thrown to the ground.

David wondered who his guardian angel was.

■   ■   ■

Pete's first thought was that a small war had erupted in the valley. The location of the shots he heard was a mystery, but the fact that there were any shots at all was enough to throw him into a panic.

He knew Marvin was somehow involved, by the unmistakable chatter of the MAC-10. Unless someone else in the valley had a MAC-10. That thought only served to amplify Pete's growing anxiety.

The MAC-10's volley had been followed almost instantaneously by four shots from another weapon that was definitely *not* a MAC-10. A pistol by the sound of it. What was going on? Had they been set up? It made no sense, but then Pete knew, most things that involved Damon did not make a lot of sense.

It was then that Pete realized who and what Damon was. The knowledge, he knew, would do him little good in his present situation, but just knowing seemed to offer some strange comfort.

Pete had been within a hundred yards of the house when the first shot split the early morning. But that shot had come from within the house. The subsequent shots had come from outside. Whatever was going on, Pete had the uneasy feeling he was about to end his criminal career in this Arkansas valley.

■   ■   ■

Jason Swann looked in awe at Billy Bob Campbell's huge body splayed across the floor of his office. Cole Branscum stood across the room where he had bolted out of his chair in response to the shot.

Swann had backed away from the wall safe as Billy Bob emptied the contents—more than a quarter of a million dollars. He'd gradually eased open the drawer of his desk, extracted a pistol, and shot Billy Bob Campbell as easily as if he'd been exterminating a rodent. *Come to think of it, Billy Bob probably fit that category rather well,* Swann thought.

Swann swung the pistol toward Cole, but Cole had had no intention of interfering in his best friend's extermination. Cole had already figured that Billy Bob was planning to kill him rather than split the money, so Swann's actions merely solved a problem for him.

With Billy Bob out of the way, he was certain he could negotiate a reasonable settlement with Swann, flee the state, perhaps even the country, and live in relative splendor for the rest of his life.

That was before the sound of gunfire erupted outside the house. Cole looked anxiously at Swann to see whether he was being set up, but the look on the small man's face was pure shock. If this was a setup, it was happening to both of them.

The two men heard the shuffling and running of feet from above. The upper floors had been thrown into their own type of panic.

Cole suddenly knew that the house was about to go out of business—permanently.

■   ■   ■

Sheriff Larsen cursed at the first shot. He knew that something had happened between Swann, Campbell, and Branscum. But panic began to well up in his chest when he heard the MAC-10. He knew that at least one of the deputies he'd sent with Gary Hantz had been spotted, possibly all three. When he heard the sound of a Beretta automatic split the cold winter air, he was reasonably certain that at least one of his deputies had returned fire.

His immediate concern now was the second man who had been closing in on the house. Where was he? Neither he nor the deputies with him had the second man in sight.

"Let's move," he barked at the men with him. The small team of officers moved quickly, sprinting from the rear of the house, headed for the front. They needed line-of-sight contact with the second man.

Larsen ran to his left, skirting the large propane tank, leaping over odds and ends lying in the yard, heading for the portico of the house. He could hear his men behind him, their boots slipping and sliding on the frozen turf and accumulated snow.

Larsen rounded the corner of the right portico. The road came into sight. The second man was no more than a hundred yards down the road, and the man was reaching for something. In an instant, Wade Larsen knew what the man had in his hand, and he knew that everyone in or near the house was dead.

■   ■   ■

David Michaels came to rest no more than ten feet from Marvin's body. Still operating on instinct, he came to his feet and began sprinting down the road toward the house.

When he heard a quick order to stop from the young deputy with the Beretta, he motioned with his hand for the officer to follow him. He ran the risk that the deputy might miss the signal or think that David was one of the killers, but when no follow-up order was heard, and no shots fired, David assumed that the deputy was racing after him down the road.

The day seemed to have darkened, if that was possible. The morning had begun with low-hanging clouds, dark and oppressive. Now it seemed more so. The evil in the valley was still here, still vibrant, still deadly.

David could hear the slogging footfalls now of the deputy behind

him. David's own boots slipped and skidded on the frozen surface of
the road. Time was running out.

He rounded the bend in the road, which paralleled the bend in the
river. Ahead of him, now in view, was the second man, his own MAC-
10 slung over his back, out of reach. The man was fumbling with something in his hand, something that David recognized immediately. What
he saw caused him to ignore a new pain in his right leg, ignore the
frozen road, ignore all else except the small box the man was holding.

When David was within reach of the second man, he launched
himself like a linebacker blitzing an unprotected quarterback.

David and Pete hit the frozen ground hard, and David was acutely
aware of a tearing in his left shoulder. Pete had been so absorbed in trying
to activate the detonator that he hadn't heard David rushing up behind
him. The impact threw him face down onto the frozen earth. A single nine-
volt battery skittered across the icy road, and the rest of the detonator
landed almost thirty feet away. The contact with the ground shattered the
box into several inert pieces of plastic and destroyed the integrated circuits.

David felt himself lose consciousness, but for no more than two or
three seconds, then he was up, his mind forcing his body to react, to
function.

Pete was still down, but moving. David could see men running
from the direction of the house—men in uniform, policemen. But they
were too far away to affect the immediate situation.

Pete recovered, groping for control of the MAC-10 as he came up
on one knee.

David did not hesitate. His body position afforded him only one
offensive option, and he took it. With his torso twisted at an angle
away from the killer, David's right leg came up, the knee bent slightly,
forcing a reverse kick into the killer's midsection, just below the solar
plexus. The only sound was of air being forcefully expelled.

The killer's eyes glazed over; his mouth flew open, trying to mouth
words that would not come from his damaged lungs. He went down,
his head bouncing once on the frozen earth, and lay still.

David's left foot slipped from beneath him with the reverse kick. With the slip, there would have been no second kick, no second chance. Had the kick not landed, David Michaels knew he would have been dead.

Men in uniform converged on him from two directions. David lay back against the cold ground and closed his eyes.

■   ■   ■

Wade Larsen and Gary Hantz reached the two men at the same time. Hantz already had his handcuffs out, forcing them onto the wrists of the man who had carried the MAC-10 machine gun. Sheriff Larsen veered to his right to recover portions of the plastic box he'd seen fly through the air.

Gary Hantz reassured himself that the cuffs on Pete were secure, then he turned his attention to David Michaels.

"You OK?"

David opened his eyes, his head still resting on the ground. He smiled at the uniformed deputy. "OK," was all he could say.

Wade Larsen approached the two men. He addressed the prone David Michaels. "You knew what this box was, didn't you?"

David pushed himself up from the ground, his body protesting, the pain a warning. He stood. "It's a remote detonation device. Probably means there are C-4 charges sprinkled around that house."

"C-4?" Gary Hantz repeated incredulously.

"I saw the other man, the one you shot, with some more. Probably find some more on this guy too."

Larsen intervened. "You know about C-4?"

David forced a smile. "It's not as ominous as it sounds. I was military. I've seen plastic explosives before."

Larsen nodded and said, "I don't doubt that part. The big question is, what are you doing here? What do you know about this valley?"

"That's another story," David Michaels answered, suddenly weary. "One better saved until after we find out where that first shot came from, don't you think?"

"I've got three more deputies corralling whoever is left in the house. I suspect I'm going to have to deal with only two of three men in there, none of whom I like very well."

David stared at the sheriff. "Sounds to me like you already know what's going on and who is behind it."

"As you just said, that's another story. One that can wait."

"I guess you're right," David agreed.

From behind them, two deputies walked up the road, a third man between them. One of the deputies staggered, obviously in pain. It was the man Marvin had shot.

"How's the chest, Carpenter?" Gary Hantz asked the young deputy.

"I'll never complain about having to wear body armor again. I'm just glad the guy wasn't using a magnum. As it is, I'll be bruised for the next month."

"Who's this guy?" Larsen asked, referring to the man between the two deputies.

"Says his name is Donald Fenwick. Head of FenMark," the deputy named Carpenter answered.

"No kidding?"

"It's true, Sheriff. And he's got a story to tell you, but I have the feeling all the facts are not going to be news to you," David said.

"I'm afraid you're right about that," Wade Larsen said. "But what is Mr. Fenwick doing out here in the middle of winter?"

"The same thing we're doing," David interjected. "Trying to clean up an evil that seems to have infected this valley."

"David?" Donald Fenwick said, offering him the small cell phone. "You said you wanted to make a call as soon as possible."

"Thanks. I want to call Janice Morgan and have her relay a message to a particular lady."

"*Sheriff* Janice Morgan from Clayton County?" Larsen asked.

"The same," David answered, taking the small phone from Donald Fenwick. He dialed the number. It was answered on the first ring. After identifying himself, he listened for several minutes, then disconnected without so much as a single word.

"What's that all about?" Wade Larsen asked.

David Michaels turned to Larsen. "I don't know how you're involved in this, but I ought to kill you right where you stand."

Larsen, despite his size and the badge on his chest, took a wary step backward. He had never in his life seen such hate in any man's eyes.

"What's happened?" Donald Fenwick asked.

"Cindy has been kidnapped. And now I know what's going on." David turned to Donald Fenwick. "I've got to get to Memphis." David began walking back down the frozen road. The other men stood stunned and watched him walk away.

"Who is he?" Gary Hantz asked tentatively.

"Would you believe a preacher?" Donald Fenwick answered.

PART III
LAZARUS

CHAPTER THIRTY-EIGHT

"He knows?" Tom Frazier asked.

"I told him what I know," Janice Morgan said. The anxiety in her voice carried over the miles, conveying the unmistakable concern she had for David Michaels.

"You didn't tell him everything, did you?"

"You haven't told *me* everything, Tom," Janice responded, exasperation replacing the earlier anxiety.

Tom Frazier sighed. Janice Morgan had every right to be upset with him.

"David's mad at you," said Janice, not waiting for a response from Frazier. "I wouldn't want to confront him right now."

"I understand."

"No, I don't think you do. David may not think you had anything to do with Cindy's kidnapping, but I suspect he feels you knew about it and didn't do anything to stop it." The accusation was clear. "That wouldn't be too far from wrong, would it, Tom?"

Tom Frazier sat back in his chair, trying to shrink into the worn leather, seeking protection that was not there. He'd been in his White House basement office for almost thirty-six hours straight, and the strain was taking its toll. Tom Frazier was accustomed to being involved in the action, used to being on the scene. But this was different, this control by proxy. He would prefer to be in Memphis, but he knew that was impossible. The scenario was set; it had to be played out the way it was orchestrated.

Frazier glanced over at Jules Goldman. The Mossad agent returned the look with anticipation, his eyebrows arching up in an unspoken question. Frazier continued his conversation with Janice Morgan.

"David Michaels is never too far from the truth," Frazier admitted. "I think it has something to do with being a preacher."

"It has to do with truth and honesty," Janice snapped.

"Yeah, Janice, I know. Those are two commodities that are sometimes rare in our business."

"My business is law enforcement, Tom. Like yours used to be. I don't know what your business is now."

"Most of the time, neither do I, Janice," Tom Frazier said wearily. "But this time it's different."

"Different enough to use a friend?"

"Different enough to use whatever is at hand. You'll understand, probably within a few days. Maybe a few hours."

"I'll accept that, but don't count on David playing the gentle pastor if something happens to Cindy."

"He's on his way to Memphis right now?" Tom Frazier asked. The implications of the question caused his pulse to accelerate despite the fatigue of the past few hours.

"With Donald Fenwick," Janice Morgan said with a feeling of satisfaction. Fenwick was a new wild card thrown into the mix and one that Tom Frazier knew nothing about.

"Fenwick? Donald Fenwick as in FenMark?" Frazier asked incredulously.

Janice Morgan smiled to herself, wishing she had one of those little phone cameras so Tom Frazier could see the smug look on her face. "The same," she replied.

"What in the sam hill is he doing in this?"

"Not much. I talked to David via his cell phone after the incident in the valley. He called me back after he calmed down. David and young Fenwick ran across each other in the forest. Or rather, according to Mr. Fenwick, David Michaels saved his life, and now Mr. FenMark feels a certain responsibility to the good reverend. Fenwick had a Humvee parked a few miles from the valley, and the two are using that. Should be in Memphis within the next few hours."

Tom Frazier placed his hand over the mouthpiece of the phone and said to Goldman, "Michaels is already on his way to Memphis. Be there in a few hours."

Goldman perched on the edge of his chair. "He's got the address?"

Frazier returned to the phone. "You gave him the address in Memphis?" he asked Janice.

"Come on, Tom. You know better than to ask me that. I may be dumb enough to get involved with you in this thing, but I'm not *that* dumb."

"Sorry, Janice. This thing is getting to me."

"David's in danger, isn't he?"

"I think so. More danger than any of us anticipated," Frazier added, casting an accusatory look in Goldman's direction.

The Mossad agent shrugged silently.

Janice Morgan heard the words, acutely aware of the emotion transmitted over the phone line. Tom Frazier was a good man and a friend to both her and David. She knew enough to know that he would never have embarked on a course of action such as this without a very good reason. Whatever that reason was, there was danger. And she could hear in Frazier's voice the additional element of uncertainty. Control had been sacrificed for exposure.

"Let me know what's going on when you can," Janice said before hanging up.

Tom Frazier slumped back in his chair, emotion and exhaustion sweeping over him in ever-increasing waves. "Your men better be in place when Michaels gets there. If this man is not who you say he is, I will personally make it my mission in life to see the Mossad thrown out of this country for the next hundred years.

Jules Goldman let a smile creep over his face. "I understand. Now lend me your phone while I check with my people in Memphis. And I will notify my boss in Tel Aviv, too, if you think the White House can afford the long-distance call."

Tom Frazier laughed, the tension broken for the moment. "You make the call; I'll get the coffee. This thing should be over by tonight."

Jules Goldman waited until Tom Frazier went to retrieve the coffee, then picked up the phone and placed an overseas call. When the phone was answered on the other end, he said, "Tonight, at the latest. It's him. There's no doubt about it. And the other man is with him. I'll let you know the outcome." Goldman broke the overseas connection, then dialed a 901 area code number. Like Frazier, he would have preferred to be in on the action, to be in Memphis this very moment, but that was impossible, so he would monitor the progress via the White House phone. When the phone in Memphis was answered, he said, "Fill me in," and he was lost in the details when Tom Frazier returned with a fresh pot of coffee and two clean cups.

■　■　■

Lazarus stormed around the freezing den. This was *not* the way things should be going. The men of *Die Gruppe* had attempted to kill him, to assassinate *him!* It was unthinkable! What was happening to the project? To him? To the men of *Die Gruppe*? The men he had trained, nurtured, tutored.

The fire in the huge fireplace had been rekindled. Dry logs blazed and crackled so loudly that he could not hear himself think. The door set in the far wall opened, and Damon entered. Lazarus felt an immediate and compelling fear. *That* was the problem. *Damon* was the problem. What was it the man had said? Something to the effect that all had taken place over the past fifty years because of *him.* That made no sense. Damon, as far as Lazarus could tell, could be no more than thirty years old, maybe thirty-five at the outside. He could not have been present fifty years ago. But something told Lazarus that Damon was telling him the truth. And the man had certainly assumed control of the current situation.

The kidnapped woman was still in the upstairs bedroom, but Lazarus was not certain any longer why she was there. Whatever it was, it was obvious Damon knew, and that was all that was important.

Damon knew everything. He had known about the attempted assassination *before* it had taken place. But that was impossible, wasn't it?

Lazarus worked his way toward the fireplace. Maybe he could warm himself by getting closer. Poland had been cold but not this cold.

In winter, the place had been ravaged by ice storms sweeping in from the Vistula River. Most Poles considered that particular portion of Poland totally inhospitable. Lazarus had considered it the perfect place. His superiors had, of course, agreed with him.

But as cold as it had been there, it had never been like this. This cold seemed to have a life of its own. It invaded, penetrated, to the very marrow of one's bones, one's soul. And unlike the cold of southern Poland, *this* cold had a character all its own, as if it was a living, breathing being. It was a cold so severe that Lazarus began to think of it as a fire which could not be extinguished.

As Damon approached, Lazarus shrank back from his presence. "I think you are beginning to understand," Damon said, as he moved into the freezing room. "It is almost over. A few more hours, and it will be finished."

"What?" Lazarus managed to ask in a weak voice.

Damon laughed, a demeaning expression that took Lazarus completely by surprise. *"What? This?"* Damon gestured with a sweep of his hand. "Everything is about over. What you thought was your life's work is *my* life's work. *That's* what's about to come to an end. In your entire, pathetic life, you have not accomplished what I am about to consummate within the next few hours. You think this world is what counts. You are wrong. Your life has been spent trying to sabotage, to undermine, to control the things of this world. My work, on the other hand, has been focused on compromising a single life, a solitary being whose impact could reach far beyond anything you can conceive of. That is where the real danger to my kind exists."

Lazarus slumped into the chair nearest the fireplace. It seemed impossible, but the cold had suddenly and inexplicably intensified. It ate at his bones, as if it were a fire about to consume him. Was there something else other than this world? Was that what Damon was talking about? Was there a hell? And if so, was there also a heaven? Had he been so wrong about his whole life? If so, was there time to change? Did he even want to?

No, he decided. What he was seeing, what he was feeling, was something he had never before experienced, but it had nothing to do with heaven or hell.

With that thought, the man known as Lazarus committed his everlasting soul to a perdition he could never have imagined.

■   ■   ■

Cindy Tolbert was not a theologian. She had heard all the debates about the power of prayer, the effects it had or did not have on future events. None of that mattered to her. She *knew* from experience what prayer could do. Prayer changed things. It was that simple and that complicated. She didn't understand how or why, but that was not her concern. Her concern was to believe, and believe she did.

The man who'd kidnapped her was named Damon. Cindy was not a linguist, either, but she knew what that name meant.

Cindy buried her face in her hands again and began praying. The supplication and praise contained in her voice found wings, piercing the seemingly impenetrable shroud of evil surrounding the house where she knelt, and shot straight to Him who hears all petitions. Instantly, Cindy felt a comfort and warmth that transcended anything earthly.

She would pray until whatever was taking place was over. She knew that would be soon.

■ ■ ■

Dr. Henry Phelps Jr. sat with his father in the older man's office. The senior Phelps's memories were clouded by recollections of an odyssey that had begun more than fifty years ago aboard a German U-Boat. It had been a long, arduous journey, but it was about to come to an end. Whatever had been the intentions of the enlightened men of *Die Gruppe,* it had not been fulfilled and never would be.

There had been a certain respect, a certain adulation for Lazarus, the man who had saved his life so long ago. Henry Phelps Sr., who had been born in Munich, Germany, as Heinrich Felpes, knew the real name of the man known as Lazarus. It was a name that would make the world sit up and take notice when it was finally revealed. The revelation would do more than expose the man; it would expose the project behind the man, and as far as Heinrich Felpes was concerned, that was not all bad.

The end had come. He hoped the world would understand, but he knew that expectation would most likely go unrealized.

CHAPTER THIRTY-NINE

A strange darkness hovered over Memphis, Tennessee, a darkness not associated with the worsening weather. Donald Fenwick urged his Humvee across the snow-covered Hernando De Soto Bridge spanning the Mississippi River. The silver-faced Pyramid, Memphis's newest sports complex, just to the left of the bridge, reflected not only the gray atmosphere but also a depressing quality set apart from the physical characteristics.

The Humvee began to slide as it started down the Tennessee side of the bridge, and Fenwick eased off the accelerator, letting the independently driven four wheels grab on the slick surface.

David Michaels sat in the right seat of the vehicle. He had been staring at the skyline of Memphis since it had first come into view from the Arkansas side of the river a few miles back. To David, the approach had signaled the beginning of a battle.

The valley deep in the Arkansas Ozarks had its own brand of evil. A depressing, despondent property possessed all who entered. But that characteristic had magically dissipated with its exposure. The depression had been replaced by a sense of expectancy, coupled with an urgency that David had not understood until he crossed the bridge that lay behind them now.

The urgency was directly related to the news that Cindy Tolbert was missing, and all reports indicated she had been kidnapped. David wondered how Janice Morgan knew not only that Cindy had been kidnapped but also the address where she was being held. And if she knew, who else knew, and why had they not done something about it?

It made no sense whatsoever. Why would anyone want to harm the petite, green-eyed Clayton County clerk? He was in love with Cindy. He wanted to marry her, to spend the rest of his life with her in the mountains of Arkansas. But he had not told another human being of his plans.

He remembered the quiet dinner they had shared in Little Rock, the gentle words which had meaning only in their context, the soft light, and the feeling of overwhelming love that had followed their intimate conversation. They had held hands over the table, desiring more but all in good time.

David had never felt anything quite like it. It had been a discovery, that revelation of love, that had left him in a state of euphoria he had never before experienced. If that was love—and he was certain it was—then he knew a magic that no magician could have ever conjured.

If Cindy was in trouble, he knew he would give his life to save her.

David was thrust back into reality as the Humvee passed the deserted campus of Rhodes College. The trees were as barren as those in the Ozark forest he and Donald Fenwick had left hours earlier. The day had slipped away during their trip to Memphis, and the flat light of a winter afternoon was gradually giving way to the even flatter purple light of the evening.

David was confused. He wondered why they were in this part of town. Then he remembered that Fenwick knew more about Memphis than he did. He relaxed and focused his attention inside the vehicle.

Fenwick guided the Humvee through snow-coated city streets, always heading east. David was not sure where they were. He had been to Memphis several times, but normally his duties carried him north to the Naval Support Activity in Millington.

The going was slow. Memphis city workers were in the process of clearing streets, but the huge amounts of snow were more than a match for the available equipment. Certain neighborhoods would have to wait.

"It's coming up on the right, I think," Donald Fenwick said.

David roused himself from his lethargy. He had been thinking about Cindy again. It would have been impossible for him to retrace Fenwick's trail.

"Drive past. Slow down, but don't stop," David ordered.

"Slow is not a problem, in case you haven't noticed."

David ignored the comment, his attention focused on the great stone house coming up on his right.

Fenwick slowed to a crawl as David examined the residence and the surrounding area. The multigabled house seemed like an edifice straight out of the pages of an Edgar Allen Poe novel. With darkness rapidly falling, the shadows cast by the various gables appeared as forms of unearthly beings come to roost. A place of gargoyles and demons. The creatures seemed to move and undulate as the darkness deepened. Lights, cold and impersonal, glowed from several of the windows. Smoke curled from one of the house's massive chimneys. Despite the evidence of warmth within, David had the feeling that the interior of the house was as chilling as the exterior.

Fenwick reached the end of the block. He accelerated slightly, the Humvee's large tires clawing at the frozen surface of the street.

"Swing around and make another pass," David said in a low voice.

Fenwick turned the vehicle around and did as he was ordered, skirting a single Memphis Light, Gas, and Water service truck with two men working on power lines, slowing as he drew even with the house.

"That's the most frightening thing I've ever seen," Fenwick whispered, almost to himself.

"That's what I'm beginning to think," David replied.

"What are you going to do?"

"Cindy's in that house," David stated matter-of-factly. "I'm going in to get her."

For Donald Fenwick, the resolve in David Michaels's voice stilled any comment he might have had. He had seen Michaels in action. The preacher had saved his life on a rock face in the middle of the Ozarks. He had seen the man throw himself at a killer intent on blowing up a house filled with people. There was not much, Donald Fenwick thought, that the Reverend David Michaels could not do if he set his mind to it.

"What do you want me to do?" Fenwick asked.

"Just stay close. A block away should do it. I'll find you if I need you." With that, David opened the door and stepped out.

■   ■   ■

He was close. Damon could feel it. His perception was acute, his recognition of his enemy's presence unmistakable.

Damon strode from the den. At this point, Lazarus was of little use to him. The man was no more than a shell—a broken, fragmented man whose life had come to nothing.

He needed the woman now. She was the lure, the bait, that would entice his enemy to his death. Of course, physical death was not his goal. He was looking for something more substantial. He was looking for the death of the spirit, of the soul, which would afford him his honored place among his peers. A year ago, one of his subordinates had failed to accomplish this very task, but he had underestimated David Michaels at that time. This time would be different.

Damon started up the stairs, heading for the bedroom where he had imprisoned Cindy Tolbert. The time had come to use her. Halfway up the stairs, he became aware of another force, a barrier thrown up, an impediment he could neither see nor penetrate. Like an invisible wall of sheer energy, the impervious wall of power threw him back. He ran headlong into the strange force and tumbled down the stairs.

Shocked by the encounter with the invisible wall, Damon sat stunned at the base of the stairs where he had come to rest. He had never encountered such a force before. But, he reminded himself, he had seldom taken on the form of a human being before, and in such a guise, even his own awesome powers were limited. But the appearance was necessary. He had to battle his enemy on even ground to claim victory.

Damon rose, cautiously climbing the stairs once again. The barrier had been halfway up, near the first twist in the staircase. He approached the area, his right hand stretched out in front of him, anticipating the contact.

When it came, it was as much as a surprise as the first time had been. His hand contacted the invisible impediment, but this time it was not the actual existence of the obstruction that surprised him; it was the feeling of absolute righteousness, like a powerful electrical jolt, which caused him to jerk his hand away as if he had been electrocuted.

Prayer! The cursed woman was praying! Angels had erected a barrier in response to flawless belief! How could one human being possess such power? As quickly as Damon asked himself the question, the answer came in a blinding revelation: the woman believed totally in the cursed Son of God! The difference was Jesus!

Damon raged at the invisible wall of pure righteousness in front of him. An earth-shattering howl of pure agony bellowed from his throat, rattling the foundation of the stone house.

Damon raced down the staircase, away from the barrier of goodness, away from the praying woman. He could still win, still defeat the one he had come to do battle with. The woman could pray all she wanted. Her faith might protect her, but it would have little effect on his coming encounter with David Michaels. The woman's faith was not transferable to the preacher. Michaels would have to stand on his own faith, and that, Damon was certain, would not withstand the onslaught of pure evil he was about to unleash.

■   ■   ■

Three Mossad agents tracked David Michaels as he stepped from the Humvee. Two agents, positioned in the utility service truck just across the road from Lazarus's house, watched as David Michaels got out of the vehicle. The third agent, out of sight in the rear of the house, was notified via radio by the senior agent in the truck.

None of the three understood completely what was taking place, but they all knew whose house this was, and regardless of what was happening, they knew they must have the man known as Lazarus.

Failure was not an option.

■   ■   ■

The sidewalk leading to the front door of the house was slick with ice. David approached the house, careful not to slip. At first, he had contemplated how to get into the house quietly. Any advantage was to be valued. But when he realized what and with whom he was dealing, he had decided to approach the house directly.

David prayed silently as he approached the great stone facade. Darkness had fallen, giving the house the appearance of a great beast. The eyes were the lighted windows on the upper floors; the mouth, the door which he now approached. Direct action was the only valid option, he knew. He was dealing with pure, unfettered evil, and there was no way to avoid such malevolence without being tarnished in the process.

David stepped onto the small front stoop. A demonic force encompassed the house, a blanket loathsome and insidious. David shuddered.

The door slowly opened, the beast's mouth beckoning the innocent. David Michaels did not hesitate. He stepped into the house as if he belonged. The door closed behind him.

■   ■   ■

Lazarus reached into the left-hand drawer of the oak desk in his den and extracted a small automatic pistol. The weapon was freezing but he did not drop it. The temperature in the room had dropped to unbearable levels despite the fire burning in the stone fireplace. Moisture collected on every surface, freezing as it accumulated, turning the room into a place of unendurable torment, but torment was something Lazarus understood.

Now he would exact his last retribution from the one who had been responsible for his lifetime of anguish and failure.

CHAPTER FORTY

As David Michaels entered the house, the same oppressive sense of evil lingered like stale smoke. But there was something more. David found the prayer he'd been praying had at some point been forced from his mind, and now he felt totally vulnerable. He'd felt the same way before, in the jungles of Vietnam, in the deserts of Iraq, and a year ago, in the streets of Little Rock, Arkansas.

In Little Rock, he had initially thought he was facing a mortal attack, an assault aimed at him by men of flesh and blood. It had turned out to be a significant spiritual battle, and he had been surprised at the twist of fate. This time there was no doubt about what he faced. Somewhere in the sprawling house was Cindy, the woman he loved. But there was someone else, he knew. Someone with more power than the minor demon he had faced in Little Rock, someone with but one objective—his absolute destruction.

As he stood in the foyer of the great house, David could feel the conflict that raged within the confines of the stone walls. There was the beast, a presence from the depths, and there was the unmistakable power of righteousness, which ebbed and flowed like a spring breeze. David smiled to himself. He understood the righteousness—Cindy Tolbert was on her knees, somewhere in the house, praying. That had to be a particularly thorny issue for the man David knew was no man at all.

Then David identified another aspect of the battle. The interior of the great house was cold, far beyond the cold produced by the weather outside.

David examined the immediate area. A grand staircase led to the upper floors, its carpeted hardwood stairs and rails glistening with frozen moisture. Small ice crystals covered the heavily brocaded walls. It was difficult to tell whether the two medium-sized chandeliers were ice-coated or not, but David suspected they were. The carpet runners covering the expensive carpets shone with the same frozen moisture. It was at once both incredible and horrendous.

David resisted the temptation to wrap his arms around his body, to warm himself. Instinctively he knew that would have been a sign of weakness, but a sign to whom?

David moved deeper into the house. The cold was almost unbearable. Doors leading from the foyer were closed, their surfaces highlighted with frozen and half-frozen globules of moisture.

David stepped carefully, aware of the ice forming beneath his boots. There was no doubt now. He knew whom he was battling, but there was no need to wait for an attack. He would initiate his own battle plan; he would pray.

Just as David uttered the first syllable of his prayer, a voice from behind him spoke, its resonance filling the room. "Welcome, David Michaels."

David turned, appalled and surprised by what greeted him.

■　　■　　■

Damon moved in behind David Michaels, cutting off his escape. When he spoke, the expected reaction did not materialize, and for the first time, Damon wondered if he had not underestimated this country preacher yet again.

When Michaels turned, the expression on his face was not the one of boundless terror Damon had hoped to see. Instead, Michaels seemed to examine him as one might examine an object on the auction block.

Damon, for the first time since he'd begun this expedition, felt fear.

■   ■   ■

"And you are?" David Michaels asked quietly, as if *he* were the owner of the house, and Damon had intruded without invitation.

The aplomb with which the question was asked further unnerved Damon. He could not speak.

"Come on. You're a man. At least for now. Who are you?" David demanded.

Damon found his voice, and with it, the hate which powered his very being. "I am Damon," he hissed. "And this is the day you will die, preacher."

David smiled, a slow, gentle smile which said more about his faith, his beliefs, than words ever could have. It was a smile that found its origins deep within his soul, where faith is kindled and the fires of love burned brightly. David took a step toward Damon. "Perhaps. That is yet to be seen. You say your name is Damon?"

Damon moved in unison with David Michaels, not willing to surrender the advantage of direct action to the preacher. "That's correct, preacher. I have come to stop you."

David's laugh split the super-chilled air like a flash of lightning. Damon was temporarily taken aback. "That has been tried before, Damon. You don't mind if I call you Damon, do you? Although, I think a more appropriate name would be the literal translation of your name from the German. 'Demon,' isn't it?"

Damon smiled. "I was right. You are a formidable foe. And yes, that is the correct translation. I took that name many years ago, when I first conceived the plan that brought you here."

David raised his right hand, stopping Damon. "That's interesting. How did you know it would be me who intervened? I assume you're the one responsible for the atrocity in the Arkansas valley?"

"That was begun by me. It's amazing what you can do with a word here, a suggestion there. Particularly when the men to whom you are speaking want to listen. It was not difficult."

"It was abominable," David said between clenched teeth. He took another step forward, noticing for the first time Damon's countenance. The demon was handsome, rugged looking, the epitome of what someone obsessed with the outward man would aspire to. "You should have been a movie star. You have the looks for it."

Damon smiled easily now. "What makes you think I haven't been what your kind calls a 'star'?"

"Yes, I suppose that is a possibility. You do have that power, don't you."

The two men were still moving toward each other, closing the distance between them like two gunfighters in an old western movie.

"What power is that, preacher?"

"The power of deception," David Michaels shot back, his smile now gone.

"Perhaps deception is too strong a word, David. You don't mind if I call you David, do you? You call me Damon, I call you David. We should be on first-name basis, don't you think?"

David's smile returned; he continued his silent petitions.

"You smile too easily, David," Damon said.

Both men stopped. The foyer moaned and groaned under the onslaught of the accumulated ice. Nothing dripped now; all was frozen. No more than ten feet separated the two adversaries.

"I smile because I recognize that trick too. Your offer of false friendship probably works very well on some. Many people in this world need that very thing. Companionship, understanding, caring. It would seem you have the capability to provide all of those," David said. Then his words turned harsh. "But that's all just a false patina, isn't it, Damon? You don't have, never will have, such an ability. That's what makes you the demon you are, doesn't it?"

The man known as Damon began to change gradually as David spoke. In the last minutes, a subtle shift had occurred, and it took David a few minutes to realize what it was. Damon was still the handsome, rugged-looking individual he had been when David had first seen him, but something *was* different. Then he had it. The eyes! It always showed in the eyes! Hadn't they been blue when he first saw the demon emerge from behind him? The demon's eyes had made a chameleon-like transformation to a bilious green.

David's mind temporally went to the sparkling green eyes of Cindy Tolbert. That green was a translucent, deep pool of color, reflecting love and understanding. Damon's green eyes were the color of the dead seaweed he'd seen floating off the beach at Torre Pines, California, when he had been stationed at Camp Pendleton. It was a flat, slimy green that more closely resembled bile than any other substance he could think of. The change had to signify something.

"That is the problem we have with you, David," Damon said, as if answering the unasked question in David's mind. "You are too intuitive. You see too much. You have recognized me for what I am. *That* is where your strength lies, in your ability to identify us."

"'Us' being the demons walking this earth in search of souls."

Damon laughed now. "You see. That is just what I am talking about. People like you make it very difficult for us to be succeed."

"By that, I take it you do not mean me as a preacher or man of God."

"Preacher is irrelevant," scoffed Damon. "A man of God, on the other hand, is very, very significant. The two are not necessarily inclusive. *That's* what makes you dangerous. We reach as many souls through what this world knows as organized religion as we do through bars, brothels, and drugs." Damon began moving again, approaching

David Michaels, slowly closing the distance between them. "And now it is time for you to die, David."

David held up his hand again. No sign of fear showed on his face or in his actions. "One question," he said, more a demand than a request from a subordinate.

"Ask it," Damon said, stopping in his tracks.

"Why this form? Why the form of a man? You could have already transformed yourself like that last one you sent to kill me in Little Rock."

"Him!" Damon's voice exploded within the freezing confines of the foyer. "That was an error of judgment on my part. I should have done that job myself, and I would not have had to waste the valley operation to drag you back into confrontation."

"That's what I'm talking about. You are obviously the master of the one you sent before. You are more powerful, more intelligent, certainly more resourceful. Why waste the 'valley operation' as you call it? Why not just come to me?"

Damon let the question hang in the cold air. In short, he answered. "I have no power to do that. *You* must come to *me.* That is the way it is. The decision to pursue whatever path on this earth is left to the individual. I cannot override a person's choices. Fortunately, it is not necessary. All that is needed is to present the options, and most follow the path of least resistance. How is it written? *Enter through the narrow gate. For wide is the gate and broad is the road that leads to destruction, and many enter through it.* Fortunately for us, those who want to enter that gate are numerous."

"But numbers are not enough. Is that it?"

Damon smiled broadly, his handsome face glistening with small sweat beads despite the bone-chilling cold of the house. His green eyes glowed. "It is never *enough,* David," he replied.

"I see. But I'm still slightly confused at your current form," David said.

"This body? I settled on this so I could eliminate you in a manner fitting this world. When your body is found, it will be just another murder among so many. A tragedy, perhaps, but only for brief seconds. Nothing more."

"You cannot kill my soul."

"I only need to stop your kind on this earth. To separate you from those who might hear, see, and believe. *That* is my only objective."

"And to do this, you have placed yourself in such a vulnerable position?"

"Vulnerable? What do you mean?"

David motioned with his arm, sweeping it around the room, indicating the world of cold surrounding them. "This. Don't you feel it? I can see it in your eyes. Even though I know that you are responsible for all this, you, too are affected by it."

"You mean the cold? Yes, I am responsible, and in this form, I can be affected by the same physical elements that affect every human, but that will only be for a short time longer. After that, I will return to my former glory."

"Only if you succeed."

The easy smile slipped from Damon's lips for a moment, an infusion of self-doubt sweeping through him at David Michaels's words.

"In your present form, I might kill you. Have you considered *that?*"

The room resounded with demonic laughter once again as Damon bellowed forth his mirth at David Michaels's suggestion. "Kill me? *You?* Do not think yourself my equal, preacher," Damon shouted. He advanced on David, his hands reaching out, his bilious green eyes glowing even brighter.

From behind Damon a door flew open, and an older man fell into the foyer where David and Damon stood. He wore a large, gray mustache, and a rumpled gray greatcoat open in the front to reveal an equally rumpled gray uniform. David caught the glint of madness in the old man's brown-green eyes.

But what made the man's entrance significant was the old Parabellum Luger he carried in his right hand.

The old man stopped when he spied David and Damon. Standing just inside the foyer, the man raised the old pistol; its barrel came up slowly, but with a certainty reflected in the intense concentration of the old man.

The old man was here to kill one or both of them, David understood.

■ ■ ■

The three Mossad agents were armed with .22 caliber, Beretta Model 87 automatic pistols, the standard issue of the Israeli agency. Each Beretta was equipped with a silencer. The agents had not transported the weapons into the country with them but had acquired them upon arrival. The risk of detection was too great at gateway airports, and unnecessary. Such weapons were easily obtained through legitimate means in the United States. It had been a simple matter to provide three different sporting arms dealers with perfectly forged documentation, fill out the required papers, and purchase the three automatics. The silencers had come from a private individual whose sympathies lay with the government of Israel, as had the fake service truck and whatever else the three agents had needed to keep track of the man living in the stone house in east Memphis. It had been a long process, finding and confirming the man's identity, but that had been done, and now their mission was drawing to a rapid conclusion.

Their orders were succinct: Capture the man, if possible, for return to Israel where he would be tried for war crimes. Failing that, kill him. One agent carried a Minicam capable of recording events as they occurred. They were prepared.

The agents had abandoned their cover at the first sight of the Humvee making its way down the street. They had watched it pass, turn around, and retrace its own tracks in the snow, then regurgitate the tall man with the short-cropped gray hair into the street.

They had been advised to expect the man, but they had not expected what they witnessed next. Accustomed to a more clandestine type of entrance, none of the Mossad agents had expected the man to approach the front door.

The two agents watched in horror as the man stepped into the entry hall, and the door closed behind him. Both were moving before the door had fully closed. One agent was speaking into a radio. His transmission was picked up by the third Mossad agent in the rear of the house. The other agent pulled a cellular phone from his pocket as he followed the first, both heading for the house entrance.

The agent speed-dialed a number, and the phone connected him to an office in the bowels of the White House.

"He's going in the front door!" the agent said urgently. With that, he pressed the "end" button on the phone and scrambled for the Beretta. This was not happening the way it had been planned.

∎   ∎   ∎

"He's in," Tom Frazier told Jules Goldman.

Goldman nodded and reached for the phone on Frazier's desk. The line was a dedicated line connected directly to the inner chambers of the Mossad in Tel Aviv.

The prime minister of Israel listening, via a secondary connection, made no response as he hung up the phone and muttered a short prayer before reaching for the cold cup of tea sitting on his desk.

∎   ∎   ∎

Lazarus stood in the foyer, his Luger pointed in the general direction of David and Damon. He'd expected to find Damon, but who was the second man? Where had he come from? It made no difference, he had come for a very specific purpose, and he would not be deterred.

∎   ∎   ∎

A commotion downstairs distracted Cindy Tolbert. Something was going on, but she'd expected that. She returned to her prayer, this time with renewed dedication. Already she knew that she'd been protected by heaven's angels. The angels had erected a barrier around her, she knew. How far the barrier extended, or how long it would last, she did not know, but her confidence in their protection had released her to pray in an intercessory fashion for David Michaels.

■　■　■

Both David Michaels and Damon stared at the pistol in the old man's hand.

Damon had turned to face the new threat. David moved swiftly, the advantage of surprise would not last long.

He sprang across the remaining six feet that separated him from the demon. Damon began to turn, but he was too slow in his human form.

David slammed his rock-hard body into Damon, catching the demon in the lower abdomen with full force. Damon went down in a heap, his face white; his green eyes dulled.

David slipped on the icy carpet runners and skidded on the hardwood floor. He went down hard, twisting away from Damon as he slid. Pain shot through him again, reminding him of his damaged shoulder.

He scrambled to his feet before Damon, advancing in rapid, small steps to avoid slipping. Damon, too, had recovered and was quickly regaining his composure.

A sound temporarily diverted David's attention. He looked to his rear now. The old man with the Luger was still there, the pistol coming up slowly but deliberately.

The shot sounded like a clap of thunder. Within the close walls of the hallway, the sharp noise had almost as much effect as the bullet.

David dove for the floor, rolling to his left, away from where the old man was standing, and came to his knees. He faced the old man who was standing over Damon.

Damon struggled to his knees just as the old man raised the gun again and fired. The force of the 9mm bullet threw the demon against the wall with the impact of a pile driver.

David stared in fascinated horror as the old man knelt down in front of the demon-turned-human.

"I am finished with you," the old man gasped.

To David, it signaled the end. The words had been forced from the old man's throat as if they might be the last he ever spoke. The rasping quality of the voice was that of a habitual smoker.

David watched Damon's putrid green eyes glaze over in death. The demon had not been able to escape his own, self-made death chamber— the human form he'd assumed to do battle with David Michaels. The demon had made a tactical error, and it had cost him his very existence.

The old man turned from the demon, his face now a mask of indifference. David saw the Luger the old man held at his side. There was no indication that he would use the weapon again, and David relaxed momentarily.

As the old man stood and turned to David, the front door of the great house burst open, and two uniformed men rushed in.

David was confused. The two men wore the uniform overalls of the Memphis Light, Gas, and Water Company. What were they doing here?

The old man reacted instantly. He brought the Luger up, but he was not quick enough.

Muffled bursts, like underpowered firecrackers exploding at a great distance, sounded three, then four times. The old man stopped in his tracks, as if a mainspring had suddenly unwound, and dropped to the floor almost gently. The greatcoat fell open, revealing the uniform he was wearing. David's mouth fell open at the sight of the gray Litewka tunic. The right collar tab was adorned with the runes of Germany's SS, the left with the insignia of a German Haupsturmführer.

"What . . .?" David began.

"Are you all right, sir?" one of the MLG & W men asked, moving toward David.

David was speechless; when he tried to answer, no words came.

The second man examined the two dead bodies. The other went to David. "Sir," he said again, "are you all right. Have you been shot?"

David found his voice. "No . . . no . . . I'm fine."

"I was worried for a moment. I was led to believe preachers in this country are seldom at a loss for words," the man joked.

David now looked at the man for the first time. "You know who I am?"

"Yes, sir. We do. And we have orders to connect you with some-one you know," the man said, as he pulled the cellular phone from his uniform jacket and handed it to David. "Just push the 'send' button. It's preprogrammed."

David did as he was told; the phone rang. It was answered on the first ring, and David recognized the voice of Tom Frazier instantly.

When the conversation was over, David disconnected. He'd not said more than a dozen words, listening as Frazier explained, very rapidly and very briefly, what had just occurred in Memphis.

David returned the phone to the Mossad agent. His attention then returned to the man in the greatcoat and German uniform. It was incredible, but the words had come directly from Tom Frazier.

"Cindy?" David said to the agent.

"Upstairs, Mr. Michaels. She's fine. Third door on the left after the head of the stairs."

David bounded up the stairs, taking them three at a time. The door was locked but yielded to his right shoulder. The force he applied shat-tered the door facing.

Cindy Tolbert was on her knees, and David feared the Mossad agent might have spoken too quickly. But when Cindy turned and saw him, her eyes lit up, glowing a beautiful emerald green.

Cindy rushed into David's arms; they kissed. Cindy clung to David, and David, in return, found himself clinging fiercely to the one woman he really loved.

Both wept. Tears of joy mingled with tears of doubt and uncer-tainty. Until this very minute, David thought, he'd really not under-stood how much he loved this woman. But now emotions overflowed, fear washed away by tears of happiness.

"I knew you would come," Cindy whispered to David, her mouth next to his ear.

"And we'll never be apart again. That's a promise," David whispered back.

Cindy wiggled out of David's embrace, stood back three feet from David, and said, "That sounds like a proposal to me."

David's smile spread across his face. "I always did say you were too intuitive for your own good."

The two fell into each other's arms again, then David led Cindy from the room. The last thing he noticed as they left the room was the warm air inside Cindy's makeshift prison cell.

EPILOGUE

The story broke that night on all the major networks. Disbelief was the first reaction, even among those broadcasting the monumental event. The wire services picked up the story, and in under thirty minutes, the news was circling the globe. Foreign news agencies quickly jumped on the bandwagon, taking the information provided, embellishing it with their own brand of broadcast journalism, and replaying the story as if they had just broken the earth-shattering news.

Tabloids, along with legitimate newspapers from every western European country, including the Scandinavian countries and the British Isles, rushed news teams to Memphis, Tennessee. Most knew Memphis as either the birthplace and home of Elvis Presley or the site where Dr. Martin Luther King Jr. had been assassinated. That had changed forever.

Both Germany and Israel sent multiple news teams, not willing to trust coverage to any one team and also unwilling to accept unknown, built-in bias which might place an unwanted twist on the coverage.

Historical records were reviewed, dissected, analyzed, and investigated from every possible angle. The inquiries finally reached the level of the State Department, which in turn quizzed the Brazilian government about the incident. The Brazilians, eager to rid themselves of any complicity, quickly contacted the coroner's office in São Paulo, demanding all records dealing with the earlier, and now obviously false, reports of the man's death. The coroner's office scrambled to produce the records showing that no conspiracy to cover up had been instigated within the confines of its hierarchy.

The many books that had been written on the subject were exhumed, their contents pored over by scholars, physicians, and laymen, all wanting to find that minuscule piece of information that may have shown, even in those early years, that the man had not died on the beach at Bertioga, Brazil.

In their Atlanta offices, CNN was putting together a two-hour special to air within the week. Three news teams were sent to São Paulo and then to Bertioga to search for whatever new information might be available, timely, and true. Of the three, truth was the more flexible element.

In Memphis, the man known as Lazarus was fingerprinted in the Shelby County morgue, and his identification was certified by independent sources, including the Israelis and the Germans. A call from the president of the United States to the mayor of Memphis accomplished what no one else could have. The obligatory autopsy, required of gunshot victims, was forgotten. The body of Lazarus was turned over to the Mossad agents to be flown back to Tel Aviv.

Among all the glittery coverage and in-depth analysis, the headlines that appeared the next morning in the *Commercial Appeal,* Memphis's daily newspaper, summed up the entire story in four words:

JOSEPH MENGELE DEAD! AGAIN!

Joseph Mengele, the notorious "Angel of Death" responsible for thousands of deaths at Auschwitz, the German concentration camp in southern Poland during World War II, died in his Memphis home yesterday when agents from the Mossad, Israeli's external security force, shot and killed him while attempting to arrest him for war crimes.

■   ■   ■

Two days after Mengele's death, David Michaels sat in his room in the Peabody Hotel on Third Street in downtown Memphis. Cindy Tolbert occupied a suite on an upper floor, courtesy of the hotel.

Tom Frazier and Jules Goldman had arrived two hours earlier, landing at Memphis International Airport and taking an airport courtesy bus to the Peabody.

Janice Morgan had driven to Memphis from Clayton, Arkansas. Instead of her usual county sheriff's uniform, she wore an attractive two-piece suit in hunter green. Her blonde hair flowed over her shoulders, and her blue eyes sparkled. No one in the lobby of the Peabody missed her entrance, and nobody guessed that she was one of the toughest and most intelligent sheriffs ever to wear the badge. That was the way she wanted it, at least today.

Donald Fenwick occupied a suite on the same floor as Cindy Tolbert, but his agreement with the Peabody was that he would pay his own way, plus gratuities for the in-house staff in exchange for total anonymity during the week he was there. The Peabody's manager assured the CEO of FenMark that additional payment was unnecessary. Discretion was their stock-in-trade, and he would not be disturbed. It turned out they were as good as their word.

A small conference room was put at the disposal of the well-known guests, and now they all sat around a highly polished oak table, surrounded by the understated elegance of the Peabody, catered to by discreet waiters, and assured of total privacy.

Tom Frazier sat next to Jules Goldman at one end of the table. David and Cindy shared one side of the table to Frazier's right. Donald Fenwick sat at the other end and Janice Morgan rounded out the group on the other side of the table, across from Cindy and David.

A nervous smile was splayed across Tom Frazier's face as he cleared his throat. He had waited for everyone, and the four-minute wait for Fenwick had resulted in an awkward silence until the CEO had arrived and taken his place at the table.

Two white-clad Peabody waiters filled all the coffee cups on the table and set out trays of pastries, then quietly withdrew from the room.

Frazier cleared his throat again. "To begin, I want to introduce Jules Goldman. Jules and I go back a bit, and it was his agency that was instrumental in tracking down Mengele."

"Mossad?" Fenwick asked.

"A very special branch," Frazier answered, "dealing with the capture and return of war criminals."

"I thought the Jewish Documentation Center handled that sort of thing." The statement came from a stone-faced David Michaels.

"Normally, that is the case," Goldman interjected. "But this was a very special case."

"We will get to that in short order," Frazier said. "Let me say right now that, while the end result of what Jules did was highly successful, I do not and will not condone the same tactics again."

"You mean using civilians to flush out criminals," David added, his face still an unreadable mask.

"Yes, well, that's another story, too, David," Tom Frazier said. "And I suppose I might as well start at the beginning."

"Please, do," Cindy Tolbert said quietly. She reached for David's hand, the touch reassuring and warm. Her gentle squeeze was returned, and she felt better.

"The beginning goes back to 1944. On 17 June 1944, the U-Boat *Eins Zwei Drei* sailed from Point de Keroman in France. It carried only one passenger, but a very important passenger. The voyage was arranged by a doctor at Auschwitz, Joseph Mengele, and our own State Department. The passage, and subsequent immigrations during and after the war, were in payment for other, more desirable immigrants."

"Scientists," David broke in.

"Scientists, mathematicians, chemists, physicists, and others. All of them vital to a growing defense force and a fledgling space program."

"So the State Department overlooked other, 'less desirable' immigrants to get the ones it wanted," Fenwick said.

"You people are much better informed than I was led to believe," Jules Goldman told Frazier.

"So it would seem. To answer Mr. Fenwick, yes. The undesirables were part of the deal to get the men and women we needed in the post-war era. 'Operation Paperclip,' which took place later, in the early fifties, was part of the overall project to get those vital to our programs into the country and working on a 'space race' that everyone knew was about to take place. It was easy to overlook a few additional people in the process."

"Doctors?" David asked.

Jules Goldman and Tom Frazier looked at each other, realizing that David Michaels had already put the scenario together.

"Doctors all," Frazier said. "The post-war state in Europe was dismal. The four-way administration in effect was less than ideal, especially as it concerned the immigration process. It was fairly easy to circumvent the process and shuttle the people we wanted into the United States. Unfortunately, it was just as easy to do the same thing with the doctors."

"I don't understand," Cindy Tolbert began. "It would have seemed physicians would have been among the professional people we wanted in the U.S."

David squeezed Cindy's hand beneath the table, then said, "Not just doctors, concentration camp doctors. Right, Tom?"

Frazier felt his face flush at David Michaels's insight. Even though he had not been part of the operation to allow the doctors into the country, he had known about it for the past few years. Even now, the knowledge seemed to put him in an unfavorable light, even in his own eyes.

"Exactly," Frazier finally answered. "All the doctors were from German concentration camps, and they were being shipped out of Germany in wholesale lots. Mengele had set up an organization within the SS, tied to other scientists, that let him know who was being sought. What type of professions, that sort of thing. It was pretty evident who the allies wanted, and it was an easy matter to convince them that doctors should be high on the list. Of course, the bureaucrats were not so much interested in 'who' as they were in 'what,' and doctors seemed to be among the elite. After all, the paper-shufflers responsible for the logistics of 'Paperclip,' and other such operations, had never seen the death houses, the ovens, the showers, or the graves. As far as they were concerned, those could have been fabrications of someone's vivid imagination. Their job was to transport bodies across the ocean, and that's what they did."

"Among those was Mengele?" Janice Morgan finally asked.

"No," Jules Goldman answered. "Mengele had gone to South America. At various times, he had lived in Argentina, Brazil, Paraguay, Bolivia, and Uruguay. He kept on the move. He knew the whole world would eventually be looking for him, and he stayed pretty much on the run until 1979."

"Bertioga," David Michaels whispered. The whispered word rang out like church bells.

"Two hours from São Paulo," Goldman confirmed, "in southern Brazil. His death was widely reported, as was his funeral. That was the end of the 'Angel of Death.'"

"Except it wasn't Mengele," Frazier said. "Suspicion had always surrounded the death. On 6 June 1985, the body was exhumed and examined by the assistant coroner in Sao Paulo, one Jose Antonio de Mello. It was all quite dramatic. Grave diggers dug up the coffin, Mello opened it, exposing the skeleton, and declared the corpse to be that of Mengele. He even held out the skull for all to see. But it wasn't Mengele. As it turns out, it was a corpse from an indigent living in the slums of São Paulo. Mengele and Mello had engineered the whole scheme. It was easy for Mello to lay his hands on a corpse. They came through the morgue on a daily basis. All he had to do was wait for one with the correct specifications, fake the drowning accident, in association with the family, bury the body, and declare Mengele's death by signing the death certificate."

David felt a shudder pulse through Cindy's body. Her hand began to sweat. He tightened his grip on her hand, putting his arm around her shoulders at the same time. After only a few seconds, he felt her relax.

"So Mengele is now officially dead," Donald Fenwick said, pulling his chair closer to the table.

"Yes. He was dead. The rest is easy to figure out. He had the money and access to obtain a U.S. passport, complete with visas and entry stamps from various countries, and enter the United States, not as an immigrant, but as a U.S. citizen."

"You're not telling us what this 'access' he had was," Janice Morgan interrupted.

"Very astute, Miss Morgan," Goldman said. "You are right, of course, in your implication. The contact was high on the list in the State Department. There was a certain paranoia at Foggy Bottom in those days. The immigrations had ceased, but the records were still there. Anyone with connections to know what had gone on could have wrangled the information out of the files. The information had to be destroyed, and for that it took someone with clout or influence."

"The original operation, the doctors themselves . . . ," David Michaels began, but never finished.

" . . . were all recruited by Mengele and authorized entry into the U.S. by Allen Dulles, the head of the OSS in Europe," Frazier finished.

"Later to become head of the CIA," David continued.

"And in a perfect position to continue the activities needed to procure the scientists and technicians needed for the defense and space programs," Frazier affirmed.

"And allow a few doctors from German concentration camps into the country, as well," Janice said.

"And allow the formation of the Lazarus Project," Donald Fenwick added, the anger in his voice barely controlled.

Both Tom Frazier and Jules Goldman looked at the FenMark executive, their mouths hanging open, their faces questioning.

"What do you know about Lazarus?" Frazier asked.

Fenwick's mouth twisted into an angry slash. "Probably as much as you do. You see, gentlemen, I am a product of that project."

The entire table turned to face Donald Fenwick. The bitterness with which he had spoken demanded an audience. Fenwick glanced in David Michaels's direction. David motioned for him to continue. It was the same story Fenwick had told him back in the dim light of the Ozark forest.

"Please continue, Mr. Fenwick," said Jules Goldman.

"As I said. I am an end result of what is known as the 'Lazarus Project.' Just to bring everyone up-to-date, the Lazarus Project was the brainchild of Joseph Mengele. That is speculation on my part, but it seems pretty evident. Is that the case, Mr. Frazier?" Fenwick asked.

Tom Frazier nodded only slightly, but it was confirmation.

"Yes, well, the project was the reason for the invasion of these concentration camp doctors. Their leader, and again I emphasize that leader was Mengele, had a dream which began back on the Vistula River in southern Poland. What I'm telling you is new information which is now supported by Mengele's death. Before the events of the last few days, I had no idea who was behind this satanic conspiracy. Now I do." Fenwick paused for effect. "With that in mind, the rest of the story is as bizarre as its creator."

A ghostly smile swept across David Michaels's face. He knew what was coming. He gave Cindy's hand another gentle squeeze and settled in for the latest version.

"I would be happy to allow our gentlemen from Washington to tell the rest," Fenwick said.

Tom Frazier, with a wave of his hand, motioned for Fenwick to continue. He was as curious as the rest of the people around the table to hear Fenwick's version.

"As Mr. Frazier said, it all began 17 June 1944. At least that was the day the project was first put in motion. It was conceived years earlier in Auschwitz. Since Mengele's identity has been revealed, it makes more sense than ever before. Mengele was obsessed with genetics. Twins were a particular interest of his, but genetics in general was his specialty."

"You are quite well-informed, Mr. Fenwick," Goldman said.

"I've done a lot of research, Mr. Goldman," Fenwick answered. "The idea that genetics could be controlled, monitored, or even altered is not a new concept. It was Hitler's driving force. His views on race dilution of the 'Aryan nation' through intermarriage are well-known. But Hitler had lost the war, and Mengele apparently thought his genetic research was important enough to continue. Not only that, but he had an end in mind."

"This Lazarus Project you're talking about," Janice Morgan interjected.

"Exactly. The plan was simple enough, at least for the warped visionaries from Nazi concentration camps. The Third Reich could be reborn again. That's not a new concept, but the manner by which it was to take place was. Nazi doctors, safely ensconced in the United States, would continue genetic research, using what they learned to exert certain pressures to compromise economic and political persons."

"Blackmail," Janice Morgan said.

"Exactly," Donald Fenwick confirmed. "My father was one of the project's victims."

Now Tom Frazier and Jules Goldman sat up straighter in their chairs. Neither man, despite the contacts they had, and the information they had ascertained, knew anything about the Fenwick story.

"I'm adopted," Donald Fenwick announced. "My father contracted with a clinic before my birth to adopt me. I'm a product of these madmen's research. Fortunately, or unfortunately, depending on your point of view, their research was more than just a little flawed. They thought that by controlling the gene pool, the reproduction of babies, they could also control the babies, and by extension, the men and women who grew from those babies."

"That's insane!" Cindy Tolbert exclaimed, the words spilling from her involuntarily. She blushed at the outburst.

"Of course it is," Donald Fenwick agreed, "but insanity is the staple of madmen."

"What's this got to do with you?" Janice Morgan asked.

"These madmen tried to gain control of FenMark by threatening to expose the illegal adoption and my birth if my father did not go along with what they wanted."

"Which was?" David Michaels prompted.

"Which was economic control of FenMark. I'm sure, if an in-depth investigation is done, we will find more children like me, more fathers like mine, and more connections to politicians, businessmen, educators, and others, all men and women of influence. Control the men, you control the country. That's what they thought."

"And the valley back in Arkansas?" This time the prompt came from Tom Frazier.

"The house in the valley was my father's," Donald Fenwick verified. "The madmen took it from him using the same techniques they thought would get them FenMark. Blackmail. My father was more susceptible to such tactics in those days. But he was not a fool. He began researching the men behind all the goings-on. He kept a record. Details, dates, names. He turned the information over to me. That's when I decided enough was enough. I had no idea where the trail would lead, but I knew it started at the old house in the valley."

"Where we met," David said.

Fenwick smiled at the understatement. "Where David saved my life. I was over my head and too dumb to know it. If David hadn't come along, I'd be at the bottom of a ravine right now."

"And David was there because of a girl in the Arkansas Children's Hospital. Right?" Frazier asked.

"Right," David answered. "That, and the fact that since finding that young girl in the belly compartment of Dean Barber's Cessna, someone seemed to want all of us dead."

"You might like to know that the house in the valley is out of business. We didn't expect Wade Larsen to be the one to clean out that rat's nest, but we'll take what we can get," Frazier said.

"I thought maybe Larsen was in on it," Janice Morgan asked.

"He was. For some reason, he had a change of heart. A rather propitious change of heart, I might add. If it hadn't been for him, those two men sent to destroy the house might have succeeded. They could have killed quite a few people."

"How many?" Cindy asked.

"That's classified for now, Miss Tolbert," Jules Goldman answered. "As soon as we can, we'll let you know."

Cindy continued, "Then that nightmare is over?"

"Almost," Tom Frazier answered. "The valley in Arkansas was not the only 'baby-factory' site. Five others exist. One in the Ozarks of Missouri, one in Tennessee's Smoky Mountains, another in the Poconos, one in the desert of west Texas, and the last north of Kalispell, Montana. All were producing babies to be used in the Lazarus Project. We have identified all of them, and as we speak, coordinated raids conducted by the Immigration and Naturalization Service, the FBI, and state and local authorities are underway. All the girls used in these 'factories' were illegal immigrants. Girls kidnapped from families who had come to the U.S. to find work. Using illegals almost guaranteed that missing persons reports would not be filed. To do so would have jeopardized the family's only source of income. It was all very clever."

"It's absolutely incredible," Janice Morgan concluded.

"What's even more incredible," David Michaels began, "is that I let you use me again without knowing it." His statement was directed at Tom Frazier.

"That was another quirk of fate, David. You always seem to find a way to get caught in the middle of whatever happens in your neck of the woods. This was no exception. I was under presidential orders not to reveal anything about the investigations."

"What would have happened if I hadn't flushed these crazies for you? I could have been killed."

"You could have," Frazier acknowledged, "but I was counting on your connection higher up to get you through this. And if He hadn't, then you would have been buried with full military honors. You've been on active duty since you got involved in this," Frazier smiled.

"I . . . wha . . . ," David stuttered, completely dumbfounded.

"I have one question," Goldman interrupted. "My agents kept running up against a man Mengele called Damon. Every time we got close to Mengele, he always eluded us, and it was usually due to this Damon. Who exactly was he?"

David Michaels felt his skin crawl at the mention of the demon. "Do you know what the word 'damon' is in German, Mr. Goldman?"

"To be honest, my Portuguese and Spanish are better than my German. Sounds strange, I know, but there it is. What does it mean?"

"Demon, Jules," Tom Frazier answered before David could speak. "It means demon."

"You know something more, Tom?" David asked curiously.

"Now I think I do. It explains this whole scenario, doesn't it? The Lazarus Project, the actions in the past few days, the encounter here in Memphis. This was all the result of this demon called Damon."

Jules Goldman raised a quick hand. "Hold it right there. We just finish figuring out what's going on with this baby factory lunacy, and now you're telling me that the boogie man is the cause of all this. You're all nuts."

"I think you may be right, Mr. Goldman. I think we all may be nuts. Doesn't make a whole lot of sense, does it?"

"None at all. But then Tom told me you were one strange preacher. I can see where he gets that now. If all of you will excuse me, I have a plane to catch back to Washington. I've been ordered to accompany Mengele's body back to Tel Aviv."

With that, Jules Goldman left the others and walked out the conference room door. Everyone waited until the door was once again closed, then looked around the table at one another. With the exception of Donald Fenwick, a mild sense of déjà vu swept over the group.

"He was after you, wasn't he, David?" Cindy Tolbert said.

"He was after someone *like* me. It didn't make any difference who it was, just that the truth be stopped."

"The truth?" Donald Fenwick asked, confused.

"The truth of Jesus Christ, Donald," David explained. "Don't ever think there's not a spiritual battle waged each and every day of this world's existence. Most people don't get to view it as directly as you have these last few hours, but it exists, nonetheless."

"That's what you were trying to tell my back there in the forest, wasn't it?"

"That's it. There are forces we can only imagine, but they all must bow to the ultimate power in the universe."

"Jesus Christ," Donald Fenwick acknowledged.

David allowed a wide smile to crease his features. "That's the beginning of salvation," he said. "The acknowledgment of Jesus' saving grace. I'm not sure I've ever gotten that across to Tom down there, but I can see it beginning to sink in."

Tom Frazier fidgeted in his chair. "The message is coming in loud and clear now. Last year, I wondered about what you told me. This year, I've seen it for myself. I think we need to talk after this meeting," Frazier said.

"Consider it an appointment," David said, his smile broadening.

"I don't need to tell any of you that what we've talked about in here is better left here. I don't have the authority to order any of you to remain silent, but take it from me, your lives will be much simpler if you can put this week behind you."

The small group nodded their collective understanding. None needed, or wanted, the notoriety associated with the death of the "Angel of Death." The death of Joseph Mengele would occupy the media for less than a month. The elimination of the real "Angel of Death," the man known as Damon, would never be reported, but his demise would affect the human race for generations to come.

■   ■   ■

As the meeting at the Peabody Hotel came to a close, agents of the FBI quietly closed the Phelps Clinic on Germantown Parkway. No explanation was ever given for the arrest of Dr. Henry Phelps Jr. or the subsequent seizure of the clinic's records.

■   ■   ■

At the same time, another task force composed of Memphis Police and FBI agents arrested every known member of a group the FBI identified only as The Group. The words *Die Gruppe* were never used or released for publication.

■   ■   ■

A furious Stacii Barrett climbed into her four-wheel drive vehicle outside the Benning County jail, promising herself she would get to the bottom of what was being called her "temporary detention" in the jail. The sheriff had apologized profusely for the error, saying only that he thought she might be able to find out what was going on from "other sources." Stacii was determined to find out who those sources were.

■   ■   ■

Gaby Ibarra felt the warm tears of relief flow down her face as her family crowded around her hospital bed at Children's Hospital in Little Rock. Explanations given to her parents had been detailed up to a point. They knew what had happened to her but not the global implications the events might have had.

As caring parents, they had been interested only in the well-being of their child. When told about the baby Gaby now carried, there had been no thought other than adoption. The legal papers had been expedited, and another daughter was added to the Ibarra family.

Now as the family crushed in upon a once again happy Gaby, the events seemed to fade into the past. Gaby hugged her father and mother, knowing that she would never be able to return the love they had already shown her and her child.

■   ■   ■

Benning County Deputy Gary Hantz rummaged through the mess on Wade Larsen's desk. The officers of Arkansas's Criminal Investigation Division had swept through the office, collecting anything and everything they thought they might need in the coming prosecution of the sheriff and his most senior officers. A strange quirk of fate had left Hantz in charge of the only law-enforcement agency of the county, and the young deputy was still in shock.

Hantz stepped around the disheveled desk and sat in the chair. A feeling of profound remorse swept over him. He and a few deputies, mostly the younger ones, were the only ones left. Despite his less than three years experience, Hantz was the senior man. The investigator from the CID had asked only that he "hold the fort" until the county's administrative body could meet and provide more substantial law enforcement coverage, but Hantz knew the county board well enough to know they would look to him to provide some of the answers, and right now all he really had were questions.

On the wall next to the sheriff's desk hung photographs of past Benning County sheriffs. He knew Larsen's would never join them.

The house in the valley had come as a surprise. Surprise? Perhaps that was too tame a word, but it was the one that came to mind.

After arresting Jason Swann and the others in the valley house and freeing what Hantz could only think of as the girls of a baby factory, the Arkansas CID had stepped in and transported Larsen and the medical staff to Little Rock. The girls were carried to Benning County Hospital and isolated in a small wing on the maternity floor. One of the girls—there had been a total of nine girls, all Hispanic—had been in the latter stages of labor, and the doctors had been concerned about her, but Hantz had heard a baby girl had been born, and the mother and child were doing well.

Larsen and the others, on the other hand, had been charged with racketeering, kidnapping, murder, and a host of other crimes. The bottom line was that those arrested could easily face life in prison if convicted, and some might even face the death penalty.

The phone rang and Hantz grabbed for it, eager to expel the troublesome thoughts from his mind. He listened while a dairy farmer complained about some high school boys crossing one of his hay fields on their way to a popular fishing hole. The boys had rutted out part of the field, and the farmer demanded that Hantz do something about it. Hantz smiled as he promised the farmer he would be right there. He rose from the chair and took one last look at the photos hanging on the wall. Maybe, someday, his would join them.

■   ■   ■

Susan Blair hung the phone up just as her husband walked through the door. She went to meet him, a huge smile on her face. Kenneth Blair felt his heart leap at the radiant smile on his wife's face. He did not need to ask what had put the expression there, but he wanted to hear the words.

"The doctor's office?" he asked quietly.

"Eight months and four days from now, you are going to be a father," Susan Blair told her husband.

"And you will be a mother," Kenneth said, taking Susan in his arms. Tears of joy mingled with soft kisses as they held each other tenderly.

■ ■ ■

"What about us?" Cindy Tolbert asked David Michaels, as he escorted her back to her suite in the Peabody. They were alone in the elevator.

"I was thinking we need to have a consultation time with an old preacher I know."

"What are you talking about?"

"Do you think the right Reverend Glen Shackleford, pastor emeritus of First Community Church in Clayton, would honor us by performing our wedding?"

"Not unless you ask me first," Cindy smiled. "I want to hear the words."

David took Cindy's face between his hands, holding it with all the care of a porcelain vase, and asked, "Will you marry me, Cindy Tolbert? I don't ever want you out of my sight again. This experience has taught me a lot, but mostly I've learned how very much I love you."

"And you can always tell our children that you proposed to their mother in an elevator at the Peabody Hotel in Memphis."

David smiled gently. "To be honest, that hadn't occurred to me, but it might be a story worth telling years from now."

The elevator door slid open as David took Cindy in his arms and kissed her. A "quack" interrupted the kiss, and David and Cindy looked down to see an entourage of ducks enter the elevator, heading for the fountain in the downstairs lobby.

David and Cindy laughed, happy to be in each other's arms, and in love.

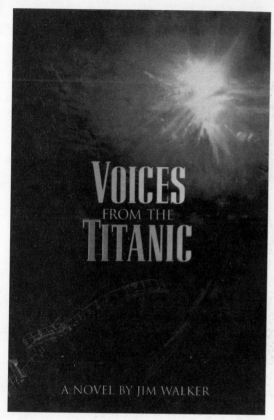

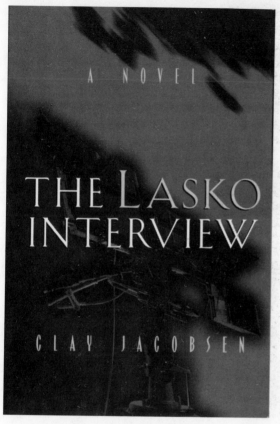

water damage
8/9/08 y/n